**“With sexy heroes and strong heroines, Killer Instincts is a not-to-be-missed experience.”***

## PRAISE FOR ELLE KENNEDY’S KILLER INSTINCTS SERIES

### *Midnight Action*

“Kudos to Kennedy for creating such passionate adversaries who are literally unforgettable!”
—*RT Book Reviews* (top pick, 4½ stars)

“Filled with wonderfully flawed characters you can’t help but love and heart-stopping, riveting suspense. . . . I highly recommend *Midnight Action* for those who enjoy their romantic suspense on the dark and steamy side.”
—*New York Times* bests[illegible] [illegible] Christy Reece

“Dangerous [illegible] romance hot enough to [illegible] puts them together and [illegible]
—**Ne*[illegible] [illegible]ian Arend



“A gripping, p[illegible] [illegible]ding tale. . . . First-class adventure, passionate desire, and fierce characters make this a very satisfying page-turner.” —*Publishers Weekly*

“An adrenaline-filled, exhilarating ride. The story is a thrilling, action-packed adventure, as well as a tender story.”
—Fresh Fiction

### *Midnight Games*

“Kennedy’s delicious third Killer Instinct romantic thriller . . . takes readers on a terrific emotional roller-coaster ride full of relentless action, heated sexual tension, and nail-biting plot twists . . . seamlessly [weaves] the romance into the mission story line. . . . Fantastic recurring characters, a deftly drawn plot, and breathless passion will leave the reader begging for more.” —*Publishers Weekly*

“An excellent addition to a very good romantic suspense series. The story has a fascinating plotline, lots of action, and an intriguing twist.” —Fresh Fiction

*continued . . .*

"So far each book has been suspenseful, heartbreaking, and full of sexy times, with *Midnight Games* being the best yet."
—Fiction Vixen

"As sexy as it is exciting. Elle Kennedy hits all the right notes in this fast-paced, adrenaline-filled third installment to her outstanding Killer Instincts series . . . action aplenty . . . spellbinding romantic suspense."
—Joyfully Reviewed

***Midnight Alias***

"Balances the gritty side of humanity with sizzling passion."
—*Publishers Weekly*

"[Kennedy] shows a real flair for penning thrillers that are passionate, gritty, and extremely suspenseful."
—*RT Book Reviews* (top pick)

"Seduction, sex, and suspense—Elle Kennedy is a master at blending all three. . . . [The] Killer Instincts series is dark, sensual, and extremely compelling." —Romance Junkies

***Midnight Rescue***

"If you're looking for a chilling, hard-core romantic suspense loaded with sensuality, military camaraderie, and dry humor, why not arrange for a *Midnight Rescue*?"
—*USA Today*

"Romantic suspense just gained a major new player!"
—*RT Book Reviews* (4½ stars)

"This was a very good romantic suspense. It had all the right elements that I look for in a book like this. The hot alpha men. The strong women they pair up with."
—Fiction Vixen

Also Available in the Killer Instincts Series

*Midnight Rescue*

*Midnight Alias*

*Midnight Games*

*Midnight Pursuits*

*Midnight Action*

# MIDNIGHT CAPTIVE

A KILLER INSTINCTS NOVEL

ELLE KENNEDY

A SIGNET ECLIPSE BOOK

SIGNET ECLIPSE
Published by the Penguin Group
Penguin Group (USA) LLC, 375 Hudson Street,
New York, New York 10014

USA | Canada | UK | Ireland | Australia | New Zealand | India | South Africa | China
penguin.com
A Penguin Random House Company

First published by Signet Eclipse, an imprint of New American Library,
a division of Penguin Group (USA) LLC

First Printing, June 2015



ISBN 978-0-451-47442-1

Printed in the United States of America
10 9 8 7 6 5 4 3 2 1

This one is for the most entertaining group
of people I've ever met: the Irish!

## ACKNOWLEDGMENTS

As always, a lot of research and preparation went into this book, and I couldn't have done it without the help of some very amazing people:

Josephine McDonnell, my Irish fairy godmother, who beta-read this book, offered valuable feedback, and made sure my Irish slang was up to par.

Brett Leary, paramedic extraordinaire, who put up with all my insane questions about shrapnel wounds.

Travis White, the best research assistant on the planet. Mostly because he sends me files with headings like *IRA For Dummies*, *International Drug Trafficking and You*, and *When in Yacht*.

Vivian Arend, my bestest friend ever, who read the book and went typo-hunting for me while waiting in the airport for a flight.

Laura Fazio, my brilliant editor, who loves this series as much as I do.

My awesome little sister, Danielle, for coming to Ireland with me and driving me around because I was too terrified to drive on the other side of the road!

And of course everyone I met and spoke to in Ireland, especially Derek, the most knowledgeable cab-driver in the whole world.

# Chapter 1

*Somerset County, England*

"Being a hermit isn't healthy, you know." Bailey paused to shoot a pointed stare at her friend before continuing to wander through the cozy living room of Paige's isolated country house.

Wall-to-wall bookshelves took up nearly half of the room, crammed with hundreds of titles that all looked well read. The lingering scent of smoke wafting out of the massive stone fireplace hinted that Paige had lit a fire recently. It was obvious that the woman spent a lot of time in this room, which corroborated Bailey's belief that her friend was a total recluse.

"Says who?" From her perch on the overstuffed sofa, Paige sipped her Merlot, unperturbed by the accusation.

Watching the other woman daintily hold the stem of her wineglass was almost jarring. With her slight frame, light-red hair, and fair, freckled face, Paige Grant was cute and delicate—and the last person you'd imagine to be a ruthless assassin. But Bailey supposed all of her colleagues were the same in that way. Sweet and harmless on the surface, tough and deadly beneath it.

Bailey herself was no stranger to death and violence. Seven years in the CIA followed by five working for a dangerous assassin had definitely hardened her. She didn't see the world as sunshine and rainbows—she saw it for what it was: cold, toxic, and treacherous, with rare moments of warmth and compassion slicing through the darkness like shards of moonlight. *If* you were lucky. She hadn't experienced many warm and fuzzy moments in her life, not as an adult, and certainly not as a child.

But right now was one of those moments. Spending the weekend in a beautiful, albeit run-down, English farmhouse, sipping deliciously smooth wine, catching up with one of her best friends. Sunshine and rainbows, all right.

"Says me," Bailey announced, returning to the couch and flopping down on the other end. "You're too young and beautiful to be hidden away here. You should be out and about, kicking ass and breaking hearts."

Paige snorted, then set her glass on the weathered oak coffee table and spoke in her crisp British accent. "First, I kick plenty of ass, thank you very much. Second, I'm not interested in breaking any hearts, but if you're hinting that I need a good shagging, then don't worry. I'm doing just fine. And third, you say all this as if *you're* a social butterfly, when we both know for a fact that you, my dear, are as big of a loner as I am."

Bailey couldn't argue with that. Loner was her middle name. But still, her friend's shut-in ways bothered her. Paige's bubbly personality was completely incongruous with a life of isolation.

"At least I attended our boss's wedding," she said mockingly.

"You did not! They eloped."

Bailey grinned. "Yeah, but I flew to Costa Rica after I heard the news to drop off a wedding present."

Paige rolled her eyes. "Yes, well, I couriered a gift. And mine was most certainly better than yours."

Curiosity flickered through her. "What'd you get them?"

"A ten-book set aptly titled *How to Keep the Sexual Fire Burning After Marriage*." Paige laughed in delight. "Noelle sent me a text message in reply. Two words. *Fuck* and *off*."

Bailey burst out laughing. She would've paid money to see their boss's face when she opened Paige's gift. Poor Noelle had already been annoyed enough that her former love turned enemy turned love again had twisted her arm until she married him. But Jim Morgan was a stubborn alpha male, and the deadly mercenary had insisted they get married . . . or else he'd drag her down the aisle kicking and screaming. And the icing on the cake—he'd talked Noelle into taking his last name, which officially made her Noelle Morgan now.

Maybe she was a jerk, but Bailey found the whole situation hilarious. She'd met Morgan two months ago in Paris after he'd reconnected with her boss, and she really liked the man. She was glad he and Noelle had finally worked through their decade-long issues.

Though their union did have one drawback.

Noelle and Morgan had joined professional forces. Which meant that Bailey and the rest of Noelle's assassins—chameleons, as they'd been dubbed—now worked for Morgan too.

"I'm still not sure how I feel about it," she confessed.

Paige furrowed her brow. "My wedding gift? Why? I thought it was awesome."

"No, not the gift—it *was* awesome. I was just thinking about our new working arrangements," Bailey clarified. "We're not mercenaries. We work alone."

"Don't worry. Noelle knows that. She said we'll still be

working solo, but if Morgan's team ever needs undercover help, they'll call us in."

Crap.

Crappity-crap-crap.

Bailey quickly swallowed the lump of unhappiness that rose in her throat, but clearly she hadn't managed to mask her expression, because Paige's blue eyes narrowed.

"What's the problem? You've helped Morgan out before. And God knows I get a call from him or Noelle at least once a week hitting me up for tech assistance."

"Which you can do from home," Bailey said, pointing to the insane collection of laptops on the long table across the room.

Cables and power strips snaked along the floor, some of them climbing toward the exposed-beam ceiling, all plugged in to Paige's command central, as she called it. The woman was a wizard when it came to computers, which was why she was on everyone's speed dial. If you wanted information, Paige Grant was your first and only call.

Unless it was the kind of information a computer couldn't find . . . in that case, that honor went to the Reilly brothers.

Aka the reason Bailey was unbelievably reluctant to call herself a member of Jim Morgan's team.

"I still don't see the issue," Paige said in confusion. "Morgan's a good guy—you said so yourself. Besides, you were the one just talking about breaking hearts. Think of all the hot single men you'll be working with. Liam Macgregor is a bloody movie star, that Sullivan guy is smokin' hot, and then there's the scary sexy badass . . . What's his name? D? Plus there's Sean—actually, wait, he's off the team—and the cute rookie—"

"Wait, back up." Bailey had frozen at Paige's last remark. "What do you mean Sean's off the team? Since when?"

"Since about a week ago, apparently. I spoke to Abby the other day and she said he suddenly quit."

"Did he say why?"

"He told Morgan he works better alone and that he was wrong to think he'd be able to function on a team." Paige shrugged. "Or something along those lines."

Bailey's brow furrowed. She supposed that made sense. Sean Reilly didn't take orders well. He was also impulsive to the core, exactly the kind of man who'd join a mercenary team and then abruptly change his mind less than two months later.

A sudden rush of bitterness flooded her chest. Yup, she was well acquainted with Sean's impulsive nature. She'd experienced it firsthand nearly a year ago, after the cocky Irishman had seduced her under the pretense that he was someone else.

*And you let him.*

It was hard to ignore the internal accusation—especially since it was one hundred percent accurate. Truth was, she couldn't lay all the blame for that night on Sean. The second he'd slid into her darkened hotel room she'd known he wasn't Oliver, Sean's equally gorgeous twin and the sweeter, more mature of the brothers. She'd *known*, yet she'd still allowed him to touch her. Kiss her.

Fuck her.

Aggravation clamped around her throat as old memories crept into her head, wicked images and seductive words whispered in a deep Irish brogue. Damn him for lying to her. Damn *herself* for playing along with the lie.

"I guess he headed back to Dublin to join forces with Ollie again," Paige was saying, oblivious to Bailey's inner turmoil. "Which is probably where he belongs. The Reilly brothers, information dealers extraordinaire, bona fide

Irish heartbreakers." The redhead slanted her head. "Didn't you go out with Ollie a while back?"

Bailey nodded, keeping her expression veiled. "Yeah, we went out a couple of times. We decided we were better off as friends, though."

"Pity. He's quite cute. Sean, too, though that's a given considering they're identical."

The conversation was veering into dangerous territory Bailey wanted to avoid. She hadn't told any of her colleagues about her night with Sean. The only person who knew about it was Liam Macgregor, who, in the past couple of months, had somehow become one of her closest friends. Figure that one out. Maybe she wasn't as much of a loner as she'd thought.

"Okay, enough man talk. This is our annual girls' getaway, remember?" She grinned at her friend. "What cheesy rom-coms did you get for us?"

Paige looked delighted. "Oooh, I ordered a bunch of them from the movie channel on the telly. You're in for a treat."

Bailey laughed as the other woman swiped the remote control from the end table and turned on the television. Back when she'd worked for the CIA, evenings like this hadn't existed in her life. She'd been a solo operative, spending months undercover and executing covert missions on foreign soil. She still did all that for Noelle, except nowadays she actually managed to squeeze in some downtime. Which was kind of comical—two assassins curled up on a couch with popcorn and wine, about to watch sappy romantic comedies. Life was strange sometimes.

"I ordered that movie about the chick who loses her memory and her hubby has to make her fall in love with him again," Paige revealed as she clicked the remote. The television was turned to a news channel, the broadcast nothing but a square box at the bottom of the screen as Paige scrolled through the channel list. "Hence the box of tissues on the table. Be prepared to sob like a baby."

Another laugh slipped out, but was cut short when Bailey noticed the line of text running beneath the news report. "Hey. Stay on this channel for a sec," she said, her good humor fading.

Paige stopped scrolling, clicking another button to bring the segment into full-screen view. "Ah, shit," the redhead murmured. "Obviously the world's gone to hell again."

Not the world—just Dublin, according to the screen. Bailey listened in dismay as the reporter quickly recapped the unfolding events to viewers who were just tuning in. There was a holdup in process at a downtown branch of Dublin National Bank. A half dozen masked, armed men had taken the bank employees and patrons hostage, and the law enforcement officers surrounding the bank were attempting to negotiate with the robbers. Apparently the situation was beginning to escalate, with reports of shots fired and hostages screaming.

"Turn it up," Bailey told Paige, leaning forward when a shaky camera image suddenly filled the screen.

Paige raised the volume, and the urgent voice of the female newscaster blared out of the speakers.

"—courageous woman uploaded a video to her social network page. We don't know how she was able to record this, but it's been confirmed that the account belongs to Margaret Allen, a twenty-one-year-old student at Trinity College. Be warned—some of these images are not suitable for young viewers."

The screen flickered for a beat before the video began to play. Immediately, loud footsteps and angry shouts filled Paige's living room. The two women watched in silence as jerky images flashed on the screen, accompanied by gruff orders from the robbers and muffled whimpers from the hostages. It was difficult to zero in on any one image—everything was moving too fast, and the men in charge wore all black, from the ski masks on their faces right down to the boots on their feet.

An uneasy feeling washed over Bailey as she focused on one of the men. Tall and broad, eye color indiscernible and voice low and deep as he issued a soft command to someone out of the camera's line of sight.

"Look at these idiots," Paige remarked with a sigh. "Do they honestly expect to get away with this?"

Bailey didn't answer. Something niggled at the back of her mind, an intangible flicker of familiarity, a sense of bone-deep dread. But she wasn't sure what was bugging her. People robbed banks all the time. People took hostages. People killed other people and did seriously stupid, dangerous shit every second of every day.

So why was this particular armed robbery making the hairs on the back of her neck tingle?

Another anguished sob echoed in the bank, followed by a male response.

"'S'okay, luv, it'll all be over soon."

The husky timbre of that voice, combined with the faint brogue, turned the blood in Bailey's veins to ice. A gasp flew out, her heart rate kicking up a notch as she stared at the screen in shock.

"Oh shit," she whispered.

Paige glanced over, big blue eyes swimming with concern when she saw Bailey's expression. "What is it?"

"That's Sean." Her finger trembled as she jabbed it in the direction of the television.

"What?" The other woman sounded bewildered. "That's nuts."

Maybe, but Bailey would recognize that voice anywhere. It haunted her dreams every goddamn night.

"It's him, Paige. One of the robbers—it's Sean fucking Reilly." Horror, shock, and confusion clawed up her throat like icy fingers. "It's *Sean*."

*Dublin, Ireland*

Well. This was his life now. Robbing a bloody bank in bloody Dublin. His ma was probably rolling over in her grave.

Sean Reilly hadn't given much thought to how he would die, but considering the dangerous path he walked on a daily basis, the assumption was he'd eventually meet a violent end. Tonight, that fate looked pretty fucking promising. Maybe the Emergency Response Unit hunkered down outside the bank's doors would swarm in with shoot-to-kill orders. Or maybe one of the snipers positioned on the perimeter would put a strategically placed bullet in his brain.

*Relax, mate. They won't risk the hostages.*

Bullshit. Sean had worked enough military ops to know there was always at least one crazy asshole on an assault team. One hotshot who thought he could take down the bad guys *and* save the innocents.

Truth be told, usually *he* was that man. His brother lectured him daily about his act-first-and-think-much-much-later approach, but Sean had inherited the reckless gene from their father, while Oliver had gotten their mother's more practical approach to problem solving. In his defense, Sean was more than capable of getting the job done, even when acting on impulse. The child's-play exercises the Garda officers underwent were nothing compared to his extensive training.

On the upside, the Irish weren't as aggressive as other folks—ahem, the bloody Americans—which meant there *was* a chance he could avoid a bullet in the head today.

The ERU rarely acted with lethal force unless the threat to innocent life was imminent, and at the moment, all the hostages were safe and sound.

Sean figured he had another hour. Two, tops. After that, the negotiator would realize the gunmen were stalling and the response unit would make their move.

If the ERU had even the slightest inkling about the dead body currently taking up space in the bank, they would've acted an hour ago.

Sean swallowed his anger as he shifted his gaze toward the long teller counter spanning the back wall. A cop. A bloody cop—literally, because the garda's head was surrounded by a sticky crimson puddle. Paddy Lynch had blown the man's forehead clean off with a sawed-off shotgun, the crazy maniac. If by some miracle they managed to claw out of this clusterfuck alive, first thing Sean planned on doing was knocking Paddy's crooked teeth out.

But at least Lynch had possessed the good sense not to shoot the undercover officer in the lobby. The garda had made his move closer to the doorway at the edge of the counter. The bullet had sent him tumbling backward, and Lynch had hastily dragged the lifeless body under one of the desks, where it remained hidden from view.

In the commotion, however, one of the tellers had dashed behind the counter and triggered the panic alarm—which was why Sean and his cohorts now had the equivalent of an American SWAT team bearing down on them.

He was definitely gonna die today.

A loud sob broke through his pessimistic thoughts, drawing his attention to a slim, ginger-haired girl crouched on the floor five feet from his scuffed boots. Another thorn in his side—the little bird had nearly been killed too, thanks to the stunt she'd pulled with her phone. Her life had been spared only because Sean had stepped in and talked Gallagher out of shooting her.

Stifling a sigh, he headed for the girl and squatted beside her. "I promise you, it'll be all right, luv."

Her head lifted slightly, big blue eyes peering up at him. She was young, no older than twenty or twenty-one. Tears stained her pale cheeks and she'd bitten her bottom lip so hard it had started to bleed.

"He's going to kill me," she whispered.

Her gaze darted toward Gallagher, who stood in the doorway separating the lobby from the rear offices. The tall man frowned when he caught sight of his accomplice chatting with a hostage, but Sean gave a brief nod to signal that everything was fine.

"He won't kill you," Sean murmured. "I won't let that happen."

A panicked breath blew out of her mouth. "He *will*. He knows I uploaded the video. He said he's going to kill me."

"You shouldn't have done what you did," Sean agreed.

Alarm filled her eyes. "I'm sorry. I'm so sorry. Please don't hurt me."

*Bloody hell.*

She truly believed he would hurt her.

How had it come to this? He was no saint, but he sure as hell wasn't a bad guy. A man who instilled fear in a young woman's eyes.

Anger bubbled in his gut as he wrenched his gaze off the redhead's tearstained face. The hot, suffocating emotion wasn't directed at the girl, but at his former employer. Why the *fuck* had Rabbit put him in this position? He'd given that bastard nothing but loyalty for more than half his life. He might have left Rabbit's employ, but they'd parted on good terms—the old man had helped Sean and his twin get their network off the ground, for Christ's sake.

Well, fuck him. Sean was officially done with that fanatic motherfucker. Rabbit had all but stomped his foot on their former relationship and ground it into dust, making it painfully clear what the Reilly brothers meant to him.

Absolutely nothing.

"I'm not going to hurt you," Sean said through clenched teeth. "I'm just pointing out that if you'd simply handed over your phone when we asked, you wouldn't have drawn any unwanted attention to yourself."

"I'm sorry," the girl whispered again.

"What's your name, luv?"

She hiccuped softly. "Maggie."

"Listen to me, Maggie. Nobody else is going to get hurt, not as long as you do what we say. It'll all be over soon."

He hoped that was true. The in-and-out heist he'd signed up for had turned into a deadly hostage situation, and it would turn into something much worse if the ERU decided to launch a full-scale assault.

They'd been trapped inside the bank for an hour, and the hairs on the back of Sean's neck hadn't stopped tingling since the response unit had arrived. He knew bloody well there was a rifle trained on his head. Probably an outdated Steyr SSG 69, the ERU's weapon of choice.

Come to think of it, Bailey occasionally used a Steyr too. Or at least she had that time he'd tracked her to Germany. He doubted she ever used the same weapon twice, though. That would mean giving law enforcement a routine, a calling card, and the woman was too damn smart to leave a trail.

But now was *not* the time to be thinking about Bailey, goddamn it.

"Delta."

The sharp address came from Gallagher, whose expression had gone dark, deadly.

Sean stared at the man's masked face and cocked his head in question.

"Leave the bitch alone and do your job," was the brusque response.

He rose to his full height, offering Maggie a reassuring pat on the shoulder before turning to monitor the status of the other hostages. There were fifteen of them, sitting on the floor against the counter like a group of preschoolers. More females than males, ranging from early twenties to late sixties. The bank's security guard sat at the end of the line, clad in his crisp blue uniform. Unfortunately for him, that uniform hadn't come with a weapon, which was something the man was no doubt cursing at the moment.

Satisfied that his charges were behaving, Sean marched across the tiled floor toward his "leader"—Rhys Gallagher, former Irish army special ops, current Irish Dagger lieutenant, and one of Rabbit's most trusted enforcers. Sean and his brother had grown up not only with Gallagher, but also with the other four men situated throughout the bank, but while the twins had left Ireland for bigger and better things, the others had stuck around to serve Rabbit, who'd been a mentor to all the boys.

Some bloody mentor he was to them now, keeping Ollie hostage and forcing Sean to do his dirty work.

Sean approached Gallagher and addressed him in a low voice. "We need to talk."

The man nodded at Joe Murray to take his place, then stalked into the corridor with Sean on his tail. They paused when they were out of sight and earshot of the others.

Sean promptly peeled off his black wool balaclava and rubbed his face with both hands. The mask had been itching the shit out of him. "Look. We got what we came for," he announced. "It's time to get the hell outta here."

"No shit," the other man snapped. "But in case you haven't noticed, we're in a real fucking jam at the moment."

They sure were, and all so Eamon O'Hare could get his hands on the flash drive burning a hole in Gallagher's back pocket. Rabbit had instructed Sean to be present when the men breached the vault where the safe-deposit boxes were stored. The Irish Dagger leader was paranoid that a mole had infiltrated his organization, but from what Sean could tell, the five Dagger members involved in the heist were on the up-and-up.

"Then we find a way out of the jam," Sean said coldly.

"What the feck do you think I've been doing? Buggering myself? I'm *thinking*, you fecking fool!" The man's Irish intonation grew deeper and less comprehensible the angrier he got. "But that fecking fasser shot a *garda*."

"Nobody said Lynch was smart," Sean muttered. "We just need to improvise."

"Ya?" Gallagher said scornfully. "Got any bright ideas?"

Sean shrugged. "We give ourselves up."

Gallagher gazed at him in disbelief. "Are you daft? You're suggesting we walk out the bloody front door? We'll get thrown in the Joy," he snapped, referring to Mountjoy Prison, the medium-security facility where most of Rabbit's men had been "guests" over the years.

"Five of us will," Sean agreed.

Gallagher hissed out a breath. "What the hell does that mean?"

"It means we got what we came for. Rabbit has his prize. And I'm no mathematician, but I'm pretty sure he doesn't need six men to deliver it. One will do the trick."

"So five of us surrender?" Gallagher sounded skeptical. "And how exactly do you see the sixth man walking away from this?"

"By pretending to be a hostage. The Garda doesn't have an exact head count of how many people we're holding here. For all they know, we could've stashed a hostage in the back for shits and giggles." Sean shrugged again. "One of us takes the flash drive and joins the hostages, the other five surrender."

Gallagher went quiet as he considered it, just as Sean had known he would. The members of the Irish Dagger were good little soldiers, prepared to martyr themselves for their leader. Rabbit spoon-fed them his bullshit, and they ate it up like it was candy. They didn't care that the world had labeled them a terrorist group. They believed in what they were doing and why they were doing it, and Rabbit made sure to remind them of it every second of the day.

"It's a sacrifice for the cause," Sean said meaningfully, knowing the reminder would override Gallagher's survival instincts.

After a long beat, the other man nodded, resignation flickering in his eyes. "A sacrifice for the cause," he echoed.

Idealistic idiot. Sean would never sacrifice himself for a losing battle. The IRA and its dozens of splinter groups were living in the past. Their sacrifices meant nothing.

People, on the other hand—Sean would give up his life for the people he cared about. Oliver. Bailey. Any of the men on Jim Morgan's mercenary team. If Macgregor or Port or, hell, even that bastard D, were in trouble, he'd risk everything to save them.

But Gallagher and his men didn't matter to him. He had no intention of dying for them, even if it meant risking an arrest. If anything, he was banking on getting pinched. Once the Garda took him into custody, he wouldn't stay there long. He had contacts in this city, allies with enough clout to ensure that he'd be back on the street in less than twenty-four hours.

Except Gallagher surprised him with his next remark. "You'll play the hostage."

Sean's eyebrows rose. Well, fuck him sideways. He hadn't thought he'd make the short list for hostage, let alone be tasked with the role.

His reappearance in his former group had been met with hostility and suspicion, particularly from Gallagher and Kelly, Rabbit's second-in-command. The crew didn't trust him, he was well aware of that, and they didn't like him anymore either, not since he and Oliver had abandoned Rabbit to deal in intelligence.

"Why me?" he asked slowly.

"Because you're the least recognizable." Gallagher lifted the bottom of his mask and rubbed the dark stubble on his chin. "We've all gotten pinched before. I don't know if the Garda is using some sort of face-recognition bullshit, but if they see me or Lynch or one of the others walk out with the hostages, someone might recognize us. You've been off the grid long enough that none of those Garda rookies would know who you are."

Jesus Christ.

He'd just been handed a winning lotto ticket.

Sean kept his face expressionless, careful not to reveal his eagerness. "Whatever you think is best," he said with a nod.

"But . . ." Gallagher frowned. "They'll be expecting six men. With you in the hostage pool, there'll only be five left to surrender."

"Because the sixth is dead." Sean arched a brow.

Gallagher instantly understood, a wry smile playing on his lips. "The cop."

"Our leader," Sean corrected. "You've been dealing

with the negotiator, but when he calls back, get someone else to talk to him. Murphy, I'd say—lad's a pathological liar. Murphy tells the negotiator that our merry band had a disagreement and our leader was taken out of the equation, and the other men are ready to give themselves up now that the head of the snake has been cut off."

Gallagher narrowed his eyes. "You're a clever little bugger, aren't you, Reilly? Always have been."

He didn't answer.

"All right. We do this, then." After a moment of hesitation, Gallagher reached into his pocket and pulled out the flash drive. "Go to the staff room and find something else to wear. I'll grab you after Murphy talks to the Garda. Then I'll bring you to the lobby at gunpoint and throw you in with the other hostages."

Every nerve ending in Sean's body crackled with triumph as Gallagher handed him the flash drive.

Well, goddamn. Maybe he *wasn't* going to die today.

# Chapter 2

Bailey spent the majority of the flight making phone calls and cashing in favors. She had no idea what to expect when she got to Dublin, but she would damn well be prepared for anything. She would've felt better if Paige had come with her, but the woman had adamantly refused. Paige shied away from any mission that might place her in the public eye, and since the bank was crawling with police and reporters, Bailey wasn't surprised that her request for assistance had been categorically denied.

Of all the women who worked for Noelle, Bailey was closest to Paige—yet she didn't have a shred of insight about the woman's past. She suspected Paige harbored secrets that rivaled her own, but she had never pushed her friend for answers. Paige would tell her eventually. Or she wouldn't. Either way, Bailey still adored the woman.

And it wasn't like she didn't have any backup—she'd already contacted a former colleague and he was hard at work on his end, gathering as much intel as he could about the bank robbery.

Bailey checked her phone again, but Rafe hadn't

checked in, so she dialed Paige's number instead. The helicopter's cabin was noisy as hell, but despite the whir of the rotors and the wind hissing past her window, she clearly heard the frustration in her friend's voice.

"I can't find a bloody thing," Paige grumbled. "The bank's system doesn't have any floor plans or schematics. I'm trying to hack into the city records to get my hands on some blueprints, but their security is surprisingly intense. Every time I knock down a firewall another one pops up."

"Shit," Bailey said. She needed those blueprints *now*. If the holdup was still in progress when she landed, she had every intention of finding a way into that bank.

"It might take a while. I'm working as fast as I can, though." There was a pause. "Is there really no way to talk you out of this?"

"Nope." Her tone was light, but the tension weighing on her chest was heavier than a block of cement.

A part of her still questioned her decision to hightail it out of England to rescue Sean Reilly, but no matter how many times the rational part of her brain tried to point out that she didn't even *like* the man, she hadn't been able to talk herself out of it.

She and Sean might not be bosom buddies, but he'd helped her out in the past. Helped her colleagues, too. And yes, he was annoying and arrogant and so reckless she wasn't sure how he was still alive, but he wasn't a criminal. He didn't rob banks, for fuck's sake, which meant that his presence at Dublin National was part of something . . . bigger. Something that could very well get him killed.

"You know what?" she told Paige. "Forget about the blueprints. I have another source I can hit up for those. I want you to focus on accessing all the security cameras in the area. I want to know where every member of law enforcement is positioned. Try to access the cameras inside the bank, too."

"Copy that."

Bailey hung up and ran a hand through her hair, once again going over the details of the robbery. It was Sean's voice she'd heard on the TV. She was certain of that. But why the hell was he inside the bank? What had that idiot gotten himself into?

"Ten minutes until descent," the pilot called from the cockpit, twisting around in his seat to give her a thumbs-up.

She nodded in return. She hadn't flown with Greg before, but Paige had, and the woman said he could be trusted. Bailey found it ironic—she had an easier time trusting a man she'd known for less than an hour than she had trusting Sean Reilly, a man she'd known for years.

Her gaze drifted out the window as she considered everything she knew about Sean. He'd been born and raised in Dublin, but he'd lived all over the world, including New York for a few years. He'd had a variety of unsavory professions—mercenary, information dealer, errand boy for an Irish gangster. His dad had been IRA and trained his sons to be soldiers for the cause, but Sean and his brother had strayed from the group, choosing their own path.

Could he be working for O'Hare again? Bailey knew that Eamon "Rabbit" O'Hare had been heavily involved in Sean's life when he was a kid. Sean's dad had been the Irish Dagger leader's right-hand man. But in the five years she'd kept tabs on Sean and Oliver, there hadn't been any indication that they were still in contact with the Irish gangster.

A frustrated groan crawled up her throat, but she choked it back. Why was she running to help him, damn it? They'd slept together. Once. And the bastard had *lied* to her. Didn't matter that he'd owned up to it immediately after. He'd still come to her hotel room that night pretending to be someone else. Just because she'd known who he was certainly didn't excuse his deception. She should be celebrating that he was in trouble, not rushing to get him out of it.

The phone buzzed in her hand, providing a much-needed distraction from her turbulent thoughts. "Hey," she said when Rafe's voice echoed in her ear. "What are we looking at over there?"

"We've got a dozen gardai front and back. Blockade on the street, but a looser formation at the rear. Two snipers street side, positioned on the rooftops. But there's got to be another one in the back. Haven't made him yet."

"I'm working on getting us more intel," she told him. "Stay in position. I'm landing in five. Rendezvous in thirty."

"Gotcha."

Rafe disconnected abruptly, but just knowing he was backing her up filled Bailey with relief. She'd worked with him a handful of times over the years, having met him when she was still with the CIA and Rafe was working in Spanish intelligence. He'd left his agency after a falling-out with a supervisor and had gone private, now operating out of the UK. She was damn lucky he'd been in Dublin when she'd SOS'd him. With Paige refusing to help, and the rest of her colleagues halfway across the globe, Bailey desperately needed Rafe's assistance.

But she needed someone else too. Someone she had no desire to get tangled up with again.

Anger and annoyance rippled through her as she scrolled through her contact list and pulled up the number. Goddamn Sean for putting her in this position. She was sticking her neck out for him, and knowing him, he probably wouldn't express an ounce of gratitude for what she was about to do.

She hesitated for a beat, then dialed. Because hell, she was already in this deep.

The call didn't connect right away. Instead, a series of clicks met her ears, which told her the call was being rerouted several times before reaching her contact. She knew the drill, though. It was the same on her end, calls bouncing from tower to tower to make it impossible for anyone to trace her. She'd always received great satisfaction from the knowledge that nobody could pinpoint her location, not even her former employer, a man with endless resources. But now, thanks to Sean, she was practically waving a flag around and begging her past to find her.

A moment later, a female voice came on the line. Absolutely delighted and more than a little smug. "Hey, stranger."

Bailey clenched her teeth. "Gwen. I need a favor."

The other woman's peal of laughter only grated harder. "Really, Bailey? Two years without a word, without so much as a *postcard*, and this is what I get? No 'How are ya?' No 'How's the old gang doing?'"

"There is no old gang," she muttered. Gwen knew damn well that Bailey had been a loner during her time at the company. She worked solo. Period. Her only contact with the other operatives had come from occasionally bumping into them on the rare occasions she stopped by headquarters to be debriefed.

"I don't have much time," she added tersely. "I'm cashing in on that favor you owe me. You know, the carte blanche you promised me when I rescued your ass from that hellhole in Uganda?"

"I was hoping you'd forgotten about that."

Despite herself, Bailey smiled. "Do I ever forget anything?"

"No. You don't." Gwen paused. "What can I do for you, honeybunch?"

"Before I tell you, you have to promise that you'll do it in a way that doesn't put me on Daniels's radar."

"Still playing cat and mouse with our boss, huh?" Gwen's tone grew mocking, and Bailey could practically see the smirk on her face.

"*Your* boss, Gwen. Not mine. And I mean it—this has to be on the DL. I don't want Daniels to know I'm back on the grid."

"All right. Tell me what you need."

"A detailed layout of Dublin National Bank, Fleet Street branch. Interior and exterior, entry and exit points, ventilation system, anything you can get your hands on. I need to know every inch of the place." She paused. "Also, any intel you might have on the hostage situation that's going down there right now."

There was a pause, followed by another thoroughly amused laugh. "Since when do you get involved in local crime bullshit?"

Bailey ignored the taunt. "You'll have to go through black channels, Gwen. I mean it. There can't be a paper trail."

"Sweetie, we both know I never leave a trail. I'm insulted you'd even suggest it." Gwen chuckled again. "But I am flattered that you think my sources are superior to yours. You can easily find this information on your own."

"Not as fast as you can," she said irritably. "Can you do it?"

"I'll see what I can do. Call you back in a jiffy."

Gwen hung up, and Bailey released a sigh. She hated that she'd been forced to reach out to that crazy bitch.

Truth be told, Gwen scared the shit out of her. The

woman was charming, highly skilled, and insanely dangerous. Her daredevil attitude reminded Bailey a lot of her colleague Juliet, but while Juliet was all about self-preservation, Gwen had never seemed to care whether she lived or died. The woman operated without a parachute. She lived and breathed danger, got off on the adrenaline of it, and that made her a massive liability.

If Gwen told Daniels about Bailey's call . . .

No, she had to trust that her old colleague would hold up her end of the deal and refrain from tipping off Daniels. Because if he got wind that she'd surfaced again . . . the bastard would be on the next flight out, coercing her into coming back to work for him. Or worse—trying to lure her into his bed again.

Not that he'd succeed. Bailey was done with the man, professionally *and* romantically. Daniels had recruited her when she was eighteen years old. He'd been her mentor. Her friend. Her lover.

Sleeping with him had been a mistake, though, only serving to illustrate that she hadn't put her past behind her like she'd thought. She'd left one controlling bastard and replaced him with another, but she'd be damned if she let Isaac Daniels have any power over her again.

Fuckin' Sean Reilly.

He owed her a frickin' fruit basket for all the trouble she was going to for him.

Gwen called back five minutes after the chopper landed in the private airfield outside the city. The car Bailey had arranged for was waiting by the hangar, and she lifted the phone to her ear as she slid into the backseat of the sedan. She'd hired a driver so she'd be able to study any schematics Gwen and Paige sent over.

"I'm e-mailing you the blueprints," Gwen said briskly.

Bailey hissed out an excited breath. "Are they up to date?"

"They're the most current plans my source could find. Best I could do on such short notice."

Bailey responded with reluctant gratitude. "Thank you. Anything I need to know about this robbery?"

"I didn't find much more than what the news is reporting." Gwen paused. "But there are a few whispers that this is the work of the Irish Dagger."

Shit. That was exactly what Bailey had been afraid of.

What the *hell* was Sean involved in?

"Okay. Thanks again, Gwen."

"We're square now," the woman said before Bailey could disconnect. "Next time you call me, it had better be to catch up. Oooh, we should go for drinks and—"

"Good-bye, Gwen."

Bailey hung up the phone, then accessed her e-mail and downloaded the file Gwen had sent. She spent half the drive into the city going over every detail of the bank.

She found herself praying that the hostage situation would still be under way when she arrived. If the cops made a move before then, Sean might very well be dead.

The peculiar clenching of her gut gave her pause. She wasn't sure why the thought of Sean dying bothered her so much. They barely knew each other. Well, outside the biblical sense.

But . . . no. She didn't want him dead. No matter how angry she was at him, she didn't want to see that cocky bastard eliminated from the face of the earth.

That's why she was hoping the Garda hadn't launched an assault. Though on the other hand, there was always the possibility that an ambush would result in arrests rather than deaths. Which was almost preferable—she'd have a far easier time rescuing Sean from police custody than getting him out of a heavily watched bank.

Her phone beeped when they were ten minutes from her rendezvous point with Rafe. Incoming e-mail from Paige, summarizing the positions of every law enforcement member in the vicinity. Paige had managed to get her hands on live security footage of the area, God bless her pretty red head. Nothing about the position of the snipers, though, but Paige's e-mail said she was working on it.

Bailey scanned the information, then rubbed her temples, trying to ward off an oncoming headache. It was enough to make her wonder if maybe she ought to bring Morgan's team into the loop. They wouldn't be able to do much, considering they were nowhere near Dublin, but they would want to know about Sean's predicament, wouldn't they? Liam and Sullivan would for sure. She knew the two of them were pretty chummy with Sean.

After a second of hesitation, she shot a quick text to Liam, promised to keep him posted, and then went back to studying the bank layout. By the time the sedan neared the Temple Bar neighborhood where the bank was located, she had a good grasp of the interior and a feasible plan, depending on what Rafe had to say.

The sun had disappeared below the horizon line not long after she'd landed, but lampposts lit the streets and cast shadows on the faces of pedestrians wandering the sidewalks. Her driver took a detour because the Garda had barricaded two city blocks, thanks to the showdown at the bank, so she was five minutes late meeting Rafe. She got out of the sedan on the street parallel to Fleet, heading for the cobblestone alley sandwiched between two darkened storefronts.

"You're late." He emerged from the shadows, his dark

eyes, dark hair, and dark stubble making it hard to see him clearly.

"Sorry. Had to take a detour."

They didn't shake hands. Didn't hug or exchange smiles. Rafe Meriden wasn't that kind of man. He always got right down to business without wasting time on pleasantries.

"The negotiator is still in contact with the gunmen," he said briskly. "He's taking the calls from inside one of the police cars parked in front of the bank."

"Has the Emergency Response Unit made any moves?" she asked.

"None. No activity inside either. I overheard one of the gardai say the shots that were heard earlier were warning shots. Gunmen fired at the ceiling when they stormed the bank to get people's attention. It's been quiet since then." He paused. "You saw the girl's video?"

"Yes," she said grimly.

Rafe frowned. "You're certain your guy's in there?"

Her guy. Hardly. If the cops didn't shoot Sean, she'd do it herself.

"Yeah, he's there." She bent down and unzipped the canvas bag she'd brought from England, rummaging around until she found the case containing her comms. She took out two earpieces, popped one in her ear, and handed the other to Rafe.

The transmitters were motion activated, so she moved her hand over the tiny device to trigger the mic. "Paige, you read?"

"Loud and clear," came her friend's voice.

"Did you get the locations of the snipers?"

"Two across the street from the bank, one in the rear."

"Be more specific," Rafe demanded. "Where's the third?"

"He's on the roof of an apartment building. If the back door is twelve o'clock, our sniper is at six."

Rafe and Bailey turned their heads inconspicuously toward the buildings to the east of them.

"Brick building," Paige said. "Second flat from the top has Christmas lights strung on the balcony."

Bailey glimpsed the blinking red and blue lights. "Got it. Thanks. I'll get back to you." She turned to Rafe. "You said there's a dozen Garda officers in the back?"

He nodded. "What are you thinking?"

"We need to take out that rear sniper, for one." Chewing on her bottom lip, she pulled up the blueprints on her phone and studied the screen. "There's a ventilation grate five feet from the back door. I need to get to it without the guards spotting me."

Rafe whistled under his breath. "You're a crazy bitch, Bailey."

"Do you think you can incapacitate the sniper and take his place?" she said slowly.

"Yes." Rafe narrowed his eyes. "But then what?"

She bit the inside of her cheek, her brain rapidly sorting through details and variables. "You'll have to create a distraction. Get the Garda's eyes off the back door just long enough for me to infiltrate the bank."

"I can do that. I've got an associate on standby."

She didn't bother asking who this "associate" was. Rafe was even more secretive than she was, and she had *a lot* of secrets.

"Can we trust him?"

"He'll do whatever I ask." Rafe paused. "What happens when you get inside?"

"I'll have to improvise, I guess. But let's cross one bridge at a time. We need that sniper removed from the equation first."

Rafe went quiet for a beat. Then he sighed. "You sure this man of yours is worth the hassle?"

Nope. She wasn't sure at all.

But she'd already come this far, and there was no backing out now.

# Chapter 3

*Turtle Creek, Costa Rica*

Liam Macgregor stared at his phone, unable to fathom what he was seeing. Maybe Bailey had gone insane. Or maybe she'd popped some hallucinogens and was tripping balls right now.

Except . . . well, fuck. Bailey wouldn't make something like that up. And although she had a pretty kick-ass sense of humor, she didn't joke around when it came to Sean Reilly. The only time Liam had ever seen hostility in Bailey's normally laid-back demeanor was when she was discussing the man.

He rose from one of the brown leather couches in the compound's massive, chalet-style living room and switched on the flat-screen television. It took no time at all to verify Bailey's story. All he had to do was turn the channel to CNN, and there it was. Hostage situation unfolding at Dublin National Bank.

There was no mention of Sean Reilly, though. According to the newscaster, the gunmen were still unidentified, all six of them, but Liam would never dream of questioning Bailey or undermining her instincts. The woman was a former CIA operative and a professional assassin. She'd had more training and battle experience than Liam, and she was capable of things that, in all honesty, scared him shitless.

If Bailey said Sean was in the bank, then Sean was in the bank.

The question was . . . *why*?

What kind of fucked-up craziness had Sean gotten himself into?

Cursing under his breath, Liam strode through the heavy oak doors and hurried up one of the twin staircases in the front parlor. The house where Liam and several of his team members resided was huge, offering endless hallways and bedroom suites, and that was just the top three floors. The basement housed a sixteen-seat theater, a fully equipped gym, a sprawling game room, and an indoor target range.

Despite its frills, the house was more secure than a military base. The hundred-acre property was surrounded by a twelve-foot electric fence and contained a top-notch security system monitored by two former Delta operatives. Running underneath the property were tunnels with escape points leading to both the jungle bordering the compound to the east and the mountains to the west, and every building was rigged with C-4 in the event that the place was breached.

Liam would consider it overkill, if not for the fact that a private mercenary squad had ambushed the team's former compound a couple of years back. Besides, with the number of people living there, precautions needed to be taken.

He raced up the stairs to the second floor, which consisted of suites belonging to Morgan and Noelle, Kane and Abby, and now Morgan's daughter, Cate. The sarcastic teenager referred to the third floor as Frat Row, since that was where Liam and the other unattached men stayed.

He rapped his knuckles on Morgan's door, but the knock went unanswered. Crap. Where the hell was the boss?

Liam was just moving away from the door when a head popped out of a doorway at the opposite end of the hall.

"Hey!" Abby Sinclair said brightly, looking overjoyed to see him.

He hid his amusement. Almost seven months pregnant and officially sidelined from all jobs for the foreseeable future, Abby had been climbing the walls for weeks now. He knew the lethal operative was bored to tears, and it didn't help that her husband was still working ops, leaving her alone for days or weeks at a time.

"Do you want to watch a movie?" she asked.

He didn't miss the pleading note in her voice, which was pretty fucking shocking, considering Abby usually wasn't very social. But since she'd been benched, Abby was willing—no, she was *eager*—to hang out with anyone who crossed her path. Apparently she was driving their security man nuts by wandering into his domain on a daily basis and trying to take over his surveillance duties.

"Can't," he said regretfully. "I need to track down Morgan. Do you know where he is?"

"No clue." Her honey yellow eyes narrowed. "Is everything okay?"

"Yeah, everything's fine," he lied. "Just need to talk to him about this bodyguard gig we've got lined up."

Abby's expression told him that she didn't buy the story, but she didn't grill him further. "Great. Whatever," she grumbled, then disappeared into the bedroom.

He didn't feel at all guilty for lying to her. Kane had ordered everyone at the compound to keep Abby's stress levels at a minimum, which meant not involving her in anything that was potentially dangerous. Like the fact that Sean Reilly was robbing a fuckin' bank.

Liam headed back to the staircase, his foot landing on the top step just as Ash entered the parlor.

"Where's the boss?" he demanded as he descended the stairs.

The dark-haired rookie grinned. "Gun range. He's giving Cate a lesson."

"'Kay. Thanks." Liam started to brush past the younger man, but Ash grasped his arm, the humor in his green eyes fading as he caught the look on Liam's face.

"What's wrong—"

Liam shrugged the kid's hand off him. "Let me talk to Morgan and then I'll fill you in."

He hurried down the corridor toward the kitchen, his bare feet slapping the hardwood floor. The steel door outside the kitchen opened onto a concrete staircase leading to the basement, and he took the steps two at a time, cursing at the ice-cold floor beneath his feet. Noelle must have turned up the air-conditioning again. Ever since she'd moved in, she'd been running the place like she owned it. Though he supposed she did, now that she was married to the boss.

Never in a million years would Liam have thought he'd be living under the same roof as the terrifying woman known as the queen of assassins, but life was funny that way.

The walls in the basement were nearly soundproof, but he heard the muffled pops of gunfire as he marched toward the target range. When he walked in, he saw Cate and Noelle at the front of the cavernous room. The younger girl held a nine-millimeter semiautomatic with both hands, aiming it at the target thirty feet away. She fired, then groaned in exasperation.

"Stop going for the head," Noelle said sharply, frowning at the eighteen-year-old girl. "I already told you, head shots require a level of precision you haven't mastered yet."

Cate threw back a challenge. "How am I supposed to master it if I don't *practice*?"

"We're focusing on the chest this week."

"I can hit any part of the chest you tell me to!" Cate protested, blowing a strand of dark blond hair off her forehead. "You know I can. Let me try another head shot."

"Fine." Noelle folded her arms over her tight red tank top. "Go right ahead."

Cate studied the target in concentration, then raised her weapon and squeezed the trigger. The shot reverberated through the huge empty room, the bullet connecting with the white space four inches from the target's head.

"Fuck!" Cate burst out.

"Language," a male voice snapped.

Liam glanced over and spotted Morgan leaning against the cinder-block wall, arms crossed as he reprimanded his daughter.

His daughter. Jeez. Liam still had a hard time wrapping his head around it, even though he'd seen Cate almost every day since Morgan had brought her to the compound.

Still, if someone had told him two months ago that deadly supersoldier Jim Morgan would be raising a teenage daughter, he would've laughed them out of town. But DNA didn't lie, and although Morgan hadn't even been certain that Cate existed before he'd finally tracked her down in Paris over the summer, the man had stepped into the daddy role with ease and confidence that boggled Liam's frickin' mind.

"Don't lecture me about language. *You* swear like a sailor," Cate grumbled at her father, accusation shining in her blue eyes. The same dark shade of blue as Morgan's. And her tone contained the same note of authority. It was damn eerie seeing them together sometimes.

"That doesn't mean I want my kid to have a filthy mouth," Morgan shot back. "It's unladylike."

Cate and Noelle both snorted.

"I have no interest in being a *lady*," Cate informed him.

Rather than answer his daughter, and without looking in Liam's direction, Morgan said, "What's up, Boston?"

Liam wasn't surprised that Morgan had known he was lurking in the doorway. The man possessed superhero senses. He could smell danger from miles away, and he always knew when he wasn't alone in a room.

Without wasting any time, Liam marched over to his boss. "Reilly's in the process of robbing a bank."

Cate's loud gasp echoed in the room, but neither Morgan nor Noelle looked particularly astounded by the revelation, which made Liam's shoulders stiffen.

"You knew about this?" he demanded.

Morgan shrugged. "One of Noelle's informants called about an hour ago to give us a heads-up."

"And you didn't think to tell the rest of the team?"

"What's the point? The situation will have resolved itself by the time any of you even get to Dublin."

Liam gaped at the other man. Morgan's blasé response was grating as fuck, and far more callous than he'd expected. Sean might have abandoned the team right before a critical op, but that didn't mean he deserved to be shunned for it.

"You *know* Sean," Liam said flatly. "He's not a criminal, goddamn it. Obviously he needs our help."

"It's not my concern," Morgan answered with a shrug.

Then he cocked his head at the two females standing nearby, as if to say, *They're all I care about.* "Reilly left. He's no longer my responsibility."

Liam's jaw fell open again. "Bullshit. He's still one of us."

"No, he's not. He made that pretty fu—cover your ears, Cate—pretty *fucking* clear when he skipped town."

Morgan's anger was palpable, and Liam supposed he understood it to some extent. When he'd first joined the team, Morgan had made it clear that there were only two rules—show up, and watch one another's backs. Reilly had disregarded both when he'd left them in the lurch and fled to Dublin in the dead of night.

"Relax, Macgregor," Noelle spoke up. Her tone wasn't gentle, but blunt. "Sean has good reasons for everything he does. I wouldn't worry about him."

"He's holding up a bank!" Liam raised his voice, unable to contain his disbelief. When Noelle remained unfazed, it triggered a spark of suspicion. "Do you know why he's doing this?"

She gave a little shrug, causing her long blond braid to cascade over her shoulder. "Rumor has it he's fallen back in with his old mentor."

"And who the hell would that be?"

Noelle spared a look at Cate, then exchanged one with Morgan, who nodded.

"Eamon O'Hare," she told Liam. "He's the leader of an IRA splinter group—the Irish Dagger. Sean and Oliver used to work for him when they were younger."

"The IRA?" Liam echoed, once again agape. "That's bullshit. No fucking way is Sean involved with them again."

"How come you don't lecture *him* about his language?" Cate said irritably, shooting a glare at her father. "And why aren't you helping Sean?"

"Because he's not my daughter," Morgan muttered.

"And stay out of it, sweetheart. This doesn't concern you."

Liam raked a hand through his hair, fighting hard to tamp down his rising anger. Morgan and Noelle might not care about Reilly, but he sure as hell did. He wasn't about to watch Sean die in an armed robbery, or stand by while the IRA fucked with him.

"I'm putting in a request for time off," he said stiffly.

Morgan met his eyes. "Request denied."

"Tough shit. I'm taking it anyway. And I want D with me."

Aggravation hardened Morgan's features. "You're pushing your luck, Boston."

"You can spare us both," he insisted. "Kane and Trevor are taking care of the extraction in Bolivia. Castle and his team are handling the Johannesburg job. D and I aren't leaving for that security gig until next month—there's no reason why we can't go to Dublin."

"Yes, there *is* a reason. Because I fucking said no."

Cate joined the conversation again, her cloudy expression darkening as she stared at her father. "You're really not going to help him? What the hell is the matter with you?"

"Watch your tone," Morgan snapped, but when her expression went stricken, he softened his. "Sean is a grown man, sweetheart. He makes his own choices, and he chose to leave the team. Which means he's no longer one of mine."

"That's *bullshit*." Her blue eyes blazed. "You like him, and he *is* one of yours. And even if he wasn't, you *owe* him."

A frown marred Morgan's lips. "How do you figure that?"

"Because he helped you get me out of France."

Cate's smug reminder hung in the air, drawing a chuckle from Noelle and a triumphant smile from Liam.

Damn, he liked the girl. Liked her a helluva lot. And there was nothing better than watching her face off with Morgan. Cate was as strong and stubborn as her father, a force to be reckoned with, and she was only eighteen. It was scary to think how unstoppable she'd be once she got a little older.

He studied Morgan's face. Saw the man's brain working, the reluctance and anger chipping away as Cate's words sunk in. Sean had been an invaluable asset during that mission in Paris. He'd worked alongside Morgan and the rest of the men to rescue Cate from the controlling clutches of her grandfather, a dangerous arms dealer who'd blamed Morgan for destroying his daughter's life. Not only had Cate's grandfather put a hit out on Morgan, but he'd turned her into a prisoner in her own home.

And Sean had played a large role in Morgan's reunion with the girl.

"Fine. You win." Morgan scowled at Liam. "You and D can go to Dublin. Ash, too."

The last-second addition put a deep groove in Cate's forehead. "Why does Ash have to go?"

"Because they'll need backup," Morgan said firmly. He arched a brow. "Would you rather everyone stay here?"

She bit her lip. "No, they need to help Sean," she murmured, but she still looked upset, and Liam knew her concern was solely on Ash's behalf.

Cate had been spending a lot of time with the rookie since she'd moved to the compound. Liam didn't think there was anything romantic between them—Morgan would straight-up murder Ash if he touched the girl—but there was no denying the two of them had formed a bond. They were ridiculously protective of each other, though whenever Liam teased Ash about it, the guy just shrugged and gave his standard response—"She's a sweet kid."

"Thank you." Liam offered his boss a nod of gratitude. "I know you're pissed at Reilly, but this is the right move."

Morgan still didn't look enthused, but he nodded back. "Just don't take too long." He paused. "And if you can get ahold of Sully, he's all yours too."

Tension hit him like a flash flood, tightening Liam's gut and bringing a rush of discomfort. Morgan didn't notice, though. He'd already dismissed him, laying a hand on Cate's arm as he led her back to the gun counter.

Noelle lingered, a small smile playing on her lips. "Say hello to Reilly for me," she drawled, and then she went to join her husband and stepdaughter.

With an unsteady breath, Liam left the room, trying not to dwell on Morgan's last words.

*He's all yours.*

The boss hadn't meant it in a . . . *sexual* way. Liam knew that. But the remark still unleashed a wave of uncomfortable memories he'd been trying hard to suppress.

Like the fact that his best friend had *kissed* him.

*Relax. You've moved past it.*

Right. They'd moved past it. Kind of.

Fine, not at all. Or at least not on Liam's part. Sullivan, on the other hand, seemed to have forgotten all about it. He'd apologized for the kiss, promised that it would never happen again, and once they'd left Paris, he'd gone back to treating Liam the way he always had.

He couldn't blame Sully, though. Liam's shocked and horrified reaction to that kiss had made it pretty damn clear where his head was.

If he was a braver man, he wouldn't have accepted the apology—he would've told his friend that saying sorry hadn't been necessary.

Because he'd *liked* it.

But the confession had jammed in his throat, and so

he'd pretended that the whole crazy encounter was no biggie. And since then, he'd tried to think of Sully as nothing more than the cocky teammate who also happened to be his best friend.

Keyword: *tried.*

Liam headed back upstairs, ignoring the turbulent emotions churning in his stomach. He wasn't gay, damn it. He liked women. No, he *loved* women. Which only made his attraction to Sullivan even more confusing. Threesomes were one thing, but fantasizing about being with another man? One-on-one? He didn't fucking understand it. At all.

He stood in the kitchen, resting his elbows on the granite counter as he took a breath to clear his head. Fuck. None of that mattered right now. Reilly was in trouble, and they needed to get him out of it.

He slid his phone out of his pocket and pulled up Sully's number, then hesitated. He hadn't spoken to his friend in a month and a half. Which wasn't out of the ordinary—Sully was always out of touch when he was out on his boat. For some reason, Morgan was perfectly cool with the fact that Sullivan skipped town for months at a time. Apparently it was the arrangement they'd made when Sully had first joined up with the team.

Sully had checked in over the radio a few times since he'd left, but Liam hadn't spoken to him personally since the . . . *incident.* It also didn't escape him that he hadn't been invited on Sullivan's little vacation; the last time Sully had done his open-water thing, he'd brought Liam along.

But hell, Liam was glad he hadn't gone this time. The two of them, alone on a sailboat in the middle of the ocean? Shit was already confusing enough.

Swallowing his reluctance, he dialed the number for Sully's satellite phone. It took several rings before Sullivan picked up, and the moment his Australian accent drawled over the line, Liam's chest squeezed. Despite the messed-up attraction he felt for the guy, Sully was still his closest friend, and he'd honestly missed him.

He cleared his throat. "Hey. It's me."

"Boston! Hey!" Sully sounded like he had no care in the world. "You should see the sunset I'm looking at right now. The whole sky is pink—it's weird, but pretty bloody awesome."

Liam had to laugh. "Instagram it. I haven't seen a nice sunset in a while. It's been raining here all week."

"Whatcha up to? Probably bored as fuck over there, huh?"

"Actually, no. Things just got interesting."

"Yeah?"

"Oh yeah." He paused. "Sean Reilly's in the process of robbing a bank in Dublin."

Silence met his ears.

"Sully, you there?"

Another long pause, and then Sullivan's grave voice slid into his ear. "I'm on my way."

*Dublin*

"This is bollocks! I'm not going to jail for this!" Paddy Lynch hissed out.

Gallagher had just outlined the plan privately to each of the men, and although none of them were too happy about it, they'd accepted the orders with resigned nods. But not Paddy. He was the hothead of the group, and Sean had expected the lad to object.

But he didn't have the patience for an argument right now. They had to make their move, and fast. The negotiator was getting wise to their bullshit requests. Five million dollars, total immunity, a chopper to take them to safety. They were the typical unrealistic demands robbers usually made, and Sean was surprised the cops were even humoring them.

The negotiator was due to ring back in fifteen minutes, which meant it was time to get the ball rolling.

"Why does *he* get to walk out of here?" Paddy's scornful gaze shifted to Sean, who kept his expression blank.

Gallagher sighed in annoyance, yet again explaining his reasoning for why Sean would be the one playing the hostage, but that didn't appease the younger man.

"Bollocks," Paddy muttered again. "I'm not surrendering, you hear me? I'm not going back to the Joy for—"

*"Mo thír,"* Gallagher interrupted.

That stopped the other man cold. "What?" he said shakily.

*"Mo thír, mo onóir, mo chuid fola."*

Gallagher's face was somber as he spoke in Gaelic, reciting the words that were guaranteed to get Paddy's attention—*my country, my honor, my blood.*

And he succeeded. Paddy went equally somber, his shoulders drooping, his fists slowly opening as his hands dangled at his sides.

"Remember those words, Padraig?" Gallagher said softly. "You took an oath."

Christ, these men and their bloody oath. Sean had recited it himself a long time ago, back when his father was still alive. Rabbit had thrown that fact at him mere days ago, reminding him of the promises he'd made, the loyalty he'd vowed, but Sean had spit it right back in the older man's face. Any allegiance he'd pledged had become null and void the second Eamon O'Hare had kidnapped his brother.

Gallagher and Paddy, however . . . the oath still meant

something to them. Their whole lives revolved around it and the ideology that had been beaten into their skulls since the day they were born.

"Live for the cause, die for the cause," Gallagher murmured, reciting the final words of the Dagger's motto.

Paddy was visibly clenching his teeth. He looked pained, upset, but the resignation that Sean had seen in the other men's eyes now flickered in Paddy's. "Live for the cause, die for the cause," he echoed.

Jesus Christ. It was fucking surreal. Sean masked his disbelief as the two men exchanged a tight hug.

"I fecked up," Paddy mumbled. "I shouldn't have aimed for the head."

Gallagher clapped his hand over Paddy's shoulder. "No, you shouldn't have."

Paddy nodded. "I got us into this mess. The alarm wouldn't have gone off if I hadn't killed the ghost. It's only right that I pay the price for my mistake."

Sean didn't know whether he was impressed or amused. Jesus, Rabbit had trained his soldiers well. Sean wondered if *he* could ever inspire that kind of loyalty in someone. His brother, sure. Maybe Jim Morgan, at least before he'd deserted the man.

But any loyalty he'd had from Morgan was gone now. The man was cold, unforgiving. When Sean had abandoned the team, he'd pretty much ensured that they wouldn't welcome him back with open arms.

Regret constricted his chest, making him want to slam his fist into the nearest wall. Maybe it made him a total pussy, but he'd been honored to earn a spot on Morgan's team. The life of an information dealer wasn't too exciting. Oliver enjoyed the work, but Sean had been tired of it. He'd found himself longing for his days as a merc, even more so once he'd started doing odd jobs for Morgan's team.

Maybe Morgan would take him back when this was all over.

*Un-bloody-likely.*

Right. Probably too much to hope for.

"Go and get Murphy," Gallagher told Paddy. "I need him to answer the mobile when the negotiator rings back." Once Paddy hurried off, Gallagher turned to Sean. "Stay here. I'll be back to grab you in a few minutes."

Sean nodded.

The second he was alone, he sank into the nearest chair around the large oval table in the bank's staff room. Fuck, he needed to get out of here. He felt like a caged animal. Trapped. Powerless. And he didn't function well in that state.

He glanced around the room, taking in the tidy row of metal lockers, the kitchenette, the closed door of the supply closet. On the back wall was a cork bulletin board littered with snapshots and postcards and notes from customers thanking various tellers for their stellar work.

Sean tore his gaze away from the board and dragged a frustrated hand over his cropped hair. Christ, he couldn't imagine working a regular nine-to-five. Being a bank teller or a manager, smiling at hundreds of people every day, dealing with their bullshit. He'd kill himself before taking a job like that.

His gaze shifted to the clock over the ancient refrigerator. As he watched the second hand tick by, that sensation of helplessness crept in once more. He'd found some clothes in one of the lockers—ill-fitting trousers, a hooded sweatshirt. He was dressed like a civilian and ready to go, but he couldn't make a single move until Gallagher returned.

Time seemed to slow down. He heard Gallagher's muffled voice in the corridor, murmuring something to

Murphy, he assumed. Everything went quiet a moment later.

He stared at the clock. Ten more minutes before the negotiator called back.

Footsteps sounded from the hall, then faded.

The clock continued to tick silently.

And then a faint creak echoed from above.

Sean froze for a heartbeat, then shot to his feet and grabbed his weapon from the tabletop, aiming it at the ceiling. The shotgun felt strange in his hands. Heavy, bulky. He was used to carrying handguns or assault rifles on a mission, but the Irish Dagger was old-school.

There was rustling overhead. Then a soft hiss, barely audible.

Adrenaline spiked in his blood, tensing every muscle in his body. Someone was here.

He kept his gaze trained on the ceiling. Studied the air vent situated above the kitchenette counter. Son of a bitch. Was the assault team making a move? O'Brien was in the security room monitoring the exterior cameras, damn it. He hadn't reported seeing someone enter or leave the premises. Unless the moron had dropped the ball, missed a breach.

And Sean couldn't alert Gallagher, because the Dagger's operation was so bloody low-rent that they didn't even use comms. He had no earpiece, no radio.

Another creak wafted from the direction of the vent. Shit. Someone was up there, all right.

Sean's boots didn't make a sound as he moved closer to the vent. He glanced at the cabinet near the door, where he'd left his mask, but it was too far away. Fuck it. At this point, covering his face was bloody unnecessary. If the ERU was making its move, then Sean's identity would be discovered sooner rather than later.

One intruder, he deduced. It was too quiet for an entire assault team to be up there. Maybe it was recon, a quick breach to better assess the situation inside the bank.

And double fuck—the intruder would have heard Sean and Gallagher talking to Paddy. Outlining their plan to surrender.

He hoped to hell that the fucker didn't have an open comm, that he hadn't alerted his team about the plan.

Sean's back went ramrod straight when another noise broke the quiet air. A metallic grind.

He narrowed his eyes, tensing even more when he saw one of the tiny bolts on the corner of the vent begin to unscrew itself.

Shit.

*Shit.*

The bolt broke free and fell to the floor with a soft *ping*. Then the opposite bolt pulled its own magic act.

Sean raised his shotgun. His breathing slowed, heart rate moving along steadily. He just had to wait. Wait for the guy to climb down. Incapacitate him before he even knew what was happening.

But it all happened too fast. The second screw was barely falling toward the floor when the metal hatch swung open and a blur of black catapulted down from the ceiling. The intruder vaulted off the counter in a swirl of speed, hitting the floor in a roll while swinging a black automatic in Sean's direction.

"Don't move a fucking mus—" The command died midsentence as a shocked hiss filled the room. *"Sean?"*

He stared at the woman crouched on the other side of the room, his jaw falling open.

*"Bailey?"*

# Chapter 4

Sean couldn't fathom what he was seeing. He had to be imagining it. Imagining *her*.

He blinked rapidly, feeling like a thirst-ridden desert nomad hallucinating a mirage. A beautiful, confusing mirage featuring the woman of his dreams.

Jesus Christ. This was no hallucination. She was actually *here*. Four feet away from him.

"What the *fuck* are you doing here?" By some miracle, he managed to keep his voice to a whisper, but he couldn't conceal his anger. Or his horror.

She was clad in all black—long-sleeve shirt, tight pants, sleek boots. Her hair was pulled into a tight knot at the nape of her neck, emphasizing her classic features and big gray eyes, and she looked as enraged as he felt.

"*Me?* Goddamn it, Sean! What are *you* doing here?"

He didn't answer. Couldn't answer. His vocal cords were paralyzed, and his brain had turned into a jumble of spaghetti noodles trying to make sense of her presence. How had she infiltrated the bank? And *why*, for Christ's sake?

He had no answers for that, and all he was capable of

focusing on was the fact that she was here. Bailey was here. His Bailey.

*Not yours. Never yours.*

The swift reminder brought a jolt of pain. No, she wasn't his. She was Ollie's.

"You need to go," he said urgently. "Right now."

"I came here for you," she replied in a fierce voice. "And I'm not leaving without you."

"Bloody hell, Bailey, *you need to go*." He stalked forward and grabbed her arm, trying to drag her toward the kitchenette. "You can't be here."

Frustration burned in her eyes. Those beautiful gray eyes that were too big for her face, giving her a perpetual doe-eyed air of fragility. But she wasn't fragile. She was tough as nails, exceedingly intelligent, and highly trained. She held her weapon with ease, and Sean knew damn well that her lithe, curvy body was probably concealing many more dangerous goodies.

It was so easy to see why his brother loved her.

He banished the thought the second it surfaced, along with the bitterness that coated his throat. Bitterness that transformed right back into rage when Bailey shrugged his hand off her and slammed her fist directly into his solar plexus.

The blow landed with a *thud*, making him grunt. For such a small woman, she was insanely strong.

"Why are you doing this? What on earth compelled you to rob a bank?"

He gritted his teeth so hard his jaw ached. "You. Can't. Be. Here."

"I already am," she shot back. "So now tell me what the hell is going on. You left Morgan's crew to join up with O'Hare again? What the *fuck*, Sean?"

He wasn't surprised that she'd figured out the Irish Dagger was behind the heist—Bailey had resources a mile long—but he didn't have time to explain himself to her at the moment. If Gallagher caught her back here . . .

". . . white flag, so to speak . . ."

The male voice beyond the door made both of them freeze.

Sean cursed under his breath. Shit. Gallagher was talking to Murphy. Which meant that he'd be returning any second to bring his "hostage" to the lobby.

Ignoring his rising panic, Sean reached out and grabbed the bottom of Bailey's shirt. "Take this off," he ordered. "Now."

"Are you kidding—"

He interrupted by yanking the shirt up, nearly ripping the fabric as he desperately tried to take it off for her. She yelped when the neck hole snagged on her ear, but Sean didn't stop. He peeled off the shirt, breathing hard as he studied the white camisole she wore underneath. It was skimpy, but not indecent. Something a woman might wear to work, rather than the all-black commando outfit she'd been sporting a second ago.

He snatched the gun from her hand and clicked on the safety, then tucked it at her waistband and pulled her camisole down to cover the bulge.

"What are you doing?" she whispered. "Why—" She halted when the sounds of footsteps came from the corridor.

Setting his jaw, Sean curled his fingers over her upper arm and dragged her toward the supply closet. He threw open the door, balled up the shirt he'd taken from her, and shoved it behind a mop bucket. The closet was tiny, crammed with shelves of coffee filters and other random supplies, but it was big enough for Bailey, and he wasted no time pushing her inside.

The footsteps got closer. Gallagher was coming to get him.

"Play along," Sean commanded. "I'm serious, luv. If you want to stay alive, you need to do everything I say."

The footsteps neared the door. Bailey's eyes widened, and then she nodded.

As the squeak of the doorknob sounded from behind them, Sean tightened his grip on Bailey's arm. He waited. Took a breath. Then wrenched her out of the closet so hard he nearly yanked her arm from its socket.

She cried out in pain, and the door opened at the exact moment Sean shook her violently. Pure venom clung to his tone as he spat out, "You little *bitch*!"

Heavy boots thudded against the floor as Gallagher appeared beside him. "What in bloody *hell* is going on?" he roared.

Sean turned to his "leader" in disgust. "I found her hiding in the closet. She's one of the tellers."

A wild curse flew out of Gallagher's mouth. "Does she have a mobile on her?"

"No, thank Christ."

Gallagher's face was still covered, but his eyes were blazing with fury, so dark they were nearly indistinguishable from the black fabric of his mask. "Are you fecking kidding me? Who swept this room?"

"Who do you think?" Sean snapped, not the slightest bit guilty for laying another burden of blame at Paddy Lynch's feet.

"Bloody wanker," Gallagher mumbled. His features hardened as he turned to examine Bailey. "Stop bawling, bitch."

Sean glanced over at her again, hiding his astonishment when he noticed her transformation. She'd slipped her hair out of its bun seconds before Gallagher's entrance, and the black waves now cascaded down her shoulders, tousled, flat on one side, as if she'd truly been hiding in a closet for the past hour.

With the tears sticking to her thick eyelashes and her bottom lip quivering like a leaf on a windy day, she looked terrified and guilty. Like a completely different person. And though Sean had seen her acting skills in action before, they never failed to impress him.

"C'mere." As Gallagher jerked her away from the closet, it took all of Sean's willpower not to unleash a right hook at the guy's jaw for manhandling her like that.

Bailey's tears fell harder as Gallagher grasped her chin with both hands, forcing her to look at him.

"You're gonna keep your mouth shut, you hear me? In five minutes this'll all be over, and until then, you're going to sit in the lobby with the rest of your colleagues and you won't say a fecking word, understood?"

She nodded weakly.

He twisted her chin, turning her toward Sean. "See this man?"

Another shaky nod.

"You don't know him. He wasn't here. When you see him again in a minute, you will pretend he doesn't exist." Gallagher released her abruptly, cursing under his breath.

He'd gripped her face so tightly he'd left red marks on her fair skin. Sean had to swallow his rage and force himself not to tear Gallagher's throat out.

"If you so much as open your mouth, I will put a bullet in your head," Gallagher finished. "Understand?"

"I understand," she whispered.

"Now, shut up and come with me." Gallagher grabbed her arm and tugged her across the room, his eyes burning with annoyance as he glanced over his shoulder at Sean. "I'll be right back."

As they reached the doorway, Bailey turned her head. Just for a split second. Just long enough for Sean to mouth the words, *Trust me.*

She gave an imperceptible nod, and then she and Gallagher were gone.

Sean stared at the empty doorway, choking on the panic that clawed up his throat like cold, brittle fingers. Everything had been on track, damn it. He'd been moments away from leaving the bank with his skin intact, and now Bailey had thrown a wrench in his plans. He wasn't stepping foot outside the building without her.

*Damn you, Ollie. She came here for you.*

The hot agony that ripped through him nearly knocked him off his feet. Bailey might claim she'd come here for him, but he knew the truth. With the intel at her disposal, she must have figured out that Rabbit had nabbed Ollie. She must have known that helping Sean was the equivalent of saving Oliver.

It stung like hell. But he had no right to be hurt. Of course she loved his brother. Why wouldn't she? Oliver was the best man Sean had ever known. Hell, he was a bloody *saint*. Sean had once watched his brother run into a burning building to save a low-life meth cooker they'd been hitting up for intel.

And he couldn't even count the number of times Ollie had swooped in to rescue *him*. The guy was perfect. Perfect son, perfect brother, perfect fucking man for a woman like Bailey.

Sean was nothing more than the speed bump that had disrupted their relationship, the asshole who'd given in to his selfish urges and taken what Bailey had been offering to his brother.

But he couldn't think about that now. Bailey might not belong to him, but at the moment, she was *his* responsibility, and he was going to bring her back to Oliver safe and sound.

Even if he died trying.

* * *

Bailey didn't struggle as Sean's cohort dragged her down the hall as if she were a piece of luggage. The masked man grumbled in Gaelic the entire time, and although she didn't know the dialect well, she suspected there were a lot of colorful curses being aimed her way. A few seconds later, he pushed her into the lobby, where every pair of eyes immediately flew in her direction.

She noted the line of terrified-looking people on the white-tile floor. She averted her gaze, heeding her captor's threat that she'd better keep to herself, but she was relieved to see that the hostages were safe. For now anyway.

"We found your little mate hiding in the back room," her captor snapped at the stocky man sitting at the end of the line.

Bailey quickly masked her alarm, forcing herself to meet the eyes of the man who'd been spoken to. He wore a gray business suit and a name tag publicizing that he was the bank manager. Shit. Sean had told his IRA buddy that Bailey was a teller.

She implored the manager with her eyes, silently begging him not to reveal that they were total strangers. He must have heard the unspoken plea, because he kept his mouth shut, his lips tightening in a thin line.

Her captor shoved her to her knees beside the bank manager. "Sit down and shut up," he said curtly.

She did both, and the masked man stalked off, leaving her with the group of fifteen ashen-faced hostages. The second he was gone, she assessed her surroundings and pinpointed the threats. Three gunmen remained in the lobby, two on opposite ends of the plate-glass window, one near the teller counter. All masked and armed with sawed-off shotguns.

The bulge at the small of her back was reassuring as

hell, as were the two knives tucked inside her boots. But the fact that Sean had let her keep her gun meant he thought she might need to use it—and *that* was not at all reassuring.

God, he'd looked so ravaged back there. Tired and pale, as if this was the last thing he wanted to be doing tonight. And that told her she'd been right. Sean wasn't a criminal. Somehow he'd been coerced into carrying out this heist.

"Who are you?"

The barely audible inquiry came from the manager beside her.

Bailey kept her gaze straight head, speaking as softly as he had, but not answering the question. "It'll be okay. It'll all be over soon."

God, she hoped she wasn't lying to him, but she didn't think she was. Because she'd glimpsed something else in Sean's eyes before, something other than desperation and exhaustion.

Determination.

He had a plan; she was certain of it. She just hoped it was a good one. You never knew with Sean, though. He was impulsive to the core, all snap decisions and rash actions without any prior thought.

She'd picked up on that recklessness the moment they'd met. Five years ago, when she'd first started working for Noelle. Bailey had taken one look at the cocky Irishman and known she'd wanted nothing to do with him. Oh, he'd been gorgeous back then, as gorgeous as he was now, with those dark green eyes and rumpled blond hair and the sexual confidence oozing from his pores. But looks meant nothing to her; they never had.

Sean had tried working the charm on her from second one, but Bailey had been immune to it. She knew from experience that charm could be deceiving. The charismatic ones always harbored the most secrets. They were the ones who hurt you the most if you let them, and so turning down Sean's numerous hookup offers had been easy for her.

Turning down Oliver, though . . . not so easy. Sean's twin was equally charming, but in an understated way. He was strong, dependable, and endearing, the kind of man you *wanted* to fall in love with. When he'd asked her out after she'd hit him up for information last year, she hadn't been able to say no. One date had turned into two, then three, but no matter how badly Bailey had wanted to make a connection with Ollie, he'd felt more like a brother than a love interest.

Fortunately, Oliver had felt the same way, and their failed love connection had transformed into a friendship she valued. At least until Sean's masquerade. After that, she hadn't been able to look at Oliver without remembering her night with Sean.

"You've caused enough trouble for one evening."

The irritated male voice penetrated Bailey's muddled thoughts. She lifted her head in time to see the masked leader march into the lobby.

Holding a gun to Sean's head.

Bailey immediately saw through the ploy. Sean was clearly feigning his fearful expression, because she knew damn well that the man wasn't afraid of anything. Hell, that was his biggest problem—*not* being afraid. Diving headfirst into dangerous situations without any regard for the consequences.

Whatever Sean and his "accomplices" had come here for, Sean was now in possession of it. And the only way to get it out of the bank was for him to deliver it himself.

Sean the robber had become Sean the hostage.

"You wasted my goddamn time," the gunman snapped. "And now you're going to sit here like a good little lad and keep your mouth shut."

Sean flinched as he was forcibly pushed to his knees, playing his part to a tee. He was breathing hard, his panicked gaze darting around the lobby like a pinball. In his khakis and sweatshirt, he looked like a terrified college student rather than the badass Bailey knew him to be.

Avoiding his captor's harsh eyes, Sean settled next to Bailey, drawing his knees up and wrapping his arms around them. The Sean Reilly she knew didn't exist at the moment. This Sean radiated weakness rather than power, and the transformation made her want to smile. Evidently he was a much better actor than she'd thought.

As the gunman marched off again, Bailey and Sean continued to stare straight ahead. She kept her gaze trained on the two men by the window. One of them suddenly made an abrupt move, taking off in a brisk walk toward the rear corridor. Voices spilled out into the lobby, laced with anger, rising in volume.

A moment later, a gunshot exploded in the air.

The sound was deafening, bouncing off the walls and mingling with the screams that erupted from the hostages. The remaining gunman at the window raced over to the frightened hostages, ordering them to shut up, waving his weapon around in a frantic attempt to calm the whimpering people. In the blink of an eye, another masked man burst into the lobby, sprinting to the window and raising his arms in the air as if trying to signal the cops beyond the glass to stand down. He held up the phone in his hand, gesturing wildly.

Bailey held her breath as silence crashed over the room. She studied Sean from the corner of her eye, saw the rigid set of his jaw, but he didn't look over.

Every single hostage jerked when the phone suddenly rang.

The man at the window relaxed, his shoulders sagging with visible relief. Then he raised the phone to his ear, his boots slapping against the floor as he retreated to the back again.

Urgent murmuring wafted into the lobby. Bailey's peripheral vision caught a muscle twitch in Sean's jaw, but he remained expressionless. The air was thick with tension, which only deepened when the gunman returned, tailed by two other men, and signaled for the remaining robbers to join them. As the five men gathered in a tight huddle, Bailey used their distracted whispering to touch her earpiece.

"Rafe," she murmured. "Abandon post. Request pickup."

She felt Sean stiffen beside her, but she didn't acknowledge him. Whatever was about to go down, she had to be ready. She and Rafe had already arranged for a rendezvous point if she needed one.

And it looked like she was about to need one.

"All right, on your feet, boys and girls." The brusque order came from the man holding the cell phone.

When nobody moved, he let out a frustrated shout. "Now!"

Everyone shot to their feet, Bailey and Sean included. God, just looking at the other hostages upset her. They were like a group of miners who'd been trapped underground for weeks. Swaying on their feet, pale and disoriented.

She donned the same petrified mask, trembling as she awaited further instructions.

The masked man pointed to the door. "Let's go."

Not a single person made a sound as the group headed for the entrance. The gunman unlocked the door, opened it, and hooked a thumb at the barricade on the street.

"Go," he told them.

There was a split second of hesitation, and then the hostages ran out the door as if the room was on fire. Bailey was jostled, shoved out of the way, and almost knocked down as a dozen people streamed past her in a mad race for the street. Two police officers in full assault gear sprinted forward at the freed captives, urgently guiding people away from the bank.

"We need to clear the area," a male voice barked. "Everybody move. *Now.*"

A hand landed on Bailey's shoulder, ushering her toward the blockade of law enforcement vehicles. Someone urged her along, pushed her forward, and she lost sight of Sean amid the crowd. The other hostages were crying with relief and stumbling to safety as half a dozen officers moved past them with military precision to form a line in front of the bank.

Where the hell was Sean?

She searched the faces around her, spotted him, and breathed in relief. Someone urged her through the line of crime scene tape, a young garda who swept his gaze over her as if assessing her for injuries.

"Are you all right, Miss?"

She quickly turned on the waterworks, blubbering incoherently as she threw herself into his arms. "Oh my God. It was so scary! I thought they would kill us!"

"It's okay." A hand awkwardly patted her head. "You're safe now. You need to go to those ambulances over there. The people there will check you out and take your statement."

Bailey nodded rapidly, feeling Sean on her six as she made a beeline for the ambulances. She didn't dare to turn and look at him, but she sensed his urgency, knew they had to make a move before they reached the emergency vehicles.

They were ten yards away when Sean halted in his tracks. Bailey turned, saw his green eyes focus on the bank doors. The five robbers had just stepped outside. Their guns were lowered, but the way Sean's shoulders stiffened, you'd think they were gunning down the police.

"Son of a bitch," he mumbled under his breath, clearly seeing something Bailey wasn't. "Damn it, Gallagher. No."

A frown marred Bailey's lips at the exact moment that all five men raised their weapons.

Shit.

Sean tried to take a step forward, but Bailey grabbed his arm, keeping him in place. "Don't. You can't— "

A gunshot cut her off, summoning a wild curse from Sean's lips.

One of the men had fired. Nowhere near the Garda officers, as far as Bailey could tell, but she knew he hadn't aimed to kill anyone.

Just to provoke.

And it worked. The police brigade opened fire as screams echoed in the night. The robbers' bodies fell like bowling pins, their blood spilling onto the pavement as they jerked and twitched from chest and head wounds. As they died in a hail of bullets that made Bailey's ears ring.

When the last body hit the ground, shocked silence crashed over the street.

"Bailey," Sean murmured. Grim, stoic.

She snapped out of her horror. Nodded.

The two of them veered past the waiting ambulances and disappeared into the darkness.

# Chapter 5

Those crazy bastards. Bloody *morons*. Sean almost wished Gallagher and the others were still alive so he could murder them himself. They hadn't needed to go out in a blaze of glory, damn it! They could have done their bloody time, trusted Rabbit to find a way to get them out.

But no, he supposed they couldn't have. The Irish Dagger had too many enemies. A stretch in the Joy for a Dagger member was the equivalent of a death sentence.

Sean stared out the car window, too preoccupied to pay attention to the city scenery whizzing by him. Christ. How was he going to explain to Rabbit why five of his soldiers had died tonight?

And how the hell was he going to get rid of Bailey? He didn't want her anywhere near this mess. It was too bloody dangerous, and Rabbit was too damn unpredictable.

She was in the passenger side of the sedan, sitting beside the dark-haired man who'd provided their pickup. Rafe. She'd introduced him as a colleague of hers, apparently trusting him enough to assist her, and damned if that didn't spark a flash of jealousy. God knew she'd refused *Sean's* help time and again. But obviously his woman was perfectly content letting a total stranger drive her getaway car.

*She's not your woman, mate.*

His possessiveness over her was too much even for him. She was *Oliver's* girl. Or at least she had been before Sean had swept in and screwed things up for them. He hated himself for what he'd done, and yet each time he thought back to that night . . . he didn't regret it. He'd wanted Bailey for so long, and for that one night, she'd been his.

Which only made him an even bigger asshole. What kind of man went after his brother's girl and didn't fucking regret it?

"My flat is ten streets west of here." Sean addressed the driver in a curt voice when he became aware of his surroundings. "You can drop me off there."

Bailey twisted around in her seat, storm clouds darkening her eyes. "Are you kidding me? You've been giving me the silent treatment for twenty minutes and *that's* the first thing you say? Drop me off at my flat?"

Sean set his jaw, responding with a cool look that only intensified her anger.

"I deserve an explanation," she snapped. "I risked my life for you tonight."

That triggered his own anger. "I didn't bloody ask you to! You shouldn't have come to Dublin."

"God. You're such a stubborn ass! You were in *trouble*."

Maybe it made him a masochist, but he found her so damn attractive when she was fuming at him. Her eyes always went from gray to metallic silver, her fair skin taking on a red flush that made her come alive.

He'd wanted her from the second he'd met her, years ago in South America. She'd been on a job and needed information about her mark, and she'd looked so tiny and delicate during their first meeting that he'd wanted to yank her into his arms and never let go. Didn't matter that she'd hated him on sight. Her standoffish attitude had been a challenge, triggering the urge to win over the elusive Bailey.

To make her his.

But he'd failed. Instead of warming up to him, she'd run straight into his brother's arms.

"I was doing just fine before you showed up," he muttered. "I got out of the bank, didn't I?" He shot her a pointed look. "Without your help, I might add."

"I don't care that you got out! I care about why you went *in*!"

The next thing he knew, she'd unsnapped her seat belt and climbed into the backseat. The car hit a pothole just as she went to sit, and her hand landed on his thigh as she tried to steady herself.

Sean's groin instantly stirred at the feel of her palm on his leg, his entire body flooding with heat. It should have been impossible, getting hard at a time like this, but Bailey had always evoked that response in him.

Seeing the look in his eyes, she snatched her hand back and settled in the seat next to him. "Why were you robbing that bank?" she demanded.

"Why else do people rob banks? For money."

A genuine rush of laughter left her mouth. "You have more money than you'll ever be able to spend. Lord knows you charge us an arm and a leg when we hit you up for intel. But fine, let's pretend you needed the money. Where is it?" She swept her hand in the air in front of him. "Where's your bucketload of cash, Sean?"

He stifled a groan. "The heist didn't go as planned. We had to abort before we could get into the vault."

"We, huh?" she echoed. "O'Hare's foot soldiers, you mean. So, what, you're suddenly back in the IRA?"

"The IRA no longer exists, luv. You should brush up on your Irish history."

Another laugh, this one heavy with scorn. "Bullshit. We both know a new splinter faction pops up every other week. There might not be an official militant republican army anymore, but the IRA fucking exists. The Irish Dagger exists. And Eamon O'Hare is still leading it, same way he's led it for decades."

Sean gave up on contradicting her. It was no secret that Rabbit was, and remained, a staunch supporter of a united Ireland. Just like Sean's father had been.

Colin Reilly had been heavily involved with the Dagger since his youth. He'd lived through the protests and riots in the seventies and eighties, witnessed the escalating violence. Hell, he'd *contributed* to that violence.

Shootings, bombings, and stabbings had been a daily occurrence in Sean's life. He and Ollie had seen their father get stitched up in the back room of O'Hare's Pub. They'd watched the Dagger members drink to successful bombings. Heard the men make plans to take down government officials or opponents of their cause.

Sean had never understood what his father was fighting for. The Reillys were from Dublin, yet they were battling over the North, a place Sean had never even visited as a child. As he'd gotten older, he'd come to understand the politics behind it, but the cause hadn't interested him and Ollie. They'd left Dublin to work as mercenaries, eventually becoming some of the most sought-out information dealers on the map, and neither one of them had looked back.

But the past had a funny way of dragging you back in.

"The question is," Bailey went on, interrupting his

thoughts, "why are you letting O'Hare call the shots again? You and Ollie quit being his errand boys a long time ago."

He might have been touched that she'd gone to so much trouble to investigate his past, but he knew damn well she hadn't done it out of curiosity. Bailey liked to know her enemies, and Sean had been placed squarely in that camp when he'd deceived her last year.

"You're right," he agreed. "We left his crew years ago."

"Then why are you working for him again?"

"Who says I am?"

Frustration clouded her face. "Stop playing games with me. You may as well tell me the truth, because if you don't, I'll just get Paige to look into everything you've been doing this past week, and we both know Paige is very good at her job."

Shit. The threat didn't bounce off him the way most threats did. Paige Grant *was* good, and the last thing he wanted was her investigating his recent movements. He'd made too many little side trips that he didn't want Bailey knowing about.

But Sean didn't want her involved in this either. Rabbit was a dangerous man. Once upon a time he'd possessed some semblance of honor, but his actions of late proved that he wasn't above using anyone he could to advance his agenda.

Still, Sean figured he could give her *something*. He'd learned a long time ago that the best lies were always rooted in truth.

"You win, luv. I'm working for Rabbit again." He met her eyes. "Happy now?"

As always, Bailey saw right through him. "Not in the slightest. I want to know what he has on you."

Bloody hell. The woman was too smart for her own good.

"That's none of your concern," he said tersely.

Triumph lit her gaze. "But he does have *something*."

"Obviously, Bailey." Sarcasm crept into his tone, along with a weight of fatigue that pressed into his chest. "I don't go around robbing banks for the hell of it, okay?"

"What's he holding over your head?"

Ignoring her, Sean peered out the window, then barked a command at their silent driver. "Turn left on the next street. There's a stretch of warehouses coming up to your right."

"Damn it, Sean," Bailey grumbled. "Tell me."

"No." His jaw tightened. "It's time for us to go our separate ways. I appreciate that you came all this way to save my ass, but it didn't need saving."

"I'm not going anywhere until you tell me what's going on."

"Why?" he shot back. "Why do you even bloody care? We're not friends, remember? You made that pretty fucking clear in Paris this summer."

Bailey's expression flickered with unhappiness. She faltered, her hands curling into fists. "I care about—Oliver," she mumbled. Stuttering on the last word, as if she didn't want to speak Ollie's name in front of Sean. "I don't want to see him suffer when you get yourself killed."

Pain sliced into his chest as her motives became clear. Of course she'd come for Oliver. He'd known that the second she'd dropped out of the ceiling back in the bank, but hearing her admit it was . . . torture.

"And I don't get why O'Hare needed you for a low-rent bank job," she went on, oblivious to the hot agony seizing Sean's throat. "It makes no sense. And even less sense that you agreed."

He pushed away the bitterness, deciding to give her another morsel of the truth. "Look, Rabbit thinks there's a rat on his crew who's feeding information to his rivals. He didn't trust his men to do the job alone, so he wanted me there to make sure he got what he needed from the bank."

"Uh-huh. All that sweet, sweet cash, right?" she said sarcastically.

Sighing, he reached into his pocket and pulled out the flash drive. "He wanted this, okay? And I got it for him. So you see? There's no reason for you to be here. I'm going to give this to Rabbit, the two of us will be square, and then I'm done with him."

Bailey went quiet for a beat. "What aren't you telling me?"

She was like a shark with a taste of blood. Sean knew she wouldn't let up, but fortunately, the car stopped before he was forced to lie to her. As Rafe pulled up at the curb, Sean tapped the back of the man's seat and said, "Thanks for the ride, mate."

He was out of the car before Rafe could respond, slamming the door to stop Bailey from following. But the blasted woman just jumped out of the other door, her boots snapping against the pavement as she angrily rounded the vehicle.

"Get back in the car," he said sternly.

She glared at him. "No." Shoulders rigid, she turned toward the open passenger window and addressed her colleague. "Thanks for the assist today. I owe you one."

Then, to Sean's dismay, she tapped the window frame to signal Rafe to drive, and the tight-lipped bastard actually did, leaving the smell of oil and car exhaust in his wake.

"Damn it," Sean burst out. "Get the fuck out of here, Bailey. I don't need you."

"Yes, you do." She folded her arms, anger coloring her

tone. "You're still playing games, but I know something is wrong. I *know* you."

The volatile emotions bubbling inside him spilled over like a volcanic eruption. "What, you think because you've had my cock inside you that it means you know me? Think again, luv."

His crude words brought a flush to her cheeks, and her expression went stricken. He knew she was thinking about their night together. The way he'd filled her. Fucked her. And now he was thinking about it too, the sheer perfection of her hot pussy clamped around him, her nails raking down his back as she moaned in abandon.

Sean's gaze dropped to her mouth, those pale pink lips that had so eagerly kissed him that night.

But of course she'd been eager. She'd thought she was kissing *Oliver*, for Christ's sake. He'd been making love to Bailey that night, but she sure as hell hadn't been making love to him.

"You don't know me," he said flatly. "You were never *interested* in knowing me, and I don't want you here."

"Well, too bad, because I'm not going anywhere."

Sean struggled to control his frustration. He'd known she was stubborn, but seeing that muleheadedness firsthand made him want to strangle her.

"I'm serious. Starting now, I'm your fucking shadow, Sean. I won't—"

"He has Ollie."

Bailey froze. "Rabbit?"

Sean pressed his fists against his sides, pissed off that he'd caved. No, that she'd *broken* him.

Without another word, he stalked toward his building, breathing in the crisp autumn air. Figured that it wasn't raining tonight. The whole bloody country was wet and misty ninety percent of the year, and the one night he could have used some fog to disappear into, there wasn't a cloud in the sky.

"What do you mean, he has Ollie?" Bailey stayed hot on his heels, following him to the key panel on the building's outer wall.

Sean sighed. "Rabbit phoned me and Ollie about a month ago, demanding we rejoin the crew. Like I said, he's gotten paranoid. He thinks he's dealing with a traitor, and he turned to us because he trusts us. Because he trusted our father."

"Did you and Ollie turn him down?"

"Of course. We're not daft. We had no interest in working for him again."

Sean tapped a series of numbers into the keypad to unlock the front door, but he didn't make a move toward the entrance. He wasn't worried that anyone would overhear them. Not only did he own the entire building, but the place was completely off the books. Sean kept two other flats in the city—the first one easy to find, the second requiring a shit ton of digging to locate, which he knew Rabbit had done. But this third loft was his safe house, where he and his brother stored the backups for all the intel they'd acquired over the years. Nobody but him and Oliver knew it existed.

And he needed to get upstairs right fucking now. He had to examine the contents of the flash drive and figure out what he was working with here.

But first, he had to ditch Bailey.

"Ollie and I said thanks but no thanks. Rabbit wasn't happy, so he decided to force our hand by sending a couple of men to nab Ollie in London."

"Why Ollie?"

Sean shrugged. "Probably because he was closer. But Rabbit knew that whichever one of us he grabbed, the other would do anything Rabbit asked to save him. And the role of savior landed on me." He took a step toward the door, keeping his body language casual.

"Rabbit threatened to kill Ollie if you didn't rob a bank?" Bailey said warily.

"Yup." He reached for the door handle. "So I robbed the bank, and I got what he wanted, and now Ollie is safe." Sean's fingers curled over the door handle. "So there you go, luv. I don't need your help. Good seeing you again, though."

He ducked inside so fast she had no time to respond, slamming the door and effectively locking Bailey out. The look on her face from the other side of the glass was almost comical. Shocked. Amazed. Outraged.

"You son of a bitch!" Her voice was muffled thanks to the barrier between them, but when she pounded her fist against the glass, the whole door shook in its frame as if an earthquake had hit the building. "Open the door! I mean it, Sean! If Ollie's in danger, then I'm damn well going to help you!"

Sean's heart squeezed as he stared at her. He knew she loved his brother, but goddamn it, didn't she realize that Oliver would want to keep her safe? Shutting her out wasn't just about sparing himself the pain and humiliation of being around a woman who couldn't stand him. Sean knew his twin would kill him if he allowed Bailey to put herself in harm's way.

"I'm sorry," he said gruffly, moving away from the door.

"Sean! For fuck's sake, come back here!"

With the regretful shake of his head, he turned on his heel and walked away.

Bailey stared at Sean's retreating back in disbelief. The son of a bitch had locked her out. She'd come all the way to Dublin to save his ass, and rather than show even a smidgen of appreciation, *he'd locked her out.*

Well, screw that. Screw his alpha male bullshit and his arrogance and his damn games. He always treated her like she was a fragile flower that would wilt and fall over from the slightest gust of wind. But she wasn't. She was an undercover operative who could kill with her eyes closed and take down men twice her size without breaking a sweat.

And he thought a measly door was going to keep her out?

Bailey stared at the lock, tempted to pull out her gun and shoot her way in. But she was in a residential area at nine o'clock at night, and she knew better than to draw attention to herself or Sean.

She walked over to the keypad instead, gritting her teeth as she yanked the plastic cover off. She was fully aware of the security camera pointing directly at her, but she didn't give a shit. In fact, she *hoped* Sean was already upstairs, watching her on some monitor so he could see that she hadn't slunk away like he'd intended for her to do. Just in case he was, she flipped her middle finger at the camera, then got to work.

It was easy to find the correct wires. Easy to rub them together and short-circuit the unit. The moment the system was down, the lock released with a loud buzz, and Bailey stormed inside the building. She had no idea which apartment belonged to Sean, but any soldier worth his salt would stick to high ground if he could do so. Quicker access to the roof, clearer visuals of the neighborhood.

She hurried into the stairwell and ran up four flights, bursting through the metal door in the landing onto a corridor with weathered hardwood floors. The hall was deserted, but she knew Sean had been there. She could smell the faint trace of his aftershave in the air, that familiar scent of spice and sandalwood, the heady, masculine fragrance she'd breathed in when he'd moved inside her. When he'd thrust into her, over and over again, summoning pleasure she'd hated herself for feeling.

There was only one door in the hall, all the way at the other end. She raced toward it, but the door was locked when she turned the knob.

Fuck that.

She didn't bother reaching into her pocket for a hairpin to pick the lock. This time she used her gun. Aimed the silenced pistol at the doorknob and blew the motherfucker right off.

When she stalked into the loft, she found Sean leaning against an exposed beam near the door, a resigned look in his eyes.

"Screw you," she said darkly. "Did you really think you'd get rid of me that easily?"

"It was worth a try." His displeased gaze shifted to the door. "Did you really have to shoot it?"

"Damn right I did. It was either the doorknob or you, and we need you alive if we're going to rescue Oliver."

At the thought of Oliver, Bailey's entire body clenched with unhappiness. God, why was *he* the Reilly brother Eamon O'Hare had decided to abduct? *Sean* was the pain in the ass.

She definitely didn't buy Sean's assertion that his former boss had chosen Ollie out of convenience. If O'Hare knew the Reilly brothers half as well as Bailey did, then he was well aware that Sean Reilly was the deadlier of the twins. The one with a higher tolerance for bloodshed and deception, the one who'd undertake any mission, no matter how dangerous.

Well, there was no way she was allowing Sean's recklessness to lead to some Irish gangster killing Oliver.

From what Bailey knew about O'Hare, the man wouldn't hesitate to harm Ollie. Although O'Hare's group was officially called the New Republicans, its unofficial Irish Dagger moniker apparently stemmed from Rabbit's penchant for gutting his enemies with a blade.

"You know, you're the most stubborn person I've ever met," Sean grumbled.

"Damn straight. And I'm not going anywhere, so deal with it." She scowled. "What's on the flash drive?"

He shrugged. "No clue."

"You haven't checked it yet?"

"I was just about to before you shot up my door," he said pointedly.

But he didn't seem concerned that anyone could walk in now, and Bailey understood why when she noticed the security monitors on the wall behind him. More than a dozen of them, displaying both the interior and exterior of the building. Sean had been able to watch her coming up, step by step, from the lobby to the stairwell to his door. Beneath the screens was a row of file cabinets spanning the entire back wall of the loft.

Bailey gave the rest of the place a cursory examination. Small kitchen, unmade futon bed across the room, leather sofa in the center, and a heavy punching bag dangling from the ceiling in the corner. Then she glanced back at the file cabinets, cocking her head at Sean. "Well, aren't you old-school."

"Ollie and I keep hard copies of every piece of intelligence we gather. We have dossiers on thousands of people." He waved an absent hand at the cabinets as he strode toward the adjacent wall, which featured a computer setup that rivaled Paige's.

Bailey studied the array of laptops and equipment on

the long desk, then shifted her gaze to the numerous world and city maps pasted on the wall. Red and green thumbtacks marked various areas on the maps, but she didn't ask what the colors stood for. People, she assumed. Operatives, spooks, criminals. Sean and Oliver knew a lot of people—and a lot of dirty secrets. They were intelligence magicians, producing data out of thin air, and Bailey had no trouble seeing why even the most secretive sorts were so willing to spill their guts to the Reilly brothers. They used their charm to lure information from unsuspecting marks, and if they ever needed to apply some pressure, the twins had the good cop/bad cop routine mastered.

Her gaze flicked back to the file cabinets. "Is there a dossier on me in there?" she asked, but she already knew the answer to that. For years Sean had been bragging about having a file on her.

"Yes sirree. I dare you to try and get it." He flashed a cocky smile.

Curiosity had her wandering over to the nearest cabinet, and she examined it closely as Sean settled on his leather desk chair and booted up one of the computers.

To Bailey's annoyance, the file cabinets were locked. And couldn't be *un*locked, not with a key anyway. Opening them required both a security code and a fingerprint on the electronic panel.

"Asshole," she muttered.

Sean glanced over with another grin. "I'll open it for you myself," he offered mockingly. "*If* you fill in the blanks in the file. I couldn't find a lick of intel on you before the age of eighteen."

Inwardly, she felt relief—the Reilly brothers were good at their jobs, and a part of her had always worried they might have uncovered her past. Outwardly, she gave him a saccharine-sweet smile. "That's because there is no intel. I'm a ghost, remember? I didn't exist then, and I don't exist now."

He narrowed his eyes. "Bailey isn't your real name."

"Give the man a gold star."

His irritation only seemed to grow, but the computer screen came to life at that moment, distracting him from grilling her further. He slipped the flash drive into the USB port, waited, then clicked the track pad.

Her dossier all but forgotten, Bailey quickly joined him at the desk. Sean's shoulders tensed when she came up behind him, but he didn't turn around. His handsome profile revealed intense concentration as he stared at the screen.

"All right, let's see what we're dealing with here."

"We?" she said, unable to contain her triumphant tone. "Ha! I see you've accepted that we're working together."

"Not one bloody bit," he said cheerfully. "But I'll get rid of you soon enough."

"Dream on. I'm helping you get Oliver back whether you want me to or not."

"Right. You're here to rescue Oliver."

She couldn't decipher the odd note in his tone. Not sarcasm, not even anger. Envy, maybe? But that didn't make any sense to her. He had no reason to be jealous of Oliver. He'd all but torpedoed their friendship by what he'd done.

"Because you'd do anything for my twin, won't you, luv?" Sean taunted.

"Yes."

"Well, so would I, and I know Oliver wouldn't want you involved in—" Sean hissed out a breath when a folder popped open on the screen.

Bailey leaned over his shoulder to get a better look,

her pulse speeding up when she inhaled his masculine scent. She ignored it, focusing on the computer monitor instead.

Dozens of icons appeared in the folder, subfolders that were organized alphabetically. Bailey furrowed her brow. She recognized several of the names and she'd barely made it halfway through the A section. How many other significant people were on this drive?

Cursing, Sean clicked on the most recognizable A name on the list—Georges Amirault.

The prime minister of France.

"Bloody hell," Sean mumbled.

Amirault's folder contained rows and rows of photographs, along with several videos. Sean clicked on a photo, and Bailey's eyebrows soared when an obscene image filled the screen. The picture showed Amirault stretched out on a canopy bed, his face visible and his features contorted with passion as a woman performed fellatio on him.

A woman that was most definitely *not* his wife, Lena, whose philanthropy and environmental activism had made her beloved in France.

"I guess we've found someone's little black book of filth," Sean said flatly.

He closed the Amirault file and opened another one, this one belonging to a prominent US senator. The video Sean clicked on was less than a minute long—and it showed the right-wing, Bible-thumping senator having sex with a man.

"Blackmail materials," Bailey said, revolted. She moved her gaze off the lewd images on the screen. "There's a scary amount of influential people on this list. Do you think all the files are as dirty as these?"

"Oh yeah." Sean opened another folder, and a second

later they were staring at a well-known European drug activist smoking crack.

Every file was just as damaging—the data was explosive, to say the least. Career ending in almost every case, and at least half were enough to send someone to prison. The men and women in those files would probably do anything to keep the information from getting out.

"Think these are O'Hare's files?" she asked.

"No. Rabbit doesn't have this kind of reach," Sean said grimly. "And his organization would've grown exponentially if he'd used any of this shit. He would've been able to expand his smuggling routes, increase his profits. He could've forced any of these politicians to throw their support into his cause."

"Whose are they, then?"

Sean went back to the Amirault file and began scrolling through the photographs of the prime minister with the unnamed woman. He enlarged one of the pictures, a shot that showed Amirault entering a skinny town house with black shutters.

With a sigh, Sean ran his finger over the house's narrow front door. "That's one of Ronan Flannery's brothels."

Ronan Flannery. Bailey had been around long enough to have heard that name before. Hard not to, considering the man ran one of the most profitable criminal empires in Europe and the UK. According to her sources, drug smuggling was Flannery's bread and butter, but he also dabbled in prostitution, loan sharking, and other shady activities similar to the rackets Eamon O'Hare ran. Except while O'Hare's power was isolated to Ireland, Flannery's was a global empire.

She wrinkled her nose as she stared at the town house in the photo. "How do you know that's Flannery's brothel?"

"Because I've been there."

She couldn't stop the bite in her tone. "A frequent visitor to whorehouses, are you?"

"It was for business purposes only." He twisted his head to smirk at her. "Would you be jealous if it was for *non*business reasons?"

"Nope."

One dark blond eyebrow cocked up. "You sure about that?"

"Don't flatter yourself." She broke the eye contact, refusing to let him see that he had, in fact, rattled her.

Sean closed the drive and popped it out of its slot, then placed it next to the computer keyboard. "Well, it makes sense why Rabbit would want to get his hands on this," he remarked, right back to business. "What do you know about Rabbit's history with Flannery?"

"Nothing," Bailey admitted. "Paige is supposed to send me a file on Rabbit, though, so I'm sure it will have all the gory details. Why? Is there bad blood between them?"

"Understatement of the year, luv." Sean leaned back in his chair and propped his hands behind his head, drawing her attention to his defined biceps and heavy forearms.

He still wore khakis and a sweatshirt, but the baggy garments couldn't hide the absolutely cut body beneath them. Sean Reilly was all muscle, big and broad and deliciously masculine.

No, not deliciously. *Infuriatingly.* She hated that she was admiring that ripped bod of his. That the sight of it was still capable of making her pulse race and her mouth go dry.

"The two of them are bitter rivals," Sean went on. "They've wanted each other dead for years."

Bailey perched on the edge of the desk. "Why haven't they killed each other, then?"

"It's a long story. Very long," he said with a tired breath. "Flannery was married to Rabbit's sister, Maureen, and he and Rabbit were tight during their IRA days. But they always had very different ideologies. Rabbit was all about his nation, uniting Ireland, getting rid of the evil British, yada yada yada."

"And Flannery?" she prompted.

"He wanted money. Power. He was just using the cause as a springboard for his own ambitions."

"Is that what started the feud?"

"No, that happened when Rabbit's sister, aka Flannery's wife, was killed in a car bomb meant for Flannery."

Bailey chewed her bottom lip. "Well, I guess it makes sense that Rabbit would hate him."

"Hate doesn't even begin to cover it. Rabbit blamed Flannery for Maureen's death, accused him of being too obsessed with his own selfish interests to protect his own wife." Sean shrugged. "And Flannery decided that Rabbit's IRA fanaticism was what killed her, and there you go—blood feud. They went their separate ways after Maureen died and built their own empires."

"Again—why didn't they kill each other?"

"According to my father? Honor. They're still family, whether they like it or not, and you don't kill family."

"So why would Rabbit want Flannery's blackmail files?"

Sean chuckled. "I said they won't kill each other—doesn't mean they can't destroy each other. Flannery's been fucking with Rabbit's network for years. Stealing, sabotaging, all that fun stuff."

Bailey pursed her lips. "Okay, so the mole Rabbit is so worried about now . . . is it possible he's right and Flannery really did plant someone on Rabbit's crew?"

"More than possible."

She went quiet for a moment, running over the details Sean had given her and combining them with what she'd already known about Ronan Flannery. "Flannery doesn't do much business in Ireland," she said slowly.

"That's Rabbit's doing."

Sean rose from his chair and ran a hand through his hair. It was short again—Bailey remembered it being longer when she'd seen him in Paris. Tousled and scruffy, curling under his ears. Now it was close cropped . . . the way it'd been last year, when they'd . . .

She shoved the memory out of her head.

"And Flannery's own doing, to some extent," Sean added, oblivious to where her thoughts had drifted. "Rabbit always stayed true to his roots, and that earned him respect and loyalty from his fellow Irishmen. Flannery? The bastard clawed his way up the ladder by screwing anyone who got in his way." Sean gestured to the dark computer screen. "And, apparently, by using blackmail and extortion. It makes sense now, the way he soared so high, so fast. But the one thing he hasn't been able to get is an alliance with the Irish."

"Why not?"

"The locals won't deal with him because they know he'll fuck them over if something better comes along, so he keeps hitting roadblocks whenever he wants to transport his merch through Ireland."

Sean's wealth of knowledge didn't surprise her—the man made a living out of gathering information. "So then it also makes sense that Flannery might plant a mole in Rabbit's crew. If he takes over Rabbit's organization, it could open a lot of doors for him." She paused. "But now Rabbit's got his hands on Flannery's dirty files. Do you think he's planning to use them to take Flannery down?

"Maybe." Sean's expression turned deadly. "I don't

particularly care either way. Rabbit can have all the filthy sex videos he wants. I just want Ollie back."

Bailey blinked in amazement. "You're actually going to give him the files? What if he exposes all the people on this drive?"

Sean looked at her as if she'd asked him what two plus two was, as if the answer was a no-brainer. "I don't give a bloody fuck about these people, Bailey. I won't sacrifice Oliver to protect the secrets of a bunch of corrupt politicians."

"So we're making a trade?"

"*I'm* making a trade," he corrected, blowing out an exasperated breath. "You don't need to be here for this. Rabbit wants this disk, I want Ollie. Easy exchange."

She crossed her arms. "I told you, I'm not going anywhere until I see that Oliver is safe."

A flash of anger lit his eyes, but she didn't give a damn if he was mad. He would just have to suck it up and let her help him.

Rather than argue, Sean set his jaw and yanked open one of the desk drawers. Bailey snuck a peek and saw that the drawer was full of burner phones. Sean grabbed one, turned it on, and started typing.

"Are you contacting Rabbit?" she asked.

He didn't answer. Kept typing.

"What are you telling him?" she demanded.

Still no answer. Sean set the phone on the desk and marched across the loft.

"Stop trying to keep me in the dark!" she called after him. "I'm here whether you like it or not."

He turned around to face her, rugged features creased with resignation. "I told him I made it out of the bank, I have what he needs, and I'm waiting for instructions about making a trade. Satisfied?"

"Did you explain that the death of his men wasn't your fault?"

"No point," he said tersely. "Rabbit doesn't want to hear excuses. He just wants to see results."

Bailey nodded slowly. "So what now?"

Sean turned his back on her again. "Now we wait."

# Chapter 6

*Thwack. Thwack-thwack. Thwack.*

Bailey tried to ignore the sounds reverberating on the other side of the loft, but it was a difficult task. Sean had been battering that punching bag for the past hour, fists slamming into leather as Bailey sat on the couch, her frustration growing by the second. Couch, bed, and punching bag. Somehow it made sense that those were the main pieces of furniture in Sean's loft, because sleeping, fucking, and fighting were probably the only things Sean Reilly was interested in. That, and gathering information.

The last thought sent her gaze in the direction of the file cabinets. She really needed to figure out a way to break into them. What kind of dirt had Sean unearthed about her?

*Thwack. Thwack-thwack.*

And why wasn't O'Hare calling back? It had been three hours since Sean had texted the man, and Bailey was beginning to get anxious. O'Hare had to have seen the news, must know by now that his men were dead. And he definitely knew that Sean was alive and in possession of the flash drive. So why wasn't he making a move? The man had gone to a lot of trouble to secure that drive, which told Bailey he was eager to get his hands on it.

Her gaze traveled back to Sean, and her pulse skipped in the most aggravating way. He'd stripped off his shirt, which left him in those ill-fitting khakis that rode so low on his hips they were in danger of falling off.

Despite her better judgment, she focused on his chest. His very bare chest, which was . . . Fine, it was truly wonderful. Roped muscles and golden skin assaulted her vision. He didn't have much body hair, save for a dusting between his heavy pecs and the dark line leading to his groin. He was built like a warrior. Tall, broad, and deadly.

Before Bailey could stop it, the memory of being underneath that powerful body flashed in her head, and she almost moaned out loud.

The sex had been good.

No, it had been more than good.

But so what? Sean had lied to her from the word *go*. He'd deceived her. And just because she'd known he was doing it didn't excuse his behavior.

What kind of man pretended to be his twin to get a woman into bed?

She jerked when his gaze suddenly locked with hers. He'd caught her staring, but he didn't comment. He simply released another one-two punch that made the black leather bag sway wildly. God, he looked . . . feral. Bloody knuckles, handsome face covered by a sheen of sweat, sleek muscles coiling from every deadly strike of his fists.

"Haven't you had enough yet?" Bailey called out, not bothering to hide how frazzled she was.

He kept on swinging.

"Seriously. You're going to fuck up your hands."

Breathing hard, he let his arms fall to the sides. He slanted his head, watching her with an expression that made her skin break out in shivers. Feral, all right.

She rolled her eyes. "What, you're in adrenaline overload? You need to hit something *this* bad? Because you're going to hurt yourself if you keep it up."

"What the hell do you care, luv?" But her words must have penetrated that thick skull of his, because he grabbed a towel from the workout bench behind him and used it to wipe his sweaty face.

Then he strolled toward her, slow, predatory. Red blotches stained the white towel in his hands as he wiped his knuckles on the terry cloth.

"You got me," he told her. "It *is* adrenaline, and you know why? Because I robbed a bloody bank today, Bailey. And when I'm feeling this way, there're only two activities that calm me down." He shrugged. "Fighting's one of them."

"What's the other?" she asked, then cursed herself for opening her stupid mouth.

Because his green eyes were gleaming now, smoldering with sin. "What do you think, luv?"

Several seconds ticked by as their gazes held.

"It's fucking," he drawled. "Pure, hard-core fucking."

Her breath lodged in her lungs. Sean's sultry gaze held her captive, making it impossible to turn away. The man radiated sexuality. He always had. It heated his eyes and rippled through his body, and whenever he directed all that sensual energy her way, her body responded.

"Would you like to help me out with that?" A mocking note entered his deep voice. "Because I'm more than happy to stop tearing up my hands and put them to better use."

She hated him. Hated that her nipples puckered against the front of her tank top, hated that he could see her response. She'd left her long-sleeve shirt at the bank, and the camisole she wore was too skimpy to hide a thing. Her breasts ached and her core pulsed, so hard she had to clench her thighs to curb the hot throb of arousal.

"What do you say?" He dragged his tongue over his lower lip, a gesture that should have been lewd, but made her heart beat faster. "Wanna help me fuck all the tension away?"

She was too mesmerized by the seductive rasp of his voice, the raw desire glittering in his eyes.

"Or maybe you can just suck me," he said silkily. "You know, just to take the edge off."

The vulgar suggestion jolted her back to reality. "Fuck you," she muttered.

"Yes, fuck me." A defiant smile curved his lips. "Fuck me, Bailey."

She stared at him.

"No?" The smile widened, taunting as hell. "Then I guess I'll continue doing the next best thing."

He tossed the towel away, bare feet padding back to the punching bag. Bailey's frustration returned in full force as she watched him pound on the bag once more.

*Thwack. Thwack.*

God, he was such an ass. Why couldn't her traitorous body see that?

She leaned her head back on the couch cushion, ignoring the arousal still coursing through her veins. Maybe she was just sex deprived. The last time she'd slept with someone had been nearly a year ago, a couple of months after her night with Sean. She'd been desperate to exorcise the man from her system, so she'd hooked up with a SEAL she'd met in the Middle East. The sex had been . . . decent.

But nowhere near as good as it had been with the arrogant asshole who was currently scraping his knuckles raw on a defenseless punching bag.

Damn it. Why had she come? Why was she *still* here?

*For Oliver,* a little voice reminded her.

Bailey took a deep breath, focusing on the twin who

was actually in danger and not the one who *was* the danger. It would all be okay. O'Hare would make the trade, Oliver would be fine, and then she could walk away and leave Sean Reilly in her dust.

Until then, she just had to do a better job of steeling herself against him.

Sean didn't want to give Bailey the satisfaction of telling her she was right, but hell, he'd definitely overdone it with the bag. By the time he finally called it quits, his knuckles were bruised and swollen, and both his hands ached when he flexed his fingers.

Rabbit was taking too long to respond. Sean knew his old boss had received his text—the phone showed him whenever a message had been read—so why the radio silence? Rabbit had to know that Gallagher and the others were dead. Did he hold Sean responsible for their suicide by Garda? Fuck. If he did, then he might've already taken it out on Oliver.

Sean inhaled slowly. No. Ollie had to be alive. He had to trust that Rabbit wouldn't hurt him, not when Sean still had the flash drive.

He grabbed his phone from the desk and checked the screen, but no new messages had come through.

"I'm taking a shower," he announced.

From her spot on the couch, Bailey swung her head around, and the sight was so fucking beautiful it hurt to look at her. He knew he'd been a dick to her before, but he couldn't help it. Being around her was torture. Knowing he could never have her, knowing the only way she'd ever view him with anything other than hostility was if he pretended to be another man . . . it was bloody torture.

"And you need to take that with you?" She gestured to the phone in his hand.

"Yup."

"Wow. You really don't trust me to monitor the phone in case Rabbit makes contact?"

"It's not about trust," he muttered.

Her nostrils flared. "Then what is it about?"

"Me. My job. Mine, Bailey, not yours. And when I set up this trade, I'll find a way to leave you behind," he said bluntly.

She smiled. "That'll be hard to do, considering I'm not leaving your side."

"'S'that so? Does that mean you're joining me in the shower, then?" Arching a brow, he unsnapped the button of his khakis.

Her eyes widened, and there was no missing the tiny spark of heat that ignited in them.

"Come on, luv. If you wash my back, I promise to wash yours."

Whatever desire he'd thought he'd glimpsed reverted right back to anger. "Sorry, not interested," she said coolly.

"Sure you aren't," he mocked.

Sean marched into the loo and shut the door behind him, too tired and pissed to concentrate on anything other than dunking his head under the spray in the tiled shower stall. He closed his eyes and let the hot water wash away all the evidence of this day from hell. No, a week of hell. He'd felt powerless and on edge ever since he'd left Morgan's team.

He didn't want this. Any of it. He didn't care about the Irish Dagger or their messed-up ideology. Let the bloody British have Northern Ireland. He didn't give a shit.

Family was the only thing that mattered to him. His parents were dead, which meant Ollie was all he had. And he owed it to his brother to handle this Rabbit bullshit.

Fuck, he owed his twin a helluva lot more than Ollie even knew. He'd betrayed his brother when he'd slept with Bailey, and the guilt had been gnawing at him for a whole year. Sean had never kept secrets from his twin until that night, and he didn't intend to keep this one forever. He would tell Ollie what he'd done. One of these days he really would come clean about it.

But the thought of Ollie being disappointed in him, or worse, not forgiving him . . . it tore his insides up.

The water muffled his anguished groan, and he forced himself to push away the guilt. He stepped out of the shower and dried off, then wrapped a towel around his waist and headed for the door. He wasn't concerned about walking around the loft half-naked. Bailey had made it more than clear that she wasn't interested in jumping his bones.

His phone beeped the second he stepped out of the loo, and his shoulders stiffened when he glanced at the message.

Bailey immediately shot off the couch. "Is that Rabbit? What did he say?"

Without a word, Sean tossed her the phone. A crease appeared in her forehead as she skimmed the message. He was so tempted to smooth it out with his fingers . . . his tongue . . . and the mere thought of putting his hands or mouth anywhere near her made his cock thicken beneath his towel.

"What does this mean?" Frowning, she read the text aloud. "'Hot tonight. Might turn up the A/C. Hopefully it'll cool down by tomorrow.'"

Sean sighed. "It means he won't meet until tomorrow night. He wants to give it twenty-four hours for the heat to die down, in case the Garda is on my trail."

"Fine. When and where will this meeting be?" she demanded.

"I guess we'll find out when he texts back tomorrow."

"So, what, we just wait around for a whole day?"

"Pretty much, yeah." Sean was nowhere near as frustrated as she was. If anything, he felt relief. Oliver would remain safe, at least for the next twenty-four hours.

He strode to the closet on the other side of the loft, while Bailey trailed after him, still frowning deeply.

"Why don't we just go in now? Do you know where he's holding Ollie?"

Sean shrugged. "I could probably hazard a guess. Rabbit has dozens of safe houses in the city, and I know the locations of most of them."

"Then why are we playing Rabbit's waiting game? Let's get Oliver, damn it."

Her eagerness to rescue his twin raised Sean's hackles. "Look, I understand that you're worried about your boyfriend, but he'll be fine. Rabbit wants the flash drive, and he won't hurt Ollie before he gets it."

"He's not my boyfriend," she muttered.

Sean's hand froze on the closet door handle. He shifted around to look at her, his gaze unwittingly dropping to her chest. She was still wearing that skimpy top, and her bra must have been paper thin, because he could see her nipples. They were a dusky rose color against her pale flesh, like rich red wine on white satin sheets. His hands shook with the need to rip that shirt off her, his lips aching to take one of those nipples into his mouth, but he battled the wild urges.

"Right, he's not your boyfriend. I guess that's my fault, huh?" he said softly.

Her mouth pinched into a scowl. "Isn't it? Because what you did that night pretty much guaranteed I wouldn't be seeing Oliver again. But that was exactly what you wanted, right, Sean?"

His gut churned with guilt. Shame. Jealousy. Anger.

Christ, he didn't even know what he was feeling anymore. Bailey's bitter expression sliced through him like a dull blade. She thought he was a selfish bastard, and she was right. He *was*.

Sean swallowed. "Are you ever going to let me apologize for that night?"

He could have sworn he saw a flash of panic in her eyes, but it disappeared before he could be sure. "You already did." She shrugged. "I didn't accept your apology."

"You also didn't let me explain."

"What's to explain? You put your ego ahead of your brother's feelings. Ahead of my feelings."

The accusation stung so badly he couldn't even defend it.

"You're not going to deny it? No, of course you aren't. God, it must have driven you crazy that I kept turning you down." Sarcasm dripped from her voice. "You just *had* to get your way, didn't you, Sean? Because it's always about the conquest for you."

He managed to speak past the lump in his throat. "It wasn't just about my ego." He gulped. "I came to the hotel to give you Oliver's message. He had to skip town for a last-minute job. I had every intention of telling you that when I showed up that night."

"But you didn't."

No, because she'd answered the door in the sexiest dress he'd ever seen. A silky black thing and high heels and red lipstick, and he'd forgotten the reason he'd come there. She'd flicked off the light, ready to follow him out the door, and in that moment, the hunger he'd felt for her—four bloody years' worth of it—had erupted like a dormant volcano, turning him into a ravenous animal. He'd wanted a kiss, just one kiss, but things had escalated so fast. So fucking fast, and the next thing he knew . . .

Yup, he was a selfish bastard, all right.

"It wasn't a conquest for me." His voice came out rough, and his pulse careened as the truth spilled out, the words he'd wanted to say for months now. "I wanted you from the moment I saw you, Bailey. You were beautiful and smart and so different from the women I'd been with in the past. Strong and elusive—"

"See, so it *was* about the conquest. The chase."

"No, damn it! It was about *you*."

She glared at him. "You pretended to be your twin brother to get me into bed. Do you honestly think I can forgive that?"

"No, but you can at least try to understand why I did it." He reached out and touched her cheek. A part of him expected her to flinch, but she didn't. She simply went still, silent, visibly uncomfortable as he gently traced the soft line of her jaw.

Her breath hitched. She didn't lean into his touch, but she didn't recoil from it either.

"I'm sorry for lying to you," he said gruffly, "but I need you to know . . . that night meant something to me." His chest went tight, achy. "I know I'm not Oliver—"

"Damn right you aren't." She stumbled backward, and his fingertips felt cold and empty without the warmth of her cheek beneath them. "And that night meant nothing, Sean."

Her harsh words made his chest ache even harder, while her cruel dismissal of their night together sparked his anger. "You can't deny it was good between us. No. It was fucking earth-shattering."

Even as he spoke the words, he knew they'd have no effect on her. She'd slept with him thinking he was someone else, for Christ's sake. If Bailey's earth had moved that night, it was because she'd believed Oliver was the one moving it.

"Wow. You really are an arrogant bastard," she snapped. "You want to hear what a great lay you are? Is that it? Then, fine. You're a spectacular lay."

His nostrils flared. "Bailey—"

"But guess what—I'm not sleeping with you again. I'm not sleeping with Oliver either, if that makes you feel better."

"Bailey—"

She cut him off with another sardonic interjection. "But I can see how important it is for you to hear that the sex was good—sorry, *earth-shattering*—so here you go: it was *awesome*. You made me come *so* hard. You're such a stud."

Her taunting set his temper off like a lit fuse. "Go ahead, be as sarcastic as you want. But don't you fucking pretend you didn't like it. I remember the way you moaned when I was buried inside you. The way your fingernails gouged my back when your pussy was squeezing the life out of my cock. I can still fucking hear your screams when you came."

Her cheeks turned red. "If you say so, Sean."

"Fuck that, Bailey. I might be a liar, but you aren't. You wanted me that night." His mouth twisted in a smirk. "You want me now."

She took a step back. "Whatever helps you sleep better at night."

Before she could retreat, he yanked her toward him and crashed his mouth over hers.

# Chapter 7

Bailey was helpless to stop the kiss. And in the back of her mind, she knew she'd goaded Sean into it. You didn't antagonize a man like Sean. You didn't question his sexual prowess, not unless you were prepared to face the consequences.

And God, the consequences were terrifying.

He kissed her like he owned her, and in that moment, he did. The kiss was rough and punishing, his tongue forcing her lips open and sweeping into her mouth with greedy precision. Electricity raced up Bailey's spine, red-hot and powerful, as powerful as the deep strokes of Sean's tongue and his tight grip on her waist.

"You want me," he muttered into her lips without breaking their mouths apart.

Oh God, she did. She craved him as badly as she had last year. She'd known it was Sean the second she'd opened that hotel room door, but he'd kissed her before she could speak, and then he'd pulled back without revealing his true identity. Pretending he was his brother, and goddamn it, but she'd let him. She'd played along because after just one second, she'd been dying for him to kiss her again. She'd wanted to experience the kind of passion she'd only ever read about.

The same uncontrollable passion swept through her now, as Sean's tongue slicked against hers, drawing a desperate moan from her throat. She heard a soft rustling sound, realized his towel had dropped to the floor. He was naked, gloriously naked, and her hands moved of their own volition, roaming his rock-hard chest.

He growled when her fingernails scraped one flat nipple, deepening the kiss as he backed her into the closet door. He rotated his hips and his erection brushed her belly, teasing the top of her mound.

*Stop this. Now.*

No, not yet. She hadn't gotten her fill yet. Her eyes were squeezed shut but she didn't need them open to explore his warrior body. Her fingers ran over his hot flesh, encountering smooth planes and roped muscles, bumpy scars that reminded her of the violent life he led.

Sean's teeth sank into her bottom lip, sending a jolt of excitement between her legs. She shamelessly rubbed up against him, sliding her tongue in his mouth as the kiss went from blistering hot to downright explosive.

*Stop. This.*

Common sense prevailed, penetrating her foggy mind. She wrenched her mouth away and staggered backward. Her breath came out in unsteady pants. Every inch of her trembled, sizzled with unquenched need.

Sean was breathing just as hard, lust burning in his green eyes, but when he spoke, it was with unmistakable regret. "Goddamn it. I lose my bloody head when I'm around you."

His muscles flexed as he bent down to retrieve his towel. He hastily secured it around his waist, but the terry cloth couldn't hide his thick ridge of arousal.

Bailey couldn't even muster up any anger toward him. She'd challenged his restraint by provoking him, and it wasn't fair to blame him for losing control.

"You're right." She could barely hear her shaky voice over the thudding of her heart. "The attraction is there."

Surprise flitted across his face.

"I won't pretend it's not, okay?" A sigh slipped out. "But I won't act on it either."

Sean met her eyes. "I'm sorry I pretended to be him. I truly am."

The earnest apology evoked a pang of guilt. It was wrong to let him apologize again. To let him think she'd been ignorant of what he'd done.

But admitting that she'd been onto his charade from moment one . . . that meant admitting she'd *wanted* him that night. It meant revealing her weakness. Exposing herself to a man she'd never intended to let get close to her.

She'd worked so damn hard to become the strong, capable woman she was now, but Sean Reilly made her feel weak. Not just with desire, but with the way he took control of every situation. Some women might like being bossed around, but Bailey wasn't one of them. Sean treated her like she couldn't take care of herself, and then he wondered why she resented him for it.

"You're in love with Ollie. I get it." His voice rippled with anguish. "I'm a shit for putting you in this position. You pushed Ollie away because of what I did, and that's not right. What I did wasn't right."

Did he honestly believe she was in love with his brother?

Bailey swallowed, searched his face, and realized that, yes, he really did believe it. The need to correct him bit at her tongue, but she choked it back. Maybe it was better if he thought she loved Oliver. At least then he'd back off. Stop tempting her with . . . with everything. His potent masculinity. His seductive taunts. His addictive kisses.

"We need to stop going around in circles," she said quietly. "Let's just put the past behind us, okay? Right now we should be focusing on getting Oliver away from O'Hare."

After a long beat, Sean nodded. "You're right."

"Look, if we're not meeting O'Hare until tomorrow night, we may as well get some sleep." She headed back to the couch, placing much-needed distance between them. "Oh, and I'll send Paige an e-mail asking her to track down any of O'Hare's safe houses that you don't know about. We can do some recon in the morning."

His features strained at her use of the word *we*. "I really don't want you involved in this."

"It's too late for that." She stretched out on the couch, reaching for the red-and-black afghan hanging over the edge. "And I'm really not in the mood to argue again."

She covered herself with the blanket. It smelled like Sean. She tried hard not to breathe, but the spicy scent of him snaked into her system and sped up her pulse again.

"For fuck's sake, luv, you can't sleep on the couch. You can take the bed."

"I'm already comfy," she murmured, closing her eyes. "Night, Sean."

She heard his aggravated expletive, followed by soft footsteps and the creak of the closet door opening. There was the rustle of clothing being slipped on, the telltale flick of a light switch, and then the mattress squeaked as Sean settled on the futon.

Bailey kept her eyes shut, refusing to look over at him, refusing to see that powerful body sprawled on the bed. She should be in England right now, snuggled up on the couch with her best friend. Instead, she'd spent the evening playing the part of bank hostage and was now having a slumber party with Sean fucking Reilly.

She had to sleep, regroup, and armor herself against the man. Most likely, tomorrow would be as strenuous as today had been, and she needed rest if she wanted to keep up with Sean.

It was weird being in his loft, his personal space, but Bailey was used to sleeping in worse, more dangerous places. Her years with the CIA had taught her to sleep with one eye open, to block out the lingering adrenaline and catch some shut-eye whenever and wherever she could get it.

She wasn't sure how long she slept. Several hours, at least, and it would've been longer if not for the loud buzzing that awoke her.

Bailey flew into a sitting position, pistol in hand as her gaze instantly sought out Sean, who dove off the futon in a blur of motion.

The loft was shrouded with darkness, but she could see him racing to the security screens. She blinked when light flooded the room, and then she bolted to her feet.

"What's that noise?" she said as she hurried over to Sean.

"Motion sensor went off." He entered a sequence of numbers on the keyboard and the buzzing stopped, but the severe set of his shoulders didn't ease. "We've got visitors."

Bailey glanced at the time stamp on the corner of the screen: 3:07. Then she shifted her gaze to the monitor Sean was staring at, which provided a clear view of the downstairs lobby. She couldn't help but be impressed when she realized Sean must have left the loft at some point to fix the security panel she'd disengaged. She hadn't heard him exit or reenter, but clearly he'd snuck past her because the keypad had been rearmed.

"Oh shit." Her breath caught when a figure suddenly appeared on the screen. A narrow face, dark eyes gleaming with displeasure. "Who's that?"

Sean looked over at her. "Ronan Flannery," he said flatly.

Every muscle in her body coiled tight. Jesus. Flannery? As in the man whose flash drive Sean had stolen?

She studied the man on the screen. Angular features, reddish brown goatee, shaved head. She couldn't see anything below his shoulders, but the thickness of his neck told her he wasn't some puny Irishman you could easily take down.

Sean typed another series of numbers, then leaned into the microphone next to the keyboard.

To Bailey's dismay, he addressed their late-night visitor.

"Yeah?" Sean said briskly.

A chuckle floated out of the speakers, and then a pleasant voice echoed in the loft. Pleasant . . . but only on the surface. The cold menace simmering beneath it was unmistakable.

"Good evening, lad," Ronan Flannery said in greeting. "Why don't you press your little button and let me in?" A deadly smile filled the screen. "I believe you have something that belongs to me."

# Chapter 8

*Porto, Portugal*

Sullivan had been dreading this reunion for weeks.

He'd known it would happen eventually. After all, he was still a member of Jim Morgan's team. So was Liam. Which meant there was no way the two of them *wouldn't* reconnect at some point.

But hell, he'd been hoping for more time. Time was a man's best friend—it was the one infallible truth Sully had discovered over the years. Death, breakups, frickin' food poisoning . . . you let enough time pass and you'd get over anything.

He wondered if his time theory applied to the you-kissed-your-best-friend-and-now-he-wants-to-fuck-you debacle Sullivan found himself in.

A groan escaped his mouth but was quickly carried away by the crisp morning wind rolling off the ocean. A bluish light blinked in the inky black sky—Morgan's jet, making its descent. Sullivan peered up at it, his breath floating out in a white wisp. Shit, it was chilly out. He zipped up his Windbreaker as the breeze picked up, cursing his teammates for scheduling the rendezvous at the crack of dawn.

The small airfield was dark and silent, not a soul around except for Sullivan and the airport owner, who was puttering around in the hangar. Sully had been killing time outside for more than an hour, wishing he had a pack of cigs or a cup of coffee—anything that would stop his eyelids from drooping in fatigue.

It had been a total bitch getting here. He'd sailed right into a squall, nearly lost a jib to the sudden and violent gusts that had repeatedly struck his boat. But *Evangeline* was a trooper. She could weather anything, and she'd gotten him to port in one piece, as she always did.

He'd docked her at a marina outside Porto, and as he stared up at the sky, he found himself longing for her. Gleaming decks and pristine white sails, a forty-five-foot slice of pure freedom.

Maybe it made him a total pussy, but he missed his boat when he wasn't on her. His entire life he'd obeyed orders, followed routines. First at the orphanage, then in the army. But there was no routine on the open sea. He never knew what to expect when he was out there.

Eventually he'd live on the water full-time. He'd do it now if he could, but that relentless itch for action always crept in sooner or later. Working for Morgan helped scratch that itch, though Sully certainly hadn't expected to land a best mate out of the deal. His friendship with Liam had crept up on him too. Who would've thunk it—the brash Australian and the reserved DEA agent hitting it off, becoming closer than frickin' brothers.

And idiot that he was, Sully had nearly destroyed the friendship with his impetuous actions.

The light in the sky grew brighter as the small jet sliced through the darkness. Lower and lower. Closer and closer.

Liam was on that jet. D and Ash too. But Sullivan wasn't tied up in knots waiting for those other two. He hadn't kissed either of *them*.

Christ almighty. What had he been thinking? Was he bloody *mental*?

He stood in silence, watching the sleek aircraft's descent. Sam, Morgan's pilot, was a pro. He landed the bird with ease, smoothly rolling down the dirt runway before coming to a stop a hundred yards from the hangar. There was no need to refuel, so Sullivan grabbed his go bag and headed for the plane.

He was two steps away when the door opened with a mechanical whir. Ash, the team's dark-haired rookie, appeared in the doorway, his green eyes alert and playful despite the fact that it was the middle of the night. Or morning, rather. Christ, it was early.

Ash flashed his trademark lopsided grin as he stuck out his hand. "Hey, Sully."

"Rookie." He grinned back and grabbed the outstretched hand, allowing the younger man to haul him on board.

"How was the vacay?" Ash asked as Sully's boots connected with the cabin floor.

"Good. Hit a couple storms, but mostly it was smooth sailing."

They moved deeper into the cabin, and Sullivan spotted D first. The tattooed mercenary was sitting in one of the plush seats with his eyes closed, but they snapped open when Sully took a step forward. Those coal black depths flickered with acknowledgment. There was a nod of greeting, and then D's eyelids snapped shut again.

Sullivan hadn't expected anything more. Derek "D" Pratt was the scariest bastard he'd ever met, and not exactly a chatter mouth.

He strode forward, discomfort tightening his chest when he saw Liam at the far end of the aisle.

"Boston," he called in greeting.

"Aussie," Liam called back, a faint grin on his face.

Sullivan stashed his bag in one of the overhead compartments and made his way across the cabin, where the two men exchanged a quick side hug that was fraught with tension that only Sullivan could feel. Or maybe Liam did too, because when he drew back, there were a hundred unspoken questions lurking in his vivid blue eyes.

Which only made Sully feel like a total shit, because he'd purposely been keeping his distance since they'd left Paris. But what the hell else was he supposed to do? Sully hadn't expected to be attracted to his friend, and he absolutely hadn't expected Liam to feel it too, but no way was he going there. Their friendship was too important to destroy over a case of misplaced lust, and he'd wanted to give Liam time to get over what had happened, to put it behind him.

"You look like a beach bum," Liam remarked.

He dragged a hand over the full growth of beard on his face. "Yeah, well, you know I don't shave when I'm with *Evangeline*. She likes me au naturel."

His teammate snickered. "Uh-huh. I bet she does."

The tension faded as they settled in seats opposite each other. Sully rested his hands on the table that was screwed into the floor between them. "Any word from Bailey?"

Liam shook his head. "Nothing since her last text. All we know is that she and Sean made it out of the bank and now they're holed up in one of his safe houses. Oh, and apparently she didn't tell Sean we're on our way. He's insisting he doesn't want any backup."

"Tough shit, because he's getting it."

Sullivan was kind of pissed that Reilly hadn't made contact with any of them yet. He'd liked the cocky Irishman from the moment he'd met him in Monte Carlo on an op a couple of years back, and he'd thought the two of them were chums. He didn't know what Reilly was tangled up in, but there was no bloody way he was letting the man fend for himself.

"Noelle thinks he's back in the IRA," Liam said grimly.

Both men buckled up as Sam called back into the cabin that they were ready to take off.

Liam continued as if they hadn't been interrupted. "One of her contacts reported seeing Sean at O'Hare's Pub in Dublin."

"Eamon O'Hare, right? The Irish Dagger bloke?"

Liam nodded.

"I remember Reilly saying he goes by Rabbit. Pansy-ass nickname if you ask me." He pursed his lips. "We both know Sean doesn't give a bloody hoot about politics. There's no way he'd willingly join up with the Dagger again."

"I agree. So does Bailey, which is why she wants our help."

Liam raked a hand through his hair, drawing Sullivan's attention to those thick black waves. The guy had great hair. Great everything, in fact. The hair, the piercing blue eyes, the male-model face that Sullivan had seen too many women go apeshit for.

The operative word? *Women.* Because Liam Macgregor was as straight as they came.

Except Sullivan had recognized the wild streak running through his friend from day one. He'd seen a man who was dying to let go, and Sullivan had helped him do that. He'd encouraged Liam to unleash his dirty side, to revel in it, turning him from a well-mannered gentleman to a filthy playboy who was willing to try anything.

But somehow he'd lured his friend to an even darker place, a place he knew Liam would regret venturing into. The man came from a big Catholic clan, for fuck's sake.

He was supposed to marry a sweet, docile female who'd pop out his kids and have dinner waiting for him on the table when he got home—not get involved with his best friend, a man who didn't even know the meaning of monogamy.

"You're not listening to me."

Liam's dry voice made Sullivan jump. "Sorry." He rubbed his beard, tired of thinking in circles. Pissed at himself for not being able to let it go, when it was the one thing he was trying to get Liam to do. "I spaced. What were you saying?"

"Just that we should try to figure out what Sean's involved in ahead of time, if we can. I think I'll contact Paige."

Sully nodded. "I'm sure Bailey already has, but it wouldn't hurt to call her."

A note of unhappiness entered Liam's voice. "I really wish Holden would come back."

The reminder of their former teammate and technological wizard brought a twinge of sorrow to Sullivan's stomach. Holden McCall had disappeared off the face of the earth after he'd lost his wife during an ambush on the team's compound a while back, and after more than a year of radio silence, Sully had given up on hearing from the grief-stricken man.

"He's gone, mate," Sullivan said roughly. "And I don't think he's coming back. Fuck, even Morgan has stopped hoping for that."

"It's that easy for you, huh? Just accepting that he's not coming back?"

Sullivan meant to keep his tone casual, but it came out gruff and thick with meaning. "I'm very good at putting the past behind me."

And they both knew he wasn't talking about Holden anymore.

* * *

*Dublin*

Bailey watched in amazement as Sean's fingers moved over the keyboard. She was no computer expert, but from where she was standing it looked like he was actually unlocking the door remotely to grant Ronan Flannery entrance to the building.

"You're letting him in?" she exclaimed.

He glanced over as if she'd just asked him if the sky was blue. "I don't have a lot of other moves."

"We can get the hell out of here, for one."

He brushed past her and went over to the overstuffed chair next to the futon, where he grabbed a threadbare T-shirt with the Manchester United logo on it and threw it on. The shirt, gray sweatpants, and bare feet made him look like he'd just rolled out of bed, and he seemed completely unperturbed that a criminal kingpin was on his way upstairs.

He caught her expression and sighed. "Bailey. If you honestly think he doesn't have his goons surrounding the place, then you need a refresher course in gangster etiquette. We wouldn't be able to get out of here without one or both of us getting killed."

"What the hell is your plan, then?"

"Don't have one. We'll play it by ear." He strode back to her, a rogue grin lifting his lips. "So . . . seeing as these might be our last few minutes on earth, how about a kiss good-bye?"

She clenched her fists to stop herself from decking him. God, his cavalier attitude drove her up the fucking wall. She wasn't used to working with someone who didn't think five moves ahead.

She, on the other hand, could find a way out with her eyes closed. She already had a car parked around the corner, courtesy of Rafe, along with the strategically placed explosives he'd planted around the building. One phone call and Rafe would set off the charges, creating a big enough distraction that she could slip away unseen.

But the determined look in Sean's eyes told her he wasn't going anywhere, and damn it, she wasn't leaving without him.

As if reading her mind, Sean chuckled softly. "I'm sure you have several escape plans in motion. Feel free to use them."

"I'm not going without you," she snapped.

"And I'm not running." He gave a careless shrug. "Look, I might as well deal with Flannery right here and now. I don't have time to be chased around by that thug—I need to get Ollie."

"Which is gonna be hard to do when you're *dead*."

He didn't get a chance to respond, because the front door swung open and then Ronan Flannery strode inside.

Bailey's fingers tightened around her weapon as the man lingered in the doorway, his tall, stocky body clad in a tailored suit. Who wore a suit at three in the morning?

"You should really get that door fixed," Flannery said politely. His voice was deep, his brogue deeper.

He took a few steps forward, flanked by four black-clad men armed with assault rifles.

"AKs? Really?" Sean sounded amused. "Don't you think that's a tad much?"

Bailey's lips puckered when Sean swiftly stepped in front of her, shielding her from the thugs. Like she was a damsel in need of protecting.

"One can never be too prepared," Flannery answered with a chuckle.

Sean approached their visitor with cautious strides, pausing when five feet separated them. He slanted his head as he studied the older man. "So. I don't mean to insult you, mate, but who are you and why did you show up on my doorstep in the middle of the night?"

He was playing dumb. Interesting. Bailey wasn't sure it was the way to go, but the ploy didn't succeed anyway. Sean's stab at ignorance simply summoned a hearty laugh from Flannery.

"You know exactly who I am, lad."

Flannery nodded at his bodyguards, who stepped back at the unspoken command. Two of them moved toward the door, while the remaining two stuck close to their boss but still allowed him some space. All four were somber faced and silent. They weren't body-builder types—only one was as tall and built as Sean—but their guns were big enough to make up for their size.

"And I know exactly who *you* are." Flannery eyed Sean. Up and down, side to side. "You look like your father."

To anyone else, it might seem like Sean was unaffected by the remark, but Bailey didn't miss the tic in his jaw.

"Colin was a good man," Flannery went on. "A loyal man." He shrugged. "Bloody shame his loyalty was misplaced."

When Sean didn't answer, Flannery's gaze shifted to Bailey. "Pretty bird you've got there, lad. Hello, sweetness. I don't remember you scowling like that when you were inside the bank, but security footage doesn't always provide the best picture."

Bailey wondered how he'd gotten his hands on the bank footage so fast, until she remembered he was a filthy-rich criminal who not only had members of law enforcement on his payroll, but apparently every important person in Europe under his thumb too.

"Put that gun down," Flannery told her. "You're only going to hurt yourself if you try to use it." He glanced back at Sean. "And good for you, finding a woman to settle down with. I remember you being a ladies' man. Nice to see you've grown up."

Sean looked like he was grinding his teeth together. "What do you want?" he said flatly.

"What do *I* want?" That inspired another laugh. "You've got some big balls, barking out demands like that. You stole something very important from me tonight." Flannery tipped his head to the side. "I assume you've seen the contents of the drive?"

"So what if I have?" Sean shrugged. "And so what if you knew my father? You don't know *me*, Flannery. You have no idea what I'm capable of."

The man smirked. "Actually, I do. Did you think I haven't kept tabs on you and your brother over the years? Think again, lad. I keep track of anyone who is or has ever associated with my old friend Eamon."

"Good for you." Sean crossed his arms. "But that also means you know if someone tells me to jump, I don't ask 'how high?'"

Flannery's features hardened to stone. "You *stole* from me, you little shit."

"Yeah, I did. Are you expecting an apology?"

Sean's reckless tone put Bailey on edge. God, the man had zero concern for his own well-being. He was telling off a criminal kingpin like it was something he did every day, and it only emphasized how irresponsible he could be.

"Yes," Flannery bit out. "I do."

"Well, I'm afraid you won't be getting one." Sean edged toward the couch, chuckling when all four bodyguards whipped up their weapons. "Relax, boys, I'm just taking a load off." He propped himself on the arm of the couch, meeting Flannery's irritable gaze. "You claim you've kept tabs on me and my brother."

"I have."

"Then you must know where my brother is at the moment."

"Indeed I do." A ghost of a smile crossed the man's mouth. "Is that how Eamon strong-armed you back into the organization? He threatened your brother?"

"We just talked about loyalty, did we not? You said my father was loyal. Well, so am I. But not to Rabbit's cause. I'm loyal to only one person, mate. My brother. And the rest of the world can go to hell."

Flannery stepped forward, nodding at Bailey. "And your sweet bird? She can go to hell too?"

Sean didn't even spare her a look. "Yes."

The dismissal stung, even though Bailey knew Sean was playing a game. Except . . . *was* he? At the moment, she had no frickin' clue what he was up to.

"It's late, so why don't we get right to the point?" Sean slid off the couch, like a lazy cat with no care in the world. "I'm not apologizing for breaking into your safe-deposit box. I had my reasons and I stand by them." He smiled. "I'm also not going to return your property."

Flannery's answering smile was indulgent, genuine even. "Is that so?"

"Oh, that is so. Very, very so." Sean marched up to one of the bodyguards, and with lightning-fast speed, he grabbed the guy's rifle.

He didn't disarm him, though. Bailey's breath hitched when Sean brought the muzzle of the gun to his own forehead.

"Go ahead and order your man to shoot." Sean was speaking to Flannery, but his gaze remained locked on the eyes of the man with the gun.

Sweet Jesus.

Sean Reilly was insane.

Next-level, cuckoo-crazy *insane*. Bailey fought to control the fear racing through her bloodstream as she watched the standoff in total astonishment. The bodyguard was as confused as she was, his gaze darting to his boss as if to say, *What the fuck do I do?*

"Come on," Sean coaxed in a low, soothing voice. "Do it. Tell him to pull the trigger. You're not going to get what you want from me, so why waste everyone's time?" He pressed his forehead into the gun barrel. Calm, defiant. "What are you waiting for? Kill me."

# Chapter 9

Sean was so tired of playing games. He knew damn well that Flannery hadn't come here to kill him. It was the reason he hadn't run when Bailey had suggested it. If they'd fled, Flannery would have just tracked them down again, and then they'd be facing off the same way they were now.

He knew men like Flannery. Men like Rabbit. They had no qualms taking a life, but they were smart enough to know that you could gain more from a live puppet than from a dead man.

Cold steel dug into Sean's forehead, but he wasn't afraid. He was bored and annoyed and ready to pull the damn trigger himself, when Flannery suddenly chuckled.

"Put that gun away," he told his thug, as if the man had been the one to raise it in the first place.

The bodyguard complied by lowering his weapon.

"And you," Flannery said, jabbing the air in Sean's direction. "Stop antagonizing my crew and trying to turn them into killers. Shame on you."

Right. Like those thugs hadn't murdered dozens—more likely hundreds—of innocent people at Flannery's command. Like Flannery hadn't committed murder himself. Though to the man's credit, he didn't *look* like a bloodythirsty killer. Nice suit, groomed goatee, fancy cologne. He looked more like a banking executive than the slimebag he was.

Flannery and Rabbit had already been on the outs when Sean was a kid, but Sean clearly remembered the man. His father had always brought him and Ollie along when he'd visited Rabbit, subjecting the boys to meetings they had no business being a part of, allowing them to witness things they had no business seeing. Sean recalled the night Flannery had walked into Rabbit's pub, hoping to strike a deal about the drug routes Rabbit and the locals were denying him. Rabbit had laughed Flannery right out of the bar, and Sean would never forget the look in Flannery's eyes. The veiled promise of death and destruction.

"Let's get down to business, shall we?" Flannery said with a sigh. "Because we both know you're worth more to me alive."

When the man made a move for the armchair, Sean glanced over at Bailey. "Grab that bottle of Jameson and some glasses, luv."

Her eyes flashed, as if she resented being treated like an errand girl. "It's three in the morning, *luv*. Should you really be hitting the whiskey?"

"Yes," he said sharply.

"Fine. I guess I will too, then." She crossed the open-concept room to the kitchen and snatched a bottle off the counter, then rummaged through the cupboards until she located some shot glasses.

She returned to the living area as Flannery and Sean settled across from each other, the former in the armchair, the latter on the sofa. Bailey poured three glasses, handed one to each man, then threw her head back and downed the remaining shot.

"A girl after my own heart," Flannery crowed as Bailey sat on the couch next to Sean.

Sean swallowed the whiskey and set the glass on the coffee table. "Say what you came here to say," he told Flannery. "Then leave."

The man chuckled. "You know, I was also acquainted with your mother, lad. And she'd be rolling over in her grave if she knew what appalling manners you have."

Sean arched a brow. "What do you want?"

"What I've always wanted."

"To see Rabbit dead?" Sean suggested.

"Fuck, no." A loud laugh boomed out of Flannery's mouth. "If I wanted him dead, don't you think I would have killed him years ago?" The laughter died as the man grew serious. "My whole life, there's only been two things I've cared about." He paused. "My beloved wife." Another pause, accompanied by a slight smirk. "And money."

Sean rolled his eyes.

"Well, at least your wife is first on that list," Bailey spoke up, her tone dry. "It's nice to see you have your priorities straight."

"Oh, I do, sweetness. I know exactly what's important."

Flannery's gaze rested on Bailey's thin tank top, slow and appreciative, and anger boiled in Sean's gut as the other man stared at Bailey's breasts. He didn't want the bastard looking at her. Didn't want him anywhere near her.

"What do you want?" Sean repeated through clenched teeth.

"I want to destroy Eamon O'Hare."

"That's a lofty ambition. I wish you luck with that."

"Wish yourself luck, lad—because you're the one who's going to do it for me."

Fucking hell.

That's what Sean had been afraid of, and he suddenly cursed Rabbit for dragging him into this mess.

"You know that second priority I mentioned? The money?" Flannery prompted. "Well, I have heaps of it. But my business continues to suffer from the lack of hospitality I receive from my fellow countrymen."

Sean snickered. "You mean because nobody in Ireland will work with you? Do you really blame them for that, Ronan? You're notorious for screwing over your partners."

The man didn't acknowledge the accusation. "I've been denied access to certain routes because of my brother-in-law. The locals are stubbornly depriving themselves of golden opportunities because of Eamon and his silly ideals."

"You believed in his cause once," Sean pointed out.

Flannery looked amused. "Who told you that? Your father? I don't give a shit about the *cause*, lad. It was always a means to an end, a way to advance my business." A dark cloud flitted through his eyes, so deadly it brought a chill to Sean's spine. "The *cause* killed my wife."

"She wasn't just your wife. She was Rabbit's sister, too."

"And did her own brother try to save her?" Flannery spat out. "No, her *brother* is the reason she was killed. She died because of Eamon and his delusions, and the bastard deserves to pay for what he did. For what he continues to do."

"And I'm supposed to make him pay?" Sean swiped the whiskey bottle and took another sip. He could feel Bailey watching him, practically see the frown on her lips. She didn't like this any more than he did, but she was wisely staying silent, and he was damn grateful she wasn't drawing any attention to herself. "I'm afraid I can't help you with that."

"Eamon went to great lengths to bring you back to Dublin. You know what that tells me? He trusts you. They all do." Flannery smiled. "Well, almost all."

Sean narrowed his eyes as a thought occurred to him. "He's right, isn't he? There *is* a mole in the Dagger."

Flannery was positively beaming now. "Of course there is."

"Good. Great. Tell your little rat to take Rabbit down. You obviously don't need me, then."

"The situation is . . . delicate. You know as well as I do that Eamon's soldiers are fanatically devoted to him. My man hasn't been making much progress in changing their minds, and he can't organize an outright mutiny. The change of leadership has to look natural."

"You want your man to take over the Dagger? Is that it?"

"Yes, and once he does, all the doors that were closed to me will open right up." Flannery shrugged. "And our friend Eamon will be destroyed."

"I hate to break it to you, but being ousted from leadership doesn't equal destruction."

The other man chuckled. "No, but the corruption of his empire will do the trick. We both know Eamon doesn't care about money—he never has." An evil gleam lit his eyes. "Imagine the sense of loss he'll feel, the crushing defeat, when his noble cause becomes just another money-driven operation."

Sean couldn't deny that Flannery had a point. Killing the cause *would* be like twisting a knife in Rabbit's chest.

"Anyway, this little chat has gone on long enough, so let's get right to the point. You're going to rejoin the Irish Dagger and turn Eamon's soldiers against him. And you're going to support my man and do whatever he asks of you."

Sean looked the man square in the eye and said, "No."

Flannery's lips curled in a sneer.

"I already told you, I only care about getting my brother back. And at the moment, *our friend Eamon*," he said sarcastically, "is playing games with my brother's life. So, as much as I know it'll displease you, I'm going to trade your little flash drive for my brother." Sean leaned back and flashed a gracious smile. "But what the hell—I'll do you a solid. If you want, I'll let you know when and where the drop will be, and you can arrange for your men to be on-site to recover your stolen goods. Beyond that, I'm not doing a damn thing."

"Yes. You are."

With a faint smile, Flannery nodded to his bodyguards, and before Sean could so much as blink, one of them yanked Bailey off the couch and raised his gun to her temple.

Sean lunged to his feet, but he shouldn't have bothered. Sometimes he forgot that Bailey was a trained operative—until the woman did something to remind him of it. Her leg shot out in a blur of speed, kicking the thug's legs from under him. The man landed on the hardwood with a loud thud, and suddenly Bailey was on top of him, straddling his thighs. Sean hadn't even seen her disarm the guard, but she was now in possession of his rifle and pressing the barrel into the man's temple.

With a bored look, she twisted her head toward Sean. "Should I put a bullet in his head?"

The other three bodyguards closed in on her, but Bailey seemed unfazed by the guns trained on her.

"That's some wildcat you've got there, lad," Flannery told Sean. "I completely approve." He made a tsking sound with his tongue. "But you know what will happen if she harms my man. And you know what will happen even if she doesn't."

Shit. He was screwed. Sean swallowed his anger as he ran over his options, but no matter which way he looked at it, he was royally screwed.

"I will kill her," Flannery assured him. "I'm not the kind of man who bluffs."

Sean's brain continued to work overtime. If he didn't agree to the terms, Flannery would kill Bailey. But the man didn't *know* her. He had no idea how skilled she was, how dangerous she could be.

Sean just needed to buy some time. Eliminate the threat to Bailey tonight and whisk her away to safety the moment Flannery was gone. The bastard couldn't hold Bailey over his and Oliver's heads if she disappeared—and Bailey happened to be very, very good at disappearing.

"Fine, I'll do it," Sean announced.

A broad smile stretched across Flannery's face. "I knew you'd see it my way."

"Let him go, luv. Nobody needs to die tonight." Sean barked the order at Bailey, who was still holding the bodyguard at gunpoint.

Anger radiated from her petite frame. Disgust, too, as if she couldn't believe he was asking her to stand down. She gave Flannery a fleeting look before meeting Sean's eyes again, and he could practically hear her unspoken plea. They could kill Flannery and his men right now. Between the two of them, they might even be able to get it done without losing much blood.

But he wasn't willing to take the risk. Not with Bailey's life on the line. And he wasn't foolish enough to believe that Flannery didn't have a dozen men posted outside with orders to attack if he didn't return.

As Bailey reluctantly released her captive, Flannery

rose from his chair and signaled to another guard, who took a menacing step toward her.

Sean swiftly blocked his path. "What the hell do you think you're doing?"

"We're taking her with us," Flannery said coldly.

A humorless laugh popped out of Sean's mouth. "Sorry, mate, but that's not happening." At Flannery's frown, he placed a protective hand on Bailey's arm. "She stays with me. If you want me to take down Rabbit, I'm going to need her help."

Flannery's laughter was equally harsh. "So be it. But if you think you can steal her away and tuck her somewhere safe, think again, lad. I'll find her. I'll find you, too, if you try to run."

"I don't run," Sean muttered.

"Your father didn't either." Flannery shrugged. "He probably should've. Might still be alive if he had." He clapped his hands together. "Well, this has been lovely, but it's way past my bedtime."

Tailed by his guards, Flannery headed for the door, then paused to shoot Sean a pleased smile. "We'll be in touch."

The second he was gone, silence crashed over the loft. The air grew thick with tension, with frustration, with Bailey's disapproval.

Sean turned away from her piercing gaze and grabbed the whiskey, taking another much-needed sip. "We're going to wait a few hours, and then I want you gone," he said gruffly. "You'll have to lie low for a couple months. We can't risk Flannery tracking you down."

Disbelief flashed on her face. "No."

He slammed the bottle on the table and advanced on her. "You *have* to go."

"Flannery is going to tell his mole about you, about

*me*. He'll know you're playing him if you don't show up there with me by your side."

Fuck. *Fuck.* She was right.

"Then you can stay only until we make the trade," he said firmly. "Once Ollie is safe, the two of you are getting the hell out of Dublin."

"And what about you?" she shot back. "Don't tell me you're actually going to do what Flannery says!"

"I don't know what I'm going to do yet. I need to clean up one mess at a time, okay? We get Ollie, and then I'll deal with the rest of it."

"We should have just killed Flannery," she said angrily.

He shook his head, choking back his desperation. "I wasn't about to do anything drastic, not with my brother's life at stake."

Bailey went quiet, her expression softening. "You're right," she finally said. "It wouldn't have been smart."

"Well, fuck me—are you actually admitting that I was *right* about something?"

"It's like an eclipse," she muttered. "Happens every so often."

He had to laugh at that, but the humor died abruptly, and his voice thickened as a confession slipped out. "I didn't mean it, by the way."

"Mean what?"

"When I told Flannery I don't care about you." He swallowed. "I didn't mean it."

She stared at him, gray eyes veiled, indecipherable. "It's late," she murmured. "We should get some sleep."

He nodded awkwardly, masking his disappointment. "Sure."

As Bailey went back to the couch, Sean headed for the bed, then stopped and turned toward her. "By the way? If you insist on staying, it's only gonna be you. I don't want anyone else involved. Not your chum Rafe, or Noelle, or any of her girls. Understood?"

She shifted her feet and averted her gaze.

"Bailey?" he said suspiciously.

With a sigh, she slowly met his eyes again. "Then I guess this is a bad time to tell you that Morgan's men will be arriving tomorrow."

# Chapter 10

Rain sprayed the windshield as Liam drove through the streets of Dublin, heading for the address Bailey had texted him. He was riding with the rookie, who was busy typing on his phone, the click of Ash's fingers cutting into the rapid swipe of the windshield wipers.

Sullivan and D were in the second car, and Liam was slightly relieved that Sully wasn't the one sitting next to him. Seeing his friend again was . . . awkward. Sure, they were laughing and joking the way they always had, but tension continued to simmer beneath the surface, that same stilted awkwardness that had plagued their friendship since the . . . *incident*.

Neither of them had brought up what happened in Paris. From what Liam could tell, Sullivan had completely pushed it out of his mind, which only made him all the more determined to do the same. He *had* to quit thinking about it. He and Sully were friends. Nothing more, nothing less. All those threesomes had simply messed with his head and triggered a case of good old-fashioned curiosity that it was now time to forget.

Curiosity.

Christ, his family would die of horror if they knew

what he'd been *curious* about. His folks were traditional as fuck. So were all seven of his siblings. Everyone in his family was happily married, and he knew they wanted the same for him, the whole home-and-hearth thing that his brothers and sisters thrived on.

But he wasn't like them. He'd always wanted more out of his life. Action, adventure, and the adrenaline high he received from both. The DEA hadn't fully satisfied those urges, but working as a mercenary did. His family didn't understand it, though.

Hell, they didn't understand *him*.

A snort sounded from the passenger seat, and Liam rolled his eyes when he saw the rookie grinning at his phone. "Seriously? You're sexting in the middle of an op?"

Ash blanched. "I'm not sexting. I'm messaging Cate back."

"You guys are getting pretty close, huh?"

"She's a sweet kid," Ash said defensively. "We're friends."

"Yeah, well, make sure it stays that way. You know Morgan will castrate you if you touch his daughter."

"I don't think of her that way," Ash insisted. "She's a teenager, for fuck's sake."

Liam flicked the left-turn signal to change lanes, then glanced over. "So what's Cate saying? Is Morgan still pissed that we left?"

"She says he's been sulking, which translates to him swearing up a storm. And she says she's worried about us."

"*Us?* Yeah, right. She's worried about you."

"Well, she worries too damn much." Ash let out a glum sigh. "Did you know she started calling me *Rookie*? You assholes have officially gotten a teenage girl to harass me."

"Dude, Ethan had to deal with it for years," Liam said with a snicker, referring to Ethan Hayes, who'd been the youngest member of the team before Ash had joined. "Just wait until Morgan recruits a new fresh-faced marine, and then you'll be off the hook."

"I'd better be," Ash muttered.

Liam reached a roundabout, a road device that was probably his favorite thing about Ireland, and took the second exit, smoothly steering the sedan through traffic. Man, Americans and their bumper-to-bumper traffic could take a lesson from the Irish—those roundabouts saved a shitload of time.

Ash consulted the GPS. "Turn right. Sean's place should be on the next street."

Liam glanced in the rearview mirror to make sure D and Sully were still on his tail, then hit the signal and took a right. The other black sedan followed suit.

Sean's safe house turned out to be a low-rise brick building, nondescript and slightly run-down. Liam hadn't expected anything fancy, though—Sean and Oliver Reilly made a living by staying off the radar.

Bailey had called earlier to fill them in about Flannery's late-night visit and the demands he'd made of Sean, so Liam kept a careful watch as they approached the building. After a quick perimeter sweep, which revealed Flannery hadn't posted any goons to watch the place, the team entered through the back stairwell as Bailey had instructed.

Liam climbed the steps with Sullivan at his six. The nape of his neck tingled at his teammate's nearness, but he shoved away the weird sensation.

When they reached Sean's loft, they found a small gaping hole where the doorknob should have been. Wooden splinters and little chunks of metal littered the floor, making Liam grin. Bailey had warned them about that, too, and he hadn't been surprised to hear that she'd shot up Sean's door. Although the woman was calm under pressure, she was also stubborn as hell, and Liam had seen hints of her fiery temper beneath her professional surface. Bailey's fire was one of the things he liked about her, though. That, and the fact that he could tell her things he didn't dare tell anyone else. He was friendly with Abby and Noelle's other women, but he wasn't close to them, not the way he was with Bailey.

Palming his weapon, Liam entered first, but there was no danger lurking inside the loft. Only hostility.

"I'm not fucking doing that," Sean was grumbling. "You're under the impression that this is a covert op, but it's not. It's the same low-rent bullshit I grew up with."

"He won't believe it unless it looks realistic," Bailey shot back.

"I'm. Not. Doing. It."

Well. Looked like nothing had changed between them since they'd last met. Liam had never seen two people argue more than Sean and Bailey. Morgan and Noelle maybe, but those two had become much less hostile after tying the knot.

Then again, Liam couldn't exactly blame Bailey for being pissed at Reilly. Back in Paris, she'd confessed that Sean had pretended to be Oliver in order to screw her. Which, in Liam's humble opinion, was a total dick move.

"Are we interrupting?" he said dryly.

Without so much as a hello, Sean looked over with a hard glare. "Yes."

Bailey, on the other hand, bolted off the couch and sprinted to Liam. "Hey! I'm so happy to see you."

She threw her arms around him and he hugged her back, ignoring the flare of anger that lit Sean's eyes. Screw that. Bailey was his friend, and he'd genuinely missed her.

"Happy to see you too, darling." He kissed the top of her head, Sean be damned. The guy would just have to deal.

"I told her I didn't need your help," Sean muttered as he stood up.

"Is that really how you're going to greet us?" Sullivan demanded. "We're here to save your ass, mate—you ought to be rolling out a bloody welcome mat." His gray eyes flickered with resentment. "A little birdie told me you left the team in the lurch."

"He did," D confirmed without an ounce of warmth in his tone. Not that he was warm to begin with, but today there was an edge of aggression that surprised Liam. D didn't usually broadcast his feelings either, but his harsh gaze made it clear that he was pissed at Reilly and not in the mood to hide it.

Truth was, after two years of working for Morgan, Liam still had no idea who D was or what made him tick. All he knew was that the tattoo-covered merc had once worked for a mysterious black ops agency, and Liam wasn't sure he needed any more details than that. D was scary as hell, which meant his background was probably equally terrifying.

"If you're waiting for an apology, don't bother." Sean met D's cold gaze head-on. "Ollie was in trouble."

"You should've told Morgan," Liam hedged. "You know he would've helped."

"I take care of my own problems. I didn't want to drag anyone else into it." Sean's green eyes flickered with displeasure as he focused on Liam's hand, which was resting lightly on Bailey's shoulder.

Since the man was already on edge about his brother, Liam gave Bailey's arm a soft squeeze before releasing her, and Sean's rigid shoulders instantly relaxed.

"Forget about him," Bailey told the men. "*I'm* happy you're here. I appreciate the backup."

Sean growled in frustration. "We won't need backup. You fellas wasted a trip."

Sullivan shrugged. "We'll be the judge of that." He moved deeper into the loft, glancing around. "Nice digs, Irish. Very . . . barren."

"I don't spend much time here," Sean said tightly.

It was obvious he wasn't the slightest bit thrilled about their presence. Wasn't very hospitable either. He didn't offer them a drink or ask about the flight. He simply crossed his arms in a pose of pure belligerence, as if daring them to stay.

Nobody made a move to go.

"So what's the sitrep?" Ash asked awkwardly.

When Sean didn't answer, Bailey fielded the question. "Eamon O'Hare got back to us about ten minutes ago. He wants the exchange to happen at his pub. Sean hands over the flash drive, Rabbit hands over Ollie."

Suspicion creased Liam's forehead. "You think it'll be that easy?"

"Rabbit's a man of his word," Sean answered, arms still folded over his chest. "He never reneges on a deal."

"Fine, let's assume it all goes smoothly," Liam said. "What then?"

"Then I deal with Flannery." Sean didn't offer any more details.

"How?" Sullivan sounded as annoyed as everyone looked.

"Not sure yet." With a shrug, Sean strode to the couch and sat down.

Liam could tell that his insolent attitude was bugging the shit out of Bailey. Hell, it bugged him, too. The Reilly brothers were secretive as hell, and of the two of them, Sean was the one with the reputation for winging it most of the time. For someone like Bailey, a woman who painstakingly planned out her missions, Sean's lack of care and preparation probably made her want to tear her hair out.

"Look," Sean sighed when he saw everyone scowling at him, "my only priority right now is making sure my brother's okay. After that, I'll find a way to remove myself from this Flannery bullshit."

A derisive noise rumbled from Bailey's mouth. "Flannery admitted to having a mole in Rabbit's group. We have to assume he'll be there when we show up tonight."

"We?" Liam asked.

She spared him a cursory look. "I'm going too."

"Okay."

Sean cursed loudly, his head swinging toward Liam. "Okay?" he echoed in disbelief. "You could at least try to talk her out of it, Boston."

"Why would I? You might be too pigheaded to admit it, but you'll need backup. And you can't do any better than her."

Bailey's look of gratitude was overshadowed by Sean's thunderous one. His eyes narrowed as he glanced from Liam to Bailey, but then he shook his head without comment.

"Anyway," Bailey continued, "if the mole *is* there, he'll be expecting you to follow through on Flannery's request. You'll need to tell Rabbit you want back in."

"I know that," he said grimly.

"You really think your old boss will believe you suddenly want to be his soldier again?" Sullivan looked skeptical as he flopped down on the other end of the couch.

After a beat, Ash moved to the armchair and took a load off, too, but Liam and D remained standing.

"That's what we were arguing about before you

showed up," Bailey explained. "I know exactly what we need to do to convince Rabbit that Sean is serious about returning to the Irish Dagger."

Sullivan's skepticism gave way to curiosity. "Yeah? What?"

"She wants me to *hit* her!" Sean roared.

The Irishman shot to his feet again and bulldozed his way to the kitchen. He snatched a fifth of Jameson off the counter and slugged the alcohol right from the bottle.

Liam and Sullivan exchanged an amused look before turning to Bailey. "How is that going to help?" Liam asked with a grin.

"Rabbit's known Sean and Ollie since they were kids, which means he knows they're protective of each other—*and* the people they care about." She flashed Sean an irritated look. "If Sean wants to rejoin the crew, he needs to give a reason that Rabbit will buy." She shrugged. "He needs to tell him about Flannery's visit."

Liam raised a brow. "And admit to being threatened into doing Flannery's bidding?"

"No, just admit to being threatened." She continued speaking as if Sean wasn't in the room, though from the guy's surly expression, it was clear he'd already heard this. "Sean tells Rabbit that Flannery tracked us down and tried to get the flash drive back. We managed to get away, but not before Flannery's men roughed me up."

D's gravelly voice rejoined the mix. "Smart."

"Smart? Jesus Christ, you people are bloody crazy," Sean snapped. He took another long swig of whiskey before slamming the bottle down. "Nobody's laying a hand on you, Bailey."

She ignored him completely as she outlined the rest of her plan. "I show up on Sean's arm with a busted-up face, his sweet new girlfriend who was kicked around by

Flannery's goons. Sean offers to help Rabbit take down Flannery in exchange for protection, and Rabbit believes it because he knows Sean would do anything to keep his girl safe. And voilà—Sean's back in the group, Rabbit thinks Sean needs him, and the mole thinks Sean is playing ball for Flannery."

Liam couldn't deny it was a solid plan—aside from the fact that she hadn't offered an endgame. "And then?"

"Then we go from there." She scowled at Sean. "How long do you want to play Flannery's game? Because the smart thing to do is skip town once we get Oliver."

"I'm not running for the rest of my life," he said darkly. "Wherever I go, Flannery will find me."

"So you intend to do his bidding?" she shot back.

"Until I figure out another way to get rid of him? Yes."

It was hard to ignore the growing tension between them. Or hell, not growing, since the tension had never gone away, never lowered in intensity. It was always there, crackling in the air the same way it had when Morgan and Noelle were in a room together, before they'd finally let go of their hatred and given in to their attraction.

Liam knew Bailey would never capitulate, though. She was secretive about her past, but whatever she'd gone through . . . it had definitely made her leery of reckless alpha men like Sean Reilly.

But that reckless alpha male had staked his claim on Bailey a long time ago, and it was no surprise when he yet again shot down her idea like a deadly sniper.

"You're not pretending to be my girlfriend," he said firmly. "I won't paint a target on your head."

"God, Sean, there's *always* a target on my head. It was there long before I met you."

Sullivan cleared his throat. "Her plan's solid, mate. If

you want to convince Rabbit you're legit, he needs to believe you're out for Flannery's blood. He won't buy it if you say it's to protect Oliver, but he will if he thinks you're trying to protect the sweet, fragile girl you're in love with."

Bailey's snicker triggered one from Liam. Bailey was the furthest thing from sweet *or* fragile, but Liam knew she could play that part if she had to. The woman was a master at transforming herself—he'd witnessed it first-hand in Paris when he'd watched her become Morgan's teenage daughter to serve as a decoy for Cate. Bailey was capable of altering not only her appearance but also her personality and mannerisms to become someone else.

It was several moments before Sean finally saw reason. "You're right." His tone was grudging as he looked at Bailey. "But you don't need to show up with a broken nose or busted lip. We'll just tell him Flannery threatened you."

"It's more effective if we show it."

He cursed. "Fine, then put on some makeup. You're good at that."

"Makeup works from a distance, or for a short conversation," she argued. "If I'm going to be spending more than five minutes with the man, it needs to be real."

"I'm not fucking hitting you, damn it!"

Bailey rolled her eyes. "Okay, then I'll just rough myself up. Easy enough."

Liam blanched as he pictured Bailey pulling a *Fight Club* and slamming her face against walls and doors. Christ. The damage could be ten times worse if she pulled a stunt like that.

"No way," he interjected. "It'll be safer if you take a strategically placed hit." Reluctance rose inside him. "I'll do it."

Sean's face turned beet red. "No bloody way, Macgregor. Lay a hand on her and I'll kill you." His enraged gaze traveled to D. "Same goes for you, you psycho. You're not touching her."

"I guess that leaves me," Sully said brightly. He was already standing up and cracking his knuckles. "Ready, love?"

"Not you either." Sean's teeth visibly clenched as he hooked a thumb at Ash. "Him."

From his perch on the armchair, the rookie's head shot up in alarm. "Why me?"

"Because you're the one I'm least likely to murder," Sean muttered. "It's easier to forgive a kid over one of these jackasses."

"I'm not a kid," Ash protested. "I'm twenty-three."

"Don't worry," Bailey said helpfully. "I'm certain you can hit like a man."

Sullivan chuckled softly.

Ash wasn't as amused. His uncertain gaze shifted from Sean to Bailey. "Fine," he finally mumbled, getting to his feet. "But only because I agree that this is a solid plan." His green eyes traveled back to Sean. "But I get a free pass for this, Irish. You're not allowed to hold it against me."

"No promises," Sean grumbled.

With a sigh, Ash approached Bailey and flexed his right hand. "What'll it be? Black eye? Split lip?"

"Go for the eye," she advised. "Easier to cover up with makeup if I need to."

The two of them moved several steps away from the group, Ash's reluctance clearly etched into his face. He looked as if he'd rather shave his own legs than lay a finger on Bailey, but she flashed an encouraging look and widened her stance as she waited.

A red vein was throbbing in Sean's forehead. His fists were clenched, like he was two seconds from diving across the room and putting an end to the insanity.

"Ready?" Ash asked, his voice lined with resignation.

Bailey grinned at the younger man. "Do your worst."

# Chapter 11

This was a bloody nightmare. After he'd received the news that Ollie had been nabbed, Sean had left Morgan's crew for a reason—because he'd wanted to keep his mates *out* of it. And now he had not only Bailey to worry about, but also the blasted men he'd been trying to protect. Sully. Ash. Hell, even that bastard D.

And Liam. Couldn't forget Macgregor, now, could he?

Was it wrong to want to strangle one of your closest mates? Because Sean did. So badly his hands ached. He hated the familiarity between Bailey and the movie-star-handsome mercenary. He'd known they'd become close in Paris, but he hadn't realized they'd kept in touch, damn it. That they e-mailed and texted and hugged—fucking *hugged*. He'd fought the urge to break every one of Macgregor's fingers when he'd seen them curled around Bailey's arm earlier.

Why did *Liam* get to touch her? Bailey had all but hurled herself into the man's arms, for Christ's sake. Why did Liam get that fucking privilege when all Sean got was a stolen kiss before she recoiled from him?

In the passenger side, Bailey was on the phone with—who else?—Liam Macgregor. The conversation was brisk, and then she hung up. "They checked out the perimeter. It's secure. There's nobody watching the pub except for Rabbit's usual sentries. No sign of Flannery's men."

"He doesn't need to watch the bar. Not when one of his men is inside it."

Sean made the mistake of glancing over at her and a burst of anger went off in his gut. Her right eye was red and swollen, the faint tinge of purple beginning to form beneath it. Ash had clocked her soundly, but not hard enough for it to swell shut. It still made Sean livid to see it.

"Relax," she said when she noticed his gloomy expression. "It's just a shiner. I've had worse."

That just made him angrier. There shouldn't have been even a lick of violence in her past. She was *Bailey*. She was smart, ballsy, and beautiful, and he hated the thought of her getting hurt.

He hated even more that he was allowing her to walk into a lion's den on his arm.

*For Oliver,* a firm voice reminded him.

Sean's fingers tightened around the steering wheel. Christ, he wanted to kill Rabbit for putting him in this position, and Flannery for twisting it into something even more fucked-up.

"So your dad and O'Hare were tight, huh?" Bailey spoke up, her tone awkward but curious.

Sean let out a weary breath. "He was Rabbit's second-in-command. They grew up together, best friends since they were six."

"Were you and Oliver close with him? Your father, I mean?"

"We worshipped him. He was our bloody hero."

"And your mom died when you were eight." It was a statement, not a question. "That must have been tough."

Her knowledge of his past didn't surprise him, since

Bailey had connections that rivaled his. But it grated a little that she knew about his background when he hadn't been able to find a damn thing about hers. The file he had contained details about Bailey's life—after the age of twenty. He knew she'd been recruited by the CIA at eighteen, but not the circumstances that led to it, or anything that had happened to her before that.

"It was tough," he admitted. "What about your parents? Alive?"

"My mother is." She didn't elaborate.

"Where did you grow up?"

"Nice try."

"What, trying to get to know you?" he said sarcastically. "Lord, the *nerve* of me."

She shrugged. Checked her phone.

"You can talk to me, you know. I'd never give away your secrets."

"What's that saying about secrets?" she said lightly. "Three can keep a secret if two of them are dead."

"Benjamin Franklin," he muttered under his breath.

"Nice. You know your American history. I guess that's because you lived in the States for three years. New York, right?" She sounded smug, as if purposely flaunting that she knew more about him than he did about her.

Sean set his jaw. "One of these days I *will* find out who you are."

"You know who I am. I'm Bailey."

"Liar. You pretty much admitted that's not your name."

Her noncommittal shrug made him want to steer the car straight into a brick wall. God knew he hit enough of those when he was around this woman.

The infuriating conversation came to an end as they reached the city's north end. Rabbit's pub was located in one of the dodgier areas off O'Connell Street, and unlike the other establishments he owned, this particular one wasn't a front for money laundering, but a legitimate business. The Garda had raided it on more than one occasion in the hopes of cracking down on Rabbit's drug network, but O'Hare's Pub was cleaner than an operating room. Some business was conducted in the back rooms, but money never traded hands, and any plans formulated there were talked about but never documented.

Sean parked at the curb and turned to Bailey. "Any chance of convincing you to wait in the car?"

She just laughed.

Of course not.

They slid out of the car. Sean was thankful for the familiar weight of the pistol at his back and the one in his boot. Bailey was also armed, but neither one drew a weapon as they approached the pub's red paint-chipped door.

D and Liam were positioned on nearby rooftops with their sniper rifles, and Ash was on the street somewhere, hidden from view. Sean spotted Sully, though. Sitting on the outdoor patio of a neighboring café and reading the paper. No doubt armed to the teeth.

Since Rabbit swept everyone for wires and mics as a rule, Sean and Bailey were going in dark, but he knew the other men were in communication with one another. And fine, maybe he felt a *tad* better knowing they were backing him up.

The interior of O'Hare's looked like any other Irish pub. Weathered wooden tables and booths, dark paneled walls, and TV screens flashing sports highlights. Only thing noticeably missing was the warm Irish welcome.

The bartender straightened up at their entrance. He was a stocky man with a bushy red beard and an icy glare that would make Satan himself shiver. Rory Smith, a longtime member of the Dagger who was obsessively devoted to Rabbit.

The group crowded around the dartboard turned around too, aiming menacing scowls in Sean's direction. Nobody spoke. They just glared.

"Evening, lads," he said wryly.

A dark-haired man rose from the only occupied barstool. Cillian Kelly, Rabbit's right-hand man, smirked at the newcomers. "Right on time," he told Sean, his pale blue eyes flicking briefly at Bailey.

"My girlfriend," Sean muttered.

The smirk turned into a broad smile. "I see."

He stiffened when the man reached out and gently brushed his thumb beneath Bailey's eye. She didn't so much as flinch, but she also didn't look happy with the uninvited touch.

Sean mentally added Cillian's name to the list of men whose fingers he wanted to break.

"I didn't realize you were whaling on your women these days," Cillian remarked in a dry voice.

"I'm not," he snapped, then forced himself to temper his hostility. "Where's Rabbit?"

"Waiting for you." Cillian swiftly moved toward the back corridor, and Sean and Bailey followed him, only to be stopped when they were out of sight of the main room.

"Spread 'em." Cillian smiled again, indicating he needed to pat them down.

"Don't bother," Sean said coolly. "We're both armed with nine mils. The lady's got a knife strapped to her ankle, and I've got a second pistol in my boot."

"Hand 'em over."

He rolled his eyes. "Do you really think I came here to fuck with Rabbit? I just want my brother, Kelly."

"Better safe than sorry," the man chirped. "Or at least that's what my ma used to say."

He highly doubted that. Sean had known the guy's mother, and the broad had always been too sloshed to form coherent sentences. Ditto for Kelly Senior. With both his parents raging alcoholics, it was no surprise that Cillian had turned elsewhere for guidance and support. He'd found it with Eamon O'Hare, who was more than happy to take lads in and use them as soldiers for his cause.

"We're not giving you our weapons, Kelly. Deal with it."

He waited for Cillian to challenge him, but the man chuckled. "Fair enough. But if either one of you draws, I'll put you down like a rabid dog."

Cillian took off walking again, heading for the closed door that led to Rabbit's domain. The moment Sean stepped into the familiar space, he searched it for signs of Oliver, but there were none. Card table, couches, telly. Rabbit wasn't one for luxuries; the shabby surroundings suited him just fine.

The man himself was sitting at the table, watching them with dark, expressionless eyes. Unlike Flannery, who'd aged tremendously well, Rabbit looked decades older than the early fifties he was. Sean supposed it was easy to stay young when you weren't getting your hands dirty—Flannery had his thugs to do that for him. But not Rabbit. He'd fought in the trenches with his men, slicing his enemies with knives and crushing them with his meaty fists.

His face bore the weathered wrinkles and scars of his lifestyle, but his lean, muscular body still rippled with power. He wore a plaid shirt, unbuttoned to reveal the wife-beater beneath it, and with his unruly gray hair and unkempt beard, he looked more like a scrub than a kingpin. But anyone who came into contact with Rabbit knew he was deadly as hell when he wanted to be.

He clasped his hands, the fingers of his right hand millimeters from the silenced Glock on the tabletop. "Why are five of my lads dead?"

Sean cocked a brow. "Because one of them was a bloody idiot."

There was a pause.

Then Rabbit sighed. "Paddy?"

"Who else?" Sean shook his head in annoyance. "The son of a bitch shot a ghost. Yep, turned out there was an undercover garda in the bank. Things went to hell from there."

Rabbit nodded thoughtfully. "And how is it you got away, lad?"

"That was Gallagher's idea." The lie flowed out smoothly, and thankfully there was nobody there to contradict him. "He knew we weren't getting out, at least not all of us. He ordered me to play a hostage so we could get the package out."

Another nod. "And the girl? Any reason she was in the bank too?"

Sean had anticipated the question. Flannery had already gotten his hands on the bank footage, so it stood to reason that Rabbit had done the same.

"That was a misunderstanding." He scowled at Bailey, who played along by wincing. "She tried to stop me from taking the job, and when I didn't listen she decided I needed *backup*." He spat out the last word, his disgust on the subject more than evident.

Rabbit's lips twitched as he studied Bailey's slight frame. Sean felt like laughing too. Every man who saw her underestimated her. She might look small and innocent, but Bailey was the very definition of *looks could be deceiving*.

"I'm sorry." Bailey directed the soft, desperate plea at Sean. "I screwed up, baby. I know that."

"We'll talk about it later," he said tightly, before turning back to Rabbit. "Where's Oliver?"

"Around." Rabbit shrugged. Made no move to get up.

Sean was aware of Cillian standing behind them with

his gun in hand, but that didn't stop him from snapping at his former employer. "Well, bring him here. I'm not giving you a bloody thing until I know my brother is safe."

The older man chuckled. "For Christ's sake, lad. You know I wouldn't hurt Ollie. You boys are like sons to me."

The words didn't appease him in the slightest. They both knew damn well that Rabbit would slit his own child's throat if it helped the Irish Dagger.

"Whatever you say, Eamon. But me? I'm not saying another word until I see my brother."

Rabbit let out an exaggerated sigh. "Tell Doherty to bring the lad," he instructed Cillian.

Sean heard Cillian's retreating footsteps but didn't turn around. The door creaked open as Kelly barked out an order to someone in the hall, and then he promptly resumed his guard duty.

"So does this pretty bird have a name?" Rabbit spoke in a conversational tone, but his gun remained inches from his hand, and the air of danger shrouding the room didn't dissipate.

"Bailey," she said nervously.

"Bailey. That's beautiful." Rabbit finally left his chair and headed toward them. He wasn't a tall man—at least five inches shorter than Sean's six-two frame—but he carried himself with deadly confidence.

Sean's jaw twitched when Rabbit clasped both of Bailey's hands in his. "I'm Eamon, luv. But you can call me Rabbit."

"Nice to meet you," she murmured.

Rabbit chuckled. "Very polite young lady you found yourself, lad. Should I be offended that you didn't introduce us before now?"

"That's because she has nothing to do with my business. And believe me, I'm not thrilled that she decided to involve herself." Sean frowned at Bailey, who meekly averted her gaze.

"Well, it looks like you punished her thoroughly for it." Rabbit didn't hide his disapproval. He was a violent motherfucker, but he possessed a peculiar moral code—a man didn't lay a hand on his woman. Ever.

Sean's lips flattened. "No. Ronan Flannery did."

Rabbit's gaze flew to his. He clearly hadn't expected that, and Sean enjoyed catching him off guard. Before Rabbit could question him, though, the door opened again.

Sean turned around, and all the air in his lungs promptly hissed out.

Oliver.

Thank fucking God.

"Ollie!" Bailey's relieved exclamation broke the silence, and then she was darting across the room and throwing her arms around Sean's twin.

He ignored the streak of jealousy that raced through him and distracted himself by studying his brother. Every hair, every feature, assessing his twin for any harm Rabbit might have caused him. But Oliver looked fine. Dark circles lined his eyes and his wavy blond hair was disheveled, but he looked more tired than hurt. And he was alive, which was all that mattered.

The twins' gazes locked over Bailey's head. Oliver nodded slightly, and unspoken conversation rapidly flowed between them.

*You okay?*

*Fine. Why the hell is Bailey here?*

*Don't ask.*

*I want her out of here.*

*Trust me, so do I.*

Rabbit watched Oliver and Bailey's embrace in fascination, then chuckled again. "Interesting. Or . . . maybe not." He smirked at Sean. "You lads always did like to share your toys when you were young."

Possessiveness reared up and hardened his jaw. "She's mine."

The fierce claim caused Oliver to look over in surprise. He released Bailey, whose expression revealed nothing as she dropped her arms from Oliver's neck and cautiously walked back to Sean.

He swallowed his bitterness. Leaving Oliver's side was probably torture for her. And having to pretend to be Sean's girlfriend when the man she loved was standing five feet away? Probably made her sick.

"As you can see, Ollie is just fine." Rabbit lifted a mocking eyebrow. "I showed you mine. Now you show me yours."

Without a word, he pulled the flash drive out of his back pocket and tossed it to Rabbit. The man had solid reflexes, catching it easily before smiling magnanimously. "Wasn't so hard, was it? And see, I'm a man of my word. You helped me, I helped you in return."

"You kidnapped my brother—that wasn't helping me," Sean snapped. "But damned if you won't help me *now*."

Rabbit turned the flash drive over in his hand a couple of times. Then he spoke, thoughtful again. "Does this have something to do with the bruise on your pretty bird's eye?"

Sean glanced at Ollie. "Take Bailey to the café next door. I'll be there in a minute."

As expected, his twin gave a resolute shake of the head. "No way."

"Just fucking do it. I don't want either one of you around for this."

The twins stared at each other again.

Sean transmitted another silent message.

*Do it, Ollie. Bailey will fill you in.*

After a long beat of hesitation, Oliver ended the stare down with a nod. "Fine."

"Go with Ollie," Sean told Bailey. "I'll be there shortly."

She clutched his forearm, playing her part of fragile, loving girlfriend to a tee. "I don't want to leave you," she whispered.

"I won't be long. I promise."

Unable to stop himself, he dipped his head and kissed her. Just the fleeting touch of his mouth to hers, but Jesus, he wanted more. He wanted to drive his tongue inside, to hear that tiny whimper she'd made last year when he'd nibbled on her bottom lip.

But he couldn't do that. Not because they were being watched, but because Bailey didn't belong to him. She belonged to the man who looked like him. The man who stepped forward now to take her hand.

Cillian snapped into a defensive stance as Oliver tried to lead Bailey to the door. Rabbit's guard dog swiftly placed himself in their path, his fingers ominously curling around his weapon.

Sean's shoulders stiffened. "Let them go."

Cillian glanced at Rabbit, who stayed quiet.

"Let them go," Sean repeated, praying like hell that he wouldn't have to draw his own weapon. "You have no need for Ollie anymore. We've got business to discuss." He shot Rabbit a pointed look. "Ronan Flannery."

The name achieved the desired result. Rabbit's lips twisted. His light brown eyes darkened with menace. Then he nodded at Cillian, who immediately stepped aside so Bailey and Oliver could pass.

Oliver's eyes found Sean's again, conveying a warning—*Be careful*—before he ushered Bailey out the door.

The moment they were gone, Sean exhaled a relieved breath.

Son of a bitch.

He'd done it. Oliver was no longer being held in some scuzzy safe house. Bailey was no longer risking her life beside him.

He'd *done* it.

"For Christ's sake, Seansy. You don't need to look so relieved." Rabbit sounded oddly defensive. "I didn't hurt him. Wasn't gonna either. The lad spent a lovely week at my flat in Ballymount. Had plenty of books and grub and fine Tullamore Dew single malt."

Sean stared at him.

"It was the only way to guarantee your cooperation, you stubborn feck!" Rabbit rubbed his beard in aggravation. "I loved your father. I love you and Ollie." He waved the flash drive around. "But the cause needs this, don't you see? I couldn't trust Gallagher to get it for me."

"Gallagher *died* for you yesterday, you bastard."

"He was working for Flannery," Rabbit said flatly.

Interesting. Was that what Flannery's mole was feeding Rabbit these days?

"You're sure of that?" Sean prompted.

Rabbit exchanged a look with Cillian, who remained stone-faced. "Pretty sure," the man replied. "Don't you see, Seansy? I needed you there to keep the men honest. And you did. You got the package. So let's just call the rest of it water under the bridge, eh? Bygones and such."

Sean laughed humorlessly. "You kidnapped my brother and blackmailed me into robbing a bank, and you're talking to me about bygones? No dice, Eamon. Only way you're going to redeem yourself in my eyes is if you help me now."

A heavy sigh rumbled out of Rabbit's chest. "Then have a seat, lad. Let's see what we can do."

* * *

"What the *hell* is going on?" Oliver hissed as he and Bailey left O'Hare's Pub.

"Let's not talk out on the sidewalk." She sighed. "Come on, we'll grab a table over there while we wait for Sean."

Oliver didn't put up an argument. He willingly followed her to the café down the street, where Sullivan was currently staked out. Neither one of them acknowledged the blond Australian, but from the tic in Ollie's jaw, she knew he'd spotted Sully. The other man nodded almost imperceptibly, a ghost of a smile on his face, then resumed reading the newspaper. Bailey saw his lips move slightly—probably reporting to the others that Oliver was okay.

The patio had a huge red awning that allowed them to sit outside without worrying about the rain, but a soft mist still floated through the air. Bailey and Oliver sat down and ordered coffees, eyeing each other across the small table.

It felt strange to be staring at a man who was identical to Sean. For the most part, the twins were carbon copies, right down to the sensual curve of their mouths and the faint crinkles around their vivid green eyes. It was only when you looked past their identical features that you began to notice the slight differences. Oliver's wavy blond hair was longer, curling under his ears and at the back of his neck; Sean's was cropped military short. Oliver's jaw was always relaxed; Sean's was tighter than a guitar string about to snap. Oliver's face was clean-shaven most of the time; Sean's was always shadowed with stubble.

Still, despite the differences, the similarities were impossible to ignore, bringing a helpless feeling to Bailey's stomach. Why couldn't she lust after *this* brother? It would make her life so much easier, and yet . . . when she looked at Ollie's mouth, she didn't want to kiss it. When he touched her, she didn't forget her name.

"Are you sure you're okay?" she asked once their coffees arrived. She studied his appearance—T-shirt, cargo pants, and army surplus coat stretching over his broad shoulders. He didn't look like a man who'd been mistreated, unless you counted the exhaustion lining his eyes.

"I'm fine. Rabbit wasn't talking out of his ass before—he didn't want to hurt me." Oliver shrugged. "He just wanted me and Sean to play ball. It would've gone the other way, you know, if it was Sean in London instead of me."

"His trust in you two is astonishing," she remarked. "Do you think that's all it really is? He wants you guys back on his crew because he trusts you?"

"I think so. Rabbit accused us of taking a shit on our father's memory when we left the Dagger, but he made sure we knew he'd always welcome us back. Except, well, we didn't *want* to come back, so he forced our hands." Oliver raked his fingers through his blond curls. "Now can you please tell me why my brother is still in there?"

Letting out another sigh, Bailey told him about Ronan Flannery's late-night visit and the man's "request" that Sean help Flannery's mole take over Rabbit's organization.

"That's bloody insane!" Oliver exclaimed. "And my brother was daft enough to agree to this?"

"He had no choice."

Wait—why was she defending *Sean*? She one hundred percent *agreed* that he was crazy for not skipping town.

"Flannery threatened to kill me if he didn't cooperate," Bailey admitted. "And Sean couldn't show up to this exchange without making it look like he's following

Flannery's orders. Whoever the mole is, he needs to believe Sean is doing what Flannery asked."

A wrinkle appeared in Oliver's forehead. "Rabbit seems to think the mole was Rhys Gallagher."

"It's not. Flannery wouldn't have been so smug and cheerful if his inside man was dead. I bet the mole planted the Gallagher idea in Rabbit's head." She paused to take a sip of coffee. God, she needed the caffeine boost. It had been a long fucking day. "Sean's biding his time until he can figure out how to get Flannery off his back."

Oliver's gaze darkened. "Did Sean tell you about Flannery and Rabbit's history?"

She nodded.

"Well, then you know it won't be easy to get Flannery off *anyone's* back, not when Rabbit is involved. And not when he finally has a real chance to destroy his enemy."

"You could leave town," she pointed out. "You and Sean. Go somewhere where Flannery won't find you. We both know it won't take much for you guys to disappear. You've got contacts in every corner of the world."

"Oh, we could absolutely do it, but I know my brother, Bailey." Oliver wrapped both hands around his mug. "He won't run. And he won't live on the run."

"Not even to stay alive?"

"Sean's the most stubborn bastard on the planet. You know that better than anyone." Oliver gave a wry smile. "Do you honestly think he'd let someone run him out of town?" He brought his mug to his lips. "No. We'll have to fight back."

His use of the word *we* didn't surprise her. The Reilly brothers were joined at the hip. They'd clean up this mess together, the way they always did.

"But you'll need to leave town, Bailey." Oliver nodded as if it was already decided, proving that he and his brother were more alike than she'd thought.

"I can't," she answered. "Rabbit thinks I'm Sean's girlfriend."

"Rabbit also thinks Flannery clocked you, which means he won't bat an eye if Sean whisks you out of town. Hell, Rabbit would probably prefer it—he wants Sean focused on the cause, not a woman." Oliver set down his cup. "And don't forget, Flannery has no idea who you really are. Sure, he threatened to kill you, but he can't kill a ghost, remember?"

The smile that reached her lips faded fast. "I expected this from Sean—I mean, he's been trying to get rid of me since I got here. But you, Ollie? Do you honestly think I can leave the two of you to fight this battle alone?"

"It would be . . . easier," he admitted. "You're a distraction, Bailey."

"To who?"

"Who do you think?" Oliver blew out a frustrated breath. "My brother's not right in the head when you're around. He won't be able to do what needs to be done if he's worrying about you."

"He doesn't have to worry about me," she shot back. "I'm perfectly capable of taking care of myself."

"I know you are. He knows that, too." Oliver shrugged. "But that won't stop either one of us from worrying."

Before she could argue with his chauvinistic logic, her cell phone interrupted them. "This conversation's not over," she warned as she grabbed the phone.

She checked the caller ID and frowned. Unknown number. Which was highly alarming, because there was no such thing as an unknown number in her life, not since Paige had pulled her techno voodoo on Bailey's cell phone. Paige's decryption chip could detect any number, even when the person on the other end was trying to hide it.

Bailey considered not answering, but the warning

bells shrieking in her head were saying she needed to take the call. Unknown variables were too dangerous—she functioned better when she knew who her enemies were.

After a beat, she picked up with a guarded "Yes?"

The voice that slid into her ear turned the blood in her veins to ice.

"Tara, it's me. I'm afraid we have a problem."

# Chapter 12

*Tara.*

It wasn't a name that many people knew. It wasn't a name that anyone *called* her, at least not in a very long time. After the CIA had assigned her the handle Bailey, only two people had continued to use her given name.

One of them was her mother.

The other was Isaac Daniels.

Bailey's fingers tightened around the phone. She noticed Oliver watching her in concern, but she quickly shook her head and pasted on a weak smile to indicate that everything was okay. Then she apologetically gestured to the phone as if to say, *I need to take this*, and rose from her chair.

She waited until she was on the sidewalk, several yards from the patio, before she spoke again. "What do you want?"

"Is that any way to greet an old friend?"

A friend? They weren't *friends*, for fuck's sake. He'd been her handler for seven years. Her lover for five. And God, what a mistake the latter had been. She'd longed for a partner, and instead she'd found herself at the mercy of yet another man who wanted to control her.

"Let me guess," she muttered, ignoring the good-natured taunt. "You spoke to Gwen."

Surprise washed over the line. "Gwen? No." A pause. "Why, have *you* spoken to Gwen?"

"Nope," she lied.

He laughed, that familiar rumble of sound that once upon a time had made her heart pound. "You're forgetting who you're talking to, Tara. I was the one who taught you how to lie, remember? And no, this has nothing to do with Gwen—although trust me, I *will* be having a chat with her once you and I are through."

"Then what's this about? Because if you're calling about a job, I'm not inte—"

"Someone ran your prints through the system."

Bailey froze. "Which system?"

"All of them," he said flatly. "AFIS, DOD, military channels, pretty much any database you can think of."

"Shit."

"Oh, it gets worse, sweetheart."

She cringed at the endearment. Every time she spoke to him, Daniels continued to act like time hadn't passed, like she hadn't walked out on him five years ago. He still viewed her as the young girl he'd recruited out of high school, the girl he'd molded into an operative and turned into a killer, only to rein her in when he decided the world was too dangerous for her. He'd been a father figure to her—God knew she'd needed one—but then he'd started *acting* like it, and not like one of those warm, supportive fathers you saw on television. He'd become a bully. Fiercely protective and possessive.

No, *obsessive.*

"When your fingerprints went online, a red flag popped up in our system," Daniels said. "Obviously your prints didn't give our mystery hacker your identity—

there aren't any files on you in the main databases—but the bastard saw the flag on our end."

"So? My CIA file is confidential. Can't be accessed without the highest security clearance, right?" But it still worried her that someone had managed to lift her fingerprints without her knowledge.

And Daniels's response worried her even more. "Right. But someone accessed the file, Tara."

A chill blew up her spine. Shit. *Shit.*

"And we both know there's only one way that could've happened," Daniels went on. "Someone in the company allowed it to happen."

"You're saying one of your people leaked my file?" She kept her voice to a low hiss, but it was impossible to control her anger. "How the *fuck* did you let that happen, Isaac?"

"Trust me, sweetheart—I'm not thrilled about it myself. Obviously there's a rat in the company, and it's someone high up on the food chain. Only senior-level staff can access the spook files."

Flannery.

It had to be Flannery—the bastard had dirt on every important person in the goddamn world. He must have someone in the CIA too.

And that someone had accessed her file. Which meant that he or she had passed the information on to Flannery. Which meant that Flannery knew her real name, her background, her—

"Oh God. My mother," she mumbled into the phone.

"I told you, it gets worse," Daniels said grimly.

Bailey was beginning to feel faint. "Are you telling me this isn't even the *bad* part?"

"I just received a call from Josiah."

"Who's Josiah?"

There was a long pause.

"Who the fuck is Josiah, Isaac?"

Her former boss sighed. "The agent I assigned to Vanessa."

Bailey hissed in fury. "You ordered surveillance on my mother? You *son of a bitch*."

"That's what happens when the woman you love disappears off the face of the world," Daniels snapped. "You do anything in your power to locate her, even if it means monitoring her mother."

"I didn't disappear," she said coldly. "I *left*. And don't play that bullshit outrage card—you knew exactly how to contact me."

"You made it clear you didn't want me to."

God, she couldn't have this talk now. She couldn't rehash the past with Daniels—it was over and done with. She didn't love him anymore, hadn't loved him in a very long time, and she wished he would just accept that.

She gritted her teeth and changed the subject back to the one that mattered. "Is she okay?"

"Your mother's fine. But someone did pay a visit to her facility, told the nurses they were a friend of the family."

"Did *Josiah* question the staff?"

He ignored the bitterness in her tone. "Of course. We're looking at a white male, early thirties, Irish accent."

Her heart plummeted as if it was weighed down with cement. Definitely Flannery, then.

"They didn't let him see her, did they?" God. The second she was through with Daniels, she was calling that motherfucking nursing home and ripping every member of that staff a new one.

"No, they didn't. You're the only approved person on Vanessa's visitors' list, and the nurses enforced that." He paused. "I posted two extra agents on-site, though."

"Thank you." Bailey almost choked on the gratitude. She hated owing this man anything.

Daniels sighed again. "Are you going to tell me what you're involved in, Tara?"

"Nothing that concerns you."

"Like hell it doesn't! I've got a rat on my team!"

"Who you wouldn't have even known about if that person hadn't run my prints," she said dryly. "So really, Isaac, you should be thanking *me*. How about we call it square, then?"

"We're not even close to being *square*, sweetheart."

"Fine, I'll toss in some extra goodies for you. I can find out who your rat is—pretty easily, actually." All she had to do was go through the copies Sean had made of Flannery's files and it would be easy to locate the person he was blackmailing in the CIA.

"How?" Daniels said suspiciously.

"You don't need to know. I'll text you with a name later, tonight most likely." She swallowed. "Thanks for the heads-up about all this. I'll take it from here."

She disconnected the call even as she heard him protesting, but Daniels didn't call back. He was a smart man, smart enough to know she wouldn't answer. Besides, if he talked to Gwen like he'd threatened, he'd know sooner rather than later that Bailey was in Dublin. She just hoped he didn't send any agents her way. The situation was complicated enough as it was without having to worry about CIA spooks shadowing her.

Taking a breath, she headed back to the patio, where Oliver's concern had only grown in her absence. "What's wrong?" he demanded.

She didn't bother pretending otherwise. "You know how you told me I should leave town?"

"Yeah . . ." His eyes flickered with wariness.

"That's not going to happen."

"Bailey—"

"Flannery found me," she cut in.

When Oliver furrowed his brow, she elaborated. "He found me, Ollie. *Me.* He knows my name, my mother's whereabouts—he sent one of his thugs to her nursing home in Virginia."

"Shit."

A cold knot of fear circled her belly. "He probably has a bunch of men stationed outside by now. With orders to kill her if Sean and I don't do what he wants."

Oh God. She had to make arrangements to move her mother—*now*. But if Flannery had found her once, the bastard might be able to track her again.

Bailey couldn't let him. She refused to let some vengeful Irish gangster anywhere near her mother. Vanessa had suffered through enough pain and torture to last a lifetime, and the only saving grace was that she couldn't even remember it.

But Bailey did. She remembered every gruesome detail of her childhood. Every second of torment she and her mom had endured. Once Vanessa's condition had deteriorated, Bailey had made sure to keep the woman hidden. It would only confuse and agitate her mom if someone showed up asking questions, if they tried to remind her of events that she'd blessedly forgotten.

Across the table, Oliver stiffened, but Bailey didn't need his body language to tell her that Sean was approaching. She *sensed* him. She'd always been excruciatingly aware of Sean Reilly's presence.

Sean reached their table, looming over them with a scowl. "Let's go."

She and Oliver rose without a word and followed him to the car at the curb. Ollie got into the passenger seat next to Sean, while Bailey slid in the back, grabbing the case she'd left under the seat and pulling out her earpiece.

She popped it in her ear as she addressed Sean. "Where are we headed?"

"The loft," he muttered.

Her hand moved over the earpiece to trigger the mic. "Liam, you copy?"

"Loud and clear, darling."

"We're heading back to the loft. Meet us there."

"No," Sean said swiftly.

She touched the transmitter again. "Hold on. Possible change of plans." She met Sean's hard gaze in the rearview mirror. "Where do you want them to go, then?"

"Tell them to find a hotel near the pub." He sounded less than enthused as he added, "I'm going to be spending some time there. So if they insist on providing backup, I want them close to O'Hare's."

She relayed the message to Liam, then glanced at Sean again. "Does this mean Rabbit bought it?"

Sean nodded.

"So what now?"

"Now we sit in silence while I fucking think about this."

She hesitated. "Listen, you should know that—"

"Not now, Bailey," he snapped. "Seriously. I can't listen to a goddamn thing right now."

For the rest of the car ride, nobody said another word.

Sean had thought he was pissed off before—and then Bailey told him about her conversation with her former CIA handler, and he understood the true meaning of anger.

"Why in bloody hell didn't you tell me this before?" he exploded as they faced off in the middle of the loft.

"Because you told me to shut up in the car," she snapped. "I was waiting for you to calm down."

"Calm down? Don't you get it? I won't *calm down* until you're out of Dublin." He shot his twin a sour look. "Same goes for you, man. I don't want either one of you involved."

With a loud curse, Oliver got right up in his face, and it was like looking into a mirror. A mirror that was blasting the same enraged expression back at him.

Ollie's fuming face only made Sean want to slug the guy, and yet at the same time, he felt like throwing his arms around his twin and thanking the frickin' heavens that Ollie was safe.

Jesus, he didn't even know what he was feeling anymore. Mad and powerless and so bloody jealous he couldn't see straight. He hated seeing Oliver and Bailey in the same room together, and he hated himself for hating it because he had no right to feel that way. He was the one who'd torn them apart, which meant it was his responsibility to bring them back together.

He'd had a plan, damn it. Rabbit had *agreed* that Oliver should get Bailey out of town to keep her safe, but now there was no chance in hell of her leaving. Bailey was fiercely protective of the people she loved, and apparently her mother topped that list.

Her *mother*. It drove him fucking crazy that Flannery had learned more about Bailey in twenty-four hours than Sean had in five years.

"I'm not leaving," Oliver said firmly. "You really think I'd let you handle this alone?"

Sean ran a hand over his scalp, stealing a forlorn look at the punching bag across the room. Wishing he was pounding it with his fists.

He turned back to Bailey, sarcasm creeping in. "Well, the cat's out of the bag, luv. Are you ready to tell me who you really are, or should I call Flannery and ask him?"

Her gray eyes instantly became shuttered. "I'll tell you whatever I think is relevant to this op."

Of course. Even when her life depended on it, she still wouldn't throw him a fucking bone.

Oliver spoke up, the anger in his eyes thawing. "What's your plan?"

"I don't know anymore," he said testily. "I had it all worked out—before Bailey dropped her little CIA bomb."

He stalked over to the closet and grabbed an empty duffel bag from the top shelf.

"What are you doing?" Bailey asked.

"Gathering my gear," he said without turning around. "We need to relocate."

"Where?"

"Rathmines." He marched to the far wall and started gathering the weapons piled on the desk. "Rabbit thinks I'm back on his crew, which means he'll get suspicious if I'm holed up somewhere that's off his grid. He knows about my flat in Rathmines, so that's where we'll stay."

"We?" Bailey echoed.

"You and me. Since apparently you're stuck with me now." He couldn't bring himself to look at her, couldn't bear seeing her black eye, not right now. Instead he turned to Oliver. "I know it's inconvenient for you, but Rabbit thinks she's my girl. We need to keep it that way."

Oliver donned a blank look. "Why would it be inconvenient for me?"

Sean stared at him, but when his twin's confusion heightened, he broke eye contact and moved to the cabinet where he stored his ammo.

"Okay," Oliver said slowly, "and what exactly do you want *me* to do while you and Bailey play boyfriend-girlfriend?"

"What you do best. Gather information." Sean shoved a handful of nine-millimeter magazines into the bag. "Give Paige a call and team up with her. Do some digging into Flannery's operation. Smuggling routes, safe houses, bank accounts—whatever helps us find a way to eliminate him."

"We can kill him," Bailey suggested dryly. "Seems like the simplest way of all."

"Trust me—I'm considering that option too. But if we off Flannery, we have no idea who'll step up to take his place or what kind of trouble they'll cause us. We'll just let it play out until the best solution presents itself, all right?"

"Let it play out?" she echoed in disbelief. "Oh my God. You're the worst strategist on the planet, Sean."

Exhaustion washed over him as he finally looked her way. "It's all I've got right now."

"Okay. So let's concentrate on the other part—Rabbit believes you're going to help him take down Flannery?"

"I already told you, yes."

She frowned. "And how do you two plan on doing that?"

"We haven't figured it out yet. Right now Rabbit is too busy basking in the glow of me rejoining his cause." Sean dropped the duffel on the floor. "Go wait in the car. I need to talk to Ollie."

Her jaw dropped so fast he was surprised it didn't make a sound as it hit the floor. "Did you seriously just order me to leave? I don't take orders from you, Sean. I'm not your servant, and I'm definitely not your submissive little girlfriend, no matter what you tell Rabbit."

"I need to talk to Ollie," he repeated through clenched teeth. "Alone."

Oliver intervened before Bailey could argue. "Please," he said gently. "I'd like some alone time with my brother too. If you don't mind."

The tender look that passed between them was like a machete to the chest. Sean wasn't sure which emotion ravaged him worse—the jealousy or the guilt. He'd screwed up whatever normal relationship they could have had, and he had no clue how to fix that.

"Fine. I'll be downstairs if you need me." But although Bailey headed for the door, it was clear she wasn't happy about it.

As soon as he was alone with his twin, Sean released the breath he hadn't even realized he'd been holding.

"I'm sorry, okay?"

Oliver sighed. "Well, that's a loaded statement. What exactly are you sorry for, baby brother?"

*Baby brother.* Sean's lips twitched despite himself. Ollie was only five minutes older, yet he never let Sean forget it.

But those five minutes . . . Christ, what a difference they made. Oliver had always been the adult in their relationship, the calm, levelheaded one who provided constant supervision for his troublemaking twin.

"I'm sorry about Bailey," he clarified.

"Again, you'll have to be a wee bit clearer."

"I'm an ass, all right? When I told Rabbit she was my girl, I knew I was coming between you again, but . . ." He shrugged helplessly. "Flannery *saw* her with me. It made sense, okay?"

"Why would I care what you told Rabbit? It was a smart play, Sean. Gave you a reason for needing Rabbit's protection, and it worked."

"At your expense." He bit his lip. "I tried, Ollie. I tried to keep her safe for you, to keep her out of this mess, but she refused to go."

Oliver chuckled. "Of course she did. She's even more stubborn than you are. But she *is* safe, Sean. She's just fine."

He hunted down the whiskey bottle, chugging a mouthful of alcohol as he slowly met his brother's eyes. "I don't understand why you don't hate me."

"'Cause I love you like a brother."

Sean snapped up his middle finger. It was their running gag, though when it'd first started, he used to retort with "I *am* your brother." Eventually he'd condensed it by simply flipping Ollie the bird.

He raised the bottle to his lips and took another deep swig. He needed the liquid courage. Desperately. Because what he was about to say . . . it was something he'd kept from Oliver for far too long.

"I slept with her."

Oliver's forehead wrinkled. "Are we talking about Bailey?"

"Who the fuck else would we be talking about?" Misery clogged his throat as he repented for a second time. "I *slept* with her."

Silence hung between them, creating a gaping chasm that Sean struggled to bridge before Oliver shut down. Before he lost the one person who mattered most to him.

"That's why she ended it with you," Sean said softly. "Because she slept with me and she felt guilty about it."

His brother continued to watch him, his expression unreadable.

"Goddamn it, I slept with the woman you love, Ollie. Would you fucking *say* something?"

"I know."

The nonchalant response threw him for a loop. "What?"

"I know," Oliver repeated. "Bailey told me about it the day after it happened."

"You *knew*? And you didn't say anything?" Jesus Christ. He'd been walking around for a whole year with a world of guilt weighing down on his shoulders, and Oliver had known the truth the entire time? "For fuck's sake, why the *hell* didn't you kick my ass?"

Sighing, his twin gestured to the whiskey bottle. Sean passed it over and waited while Oliver took a quick sip.

"Look, I wasn't exactly thrilled that you pulled a twin switch on her, but I can't say I was surprised. Besides, *I* was the asshole in the equation. I knew how you felt about Bailey, and I still went out with her."

Bloody hell. *Oliver* was taking responsibility? Talk about taking the good-twin persona to new extremes.

"The blame's all on me," Sean insisted. "*I'm* the asshole. You were dating her, and I slept with her anyway."

"Sean—"

"Why aren't you hitting me right now?" Disbelief rippled through him. "What the fuck is the matter with you, Ollie? Are you applying for sainthood or something?"

"Would you cut it out with that crap? I'm not a bloody saint, brother. And here's another news flash for you—I was never in love with Bailey. And she was never in love with me."

Sean's breath hitched before seeping out in a shaky rush. "Bullshit."

"Truth," Oliver corrected. "The night I asked you to cancel my dinner with Bailey? It wasn't a date, you idiot. We were meeting up as friends."

"Friends."

He didn't believe it for a second, but Oliver was adamant. "Yes, *friends*. Before that, we'd gone on a few dates, made out once—"

Damned if his chest didn't clench with anger.

"—but the spark wasn't there. The first time I kissed her, she burst out laughing. Whenever I'd touch her, she'd draw back awkwardly. Definitely wasn't good for my ego, but truth was, I wasn't feeling it either. We decided we were better off as friends and that's all we were those last few months." Oliver shrugged. "She wasn't guilty about sleeping with you, Sean." He paused. "She was just pissed off."

Yeah? Well, that just pissed *him* off, because he knew

damn well she'd enjoyed every second of that night. She'd moaned so loudly he was surprised nobody in the hotel had filed a noise complaint. She'd clawed his back so hard it'd left marks.

But not only had Bailey denied liking it, she'd gone ahead and let him think she was in love with his brother.

And now he found out she and Ollie had only been *friends*?

"You're saying I didn't screw up your relationship?" he said in dismay.

"We didn't have a relationship." Oliver smirked. "But I'm not saying you didn't screw up. Because you did. Big-time. You lied to her, and you know Bailey doesn't forgive easily."

No kidding.

"Look." Oliver softened his tone. "I don't know what's going on with you two—that's for you and Bailey to straighten out—but you need to put it on hold until we figure out what to do about Flannery and Rabbit."

Oliver was right. Oliver was always right.

But Sean was still sifting through the wreckage of the shocking bomb that had just been dropped on him. Bailey didn't love Ollie. She hadn't, not even back then.

He'd thought she was denying her attraction to him because of her feelings for his brother, but now he had to face the bleak truth. She was holding back because of *him*.

Because she didn't want *him*.

Jesus. The thought of going downstairs and seeing her . . . being around her and smelling her sweet lavender scent and looking into her big gray eyes, all the while knowing she didn't want him . . . He wasn't sure he could handle that at the moment.

"Will you drive Bailey to the flat?" He let out a tired breath. "I want to stick around here for a bit longer."

Oliver narrowed his eyes. "Why?"

"Because I need some time to think. I can't keep a clear head around that woman, okay? I just need to figure some shit out before this bloody charade begins."

Oliver started to shake his head, but Sean cut him off before he could object. "Rabbit isn't expecting me back until tomorrow. We've got the whole night to regroup."

"Fine. I'll drive her. But don't take too long." Oliver hesitated, then moved in to hug him, clapping Sean on the back before heading for the door. "I'll see you later, baby brother."

Sean waited a full two minutes, until he was certain his brother wasn't coming back, and then he reached for the whiskey again.

Fuck thinking.

That was the last thing he wanted to do right now.

# Chapter 13

So far, so good. The awkwardness Sullivan had been anticipating was almost nonexistent, just the merest trace of tension beneath the surface, but not enough to put him on edge. He and Liam had teamed up for the evening's recon, and the easy camaraderie they'd shared since the moment they'd met in New York was still there, making it easy to forget the other bullshit.

And yeah, maybe he was making a conscious effort not to look at Liam's mouth, but hell, it was definitely helping him to stay focused.

"What do you think they're talking about?" Liam picked at the potato wedges on his plate, taking a tiny bite out of one.

They'd been trying to stretch out the meal for as long as they could, ordering a revolving door of light appetizers and constant coffee refills as they kept tabs on the two men across the room. Now that Reilly was "working" for Ronan Flannery, Morgan's men had been tasked with following some of Rabbit's higher-ranked lieutenants to try to uncover who Flannery's mole might be.

Technically it was supposed to be one-on-one coverage, but Sully and Liam's targets—Doherty and Doyle—

were having dinner together at a restaurant in the ritzy village of Howth, which Sully found perplexing. According to the Reilly brothers, O'Hare's Pub served decent food, yet their targets had chosen to dine as far away from the pub as possible.

Maybe there were *two* moles? Sullivan glanced at the back table, noting the hushed conversation between the Irishmen. It looked serious, but not confrontational.

"No clue," he said in response to Liam's question. "But now I'm wondering if Flannery has two inside men." He shrugged. "Maybe they're whispering about their dastardly plan to take down O'Hare."

"Christ, it's so weird hearing you talk like that." Liam lowered his voice as he commented on Sullivan's East Coast accent.

"It takes away from my natural charm, huh?"

"It's fucking surreal. You sound like me."

Sullivan grinned. He'd spent enough time with Liam that he'd perfected the Boston inflection. He was using it now so that anyone who overheard them would think they were just a couple of American tourists catching a bite together.

"Man, I can't wait to get back to Bahston and see my motha," Sully drawled. "I left my cah in the cah pahk. I wanna stop by Hahvad campus and—"

"Oh, shut up." But Liam was laughing.

Sullivan's answering laughter died the second he heard the click of high heels behind him. Before he could blink, a blur of red hair and shapely curves slid into the seat next to him.

"Evening, lads." The redhead curled her fingers around the back of Sullivan's neck and pulled his head in for a quick kiss. "Hey, baby, I missed you."

It took a few head-scratching seconds to realize that he was looking at Isabel Roma.

Sullivan chuckled as the confusion gave way to joy. "Why, hello there, love."

"Sorry I'm late," she chirped. "The taxi was late." She spoke in a flawless Irish accent, which told him she was pretending to be a local, then.

He and Liam exchanged amused grins, but neither man commented on her presence. Evidently Bailey had recruited another operative for this job, and it made sense that she'd called Isabel. The woman was a master of disguise—Sully didn't even recognize her with that curly mop of red hair and the bright green contacts. And her face looked fuller than usual. Makeup, most likely, or maybe those cheek inserts he'd seen her use on previous jobs.

"What did I miss?" she said softly.

She snuggled close to Sullivan and he played his part by slinging his arm over her shoulder. "Not much. Our friends are enjoying a nice seafood platter."

Liam signaled for their waiter, who hurried over to take Isabel's drink order. She hit Sully hard with PDA as she skimmed the cocktail menu, resting her palm on his thigh and stroking gently, which made him hard. Yup, he was a man so he got hard, even though the hand doing the stroking belonged to a teammate's wife.

Once the waiter was gone, Isabel brought her lips close to his ear. "Thought it would look less suspicious if one of you had a girlfriend. Otherwise you guys look like two thugs scoping out the place."

"Not complaining in the slightest," he replied, licking his lips seductively.

She rolled her eyes at the lewd display.

"How's Trev?" Liam asked. His features had tensed, and Sullivan suspected his friend knew damn well where Isabel's hand was resting.

"He's good," she answered. "Down in South America

with Kane at the moment. We had to kennel the dog because we're both out of town."

Sullivan raised an eyebrow. "You have a dog? Since when?"

"Since it showed up on our doorstep begging for scraps and then refused to go away." She sighed. "The damn thing guilt-tripped us into becoming dog owners."

"What'd you name him?"

"Chad."

Both men snickered.

*"Chad?"* Sullivan repeated.

"Hey, don't look at me. Trev named him and I didn't care enough to argue about it." She discreetly did a sweep of the room. "So who are we watching?"

Liam gave a subtle nod.

Isabel's gaze made contact with Doherty and Doyle's table, and then she turned back with a faint grin. "Aw, they're sweet. How long have they been a couple, you think?"

Sully didn't miss the alarm on Liam's face. "What makes you think they are?" Liam said slowly.

"Are you kidding me? I can feel the sexual tension from here." She rolled her eyes. "And they're playing footsies under the table."

Sullivan snuck another peek at Rabbit's men, who were still talking in low voices. How the hell had he missed that they were gay? Above the table there was nothing untoward happening, but below it . . . Hot damn. Isabel was right.

Well, now it made sense why they'd decided to dine on the other side of the county tonight. They were probably trying to hide their relationship from the rest of Rabbit's macho crew.

Across from him, Liam was also studying the men, a crease digging into his forehead, and Sullivan could pinpoint the exact moment when Liam's thoughts shifted. When his friend accessed the memory they'd both been pretending to forget.

Their eyes locked for one brief second, and then Liam gave a strangled cough and reached for his drink.

It was too late, though. Sullivan's mind had already conjured up the same damn images.

Lord . . . he would never forget the lust he'd glimpsed burning in his friend's eyes back in Paris. It had incinerated the air, not just before and during that blunder of a kiss, but after it, too.

It was the *after* that troubled Sullivan the most. He'd made a move on Liam out of sheer frustration, because he'd been angry and horny and astonished to find his best mate looking at him like that. Afterward, Liam had pretended that it was no biggie, easily accepting Sully's apology and acting like things were cool, and Sullivan had been happy to play along.

But he was no dummy. His friend still wanted him. He *knew* that, and if it were anyone other than Liam, Sully would be all over that like white on rice. He loved sex, and the fact that he was bisexual only doubled the pool of potential fuck candidates. Women, men, it was all good, as long as everyone was enjoying themselves.

He couldn't screw Liam, though. Nope, couldn't do that to his friend.

Besides, the worried flash in Liam's eyes when he'd realized that Doherty and Doyle were buggering each other? It spoke volumes.

It told Sully that even if he *was* interested in redefining their friendship, Liam was nowhere close to being ready for it.

Nearly eleven o'clock, and Sean still hadn't returned. Bailey had to admit she was getting worried. And it didn't help that Oliver was gone too. After he'd dropped her off at the one-bedroom flat in Rathmines, he'd hurried off to meet with some contacts. Ollie hadn't given any details, but she knew he was on the hunt for information.

She, on the other hand, was sidelined. Left alone to twiddle her thumbs while Sean spent the night "thinking." She'd wanted to join up with Morgan's men to help with surveillance, but Liam had told her they had everything covered. All of Rabbit's top soldiers were being watched, including Cillian Kelly, who, frankly, creeped her the fuck out.

She hadn't liked the way he'd looked at her earlier, or the feel of his hand on her face when he'd examined her bruise. His touch had made her skin crawl, and that worried her. Bailey's instincts never failed her, and right now they were telling her that Cillian Kelly was a threat.

When she heard footsteps nearing the apartment door, she automatically reached for her Beretta. The gun trained on the door when it opened, then lowered when Oliver strode inside.

Relief and disappointment mingled in her belly, but she refused to dwell on the latter. So what if Sean was still AWOL? He wasn't her boyfriend. If he wanted to sulk in his loft all night, he could go right ahead.

"Hey," she greeted Sean's twin. "How did it go?"

"I put out some feelers." Oliver paused. "Though I'm not sure what I'm putting out feelers *for*. My brother was pretty bloody vague about it."

"Because he doesn't have a plan," she muttered.

"Sure he does. He just hasn't come up with it yet." Oliver ducked into the small kitchen, then popped back out holding a bottle of water. He twisted the cap off, and his strong throat bobbed as he drank nearly half of it.

"Is he always like this?" she said irritably. "Flying by the seat of his pants?"

"Pretty much, yeah." Oliver grinned. "He's not a planner. But he happens to be the best improviser I've ever known."

"You two were mercs at one point—he must have known how to follow orders back then."

"I didn't say Sean can't follow orders. He's just not great at the whole planning thing. But if you're on a mission with him and it goes haywire? He'll get you out. Trust me—my brother's damn good at acting on impulse."

"Good for him, but that's not how I work," Bailey grumbled.

"I know that, sweets. But this is Sean's game, so we play by his rules."

That's what she was afraid of.

Oliver flopped down on the other side of the couch. "So . . . are you going to tell me why you lied to him?"

Her mouth fell open. "Me? How did *I* lie?"

"Well, Sean's under the impression that you and I are madly in love, so yeah, *somebody* must have told him that." He offered a pointed look.

Bailey's cheeks heated up. "I didn't tell him that." She paused. "But I didn't correct him when he said it."

"That's the same thing as lying." He shook his head. "It was cruel to let him think it. You know he's crazy about you."

Argh. It was always about Sean, wasn't it? *His* feelings, *his* orders. But what about *her*? The man refused to take her feelings into consideration. And neither did Oliver, apparently.

"I don't want to get involved with him," she said darkly. "I never did."

"Oh, come on, are you honestly telling me that the

night you slept with him you truly thought he was me? From start to finish?"

She faltered. Her cheeks burned hotter.

"That's what I thought." Oliver chuckled before going serious again. "My brother's a good man, Bailey. He has his flaws, sure—"

"Flaws? He's a frickin' Neanderthal!"

"Yes, he's possessive. He's overprotective and stubborn and hotheaded." Oliver shrugged. "But so are all the men on Morgan's team, and you seem to like them just fine."

The words evoked a spark of guilt. He was right. Morgan's men were alpha to the core, and she didn't begrudge them that. But they also didn't treat her the way Sean did. Like she needed a bodyguard, or a handler, or a man to guide the way.

"I'm not interested in Sean, okay? And I'm certainly not interested in sitting around and doing nothing when we could be strategizing. Where the hell is he?"

"Knowing my brother? He's getting thoroughly sloshed right now."

She hollowed her cheeks in anger. "Are you kidding me? Why would he do that?"

Oliver shot her a meaningful look.

"Unbelievable. Really? Because of *me*? Well, fuck that," she snapped. "He can't use me as an excuse to get drunk in the middle of a job. A job, I might add, that would be over in a heartbeat if he just kills Flannery."

"You know better than that," Oliver said gently. "Actions have repercussions. You can't kill a man like Flannery without putting a lot of careful thought and preparation into it."

"Fine," she conceded. "But that's my skill set, Ollie—thought and preparation. Give me a couple days and I could take out Flannery without any of it blowing back in our faces."

"Sean's game," he reminded her.

"Right, and Sean's rules." Setting her jaw, she got to her feet and fixed him with a hard look. "I'm taking the car. Where are the keys?"

"Where are you going?"

"Where do you think?" She glowered at him. "And don't give me that shit about how you need to stay with me until Sean gets here. I don't need a handler. I had one for seven years and I'm done with it."

"I wasn't going to give you shit," he said lightly. He reached into his pocket and tossed her a set of keys. "I think it's a good idea for you two to clear the air. It's the only way you'll be able to focus on what needs to be done."

What needed to be done? She still had no clue what that was. Sean had agreed to take down Rabbit to appease Flannery, but how long would he play nice with Flannery? And what happened when the gloves came off?

She stifled a sigh, deciding to save those questions for Sean. Then, feeling guilty for being so grumpy, she leaned in and kissed Oliver's cheek. "I really am glad you're okay."

"Thanks, sweets." He let out a breath. "And do me a favor? Go easy on him when you get there. He's not the most pleasant guy when he's bolloxed."

Wonderful. Sober Sean was asshole enough. Now she had to contend with Drunk Sean?

She really should have stayed in England.

The loft was dark when she entered it nearly thirty minutes later. She didn't see him at first. Not until her eyes adjusted to the darkness and she made out his long, muscular frame in the shadows.

He was sprawled on the couch, one thick arm propped behind his head, the other holding the whiskey bottle from last night—except now its contents had been reduced to nearly nothing, only a few mouthfuls remaining.

He was bare chested, wearing sweatpants that rode dangerously low on his trim hips, and his deep brogue broke the silence as she approached. "I was wondering when you'd show up."

Bailey slipped her gun from her waistband and placed it on the table. "Oliver said you'd be drunk."

"I would be," Sean agreed, "if there were any more liquor in this place. But I was too lazy to go and buy another bottle."

She walked over to the upright lamp near the couch and flicked it on. Light illuminated the cavernous space, revealing the slight flush on Sean's cheeks. He had surprisingly high cheekbones for a man. It was . . . sexy. Too damn sexy.

"You look drunk to me," she remarked, doing her best not to let her gaze linger.

He snorted. "You think half a bottle of Jameson would get me plastered? I'm Irish, luv. Takes a lot more than that."

She hesitated before settling in the armchair. It was still too close for comfort. Close enough that she could smell Sean's spicy aftershave every time she inhaled. Close enough that she could make out every hard ripple of his chest, every faded scar.

She wasn't looking forward to dredging up the past, but she knew it needed to be done.

"Sean—" she started.

"He was always their favorite, you know."

The abrupt interruption brought a frown. "What?"

"Ollie. He was my ma and da's favorite." Sean leaned over to drop the bottle on the table before rolling onto his back again. "This one time—we were five, maybe six years old. We'd just started learning basic math stuff in school, you know, like you've got four bananas and you take away two bananas so how many bananas are left. The first quiz we did, Ollie got every question right. I got about half right. No, maybe more. Two-thirds, I'd wager."

He rubbed his eyes and sat up, drawing her attention to his chest. God, his muscles were so defined it was like they'd been carved from stone.

"Anyway, we went home and showed our quizzes to Ma, and she gave us big bear hugs and told us we'd both done exactly what she'd expected us to do." He chuckled harshly. "She expected Ollie to get a hundred, and she expected me not to. Guess she knew who the smart banana in the family was."

Bailey's frown deepened. "That's not a very nice thing to say to your kids."

"Oh, don't worry. She loved us both. I know she loved me. But she was prouder of Ollie. He was always better at everything." Sean shrugged. "Guess what I'm saying is, it made sense to me that he was the one you wanted. And that even when you're not with him, I'm still not someone you want."

Damn it. Her heart wasn't allowed to clench like that. He wasn't allowed to say things like that.

"But I wanted you from the moment I saw you." Sean's gaze found hers, green eyes hazy with alcohol and regret.

"Trust me—you made that more than clear."

"I wanted you for more than a fuck, Bailey."

She swallowed. "I know."

Bitterness colored his tone. "But you didn't. You didn't want a fuck, and you didn't want more."

Her throat closed up on her, making it difficult to get any words out. "I'm not who you think I am," she mumbled, averting her eyes. "You have this image of who I am, but you really have no idea."

"You haven't offered to fill in the blanks." There was an edge to his tone.

Because it wouldn't make a difference, damn it. He knew what she did for a living and yet he still treated her like she needed rescuing. She would never be an equal to this man. Or worse, he might end up resenting her independence, her strength, and she knew exactly what men were capable of when they felt like the women in their lives had more power than they did.

"Knowing won't change anything," she said aloud. "We're not the same, Sean. We think differently. We have different ways of getting things done. All we do is fight."

"You're the only one fighting, luv."

The pitch of his voice lowered, became seductive, and Bailey suddenly felt very, very tired. "I can't give you what you want, okay? I don't want a relationship."

"You don't want a relationship with me," he corrected.

She didn't answer.

"You admitted yesterday that you're attracted to me. Were you lying?"

She found the courage to meet his eyes again. "No. But lust is one thing. A relationship is a whole other matter."

"Give me the lust, then."

She blinked. "What?"

"You heard me. If you don't want to get involved with me, then fine." His eyes gleamed. "Just fuck me again."

Her lower body clenched. Hard. And her nipples tightened painfully. She shouldn't be aroused, this tempted to surrender to him, but she was.

"You're drunk," she murmured.

"I already told you—I'm not drunk. Buzzed, maybe. But I know exactly what I'm saying and exactly what I want."

"And I already told you—I can't give you what you want."

He waved a dismissive hand. "Forget that. A relationship is off the table—I heard you loud and clear, luv. But sex isn't. Sex is very much on the table."

"According to you."

He lazily slid off the couch like a golden cat, muscles flexing as he bridged the distance between them. He loomed in front of her, six-plus feet of pure temptation. Those sweatpants were practically falling off him. She stared at one sleek hipbone and she wanted to put her mouth on it. Drag her tongue over his hot flesh and taste his masculine flavor.

"You want it," he said huskily. "I can see it in your eyes."

"So, what, you want to have a fling in the middle of an op? Is that it?"

He gave a careless shrug. "I won't be glued to Rabbit's side. We've got plenty of time for other . . . activities. And it doesn't have to be a fling. One night is fine too."

Bailey bit the inside of her cheek. "Why? What's the point?"

The fierce look in his eyes robbed her of breath. "Because I *want* it. I want to be inside you again, and this time, I want you to know exactly who's fucking you."

Bailey almost revealed the truth biting at her tongue, that she'd known all along that she wasn't in bed with Oliver, but her vocal cords were paralyzed. The look in Sean's eyes was too intense. Smoky lust and flinty determination. Hot need, so potent it seared right through her clothes and heated her skin.

He slid to his knees in front of her, inching closer to

rest both hands on her thighs. The warmth of his touch seeped into her body and made her feverish, achy. Arousal gathered between her legs, tightening when his blunt fingertips traveled to her waistband and dipped beneath it, lightly stroking her hips.

"I like these pants, luv. But they're getting in our way, don't you think?"

This had bad idea written all over it. In permanent marker. Bailey was well aware of that, but she couldn't stop staring at his hands, just inches from her aching core, and his mouth, curved seductively as he waited for her answer. She knew exactly what that wicked mouth was capable of. The pleasure it had to offer.

"Well?" he prompted, toying with the elastic of her leggings. "What should we do with these pants, Bailey?"

One teasing stroke of his fingers over her belly, and a breath shuddered out of her lungs.

"Take them off," she choked out.

# Chapter 14

Her skin was like silk. Smooth and supple and porcelain pale, a sharp contrast to her jet-black hair. Her eyes were a mixture of the two hues, black and white combining to form perfect slate gray. Like an overcast sky, not dull and flat, but like that moment before a storm rolled in and lightning prepared to strike. Power held in check. Passion on the edge.

But not for long. Because he was about to unleash that passion.

Sean peeled her leggings off, groaning when he discovered she wasn't wearing any panties. No bra either, judging by the puckered nipples poking against the front of her black T-shirt.

He'd expected a rejection, but he hadn't gotten one. He got a blatant invitation instead as Bailey parted her legs and exposed herself.

His mouth ran dry, his hands shaking like a train hurtling along an old wooden track. He hadn't slept with anyone since Bailey. He'd spent the whole year resorting to self-gratification, every jack-off session involving his very vivid memories of this woman. Now the real thing was in front of him, and he was dangerously close to losing control.

"So beautiful," he rasped.

He stroked her inner thighs before spreading her legs wider so his gaze could soak in the sight of her delicate pink pussy. Then he lifted his head and their eyes locked, and her dilated pupils inflated his ego. She wanted him—*him*—and her hazy expression proved it.

And Lord, there was even more proof between her legs. Wetness coated his fingers when he brought them to her opening, toying with her slick flesh.

Without breaking eye contact, he dragged his hand upward and rubbed his wet fingertips over her clit. It swelled beneath his touch, pulsing in time to her heartbeat. Her very erratic heartbeat, which was thudding nearly as fast as his.

He stroked little circles over that swollen bud, and her answering moan was like music to his ears.

"I've wanted to touch you like this for so long," he said roughly. One finger traveled south again, inching into her hot channel but not filling her completely. "I've been thinking about this pussy for a year, luv. A bloody year."

She still didn't speak. Her lower body moved, hips rising to try to increase the contact between them.

He gave her what she wanted, pushing his finger deeper. When her inner muscles clamped down, his dick jerked in his sweats, throbbing with anticipation and desperate for relief.

But not yet. He wasn't taking his pleasure until he had Bailey's complete and total surrender. Her big gray eyes remained focused on his face, but he had to be sure that she knew what she was doing. That she knew precisely whom she was doing it with.

"Say my name," he commanded.

Her eyes flickered. Displeasure. Resentment. Resistance.

When she didn't comply, another finger joined the first, and he drove them in and out at a rapid pace.

A throaty cry left her mouth, but when she started rocking into his hand, he withdrew, and the moan dissolved into a whimper of disappointment.

"You're not getting any more. Nothing, Bailey. Not until you say my name."

Her throat dipped as she swallowed, her shoulders sagging in defeat. "Sean," she whispered.

"Louder. Again."

"Sean."

He gave her his fingers again, and she was so wet it was easy to move them inside her, to curve them so that he stroked the top of her channel with each smooth glide. His thumb tended to her clit, offering the pressure she wanted, the tight friction he knew she needed.

"You're going to say my name again," Sean muttered. "All fucking night, Bailey. You're going to say it again and again, and you're going to scream it when you come."

Her breathing grew labored, eyes wide as he fingered her furiously. Their previous encounter had taught him what she liked—and it sure as hell wasn't slow and sweet. She liked it rough. Liked it hard. He added a third finger and increased the pace, and her head lolled to the side.

"Oh *God*."

He stopped. Frowned.

"Sean . . ." she corrected herself desperately, and that final sign of surrender fueled the lust burning in his groin.

"Again," he ordered.

"Sean . . . ohhhh . . . Sean . . ."

His name intermixed with her moans of pleasure. His fingers were soaked as he fucked her with them. He felt her muscles tighten, her pussy tremble, and he knew she was close.

He also knew exactly what it would take to get her there.

He dipped his head and tongued her clit as he fingered her, and she convulsed so hard the armchair shook.

*"Sean."*

There it was. His name on her lips as she climaxed, her orgasm on *his* lips as he got her there.

He sucked her clit as the orgasm shuddered through her body, and when she grabbed the back of his head and rocked into his face, he grinned against her hot, quivering flesh. Oh yeah. She could deny it all she wanted, but he knew that no man had ever made her come this hard.

She finally grew still, her hands relaxing their death grip on his head, and Sean eased back on his knees and licked his glistening lips. No flavor in the world compared to the taste of Bailey. She was sweet and tangy and addictive. He'd gotten his first fix a year ago and had waited so long for another hit. Now that he had it again, he wasn't going to give it up anytime soon.

"That was just to take the edge off," he said in a low voice. "I'm going to make you come again tonight, luv. And you're going to say my name every time. Understood?"

She nodded, looking stunned. Confused. As if she hadn't expected to come apart like that.

He yanked her to her feet and tore her shirt off, then crashed his mouth down on hers in a punishing kiss. She kissed him back eagerly. No, hungrily. Frantic hands shoved his sweats down his hips, and then her fingers dug into his ass and he groaned into her lips.

His cock was trapped between their bodies, leaving a streak of moisture on her flat belly. He rotated his hips and ground against it, growling when her tongue slicked over his. "Mine," he muttered. "You're mine, Bailey."

She broke the kiss, anger blazing in her eyes. "I don't belong to anyone."

"You do tonight." When she tried to back away from him, he touched her face, gently curling his hand under her chin. "It goes both ways, luv. Because tonight I belong to *you*."

Surprise flitted through her expression, deepening when he took her hand and placed it directly over his heart so she could feel its irregular pounding. "Feel that, Bailey?"

She nodded wordlessly.

"That's how badly I want you." He swallowed, oddly nervous now. "That's how terrified I am that you might change your mind and walk out the door."

Her breath hitched, gaze flying to his.

"I know I come on too strong sometimes, but I just want you to know that I . . ."

He trailed off, trying to find the right words, but Bailey didn't give him the chance. Suddenly she was kissing him again, her earlier hesitation gone and her urgency returning as she slid her tongue into his mouth and looped her arms around his neck.

"Stop. Talking."

Her whisper was muffled against his lips, and his answering chuckle was muffled by hers.

"What would you have me do instead?"

"For starters? Put your mouth to better use." She grasped the back of his head and brought it down to her breasts.

Sean groaned as he took one nipple in his mouth, sucking hard enough to make her cry out. He drew back, gauging her expression. "Too rough?" He raised a brow. "Or not rough enough?"

She responded by raking her nails over his scalp and pushing her breasts closer to his lips. Laughing, he captured her other nipple and lightly sank his teeth on the distended bud, and her moan of pleasure sent electricity racing up his spine.

"Trust me, baby. I remember what you like," he whispered, his tongue licking a path around her areola. "I memorized every second of our first night together."

Then he scooped her into his arms and carried her to the futon, proving to her that he did indeed remember. He tormented her with his tongue. His lips. His teeth—oh yeah, she liked the teeth. And she liked using hers on *him*.

His head reared back in pleasure-laced pain as she bit his shoulder, deep enough to draw blood.

"I have a good memory too," she said breathlessly. "I'm not the only one who likes it rough."

Sean's chest clenched because he knew she wasn't remembering *him*. Last time they were together, she'd thought he was Oliver.

"My name," he squeezed out, strangled, urgent. "Say it."

"Sean." Her tone changed, softened, as if she'd read his mind and saw the old doubts and insecurities creeping in.

But then she brought her hand between them and gripped his cock so tight he saw stars.

"Sean," she repeated, smug and throaty.

His lips found hers in a greedy kiss, tongue stroking her mouth in time to the hand stroking his dick. His body was on fire. Heart thudding with excitement, blood burning with need. But the fast pumps of her hand weren't enough. It wouldn't be enough until he was inside her. Where he belonged.

He abruptly rose onto his knees, fisting his cock as he brought it toward her mouth. "Suck me," he rasped. "Get my dick nice and wet so I can put it inside you." Then he faltered. They hadn't used condoms last year, but he realized he couldn't just assume she'd want to do that again. "Unless you want me to grab a rubber?"

Bailey flicked her tongue over the tip of his cock, and it

took all his willpower not to thrust into her mouth. Shaking her head, she licked her lips as she peered up at him. "I'm on birth control. And clean, just like I was last year."

"Me too," he said gruffly. "I, ah, haven't slept with anyone since you."

Her eyes widened. "Seriously?"

"Don't look so shocked." He couldn't stop the edge to his voice. "Not everyone is as slutty as your good chum Macgregor."

She laughed. "Jealousy isn't an attractive quality in a lover, you know."

"Tough luck. Because I *am* jealous. I'm jealous as hell." As the truth poured out before he could stop it, he suddenly wondered whether she'd like him better if he censored himself, if he curbed that blunt honesty that spilled out whenever she was around. But then her mouth closed around his cock and his brain shut down like a broken furnace.

"You have no reason to be jealous of Liam." Her soft breath tickled his shaft. "I've never sucked him off, if that's what you're worried about. Never slept with him either."

He'd known that, but hearing it loosened the tight knot in his chest.

Then she licked him again, and his muscles seized right back up. Her tongue was incredible. Dancing over his throbbing flesh as she worked him. Excruciatingly slow, as if she planned on torturing him all damn night. When those soft, teasing glides turned into the hot, wet suction of her mouth, his balls tightened, and he choked on a curse.

"No. I want to come inside you."

He pulled out, his cock weeping when the cold air met it, but he didn't suffer long. He covered her body with his and with one hard thrust, buried himself deep.

Bailey's nails scraped his back as he began to move. Thank God she didn't have those manicured talons other women liked to grow or she would have ripped his flesh apart. Not that he'd mind the pain. Her urgency matched his own. The furious rise of her hips met him thrust for thrust. Maybe next time he'd take it slow, but right now, it was a race to the finish. A violent storm of need and lust that raged between them, threatening to consume them both.

Sean's heart damn near burst when release blasted through him. The sizzling rush of pleasure had him sagging against her, but he kept pounding his hips forward, over and over until she cried out and joined him in that hot, mindless place that had turned his muscles to jelly.

They lay there for a moment, panting to catch their breath, their bodies glued together by sweat and sheer exhaustion. And then Bailey exhaled, and he felt her shut down beneath him.

She shifted and rolled away, and Sean experienced genuine loss the second he left the warmth of her body. He hadn't expected her to cuddle, but he hadn't thought she'd freeze him out either.

Her expression grew somber as she met his eyes and said, "You're wrong."

God, she could barely breathe. She was reeling from her second orgasm of the night. Stunned by the knowledge that Sean Reilly still had this power over her.

"Yeah?" he said warily. "Well, I'm wrong about a lot of things, so you'll have to be more specific."

She swallowed. "When you said we belong to each other. You're wrong."

A mocking glint lit his eyes. "Am I? Because it didn't feel wrong when my cock was buried inside you."

No, it hadn't, but that word—*belong*—it brought back memories that cracked her chest wide open. Sean wasn't the first man to say that to her. He wasn't the first man who had thought he could do whatever the hell he wanted to her because she was *his*.

Trapped. That was how she'd felt at home. And with Daniels. And now with Sean.

Her desire for him held her captive, tied her to him. She'd never experienced anything like it, and she hated the powerless sensations that arose when she was with Sean.

"I won't pretend that you don't make me feel good," she said tightly. "And you know how to make me come, I'll give you that. But that doesn't mean you own me, or my body. I'm *choosing* to have sex with you."

"Gee, I'm so bloody flattered that you'd bestow such a wonderful gift on me." He narrowed his eyes. "But what if I want more than your body?"

"You won't get it." She stared at him in accusation. "You said you understood that."

"Oh, I understand, all right." He sat up, resting his blond head against the wall as he stared back. "But when we're around Rabbit, you *do* belong to me."

"I already said I'd pretend to be your girlfriend," she muttered.

"Well, you're going to need to do more than hold my hand and stick your tongue in my mouth. I don't want you on that man's radar, which means that when Rabbit is watching, you need to be meek and silent and obey every word I say."

His sharp tone raised her hackles. She understood why they had to put up that pretense in front of Rabbit, but she still resented being ordered rather than *asked*.

"Yes, sir."

She started to get up, but he pinned her with his naked body, propping his elbows on either side of her head as a smoky look darkened his eyes. "What's your hurry?"

"We need to get back to the other flat."

"No. I haven't had my fill yet."

She became aware of the thick erection trapped between them. Long and hard, pulsing against her belly. She tried to fight the rising arousal, ignoring her swelling clit and tingling breasts, but she might as well have been asking the sun not to rise.

"You got what you wanted," she protested. "I slept with you again. And trust me, I knew who I was with the entire time. We're done here."

"Are we?"

His hand found her breast, and when her nipple hardened against his palm, she cursed her body for betraying her. She was already wet again, anticipation surging through her veins and pulsing in her core.

Sean smiled. Slow and wicked and full of sinful promise. "I don't think we're done at all, luv."

Pleasure shot through her when he pinched her nipple, lightly twisting it between his thumb and index finger.

"Yes," she gasped.

He chuckled. "Yes, we're done, or yes, that feels good?"

Goose bumps broke out on her skin as his hand moved between her legs. An anguished moan slipped out when he stroked her most sensitive place.

"We're not done," she whispered.

"That's what I thought."

His mouth captured hers in a reckless kiss, and then it was gone, traveling down her body and leaving shivers in its wake. He circled her clit with his tongue, hot and insistent, teasing and probing until she was reduced to a moaning, panting mess.

He lifted his mouth slightly. "Remember the rules, Bailey. You say my name when you come."

He was primal and infuriating, and goddamn it, she was helpless to deny him. Orgasm hovered beneath the surface, and as hard as she tried to fight it, it still broke free, ripping through her body and shattering her mind. When she exploded, it *was* his name she called out.

And she hated herself for it.

His ragged breathing fanned over her sensitive flesh. She felt his excitement thickening the air and knew he would be inside her soon. She *wanted* him inside her.

In the back of her mind she wondered if she would ever *not* want this man, but then she lost the ability to think altogether because Sean climbed up her body and plunged deep, and a wave of pleasure swept her away to a plane of mindless bliss.

His thrusts were as urgent as before, hard enough to shake the futon frame, to make her gasp for air and cling to his shoulders. Sean was the only man she'd slept with who didn't hold back during sex. Who didn't treat her like she might break, or shy away from the rough play she enjoyed.

He came moments after her second climax, groaning her name as he shuddered. This time when he rolled over and pulled her to his chest, she didn't move away. She lay nestled at his side, struggling to steady her breathing, wondering why the sex between them was always so damn explosive.

It was several minutes before he released her so he could duck into the bathroom to grab a wet washcloth. Bailey didn't say a word as he cleaned her up. His touch was almost reverent as he swiped the warm towel over her core.

This was what confused her the most. The tenderness,

completely incongruous with his overbearing personality. It was so much easier to keep her defenses up when he was being a jackass—

They both froze when a creak echoed through the loft.

"Don't stop on my account."

Bailey's head shot toward the mocking voice of the man standing in the doorway.

It was Cillian Kelly.

# Chapter 15

Why the *fuck* hadn't his security alarm gone off?

Sean dove off the bed, his feet slapping the hardwood at the same time Cillian raised a gun in his direction. He didn't have time to reach for the gun on the bedside table. And he couldn't even throw a blanket over Bailey's naked body because she was lying on the damn thing. Fully exposed to Cillian's glacier blue gaze, which wasted no time sweeping over her pale curves.

Cillian glanced back at Sean. "You won't be needing your weapon." He smirked at Sean's groin, the jutting hard-on that had gone from a lust-induced erection to a danger-fueled boner. "Or your gun," he added, looking amused by his own joke.

As Bailey reached for the edge of the bedspread, Cillian cocked his pistol at her. "No. Don't cover up. I like your tits."

Fury pounded into Sean like steel fists. He was going to rip out that son of a bitch's throat for saying that. For *looking* at her like that.

"I suggest you take your eyes off my girl's breasts," he said coldly. "Unless you'd like me to cut them out of your face."

Cillian chuckled. "You were always a possessive bastard, Reilly."

"And you were always a sick fuck. I remember you liked to watch—that was your kink, right?"

The other man just smiled. "All right, you win. You can both put some clothes on. We need to have a little chat."

Wholly aware of the weapon pointed at them, Sean tossed one of his discarded T-shirts at Bailey. He shielded her from view as she slipped it on, and when she stood up and he saw the shirt hanging to her knees, he was suddenly reminded of how small she was.

Cillian was still watching her. No, leering at her, in a slimy, predatory way that pounded the last nail in his coffin—Sean was going to kill him. Maybe not tonight. Maybe not tomorrow. But he *would* die.

Sean wasn't going to lose a wink of sleep over it, either. He'd never liked Kelly. The man had joined Rabbit's crew a few years before Sean had left it, and it hadn't taken long at all to see that he was a violent, sadistic asshole.

"What are you doing here?" Keeping a close eye on Kelly's gun barrel, Sean tugged on his sweatpants, then strode to the security monitors. He cursed when he spotted the black screens. "What'd you do to my system?"

"Disarmed it, obviously." Cillian rolled his eyes. "That's what happens when you rely on wireless technology to keep you safe." He waved toward the couch. "Sit down. Both of you."

Lovely. His living room was about to host yet another unwelcome tête-à-tête.

Had Rabbit sent Kelly? He must've. Which meant that Rabbit hadn't bought Sean's sudden decision to rejoin the group the way he'd led Sean to believe.

Shit.

The three of them sat down, Cillian occupying the same armchair Flannery had used last night. He rested his gun on his thigh as he confirmed Sean's discouraging thoughts.

"I know what you're up to, Reilly."

"Yeah?" Sean shrugged. "And what am I up to, Kelly?"

"Returning to the fold, begging Rabbit for his protection so you can keep your little bird safe." Cillian arched a brow at Bailey. "But you don't need a man to keep you safe, do you, sweetness? From what I hear, you can handle yourself just fine."

"Oh really?" she said evenly. "Who told you that?"

"My employer."

Sean sucked in a breath as something niggled at his brain. He studied the other man intently. Then cursed out loud.

"Bloody hell. You're Flannery's mole."

"Mole?" Cillian frowned. "That's a very unflattering word. I prefer . . . *trusted observer*."

The revelation made Sean's head spin. Fifteen years. Cillian Kelly had served Rabbit for *fifteen* years. He was a vital cog in Rabbit's organization, and the first lieutenant Rabbit had truly trusted since Sean's father had died.

"You've been working for Rabbit's enemy this whole time?" Sean couldn't contain his disbelief.

"Of course not," Cillian answered. "Jeez, Reilly, do you really think it would take me that long to do my job?" He set his gun on the table, as if he no longer needed to keep up a menacing front now that he'd revealed himself. "Not that Ronan didn't try to recruit me sooner. He tried. Approached me about ten years back, but I turned him down."

"What finally changed your mind?" Sean demanded. He found himself oddly angry on Rabbit's behalf, which was all sorts of fucked-up because he didn't give a shit about Rabbit.

"What do you think? Money." Cillian snorted in derision. "The Dagger has been spinning its wheels for years now. Rabbit has no interest in expanding our interests. He's perfectly content with the status quo. His low-rent operation and feckin' rackets that earn us peanuts. The man has no concept of ambition."

"Rabbit was never ambitious," Sean pointed out. "His goal has always been to unite the country. He earns enough to fund the organization, but we both know he doesn't care about money."

"You're right. I did know that." Cillian shrugged. "But I decided I didn't want to live in the gutter anymore. Once I take over, we'll start making changes. Forget the feckin' politics. The end goal is gonna see us become very rich men, Reilly. Rabbit can't make that happen, but I can." He cast a meaningful look. "*We* can."

"I don't need any more money," Sean said coldly. "And for the sake of full disclosure, you should know I'm not planning on being Flannery's errand boy for long. I agreed to help him take down Rabbit, but after that, I'm done. I won't be sticking around."

"Pity. I could use someone like you by my side."

His jaw tightened. "Someone like me?"

"You know, smart. Calculated. Ruthless enough to get shite done without worrying about right or wrong."

"You don't know a damn thing about me, Kelly."

"I know that six men robbed a bank and only one of them walked out. And I know it wasn't Gallagher's idea, as you led Rabbit to believe." Cillian chuckled. "Only thing you've ever cared about was yourself. Saving your skin, and your brother's. And now your girl, apparently. I see you're widening your little circle of people you give a shite about."

"Is there anything else you want to discuss tonight?" Sean said abruptly.

Cillian looked from Sean to Bailey, then gave another chuckle. "Nah, I've done what I came here to do. Just wanted you to know whose team you're playing for."

Yeah, fucking right. The only team Sean had ever played for was his own, and Oliver's, and fine, Bailey's too. If Cillian thought they were now best buds because Flannery pulled both their strings, he was going to be sorely disappointed.

Cillian stood up and shoved his weapon at the small of his back, then smoothed out the tails of his button-down shirt. "I suggest you get your alarm system back online." He winked. "You never know who might break in. And I'll see you at the pub tomorrow—we've got a lot of work to do."

When Sean didn't answer, Cillian focused those ice blue eyes on Bailey. "I look forward to seeing more of you, luv."

Sean stiffened. Luv? Like hell she was. Only *he* was allowed to call her that.

He quickly added *cut out tongue* to the growing list of mutilations he'd be giving Cillian.

"Enjoy the rest of your night, Reilly. Fuck her nice and hard for me."

Miraculously, Bailey managed to keep from exploding until *after* Cillian had gone, but when she did, the volume of her voice nearly shattered Sean's eardrums.

"*Fuck her nice and hard for me?* Are you kidding me! Are you fucking *kidding* me, Sean! That man is *disgusting*!" She groaned loudly. "Goddamn it, why did I come to Dublin?"

He glowered at her. "I've been wondering the same thing for days."

But he knew the answer to that—she'd come to save

his ass. And as a result, she'd become a player in a game none of them wanted to play.

He felt like begging her to leave again, but he was scared that if he opened his mouth, he might end up begging her to *stay*. No matter how badly he wanted to protect her, he didn't want her to leave him again.

What he wanted was to implore her to give him a chance. A real chance to prove that he could be more to her than a good lay.

But the plea got stuck in his throat. Reilly men didn't talk about their feelings, especially with women. His father had always warned him that loving someone too hard would only destroy you in the end—and God knew that love had definitely destroyed Colin Reilly. When Sean's ma had died, it had broken his father. It'd made him reckless, led him to accept the higher-risk jobs that he usually handed off to other soldiers. Colin had put his life at risk because he simply hadn't given a shit anymore, and Sean knew his father had died long before the car bomb killed him.

That was what women did to you. That was what Bailey did to *him*. She consumed his thoughts. Caused his composure to unravel like an old sweater. Triggered the obsessive urge to protect her. Hell, just the sight of her in that oversize T-shirt made him want to pull her into his arms and never let go. But he knew she'd probably draw back if he tried—

*Whenever I'd touch her, she'd draw back awkwardly.*

His brother's confession suddenly seared into his head, and now that the whiskey was no longer clouding his mind, he was finally able to comprehend its meaning.

*The first time I kissed her, she burst out laughing.*

*Whenever I'd touch her, she'd draw back awkwardly.*

Son of a bitch.

She'd known.

The night at the hotel . . . she'd *known* he wasn't Oliver. She *must* have. Unless she'd developed a sexual attraction to his brother overnight, but how likely was that? She'd been seeing Oliver for months, after all. She'd already kissed him, known what it felt like—and what it didn't feel like.

But she hadn't laughed when Sean had kissed her, and she certainly hadn't drawn back from his touch.

A slow grin stretched across his mouth.

"What are you smiling about?" Bailey said warily.

The smile widened, but he wasn't quite ready to confront her about his thoughts, so he shrugged and said, "Nothing important."

But Jesus, it *was*. It was more important than he knew what to do with at the moment. The realization had elicited a rush of . . . something he couldn't decipher. Something that floated through him like a feather and lightened his heart. It took him a moment to figure out what it was, and once he did, he grinned even harder.

It was hope.

The following afternoon, he and Bailey walked into O'Hare's Pub and found it bustling. The bar wasn't open to customers yet, but Rabbit's men were all there, crammed into booths or sitting at tables as they ate their lunch and drank their Guinness.

Every pair of eyes swiveled toward Sean when he strode inside. Voices lowered to gruff murmurs, which brought an inward groan, because clearly earning these men's trust would not be an easy feat. The guys who'd been around during his Dagger days remembered how he'd abandoned the cause, and the new soldiers were taking their lead from the older ones, pointedly avoiding Sean's gaze as he headed for the nearest table.

He greeted the men with a nod. "Rabbit around?"

"Stepped out," Callum Quinn muttered.

Shit. Well, at least Cillian wasn't there either. Sean didn't want anything to do with that perverted motherfucker.

Though he couldn't deny that Kelly had made their job a helluva lot easier by revealing himself to them. Sean had hoped Morgan's men would leave now that the mole hunt was over, but no such luck. When he'd suggested it to Sullivan over the phone that morning, the stubborn Australian had told him to fuck right off. Apparently D and Ash had teamed up with Oliver to gather intel, and Sully, Liam, and Isabel—who the *hell* had called Isabel?—were handling surveillance in case Sean and Bailey needed backup.

Sean signaled to Rory behind the counter, who scowled at him when he ordered a Guinness. He doubted he'd ever see a pint glass, but he still sat in the empty seat next to Quinn as if he belonged there.

The older man stiffened, then shoveled some shepherd's pie into his mouth without uttering a word.

Sean sighed and looked at Bailey. "Go sit at the bar, luv. I need a moment with the fellas."

She wandered away like an obedient girlfriend and slid onto a stool at the bar. She kept her back turned to them, but Sean knew she was listening to every word, aware of every person in the dim-lit room.

"I get it," Sean announced as the silence dragged on. "I'm back, and you don't like it."

"It's not our place to like it," Robbie Doyle said dourly. "Rabbit calls the shots."

The rest of the room remained silent, and Sean's frustration grew. "I know you lads are pissed at me for skipping town, all right? But I never got a chance to share why I left." It was true—he'd been completely shunned after he and Ollie had quit the crew. None of the men had spared them even a second to state their case.

He looked around the table, saving Quinn for last. Quinn's opinion carried the most weight with the other men, and if Sean was going to win them over, he needed to start with the ginger-haired behemoth at his side. "I'm just asking for a chance to explain now."

There was a long silence. Quinn picked up his beer and took a swig, then slammed the pint glass on the table.

"Let's hear it then, lad."

The story he'd concocted flowed out smoothly, just as he'd rehearsed in his head. "I never saw this as my cause," Sean confessed. "My father . . . it was his thing, y'know? Me and Ollie, we worked for Rabbit because Da worked for Rabbit. We did what they asked without question, but . . ." He shrugged. "We started to question it. Started to wonder if maybe we were just sheep, following orders because it was expected of us and not because we truly believed in what we were doing."

No one spoke, but he was gratified to see a few grudging nods. These men understood. They'd all joined up for the same reason he had—because their dads had fought for the cause, because their granddads had fought for the cause, because their whole bloody family had fought for the cause.

"And, well, you know me," he said ruefully. "I've always been a stubborn son of a bitch. Once I decide something, nobody can talk me out of it. I convinced Ollie that we needed to go off on our own, and so we did."

"But now you're back," Quinn said gruffly. "Why's that, lad?"

"Because I realized where my roots are. Where I belong—*here*. There's a reason I still keep a flat in Dublin. It's my home."

Quinn's cheeks hollowed. "Ya? 'Cause I don't recall you coming *home* all too often these past eight years."

"I had a job to do, and that job meant traveling the world. It's how Ollie and I made money. It's how we got the reputation for being the guys who could get the intel nobody else could. But . . . turns out those are empty accomplishments, y'know? What else have I really achieved other than feeding intel to scumbags and spooks?"

He feigned unhappiness, reaching for an empty beer bottle and absently toying with the label, which had been loosened by condensation. It was so easy to play his part. To play any part, really. Bailey might be the chameleon of the two of them, but he was far from an amateur. An information dealer had to adapt, cozy up to folks to get them to talk, be whoever he needed to be in order to unearth people's secrets.

"I met my girl in America." He nodded toward Bailey. "I knew the moment I brought her here that I wanted us to stay in Dublin."

"This would be a real nice story, lad—if we didn't know that Rabbit had to twist your arm to come back. Only reason you're here is 'cause we nabbed Ollie."

"You're right." He met Quinn's sardonic gaze head-on. "I came for Ollie. I wasn't planning on rejoining the crew. And then I watched five men I grew up with get shot and killed in front of my eyes."

The mood at the table immediately went somber. It was Irish tradition that you couldn't mention the dead without toasting them, and so Sean wasn't surprised when Finn Doherty abruptly raised his glass.

"Gallagher and the boys," Doherty murmured.

"Gallagher and the boys," the others echoed.

As the men drank, Sean waited a moment before speaking again.

"Rabbit has lost sight of the cause."

Alarmed looks appeared all around him, along with a deeply suspicious glare from Quinn. "You're talking out of your ass, son."

"Am I? Because from what I see—no, from what I *know*, Gallagher and the others weren't in that bank to steal money for the Dagger. They robbed it because of Rabbit's personal vendetta against an old enemy."

Sean held his breath as he allowed the information to sink in. He wasn't sure if Rabbit had told the crew about the real reason for the heist, and he knew he was risking Rabbit's wrath if the men *didn't* know, but revealing it was necessary for Sean's plan.

To his relief, nobody looked surprised.

"Taking down Flannery is good for the cause," Quinn said tightly.

"How?" Sean challenged. "The man is untouchable. Believe me, I wouldn't shed a single fucking tear if he dropped dead—the bastard laid a hand on my woman, and one of these days I'm gonna make him pay for that. But Rabbit doesn't want his old friend dead. He wants to waste his time—*our* time—trying to topple Flannery's empire. But we should be focusing on the real goal—reclaiming our country." He looked around the table angrily. "My father died for the Dagger. He *believed* in it. Rabbit used to believe in it too, and that's why I'm back, to lead him down the right path again."

His speech resulted in silence.

And then Quinn sighed. "Colin was a good man."

"Yes, he was." Sean shook his head in disappointment. "So's Rabbit, when he's not playing out revenge fantasies that mean nothing to the rest of us. Gallagher and Paddy and the other boys already died for Rabbit's vendetta. Well, I'm not gonna let anyone else die in vain. If that means coming back to guide the old man, then I damn well intend to do that."

"You've got some mighty big balls saying all this shite, lad."

Quinn's chuckle set off a round of laughter from the others, whose stony expressions had been chipped away by Sean's passionate appeal.

He glanced at each man again, arching his eyebrows in defiance. "I don't need any of you to trust me. I'm not asking you to. But you're all gonna have to suck it up and deal with me being around, because I refuse to stand by and watch Rabbit destroy my father's legacy."

There were some murmurs of approval from the neighboring table, which was occupied by some of the younger men who'd been listening in.

It was hard to contain his satisfaction. They'd bought it.

And not only that, but his little diatribe had set Flannery's plan in motion as well. Sean had just shown them that Rabbit wasn't the loyal leader he claimed to be. That he'd gotten his own men killed for the wrong reasons.

He hadn't planted enough seeds of doubt to cause the crew to abandon Rabbit, but it sure as hell was a start.

"Well, then I guess we'll deal with ya," Quinn grumbled. "Seeing as we have no choice." But the redheaded man was smiling, and then he clapped a meaty hand on Sean's shoulder. "It's good to have you back, Seansy. Gotta admit, things were getting a wee bit boring around here."

Sean grinned. "Happy to liven them up, Callie."

"You gonna introduce us to your lass?"

Shit. This was the part he wished he could avoid. But he'd made his damn bed, and now he had to lie in it.

"Bailey, luv, c'mere and meet the boys."

She approached the table tentatively. Her fitted jeans and thin sweater showed off her slender curves, and her dark hair was loose and slightly damp from the mist they'd encountered outside earlier. But it was her eyes that drew everyone's stares. Those huge gray eyes that dominated her face and lent her a fragile air that softened every hard expression at the table. Sean had seen it happen dozens of times before. Bailey was damn good at using that misleading fragility to disarm the people around her and make them believe she wasn't a threat.

He patted his lap, and she sank onto it without hesitation.

"It's nice to meet you all," Bailey murmured after Sean made the introductions. And then she smiled, and if there'd been a puddle nearby, every man in a five-foot radius would've ripped the shirt off his back and laid it on the ground to save her delicate feet from getting wet.

"Lord, you have the smile of an angel," Quinn breathed, and Sean was amused to find the older man honest-to-God blushing.

"An angel," Patrick O'Neill chimed in from the other end of the table. "Which raises the question—what are you doing with Seansy?"

The other men guffawed.

"Are you saying Sean's the devil?" Bailey said with a twinkling laugh.

"Oh, he's devilish, all right. The lad raised hell the second he was able to walk." Quinn grinned, then glanced at Sean. "She's not your usual type."

Bailey looked curious. "What's his type, then?"

"Fast and loose," Doherty piped up, and the men chortled again.

"What was the name of that red-haired bird you were seeing back in the day?" O'Neill asked. "Pearl? Penny?"

Sean stifled a sigh. "Peggy."

A cacophony of hoots erupted all around him.

"Ah, Peggy," Quinn drawled. "Lovely girl. Great arse on that one." He waggled his eyebrows at Bailey. "She drove our boy Sean crazy."

Bailey smiled. "Yeah?"

"Oh ya. Flirted with anyone with a co—" Quinn stopped as if remembering he was in the presence of a lady. "The lads, ah, she flirted with all the lads. Only did it because she knew it peeved Seansy right off."

"And he'd beat the piss out of anyone who flirted back," O'Neill said with a snort.

Sean felt Bailey stiffen in his lap, but he didn't defend himself against the claim. He knew she thought he was reckless and violent, but hell, what else was a man supposed to do when someone was hitting on his girl? Shake their hand? Colin Reilly had taught his boys to solve their problems with their fists, and that was one Irish tradition Sean didn't mind upholding every now and then.

"How long were you and Peggy together?" Bailey asked, her body relaxing as laughter continued to echo around them.

Sean shrugged. "Three years, on and off."

"Really? I can't imagine you in a long-term relationship."

"There's a lot you don't know about me, luv." He couldn't resist leaning in to nuzzle her neck. She didn't stiffen this time, but he heard her breath hitch. "I'm looking forward to showing you all of it."

More hoots broke out, turning to catcalls when Sean gave in to temptation and kissed her. As his lips brushed Bailey's, Quinn poked him in the ribs.

"Get a room, lad. You're making the rest of us jealous."

Sean reluctantly withdrew his mouth, but he kept one arm solidly around her waist, stroking her arm as Quinn focused his attention on Bailey.

"So you're American, eh? Where from?"

"Virginia. But I haven't lived there in years. My family traveled a lot when I was growing up."

The revelation put Sean on alert. It was impossible to

know if she was feeding them a story or telling the truth. For all he knew she'd created an entire fictional life to prepare for the role of Sean Reilly's Submissive Girlfriend, but he'd detected a chord of truth just now.

"Is your family still around?" Quinn asked.

She shook her head. Then corrected herself by nodding. "Well, my mom is. But she's in a nursing home."

Her voice quavered, and Sean knew she was thinking about the man Flannery had sent to her mother's facility. He'd heard her on the phone earlier making arrangements to transfer her mother, but when he'd asked for an update, she'd simply said that it was taking time.

Next to him, Quinn frowned. "How old is your ma? You don't look nearly old enough to have a mother in a nursing home."

"Ah, no. She's not there because she's old." Bailey visibly swallowed. "She's got early-onset Alzheimer's."

The mood at the table sobered. "I'm sorry to hear that," Quinn said gruffly.

"Thank you. It's been . . . tough."

She was definitely telling the truth. Sean could see it in her eyes, and he snatched up the meager details she'd offered like a prospector who'd discovered nuggets of gold in a creek bed. It was bloody impossible to pry any details from this woman—in fact, he was kind of insulted that she'd willingly handed them out like business cards to a group of strangers, when he had to work so hard to gain even a glimpse of insight.

The conversation was interrupted when the front door swung open, and every head turned as Rabbit and Cillian entered the pub.

Rabbit greeted his crew with a nod before shifting his brown eyes to Sean. "Seansy," he barked. "Need to have a word with you."

"All right." He gently moved Bailey off his lap, hesitating as he met her wary gray eyes. "Stay out here, luv. The lads will keep you company."

He was damn reluctant to leave her, but Quinn shot him a reassuring smile. "I'll take care of the lass." The older man pulled Bailey down beside him and threw an arm around her shoulders. "I'll even make sure O'Neill doesn't steal her away while you're gone."

The butt of Quinn's joke was quick to protest. "Hey! I *never* poach other men's girls."

Quinn snorted. "Ya? 'Cause I know three lads who might disagree with that."

Sean left the men to their raucous laughter and followed Rabbit and Cillian toward the rear corridor. With Rabbit walking ahead of them, Cillian took the opportunity to give Sean a hard look, and Sean could practically hear the man's silent order to back him up.

But . . . back him up on what?

What the hell were those two up to?

A minute later, the three of them settled around the table. It reminded Sean of all the times he'd seen his father sitting in this very chair. When he and Ollie were kids, they would hang out at the pool table while the men talked in hushed voices, discussing whatever dangerous plans needed to be discussed. Now he was the one at the table, which felt so bloody wrong and yet so bloody right at the same time. Figure that out.

Rabbit got down to business, his gaze flickering with displeasure. "Cillian here thinks I've gone soft."

Sean hid his surprise, not daring to glance at Flannery's "trusted observer." Instead he focused on Rabbit. "Is that so?"

"What do *you* think?" Rabbit's voice was deceptively calm. "Have I gone soft?"

He took a second to formulate his answer. "Well, I

don't know about soft, but I do think you might be losing sight of what's important."

"What the feck is that supposed to mean?"

"It means five of your men were shot down in a hail of bullets so you could have some leverage over Flannery." Sean folded his hands on the splintered tabletop. "The way I remember it, your people used to die for Ireland. Not for personal bullshit."

Rabbit's nostrils flared. "It's all connected, son. We get rid of Flannery, we rid ourselves of a threat to our country." The man waved a dismissive hand, his go-to response when someone disagreed with him. "But we're not here to discuss my brother-in-law."

Sean found it interesting that Rabbit still considered Flannery family, even though his sister's death had effectively severed the link between them. Then again, family ties meant something to the Irish. Even when you hated that family.

"We're here to discuss the cause. You know, the one you claim I'm neglecting," Rabbit said scornfully. "Cillian thinks we need to remind our fellow countrymen that the Irish Dagger still wields the same power it always has."

"And how does Cillian suggest we do that?" He continued to ignore the man next to him, feeling Kelly's frown boring into his face.

"How else?" Cillian spoke up. "Intimidation. We need to show them that the Dagger is still in control."

"And who exactly is *them*?" Sean asked dryly.

Rabbit's voice lowered, as if he was worried someone might overhear. Which was ridiculous because he swept the room for bugs every hour and kept a man posted outside the door. "We're going to hit a pub near the college."

Alarm shot through him. "The *college*? As in, civilian targets? Are you insane?" In the decades since the organization's formation, the Irish Dagger had never targeted innocents, and Sean was horrified to hear they were even entertaining the idea.

"The political science faculty practically lives at that pub," Rabbit said briskly. "The people who are supposed to be preaching nationalism—"

"What kind of intimidation tactic are you thinking of?" Sean cut in. "IED?"

Cillian nodded. "Car bomb, parked outside the pub."

"Why Dublin? Why not Belfast?"

"North, south, it doesn't matter anymore. The results will be the same."

Sean narrowed his eyes. "With a call ahead?"

Rabbit narrowed his eyes right back. "Do we do it any other way?"

Well, at least there was a bright side. For the most part, the IRA avoided Irish casualties at all costs. Their tactics had always been to phone ahead after a bomb was planted—that way, the target area could be evacuated while the terror was still inflicted, showing that the IRA could get to anyone, anywhere and anytime. Unfortunately, many of the splinter groups had chosen to break that golden rule over the years.

Luckily, it looked like the Dagger wasn't one of them.

"When?" Sean asked.

"Tomorrow afternoon." Rabbit pursed his lips. "What are your thoughts about this?"

"Does it matter? It sounds like you've already made up your mind."

"I'd still like to know your opinion."

His opinion? This was a bloody *terrible* idea. The last thing he wanted to do was instill fear in his own people. For Christ's sake, the IRA had been a dead cause for decades. He had no clue why people like Rabbit continued to cling to it.

But he'd been ordered to back Cillian up, and although the man wasn't looking at him, Sean could feel the waves of menace rolling off the other man's body. The implicit reminder that if he didn't play ball, Flannery would be very, very upset.

"It might help you placate some of the guys," Sean relented.

Rabbit spoke with a biting edge. "And why would they need placating?"

"I'm not the only one who's been wondering if you've lost sight of the cause. This'll show everyone you're still invested."

Rabbit mulled that over, then gave a decisive nod. "We go ahead, then." He scraped his chair back, glancing at Kelly. "You and Reilly will head this up. Bring Quinn into the loop."

"Where are you going?" Sean asked warily.

"I've got other engagements to tend to." Rabbit didn't elaborate. "I won't be back tonight. Make your plans, and then take the night to reconnect with the crew." A slight smirk lifted his lips. "I'm not the only one they're questioning, Seansy."

Shit.

He had no interest in spending his evening planning a bomb threat *or* hanging out with the crew, but clearly he didn't have a choice in the matter.

Once Rabbit left, Cillian turned to him with a broad smile. "Nice work. Getting the men to doubt Rabbit's loyalties? Very smart."

Kelly waited as if he was expecting a thank-you, but Sean didn't offer one. He stood abruptly, taking a step to the door. "I'll grab Quinn, and then I'm driving my girl home. I'll join you lads after."

"Any reason your girl can't handle a motor vehicle by herself?" Cillian scowled. "I don't have time to wait for you to play chauffeur. I need you here." A pause. "Our boss needs you here."

No mistaking which "boss" he referred to—and it sure as hell wasn't Rabbit.

"I'll walk her out to the car, then," Sean muttered. "I'll be right back."

He found Bailey at the table next to Quinn, laughing at something Robbie Doyle had just said. The men seemed thoroughly charmed by her, but Sean wasn't feeling too merry as he reached for her arm.

"Time for you to go," he told her.

She wrinkled her forehead. "Is everything okay?"

"I have to take care of business." He nodded at the redheaded man. "Quinn, Kelly's waiting for you in the back. We've got matters to discuss. I'll join you after I walk my girl out."

Quinn nodded back.

Sean tried to keep a casual demeanor as he ushered Bailey out of the pub, but the moment they stepped onto the sidewalk, the tension returned, seizing his muscles and triggering Bailey's frown.

"What's going on?" she demanded.

"Nothing." Sarcasm dripped from his next words. "I'm about to spend the night talking intimidation tactics and reconnecting with the boys."

"Alone?"

"Yes. Alone."

She shook her head. "I'm not leaving you."

"You don't have a choice." Anger bubbled in his stomach, hardening his tone. "Go back to the flat, Bailey."

She studied his face intently. "What kind of intimidation tactics?"

He let out a ragged breath. "Rabbit wants us to plant a car bomb near Trinity College."

"*What?* And you agreed to it?"

"What fucking choice did I have? Cillian was beside me the whole time and I have to back him up, remember?" He glimpsed the worry in her eyes and sighed. "The explosives won't go off, luv. The Dagger calls ahead."

"You mean tips off the Garda about the bomb?"

"It's the IRA way. The bomb squad shows up and disables the IED before it detonates, and the Dagger proves its point—that nobody is untouchable as long as we're around."

"That's utter bullshit," she grumbled.

"I'm not saying I support it. Just that you don't have to worry about innocent people dying, okay?" Impatience rippled through him as he took her arm and guided her to the car. "Go, Bailey. There's nothing for you to do here."

"Right. Because you've got everything covered, apparently."

"What the hell do you want from me? I can't bring my girlfriend to a fucking strategy meeting. That's not how the Dagger operates."

Her gray eyes blazed. "Out of curiosity, do you consider all women less than your equal, or is it just me?"

He felt a headache coming on. "This has nothing to do with bloody gender equality. You think I don't recognize that you'd be an asset in the planning of something like this? I *know* you would be. But it's not my call. If they wanted you to stay, I'd let you stay."

She hit him with a dose of sarcasm. "Oh, you'd *let* me? How nice. And I call bullshit on that, by the way. You've been trying to force me out of town since I got here."

"Because I wanted to keep you safe!" he shot back. "I wanted to keep you safe for *Ollie*, damn it. He already lost you once because of me, or at least that's what I thought—" He stopped abruptly, his temples throbbing even harder.

They couldn't have this damn argument right now. Someone in the pub might be watching them from the window. Hell, it was bad enough that Macgregor was lurking somewhere nearby, witnessing every second of this.

"Look, I don't have time to argue with you," he snapped. "Get the hell out of here, Bailey."

"Fine, you want me gone? I'm gone." She flung open the driver's door, angrier than he'd ever seen her. "I'll see you later at the flat. Or maybe I won't. I'm sure you'll do whatever suits your fancy with no regard for your *girlfriend*, right, Sean?"

He gritted his teeth. "I'll be back later tonight."

Then he turned on his heel and walked back into the pub.

# Chapter 16

"I absolutely hate him." Bailey irritably slid into the booth and snatched the drink menu. She needed a stiff drink, pronto. Otherwise she would lose her temper again, and she couldn't afford to do that in the middle of a crowded pub.

In the seat across from her, Isabel looked like she was fighting a smile. "No, you don't. You don't hate people, remember? You get along with everyone."

"Sean's the exception to the rule," she muttered. "He's a damn Neanderthal, Iz."

"Ha! And my husband isn't?" Isabel's bright green eyes sparkled as she ran a hand through her red hair, and if Bailey hadn't known the woman for years, she might actually believe she was having afternoon drinks with her new Irish gal pal, "Izzy O'Malley."

The waiter came by, raising a bushy eyebrow when both women ordered bourbon, as if he'd expected to scribble down *daiquiri* or *appletini* on his little notepad. Well, screw that. Bailey had never ordered a sissy drink in her life.

"Trust me," Isabel added after the waiter left. "Trevor gets crazy overprotective when I'm on a job."

"But you're married to him. He's allowed to be overprotective. Sean and I aren't even together."

"Uh-huh. So then you *haven't* slept with him again?"

"Nope."

"You used to be an accomplished liar. What happened to that?"

Bailey felt herself blushing. "Fine, I slept with him again. But that doesn't mean we're together, and it doesn't give him the right to control me."

*Was* he trying to control her, though? She didn't even know anymore. Didn't know if Sean was truly on some kind of power trip, or if she was simply scrambling to find excuses to keep him at arm's length.

*I wanted to keep you safe for Ollie, damn it. He already lost you once because of me.*

His aggravated words buzzed in her mind, but she had no idea what to make of them. Did he honestly expect her to believe that his overprotective bullshit stemmed from his desire to protect his *brother*? She knew the twins were close, but that sounded like an excuse to her. Sean's way of justifying his alpha assholeness.

"He does get a little . . . *intense* when you're around." Isabel sounded perplexed. "I mean, I've known Sean for years. He's a raging flirt. Total ladies' man, and that killer smile of his? Watch out. But he's different with you. He's . . ."

"A barbarian," she said darkly.

Isabel laughed. "Yeah, I guess that's a good way to describe it—you *do* bring out his savage side."

"Lucky me."

"But that just tells me he's fallen hard."

Bailey smothered her alarm. "He hasn't fallen for me. I'm just a conquest for him, and five years of rejection has made him determined to break me."

A groove dug into Isabel's forehead. "Sean doesn't break people."

"Yes, he does. You think you know him, Iz, but I know him better." The confession slipped out before she could stop it. "I tailed him for two months earlier this year."

Isabel's jaw dropped. "You did? *Why?*"

"I wanted to find out what he was up to," she said defensively. "He pretended to be Oliver to get me into bed, Iz, and then he started calling and texting all the time, asking me to meet up so we could 'talk.' I didn't trust him."

"Fair enough." Isabel looked amused now. "So what'd you find on your fact-finding mission?"

"Well, I saw how he gathers his intel, for one. He definitely uses that killer smile you mentioned and charms information out of his sources. But he also roughed a lot of them up." She frowned. "Ollie told me once that Reillys solve problems with their fists. I don't condone that."

Her colleague hooted. "Says the contract killer."

"Hey," she protested, "the people I take out are scum."

"And the people Sean hits up for intel are also scum. We live in a scummy world, Bailey."

Their drinks arrived at the same time Liam's voice filled Bailey's ear.

"You ladies have an admirer," he said softly.

At first she thought he was referring to their waiter, but the young man had already darted off. Bailey's hand moved to activate her earpiece, but Isabel beat her to the punch. She'd forgotten that her colleague could hear Liam too.

"Does he have any friends?" Isabel kept her gaze on Bailey as she addressed Liam.

"Flying solo," he reported. "But he's armed, judging by the very obvious bulge under his shirt."

Bailey was troubled by the update. She always sensed when someone was tailing her, which told her that the man on their tail had taken up his post only today. Made sense, though. This was the first time she and Sean had separated—Cillian must have told Flannery to put a guard on her.

"Recognize him?" she murmured to Liam.

"Nope, but I snapped a pic and e-mailed it to Paige. She'll find out who he is and get back to us."

"On a scale of one to ten, how bored are you right now?" Isabel teased him. "You must have drawn the short straw to get stuck with chick surveillance today."

"Yeah, I'm *stuck* watching two beautiful women, darling. God, the torture." His deep voice rippled with sensuality.

Bailey grinned at Isabel. "He's loving every second of it."

"Sully's the one who has to stare at Reilly's ugly mug all day," Liam drawled. "So I definitely got the better gig. Show me some skin, ladies."

Bailey didn't know where he was positioned, but it must have been close enough for him to see them through the plate-glass window. She was tempted to give him a little wave, but she resisted the urge.

"Keep us posted about our friend," Isabel said. "We're cutting off the feed so we can resume our girl talk."

"No, keep it on," he begged. "I *love* sexy girl talk."

"Nobody said it was sexy, you pervert." Isabel touched her ear, then flashed Bailey a grin. "So, how was the sex?"

She instantly donned a casual look. "It was okay."

"Just okay?"

One arch of Isabel's brow, and Bailey caved like a broken roof. "Fine, it was good."

Ha. More like incredible. Phenomenal. Mind-blowing.

But she refused to give Sean the satisfaction of voicing any of those annoyingly accurate adjectives.

"Why are you fighting him so hard?" Isabel asked gently.

Bailey gulped some bourbon.

"Seriously, hon—why?"

The alcohol loosened not only the knot in her insides, but her tongue as well. "Because he's everything that scares me in a man."

That got her a sad smile from Isabel, who knew enough details about Bailey's childhood to understand the meaning behind the confession. "We've all been hurt by our pasts, hon. It's hard to put old traumas behind you."

Hurt? The word didn't come close to describing what she'd gone through. But Isabel was wrong—Bailey *had* put the past behind her. She didn't wallow about it, or cry herself to sleep every night. Every grisly thing she'd experienced had shaped her into the person she was now. She'd *learned* from her past. It had showed her what she wanted out of life, who she wanted to be . . . and whom she didn't want to be with.

God, she wished she could make sense of her feelings for Sean. She couldn't deny that she was wildly attracted to him, but was it just a case of lust? Or was it something more?

No, it couldn't be anything more than that. He was bossy and annoying and too damn cocky for his own good. She couldn't possibly have actual feelings for the man.

*So why did you come all the way to Dublin to help him?*

Bailey swallowed another gulp of bourbon, unable to defend herself against the internal taunt. She couldn't even use Oliver as an excuse for racing to Dublin, because she hadn't learned he was in trouble until *after* she'd snuck into the bank.

Did a woman really go to this much trouble for a man she didn't care about?

Damn it. She was so fucking confused.

"He's too unpredictable, Iz," she said. "I can't open that door, okay? I just can't."

"I get it." Isabel hesitated. "But you're wrong about what you said before—he *does* love you."

Ignoring the tight clench of her heart, Bailey picked up her glass and downed the rest of her bourbon. "I don't care."

There was nothing more uncomfortable than watching another man ejaculate. Well, unless you were into blokes. Then you'd love it. But Sean couldn't say he was entirely comfortable seeing Patrick O'Neill orgasm ten feet from his face.

O'Neill groaned in ecstasy as the prostitute in his lap rode him like a bitch in heat. The bastard even had the nerve to wink when he caught Sean's eye.

Sean lowered his gaze to his pint glass, wishing like hell he could get out of there. O'Hare's was closed to the public for the private party. Or *morale booster*, as Cillian had referred to it. Only the younger men filled up the main room, though Quinn had apparently been in the mood for some fun, because he'd stuck around too and was in the process of getting blown in one of the back booths, fortunately hidden from view.

Sean was used to these kinds of raunchy scenes. The men on Rabbit's crew had simple tastes—they liked to fight and drink and fuck. *Especially* the latter. When Sean was a teenager, he'd been more than happy to join in on the fun. Ollie, too, though they'd drawn the line at tag teaming women, no matter how many times a pretty girl tried to lure them into it. Apparently boning twins was a fantasy for a lot of chicks. For him and Ollie . . . not so much.

"You know, you'd do a better job of convincing the men if you dipped your wick in a pussy or two."

Cillian's low voice made him tense. The man stood next to Sean's barstool, watching the sexual festivities in boredom.

"I have a girlfriend," he mumbled.

"I'm sure she won't mind."

Sean glanced at the naked women littering the room, picturing the look on Bailey's face if he admitted to "dipping his wick" in a prostie. "She'd rip my balls off," he said dryly.

Cillian chuckled. "I envy you. There's nothing hotter than a high-strung filly. Makes it all the more rewarding when you break her. When you show her who's boss."

Sean bristled. He had no desire to "break" Bailey. He *liked* her fire. He liked the way she challenged him, argued with him. Though sometimes he wished she didn't argue *so* much. He wished she would . . . Fuck, he didn't even know what he wanted anymore.

No, that wasn't true. He wanted *her*. Just her.

But she refused to give that to him.

"I've actually got a filly waiting for me in the back," Cillian told him. A dark eyebrow propped up. "If you want to join me."

"I'll pass."

"Suit yourself."

As Cillian wandered off, Sean slid off his stool. Definitely his cue to leave. There was no reason to stick around now that Flannery's trusted observer wasn't watching his ass like a federal prosecutor.

He made his way to the door, only to get intercepted by two crew members he didn't know well. They forced him into a conversation about football. The irony didn't escape him—here they were chatting about the Red Devils while everyone else was screwing their brains out. But these boys were in their late teens, and clearly overwhelmed by the hedonistic activities happening around them.

They also knew exactly who Sean was, and he was uncomfortable with the way they looked at him. Like he was their idol or some shit. He knew his reputation, both as a lethal fighter and as a ladies' man, was legendary around these parts, but he hated that these lads viewed him as some kind of superhero.

Still, he used the Manchester United discussion to sneak in a few barbed comments about Rabbit, which caused both lads to fidget awkwardly, as if they didn't know how to respond. Hell, they were so damn young. They had no idea what they were even fighting for.

"Sorry, lads," he said a short while later. "I have to go. My girl's waiting for me at home."

They grinned knowingly and drifted off, and Sean was two feet from the door when he realized he'd left his coat in the back when he'd been strategizing with the men earlier. Normally he'd say fuck it, but it was pouring buckets outside, and his already shitty mood would only get shittier if he went out there without a coat and got soaked to the bone.

Loud slapping noises met his ears when he approached the closed door at the end of the rear hallway. Lovely. Cillian and his *filly* had gotten started.

It took a second to register that he wasn't hearing sex. The sharp slaps were not the sounds of flesh meeting flesh, of bodies coming together in a frantic fuck. Cillian was spanking the hell out of that woman.

Sean rapped his knuckles on the door, then strode through it without waiting for a response. He walked in just in time to see the hard strike of Cillian's palm against a round backside.

Jesus. The woman's ass was a shocking red contrast to her lily-white skin. Sean could even see the imprint of Cillian's hand.

She was bent over the arm of the couch, but she whirled around in startled surprise at Sean's entrance, and he didn't miss the red marks on her breasts, as if Cillian had squeezed the hell out of them. He also didn't miss the tears streaking down her pale cheeks.

"Everything all right in here?" he said roughly.

Cillian smirked. He was fully clothed, but a visible erection strained against his fly. "Ah, you decided to join us after all?"

"I forgot something." Sean headed for the table with stiff strides and grabbed his jacket, then spared another glance at the prostitute, who'd draped herself over the couch again. "You all right, darling?" he repeated.

She nodded, a little too fervently.

"Amelia is just fine," Cillian answered for her. "Isn't that right, sweetness?"

Her head bobbed up and down again, but tears continued to slide down her face.

Sean hesitated before leaving. He supposed he could interfere, but the woman was a professional. Her specialty was probably catering to sick fucks like Cillian, who liked a side order of violence with their sex.

Christ, he just wanted to get out of there. He wanted to see Bailey.

Ignoring the smacking of flesh and the prostitute's squeal of pain, Sean marched out of the room without looking back.

Sean was angry. Bailey sensed it the second he strode into the apartment, but he snubbed her completely, not even a look in her direction as he stalked into the bathroom and slammed the door behind him.

When the shower came on, she released a frustrated breath. Why should she care if he couldn't be bothered to say hello to her? She was just his pretend girlfriend, after all.

Except . . . damn it . . . she *did* care. She hated being shut out, even though she knew damn well she was doing the same to him.

She marched into the bathroom without knocking, her pulse kicking up a notch from the sight of Sean's naked body in the transparent shower stall.

His head turned, gaze locking with hers through the glass. "What do you want?"

Anger spiked in her blood as she threw open the door. Water slid down his muscular body in soapy rivulets, clinging to his pecs and abs, sliding lower, to his . . . no, she refused to glance south. No doubt he was sporting a raging hard-on. The man was virile and sexual and too damn tempting.

She raised her voice over the rush of water. "What happened tonight?"

"Nothing." He glided the bar of soap lower, lathering the groin she was making a pointed effort not to look at.

"Is the bombing all set to go?" she said sarcastically.

"Yes." He turned toward the spray to rinse off the soap, flashing her his bare ass.

Damn it, he had a great ass. Not one of those pancake butts you couldn't grab onto, but round and taut and delicious. She could still feel those firm buttocks flexing beneath her fingers when he thrust inside her.

*Focus.*

Right, this was not the time to be ogling the man's backside, no matter how spectacular it was.

"You're really going through with it?" she demanded.

He kept his back turned and said, "Yes." The tone of his voice brooked no argument.

Bailey spun on her heel and left the bathroom before she gave in to the urge to smack him.

A car bomb. He'd agreed to plant a damn car bomb and it didn't faze him in the slightest.

She grabbed her phone from the coffee table and distracted herself by checking the screen, but Daniels hadn't texted her back. Since she'd had time on her hands tonight, she'd spent hours poring over the copies of Flannery's files, until she'd finally located the CIA's potential rat. She'd sent Daniels the information and he'd said he would check it out, but the man was taking his time getting back to her.

Not that she cared. If it were up to her, she'd be just peachy never hearing from Isaac Daniels again. But she owed him for giving her the heads-up about Vanessa.

And talk about someone else taking their sweet-ass time—the director of her mother's facility was dragging his heels on the transfer. Ironically, it was the security measures Bailey had implemented in the first place that were coming back to bite her in the ass. Dr. Levinson insisted she had to sign the permission papers in person, which she couldn't exactly do at the moment. Luckily, there were three CIA agents watching the premises, and Flannery's thug didn't seem inclined to make a move, but she would feel better once Vanessa was off Flannery's radar.

Sean reentered the living room a few minutes later. Buck naked. He'd dried off, but his hair was still wet, droplets clinging to the short blond strands and falling on his forehead.

When Bailey didn't speak, a frustrated noise rumbled out of his mouth. "What the hell do you want me to say, Bailey? They're going to plant that bomb whether or not

I help them. Cillian's watching me like a hawk and reporting everything I say back to Flannery. Rabbit's watching me just as hard. So yeah, hard place, meet rock. That's where I'm fucking at right now, okay?"

He sounded so upset that her anger thawed, replaced by a reluctant pang of sympathy. She supposed he didn't want to be in this situation any more than she did.

"Oliver checked in earlier," she told him. "He tracked down Flannery's hush-hush Dublin address, a mansion in Dalkey. He's trying to get his hands on the blueprints and security protocol."

"Yeah, he texted me the same thing."

Sean disappeared into the kitchen and returned a moment later with a glass of water. She watched his corded throat work as he drank, and then her gaze moved lower, resting on bare chest, and even lower, focusing on the long cock jutting from his groin.

"Are you going to put some clothes on?" she blurted out.

"No. Are you going to take yours off?"

"No."

"Right. Of course not."

His surly tone annoyed her. "What, you think I'm going to throw myself into your arms and beg you to fuck me?"

"You won't have to beg. Just say the word and I'll be inside you again." His hooded eyes roamed her body as if he could see right through her clothing. Hot and sultry and gleaming with promise.

Bailey gulped.

He shrugged. "It's all right, luv. I know you won't say it."

"I just don't see the point in having sex again when we both know this isn't going anywhere."

"If you say so."

She clenched her teeth. "What do you care anyway?

You wanted one night, remember? You wanted me to know who I was with," she mimicked. "And I did. You got what you wanted."

Something indecipherable crossed his eyes, but she couldn't for the life of her interpret that cryptic look.

"What is it now?" she muttered.

Sean set down his glass and advanced on her like a predator. A very naked, very determined predator.

"I'm just wondering how long you're going to keep lying to me. I mean, I know why you are, but I'm curious to see how far you'll take it."

"As usual, I have no idea what you're talking about."

His mouth curved in a smile. "You knew who I was last year."

Panic jolted through her, bringing a swift denial. "I didn't—"

"You *knew*," he interrupted. "You knew from the second I walked into your hotel room to the moment I came inside you."

Before she could avert her eyes, he grasped her chin and forced her to look at him.

"You knew I wasn't Oliver. You pretended to be shocked and horrified when I told you afterward, but you were faking it, weren't you, Bailey?"

She could have tried to lie again. But what was the point? Sean had clearly figured out the truth, and he'd only keep pushing her if she didn't own up to it.

"Yes." She exhaled in a rush. "I knew."

Triumph flared in his eyes. His thumbnail scraped the edge of her jaw, slow and sensual. "Don't worry, luv. I'm not angry with you. I understand why you lied. You needed to give yourself an out."

She tried to back away, but his fingers curled around the nape of her neck, rooting her in place.

"You wanted to fuck me but you couldn't let me know

it, could you? Because that would mean admitting that I could get to you, that I made you feel things my brother never made you feel. But you found yourself a loophole, didn't you, baby? You took what you wanted from me that night, and then you pleaded ignorance." He mocked her with his tone. "You're scared of me, Bailey."

Her gaze flew to his. "I'm not scared of you."

"Yeah, you're right. You're not scared—you're bloody *terrified*. You're terrified of how good I make you feel. You think it gives me power over you."

She sucked in a shaky breath.

"But for a smart woman, you're pretty fucking dense sometimes." His hand dropped from her neck. "Don't you know by now that you have just as much power over me?"

Bailey blinked in surprise, but Sean had already walked away, ducking into the hallway as she stood there, struggling to breathe. She didn't hear the bedroom door close, but the mattress squeaked as if he was stretching out on the bed.

It occurred to her that he hadn't offered her the use of the bedroom this time, though that was probably because he'd known she'd reject the idea. Sleeping on the couch allowed her to keep him at arm's length.

But there'd be no sleep for her anytime soon. It was only eleven, and she wasn't tired. She listened to the sounds of traffic on the street below them, trying to make sense of everything he'd said. He was right. She *did* have power. And not just to turn him on. She had the power to choose how much of herself to give him. The power to push him away if he got too close.

Her wobbly legs carried her to the bedroom before she even realized it.

"What do you want now?"

His deep voice drifted toward her in the darkness. He

was a shadowy blur on the mattress, but she could feel his gaze burning into her.

She sighed. "Can we please just call a truce?"

"We're not at war, Bailey. You're the only one who's fighting."

She approached the bed, uncertain, unhappy. She sat on the edge and fumbled for the lamp on the night table; she located the switch, and pale yellow light flooded the room, revealing Sean's naked body. His cloudy expression.

Bailey took a breath. "I fight you because . . ." She searched for words. "Because . . . I just do. You piss me off."

His lips quirked. "I piss everyone off."

"I hate being kept out of the loop," she admitted. "You're always shutting me out or keeping me in the dark. I don't like it, okay?"

"Christ, don't you get it? *I* hate that you're caught up in this mess. This bloody mess that I shouldn't even be in. I have no loyalty to Rabbit *or* Flannery, yet I'm stuck between them like the damn meat in a really shitty sandwich." He rubbed his eyes, his voice coming out hoarse. "I'm gonna have to kill him, Bailey."

"Which one?"

"Flannery, for now." He groaned. "But certain measures need to be in place before I do it. I want Ollie somewhere safe. You. The others." He paused. "Your mother."

"I'm arranging for a transfer," she reminded him.

He searched her face, a crease of hesitation furrowing his brow. "Does . . . does she really have Alzheimer's?"

Bailey's throat tightened, making it hard to speak. So she settled for a nod.

"I'm sorry, luv."

"Yeah . . . I used to be, too." She swallowed hard. "But lately I think she's better off."

Shock filled his eyes. "You don't mean that."

"Yes, I do." Needles of pain pricked her chest. Her heart. She knew she sounded callous, but she was being honest. "At least this way she doesn't have to remember."

"Remember what?" he said softly.

"Everything that happened to her."

"To her, or to both of you?"

She fought her discomfort. She didn't talk about her childhood. Period. But the rare tenderness in Sean's eyes coaxed the confession from her mouth.

"Both of us. But Mom suffered more than I did."

His expression became knowing. "Your father?"

Bailey's head jerked in a nod.

"He beat her? Beat you?"

Another nod.

She saw his fists curl into the sheets, as if the thought of anyone laying a hand on her enraged him.

"My beatings weren't as bad, or as frequent. Usually he focused on Mom. Tormented her." Involuntary shivers traveled up her spine. "But a lot of the times he'd force me to watch."

Sean sucked in a breath. "Are you serious?"

"He said he was trying to teach me a lesson." Bitterness combined with the lingering horror to form a queasy knot in her stomach. "He wanted me to witness every horrible thing he did to her. He wanted me to see the cuts and the bruises and the broken fingers and the ci—" She wheezed out a breath. "Cigarette burns. He wanted me to learn."

Sean's face painted a picture of pure revulsion. "To learn what, for Christ's sake?"

"What happens when a woman tries to be more powerful than her husband."

"How did she try to do that?" Sean asked in confusion.

"She didn't try—she *was*. Her job was more important than his. She couldn't help—" Bailey stopped. Her choice, she reminded herself. *She* got to decide how close Sean was allowed to get. And they'd just reached the line in the sand.

"What did your mother do for a living?" he pressed, but Bailey was done talking.

She placed her palm on his chest, stroking the light dusting of hair between his pectorals.

"Damn it, don't distract me. Talk to me."

"I don't want to talk anymore." Her hand glided down his stomach, and his abdominal muscles tightened beneath her palm. She reached the dark blond curls at his groin and grasped his semihard cock. One soft stroke and he was steel in her hands. Fully erect, precome oozing from his tip.

"*Talk* to me," he ordered.

"No."

He tried to move out of her grasp but she squeezed him harder, drawing a wild groan from his throat. When she leaned forward to take him in her mouth, his hips shot off the bed, seeking deeper contact.

It wasn't fair what she was doing, but knowing that didn't stop her from doing it. She'd given him enough insight tonight. Now it was time to armor herself again, to slam the door Sean kept trying to barrel through.

He shuddered when she sucked on the crown of his cock. "Bailey . . . you're being . . . an asshole . . . right now."

"Deal with it," she murmured. Then she licked her way down his shaft and flicked her tongue over his tight sac.

The distraction ploy worked. Soon he was cursing under his breath and thrusting into her mouth. Pleasure stretched his features taut as his hand tangled in her hair, guiding her along his shaft. He tasted soapy and salty and *male*, and Bailey couldn't control the arousal that gathered inside her, throbbing in her sex and tingling her nipples.

She sucked him hard and fast, knowing what he liked, using that knowledge to summon groan after groan from his lips. She grazed her teeth on his sensitive underside and he grunted in pleasure.

But when he spoke, it wasn't to urge her on. It was a command to stop. "No," he said in a tortured voice. "You don't get to do this."

"You don't get to stop me."

She took him all the way to the back of her throat and his violent curse triggered her muffled laughter against his cock.

His hand fisted her hair, pulling to the point of pain as he yanked her head up. "You think I shut you out? Well, take a good look at *yourself*, Bailey. You'd rather blow a man you don't like than offer one measly detail about yourself. Let me *in*, damn it."

Bailey took off her T-shirt and pajama pants and straddled his hard thighs. "You want me to let you in? Fine. Here you go."

She impaled herself on his cock and he moaned so loudly she had to laugh again, but the humor died the second he thrust upward and filled her to the hilt. God, she couldn't think straight when he was inside her. He was the addiction she desperately wanted to cure herself of.

Sean's movements stilled as he brought a hand to her face, gently stroking the fading bruise beneath her right eye. "I hate seeing this."

"I've had worse."

His thumb moved in a soft caress. "I hate hearing that even more."

Damn it, the tenderness was too much. She liked him

better when he was rough. Crass. Made it easier to remember that this was only sex.

She distracted him again by leaning forward and bringing her breasts to his mouth. And it worked—his tongue darted out for a taste, flicking one distended nipple before he sucked it deep in his mouth. Each time she lowered herself on his cock, that thick shaft stroked her inner channel, and her clit rubbed against his pelvis, until the pleasure grew too intense, sending her sagging onto his hard chest.

Bailey ground herself against his lower body, frantically, mindlessly, her body aching for relief.

"That's it, luv." His hands stroked her back, his raspy voice coaxing her to the brink. "Come all over my cock."

She exploded in a fiery rush, gasping for air as the orgasm blew through her body. Everything stopped working. Her brain, her lungs, her limbs. And her pussy spasmed harder when she felt the wet warmth of Sean's release flood her channel. His cock pulsed in time to his rapid heartbeat, which vibrated in her breasts and matched the fast pace of her own.

Strong arms held her against him. He was still inside her, hard as a rock, the heat of him burning her from the inside out.

The lips that brushed her ear were soft and warm, but his words sent a chill up her spine. "You're going to let me in, Bailey. I won't stop pushing you until you do."

"That's not what this is about," she whispered.

"Yes, it is."

Caveman Sean was back, but when she tried to disentangle from his arms, his grip tightened.

"You still don't understand, do you? We're good together, baby. We *fit*," he said fiercely. "I won't go away until I know everything about you. I won't go away even when I *do* know. I'll always be here, and you *will* let me in."

Terror shot through her at the thought that he might be right.

But no. It wouldn't happen. Not if she kept him at a distance, where he belonged.

"Tell me what you're so afraid of," he said thickly. "Just tell me, and we'll talk through it. We'll work past it."

He slid his fingers through her hair and tugged her head up. The raw, naked emotion in his eyes made her heart race in panic. Breathing hard, she wrenched his arms off her and stumbled off the bed.

"Running away isn't going to change what this is. You can hide from me, but we both know it won't work, Bailey. Because I'm with you even when you're alone."

Her hands trembled as she grabbed her clothes.

"Stay," he pleaded in a hoarse voice. "Stay and let me in, damn it."

His sorrowful sigh was the last thing she heard before she hurried out the door.

# Chapter 17

"It's done." O'Neill was downright gloating as he strode into the pub.

Sean glanced up from the table he was sharing with Quinn and Doherty, trying not to flinch at the cat-killed-the-bloody-canary grin on O'Neill's face. The man had been tasked with driving the explosives-filled car and parking it in front of Trinity Pub, and Sean was disappointed that O'Neill had followed through. A part of him had hoped O'Neill would chicken out or screw up.

Because whether or not the damn thing went off, Sean didn't feel right knowing there was a bomb in an area teeming with civilians and college kids.

From the corner booth where she sat with her laptop, Bailey lifted her head and met his eyes, and he saw the same unhappiness he was feeling reflected on her face. Then she scowled and turned back to the computer screen, the rigid set of her shoulders revealing that she was as unhappy with *him* as she was about the car bomb.

She'd barely said five words to him all morning. She'd just fiddled around on her laptop in silence, pretending to do the graphic design work she was using as her occupation cover. Or maybe not pretending—Sean had stolen a few peeks at her screen earlier, and the fake advertisement she'd created had looked pretty damn good. Not that he was surprised. The woman was good at everything.

Well, except for talking about anything important.

He'd pushed her too hard last night. He knew that. But he wasn't going to back off either. He'd spent five years playing it cool and subtle, and where had that gotten him? Absolutely nowhere. The bulldozer approach came with a greater risk of losing her, but it had already produced more results than any of the other strategies he'd tried in the past.

"Where's Rabbit?" O'Neill asked as he shrugged out of his coat.

Good fucking question. Since Sean's return to the Dagger, Rabbit had been AWOL more often than not.

"He had an errand to take care of," Quinn replied. "Should be back soon."

An errand? Or something more sinister?

But fuck, who cared? At least Rabbit wasn't with Cillian, who was currently holed up in the back room. Smacking a woman's ass raw, no doubt.

Every time Sean turned around, Kelly was whispering in Rabbit's ear like Iago in an Irish production of *Othello*. He didn't trust the twisted bastard, and not just because Cillian worked for Flannery.

"I'll be right back," he said abruptly. "Wanna check on my girl."

He left Quinn and O'Neill to their own devices and approached Bailey. She was frowning at her phone but tucked it away before Sean could sneak a peek at it.

"Should I be jealous?" he mocked, raising his brow.

"Aren't you always?"

He slid onto the bench seat across from her. "Who was that text from?"

"No one you need to worry about." Her gaze lowered to the laptop screen.

"Who was it from?" he repeated sternly.

There was a pause, then, "My old handler."

No one he needed to worry about, his ass.

A deep frown puckered his brow. "Isaac Daniels, you mean."

If Bailey was surprised that he knew the man's name, she didn't show it. "Yes." She glanced at Rabbit's men, then lowered her voice. "I went through Flannery's files last night and found three CIA agents who could've leaked my file. Daniels just confirmed which one of them it was. He wanted to thank me for the heads-up."

"I'm sure he did." Sean ignored the burst of jealousy that streaked up his spine. "Guess he's gonna be doing some firing today."

She gave a wry smile. "People don't get fired from the CIA. They get executed."

"I was being facetious."

"Oooh, look at you and your big fancy words."

"I'm a bloody wordsmith, baby. A genius, actually—I even graduated from high school."

A laugh popped out of her mouth, and then her eyes darkened, as if she was annoyed with herself for showing amusement. "Shouldn't you be sitting with your best buds and discussing your next terrorist attack?" she grumbled.

"Nah, I'd much rather sit here with you and discuss your ex-lover."

Her jaw twitched.

"What, luv, you thought I didn't know? Flannery's not the only one with *files*, remember?"

She leveled him with a scathing look. "Congratulations, you know I fucked my boss. Gold star for Sean."

"You didn't just fuck him. You lived with him for four

years." Sean slanted his head. "I tailed him a few years back, you know. Got a lot of pretty pics, too. He's . . . hell, he's prehistoric. How old was he when you first hooked up? Ninety?"

"Forty-eight," she said stiffly.

"Jesus Christ, Bailey. You were eighteen years old."

"Twenty, actually."

"Still makes him a dirty old man."

Sean wanted to ask what the hell she'd seen in the wrinkled perv, but Rabbit chose that moment to return from his mysterious errand.

"Reilly," he called. "A word."

Though he was reluctant to leave her, Sean slid out of the booth and walked over to Rabbit, who led him out of earshot of the others.

"Kelly tells me we're all set."

"That's what I hear," Sean said indifferently.

"You don't like this."

He met Rabbit's gaze head-on. "No, I don't. I don't fuck with innocents, Eamon."

"No?" The older man smirked in Bailey's direction. "Seems like you fuck innocents just fine."

"Yeah, but she's not sitting in Trinity Pub at the moment, now, is she?"

Rabbit's eyes stayed focused on Bailey. "She means a lot to you."

"I wouldn't be here right now if she didn't."

"I see . . . But, well, I hope she's not the *only* reason you're here." Rabbit's voice went oddly gruff. "I'm glad you're back, Seansy. Every time I look at you I see your father. You're so much like Colin, y'know that? Not just the resemblance either. You have his strength. His loyalty." Rabbit paused. "I miss him."

"Yeah," Sean said hoarsely. "Me too."

His childhood hadn't been flowers and sunshine—

that was impossible when your father was tangled up with the IRA—but that didn't mean Sean lacked good memories of his old man. He did miss him. A helluva lot.

But he had no interest in commiserating about it with Eamon O'Hare.

"Don't you have a call to make soon?" Sean deliberately tapped his tactical watch.

An unreadable look crossed Rabbit's expression before he nodded. "You're right. I do. I'd better get on that."

"I don't like this." Sullivan voiced the uneasy admission into the comm as he monitored his surroundings.

As usual, he was the one out in the open, sipping a coffee on the street-facing patio of Trinity Pub, while Liam and D worked their sniper magic on rooftops across the thoroughfare. D was back on surveillance duty because Oliver Reilly had effectively fired him, claiming that the sullen-faced merc was so intimidating that he scared the shit out of any source they tried talking to. Ash was apparently suited for the job, though, because Oliver had kept the rookie.

With Isabel watching O'Hare's, Sullivan was left playing foot soldier alone. Normally he didn't mind being the eyes on the street, but today, the back of his neck was tingling and he couldn't fight the rattled feeling that something was amiss.

"Not sure I blame you," Liam murmured back. "I wouldn't want to be sitting ten feet from an IED either."

Sully's gaze shifted to the blue sedan parked directly in front of the patio. There were five spaces along the curb; three were occupied. The sedan was sandwiched between an SUV and a hatchback.

It was half past eleven. The lunch crowd would start pouring in around noon, but half a dozen patrons already loitered on the patio. Sullivan was amazed by the number of morning drinkers in this bloody country.

He kept his eye on the sedan, half expecting the thing to blow up at any second and rip him to pieces. One of O'Hare's men had parked the vehicle more than an hour ago. He'd fed the meter and disappeared around the corner, leaving a ticking time bomb behind him. Literally.

Sean insisted that the Dagger always tipped off the cops, but . . .

Sullivan's entire body continued to hum forebodingly.

"When's the call supposed to come in?" The fancy-pants Bluetooth lodged in his ear gave the impression that he was on the phone, but he still spoke in a low voice.

"Twenty to," Liam answered. "Just stay put. It'll all be over soon."

Liam's voice was reassuring, easing Sully's nerves. Slightly. His neck was still prickling like a motherfucker.

People began approaching the pub. Students mostly, with the odd older patron here and there.

For the first time in days it wasn't pouring out. Fuckin' Ireland. It was October—it should have been cold and rainy, for Christ's sake. But no, today just *had* to be dry and cloudless. And warm, damn it. Warm enough that folks were taking advantage of the nice weather and filling up the patio.

"I'm not seeing any Dagger members," D reported brusquely. "Boston?"

"None. Wasn't expecting any, though. They've got no reason to stick around." Liam paused. "The area will be crawling with Garda soon."

It'd better be. Reilly had said the bomb was set on a timer scheduled to go off at noon. Or rather, *not* go off at noon. Bloody terrorists and their scare tactics.

Sullivan checked his watch: 11:34. Six more minutes and the call would go through.

He absently rubbed his right forearm. Beneath his sleeve was the tattoo that spanned from his wrist to the inside of his elbow, one line of black script that spelled out the name that always brought him comfort.

Liam's knowing chuckle filled his ear. "I see what you're doing, dude. Jeez, you can't go even a second without thinking about that damn boat?"

An uncharacteristic snort came from D. "You kidding me? He'd fuck that thing if he could."

Sullivan ignored their soft laughter and flattened his palms on the tabletop. His teammates thought he was a pansy-ass for having the name of his sailboat inked on his flesh, but they had no bloody clue. Evangeline the woman had come long before *Evangeline* the boat. And *she* was the one from whom he drew comfort.

The feed went quiet. Sullivan pretended to text on his phone. As the minutes ticked down, his agitation doubled, then quadrupled when a guy in a baseball cap approached with a golden retriever and proceeded to tie the dog's leash around the lamppost two feet from the blue sedan.

As the kid ducked into the pub, Sully let out a soft groan. "Bloody hell. He left the dog out here."

"Take a breath, Aussie," came Liam's quiet reply. "There's time."

Sully inhaled deeply. "Is Reilly at O'Hare's?"

"Affirmative. Bailey's with him."

"Get him on the line. Find out what's going on over there."

Another glance at his watch revealed it was 11:40. The Dagger would be calling law enforcement now. *Should* be calling now. And the nearest Garda station was four minutes away by car—Sullivan had checked. Which meant that four minutes from now, sirens would wail, civilians would be evacuated, and a bomb squad unit would speed in to save the day.

"Sean says the call went through," Liam reported.

The pressure in his chest dissipated. Some of it anyway. No police sirens sounded, but he heard them in his own head, damn it.

Shit. His internal warning system had been triggered. That wasn't good.

The seconds continued to tick by.

"Something's wrong," he hissed. "Call Sean again."

"There's still time," Liam assured him.

His watch read 11:44.

There wasn't a Garda vehicle in sight.

"You're wrong, Boston." He couldn't fight the urgency in his tone. "*This* is wrong."

"Fuck. Your Spidey senses are tingling?"

"Big-time."

"Maintain your position. Calling Sean."

Sullivan exhaled in a slow rush, appreciating that Liam hadn't put up an argument. But Liam knew as well as he did that a soldier's instincts were too critical to ignore. If one of your teammates had a bad hunch, you bloody listened to it.

Liam's perplexed voice rippled through the comm a few moments later. "Reilly insists the call was made."

"Did he make it himself?" Sullivan demanded.

"No, but—"

"Then the fucking call wasn't made."

Eleven forty-nine. His frantic gaze flew to the blue sedan. Bloody *hell*.

"The Garda isn't coming, Liam. We need to clear the area. *Now*." Sullivan inhaled a calming breath. "D, you copy?"

"Loud and clear," was the grim reply.

"Put in an anonymous call to the Garda. Tell them to send a bomb unit."

"Roger that."

"Liam, get your ass down here. ASAP."

"On my way."

It was 11:51 now. Nine minutes until the timer reached zero. Nine minutes to clear the street. Or maybe the civilians would be safer inside? Sully's brain raced a million miles a second as he struggled to find the best way to handle this.

He had no clue how big the bomb was—five hundred pounds of explosives? A thousand? The blast radius would be . . . fuck, it could be anything. Required at least a two-thousand-foot outdoor evacuation distance. No one could be anywhere near the pub—hell, the entire stretch of street—when that bomb went off. But people might have a better chance of survival inside. Easier to avoid injury from flying shrapnel and debris. And how close was the bomb to the fuel tank? The explosion could be ten times worse if the gasoline ignited and released a fucking wall of fire.

Shit. Motherfucking *shit.*

"Bomb threat's been called," D said briskly.

Eight minutes.

Sullivan shot to his feet, knocking his chair over in the process and drawing several confused stares. He couldn't create a panic. Couldn't shout, "There's a bomb!" and watch folks stampede one another to death. It had to be done quietly—but *fast.*

He grabbed the arm of the passing waitress and brought his head close to her ear. "We need to evacuate this patio, love."

Her eyes widened. "W-what? Why?"

Stifling a groan, he discreetly lifted up the bottom of his shirt to flash the bogus police badge clipped there. "I'm undercover," he murmured. "And I'm telling you right now—this place needs to be cleared out. A bomb threat was just called in."

She gave a horrified gasp, and he swiftly covered her lips with one finger. "Don't raise a panic, love. Just take a breath and help me get these folks off the patio."

The fear in her eyes was unmistakable, but she nodded weakly and did what he asked. For the next minute, the two of them moved from table to table, urging the patrons away from the pub.

"Walk," he whispered to each one. "But walk fast, damn it. Get as far away from here as possible."

By some miracle, they followed his instructions. People started to leave the patio in brisk strides rather than a full-out run, but the rapidly emptying space caught the attention of pedestrians and the patrons inside, and within seconds, pandemonium broke out.

"What's going on?" A woman hurried out of the bar and grabbed Sullivan's sleeve.

She wasn't the only one. People streamed out of the pub, crowded on the patio, gathered on the sidewalk—exactly where he didn't want them to be, damn it.

Admitting defeat, Sullivan cupped his hands around his mouth and shouted, "Everyone clear the area! *Now!*"

As bodies jostled one another and feet pounded the pavement, Sullivan found himself surrounded by a panicking mob. Frightened voices echoed all around him, flashes of clothing and the scent of perfume, cologne, and sweat. An undulating mass of bodies radiating fear and terror.

Relief crashed over him when he registered the shriek of sirens. Oh, thank fuck. The Garda was on the way.

"Move! Now! Get away from the sidewalk!"

Liam's voice, shouting at the blur of people bumping into one another and running for their lives.

Sullivan checked his watch—five minutes left. Too many people on the sidewalk. Too many fucking people. He and Liam hurried to usher them away, but every second that ticked by intensified the urgency and desperation.

Flashing lights and earsplitting sirens broke onto the scene, car doors slamming as uniformed men swarmed the sidewalk and joined the evacuation efforts.

Three minutes.

D was there now, barking orders to the crowd in his gravelly, scary-as-fuck voice.

An armored van whizzed up. Tires screeched and the stench of burning rubber filled the air. The bomb squad. Too bloody late. They were never going to disarm that thing in time.

Sullivan's pulse drummed a frantic rhythm in his ears as he worked to clear the area. The heat from the throng of bodies caused perspiration to stream down his neck and forehead. From the corner of his eye he saw D pushing a group of young college students toward the street, commanding them to run.

Two minutes, damn it.

Three men in protective gear were already at the sedan, probing the undercarriage.

The street was almost clear. Sullivan looked around in astonishment at the deserted patio, the sidewalk, the road. Garda officers burst into neighboring storefronts where there were still people inside, shouting orders to steer clear of the windows and doors, to take cover in the rear of the buildings.

One minute.

"*Sully.* We need to go." Liam's sharp command penetrated his inspection of the scene, and then a strong hand clamped on his arm, dragging him away from the sidewalk.

A high-pitched whine sliced through the roar of voices.

Sullivan halted in his tracks. The dog. The fucking *dog*.

"Go," he shouted to Liam. "I'm right behind you."

Liam nearly got hold of Sullivan's sleeve, but Sully lurched forward, leaving his teammate behind as he sprinted back to the sidewalk. The long-haired retriever was on its feet, circling the lamppost it was tied to as frightened whines tore out of its mouth.

"Sully! Get the fuck back here!" he heard Liam yell, but he ignored the desperate command.

His fingers trembled as he hurriedly undid the knot in the leash. His peripheral caught the bomb unit by the car. He didn't check his watch. Knew there wasn't much time left.

"It's okay, buddy. I got you." A second later, he heaved the sixty-pound canine into his arms and ran.

Liam stood a couple of hundred feet away, visible relief in his blue eyes as Sullivan came hurtling toward him.

He was halfway to Liam when the explosion rocked the street. There was no time to register the shock or horror or amazement. Next thing he knew, he was flying. Soaring. Suspended in the air as time stopped and white heat suffused his body.

Pain. No, *agony*, ripping through his left arm and fogging his brain, and then he was no longer freefalling. He was just falling. His head bounced off the hard ground like a basketball.

And the lights went out.

# Chapter 18

Sullivan regained consciousness to find a pair of worried blue eyes staring down at him. He blinked, then groaned, realizing he was lying on one of the twin beds in the hotel room he was sharing with D.

"W-what . . ." His voice sounded hoarse. "What happened?"

"A bomb went off."

His teammate's droll response brought a rush of choked laughter from his chest, which sent a shooting pain to his right temple. "No shit, Boston."

As the threads of grogginess wound together into a state of alertness, he became aware of the throbbing pain in his left shoulder. And the fact that he was bare chested. He glanced at the nightstand and saw scraps of black fabric draped there, along with an eight-inch KA-BAR, the blade gleaming in the sunlight streaming into the room.

"Did you cut my shirt?"

"Yup. Needed to assess the damage." Liam sighed. "Think you can sit up? 'Cause we definitely need to do something about *that*."

"About what—" He cursed when his gaze found what Liam was looking at.

The jagged piece of metal sticking out of his arm.

"Aw, shit." Well, at least the pain made sense now. "You waited until I was awake to pull it out, you bloody sadist?"

"I was worried you might thrash around and I wouldn't be able to hold you down."

He wearily sat up, glancing around the room. "Where's D?"

"Went to O'Hare's to join Isabel. There's a chance they might need to drag Reilly outta there. He's ready to rip Rabbit's throat out."

"I'm ready to do it myself," Sullivan muttered.

That son of a bitch hadn't tipped off the Garda. He'd sat by and allowed the bomb to go off, killing dozens—

"How many casualties? And how long have I been out?"

Liam rose from the bed and headed for the bathroom. "Thirty minutes or so, and there isn't an exact casualty count yet," he said over his shoulder. He ducked out of sight, returning a moment later with a black canvas med kit. "But we know there's at least ten. Four bomb squad members, two gardai, four civilians."

Ten people. *Ten* people had died today. Maybe more.

Liam carted the bag to the bed and unzipped it. "Your dog's all right, though. The owner was running all over the place screaming *'Winston'* at the top of his lungs. He was bawling his eyes out when he finally found the mutt."

The news didn't alleviate even an ounce of Sullivan's fury. *Ten people dead* trumped *man and dog reunited*, though he supposed he *was* glad he hadn't risked his life for nothing.

"D and I got you out right before the media showed up. The place is crawling with news vans now, press helicopters, too. They're calling it a terrorist attack."

"That's because it was," he said darkly.

As his teammate removed supplies from the med kit, Sully examined the shrapnel poking out of his arm. It was a small square of metal, two inches by two inches, and curved at the top. Damn thing was going to leave him with a horseshoe-shaped scar. Bloody wonderful.

He winced when Liam pulled out a pair of forceps and a handful of gauze. "Has the Dagger taken responsibility for the attack yet?"

"No, but I imagine they will soon." Liam snapped on a pair of latex gloves. "Ready?"

"Fuck, no. Just leave it in. Eventually it'll just become part of my skin, right?"

That got him a chuckle. "Stop being a pussy. I'll be gentle, I promise."

He sighed. "Make it fast. And if I pass out, do me a favor and don't revive me until you've finished stitching me up."

"Pussy," Liam taunted again.

Unfortunately, Sully *didn't* pass out. Instead he almost bit his tongue clear off when Liam clamped the forceps on the top of the jagged piece and began extracting it from Sullivan's flesh. Slowly.

Black dots flashed in his vision, hot pain shooting from the top of his arm to the soles of his feet.

"Son of a *bitch*," he ground out.

"Almost there," Liam murmured.

Several agonizing seconds later, the shrapnel was out, and both men cringed when a flap of Sullivan's skin folded downward, hanging loosely from his biceps.

Liam snickered. "Christ. That's fucking gross."

"You've got the worst bedside manner on the planet," Sullivan grumbled.

"Come on, you've gotta admit it's *gross*."

"My ego is weeping right now, Boston. You know how important my dashing good looks are to me."

Liam rolled his eyes. "It's not like you got shrapneled in the face. Chill."

Sullivan clenched his teeth as his teammate cleaned the wound. His arm was on fire. Every swipe of that antiseptic-soaked rag brought a streak of pain, and when Liam brought out the tweezers and used them to pick pieces of dirt and debris out of Sullivan's raw flesh, nausea scampered up his throat and made his eyes water.

By the time Liam busted out the needle and thread, Sully's entire body pulsed with a dull, relentless ache. His friend stitched him up, then stabbed him with a syringe of antibiotics and sat back to admire his handiwork.

"Look at that," Liam said with a pleased nod. "That'll leave a great scar, man."

He studied the neat, tight line of U-shaped stitches and had to give Liam credit. "Your technique's gotten better."

Liam dug into the bag and pulled out a small penlight. Smirking, he flicked it on and shined it right in Sullivan's face. "All right, Aussie, follow the light."

The light sent another shooting pain to his temples. "Turn that fucking thing off."

"We need to check you for a concussion."

"I don't have a concussion."

"You were unconscious for thirty minutes and you've got an egg-size lump on the back of your head. Though it'd probably be twice the size if your skull weren't so damn thick. Now, follow the light or I might decide to rip those stitches out and redo them."

Scowling, he humored his friend and followed the bloody light.

"Any dizziness? Nausea? Double vision?" Liam prompted as he clicked the penlight off.

"Nope. Because I don't have a concussion."

"What's the date today?"

"October sixth—wanna know how I know that? Because I don't have a bloody concussion. So take off your Florence Nightingale panties and pull on your man pants, and let's go help D and Isabel."

When he tried to get up, Liam planted a palm in the center of Sully's chest. "You're not going anywhere. You know the drill—twenty-four hours' sabbatical to make sure you're not concussed."

"I'm not concussed, damn it!"

"Twenty-four hours, Aussie." The stern look on Liam's face indicated that arguing would be futile.

"Twelve hours," he countered.

"Eighteen and that's my final offer."

They stared at each other, but Sully knew Liam wouldn't back down. The guy was stubborn as fuck when he wanted to be. And he suddenly became aware that Liam's hand was still on his chest. Big and warm, pulsing with power.

Sully cleared his throat and eased backward against the pillows, causing Liam's hand to withdraw. "Fine. I'll stay put. But you have to go."

"Not going anywhere, Sully. What happens if I go and you try to stand up and get dizzy? Crack your head on the corner of the table and do more than pass out this time? Someone needs to monitor you."

"No, someone needs to back up Reilly," he shot back.

"Someone will. Ash and Oliver are relieving us." Liam rummaged in the med kit for a bottle of oxycodone. He shook out two pills and slapped them in Sullivan's hand, then pointed to the water bottle on the nightstand. "Take these. They'll help with the pain. I need to call Reilly."

As Liam went to make the call, Sullivan twisted open the bottle and shoved the painkillers back inside. Then he leaned his head against the bed frame and closed his eyes, cursing Eamon O'Hare for everything the bastard had put him through today.

Sean was ready to strangle someone with his bare hands. He'd never experienced rage so visceral as he had while staring at one of the televisions mounted on the wood-paneled wall, watching a parade of gruesome images flash across the screen.

The bomb had gone off.

It had *gone off*. As in, exploded. As in, Rabbit had fucking *lied* to him.

Sean flew across the room like a tornado, directing all that volatile energy at Rabbit, who'd ducked into the back before the chaos had erupted. He heard Bailey's footsteps behind him but he didn't turn around. Couldn't stomach seeing the contempt in her eyes again.

When Macgregor had called to let them know the area wasn't being evacuated, Sean had had a bitch of a time stopping her from getting in the car and speeding to the scene. He'd known rushing over there wouldn't achieve a damn thing. They wouldn't have made it there in time, and they'd had no way of stopping the explosion.

"You son of a bitch!" he hissed as he stormed into the back room. "You didn't make the call!"

Rabbit looked up from his chair. He had a pint of lager in his hand and a vacant look on his weathered face. The accusation didn't even penetrate, didn't evoke a reaction.

It was Cillian who spoke, carefully advancing on Sean the way one would approach a feral animal.

"No," Cillian said calmly. "We didn't."

Sean breathed through his nose, trying to control the waves of fury eddying in his gut. "Why. The. Hell. Not."

Cillian shrugged. "Because that line of thinking never

helped us in the past. Welcome to the twenty-first century, Reilly."

Holy bloody hell. Was the man *for real*?

"It's time to change direction. If we want to make a statement, then we need to actually *make a statement*."

"By killing innocents?" Sean spat out. "Jesus Christ! They're reporting *ten* dead. And thirteen injured. What the hell is the matter with you?" He launched the accusation at Rabbit, who just sat there, unmoving, unblinking, un-fucking-concerned.

"Calm the feck down, Reilly," Cillian snapped. "You're scaring your woman."

The last comment held a mocking note, as if Cillian was well aware that Bailey wasn't afraid—she was livid.

Sean glanced at the doorway, where Bailey stood, as expressionless as Rabbit. Oh yeah, she was furious, all right. He could see it in the barely controlled trembling of her body.

She blamed him for this. It was pretty damn obvious, especially when she turned her head the moment he looked at her.

His attention moved back to Rabbit, and he shot the man an icy glare that could have frozen melting butter in a hot pan.

"I didn't sign up for this," Sean announced. "You hear me, old man? I didn't sign up for this, and I don't intend on sticking around to see whatever crazy bullshit you plan on doing next."

Rabbit's veiled eyes finally revealed a flicker of emotion. Either Sean was imagining it, or that peculiar gleam was actually *pride*, but he was too pissed off to deconstruct Rabbit's expression.

"I'm done with you, Eamon." Sean's incensed gaze shifted to Cillian. "I'm done with both of you."

"Reilly—" Cillian started.

He was done listening. His boots made furious tracks in the floor as he marched over to Bailey. "Come on, luv, we're outta here."

She followed him without a word, her black hair whipping behind her as she matched his breakneck pace down the hall.

Sean ignored every single man in the main room, most of whom looked stricken and shocked by the outcome of the morning's "scare" tactics. Sean waited for Bailey to collect her laptop and purse, then gripped her arm and ushered her out the door.

They'd just stepped onto the sidewalk when Cillian stalked out of the pub. "Reilly," he called sharply.

Sean's hand fell from Bailey's arm. "Wait in the car," he told her.

For once, she didn't argue with him.

"You need to walk your ass back inside," Cillian ordered.

He damn near snarled at the other man. "You don't get to give me orders, Kelly. Not after what you did."

A ghost of a smile appeared. "I did what was necessary. And if you were using that big brain of yours, you'd agree it needed to be done. Now, send your filly home and join us inside. It's time to discuss our next move."

Sean laughed. "I told you—I'm done. You can pass that message along to your boss, too. As of this moment, I'm through with being anyone's puppet."

Frigid blue eyes locked with his. "If you get in that car, Reilly . . . you *will* regret it. I'm giving you a chance, right here and now, to save yourself. And your brother. And that feisty filly of yours. Come back inside, and I'll forget all about this little tantrum. I won't even tell the boss about it." Cillian's smile held no trace of humor. "But if you leave, I can promise you this—a world of hurt will come crashing down on you."

Sean turned away from the other man. "Fuck you, Kelly." It wasn't the wittiest parting speech he'd ever come up with, but it was all he had at the moment.

Cillian's last words, however, sent a chill up Sean's spine as they softly floated toward his retreating back.

"All right, Reilly. Have it your way, then."

# Chapter 19

"So what now, Sean? What's your next big plan? Do we blow up a government building? A supermarket? Or maybe we should set some C-4 outside an orphanage—nobody's more innocent than a child, right?" Bailey couldn't contain the anger-laced sarcasm that poured out of her mouth. It spilled out like snake venom and did what she'd intended—paralyzed every muscle on Sean's face and flooded his eyes with anguish.

But when his broad chest shuddered as if she'd shot him, regret instantly spiraled down to her stomach. The feeling came too late, though, because Sean was already stumbling out of the room.

She stared at the empty doorway, choking on the guilt that crawled up her throat. Damn it. *Damn* it. She shouldn't have fired those cruel words. She knew it wasn't his fault that those people had died today. Deep down she really, really knew that, but the horror brought on by the successful terrorist attack had eclipsed the rational part of her brain.

If Sean hadn't supported Kelly's plan . . .

If he'd insisted on tipping off the police himself . . .

If . . .

*Screw the ifs,* a sharp voice reprimanded. *You don't operate on ifs.*

No, she didn't. She operated on *facts*. And the facts were—Sean had been *forced* to back Cillian up. He hadn't wanted to see those civilians die any more than she had, and blaming him for the explosion was a dick move on her part.

With a frustrated groan, she hurried to the corridor and threw open the bedroom door.

Then she froze.

Sean was . . . destroyed. Oh God. Her venom had destroyed him.

"I'm sorry," she whispered.

His head stayed buried in his hands, broad shoulders hunched over as he sat on the edge of the bed, trembling like a leaf.

Lord, he wasn't allowed to be vulnerable like this. She was better at controlling her emotions when he was an overbearing caveman who ordered her around with hard looks and even harder words.

"Sean . . . "

He didn't look up. She wasn't sure she wanted him to—she was too scared of what she might find on his face.

As her heart squeezed painfully against her ribs, Bailey approached the bed. She hesitated before finally sitting beside him.

He flinched when she touched his shoulder.

"Get the fuck out of here, Bailey." His deep voice was muffled against his hands.

"No." She skimmed her hand between his shoulder blades before moving it to the nape of his neck, gently stroking the soft hairs there. "Look at me."

"No. Get out."

Her fingers slid through his short hair and onto his

forehead, then lower, tentatively brushing over his cheek. The moisture she felt on her palm brought another tight clench to her heart.

"Look at me," she begged.

He did. Finally raising his head and letting her see his red-rimmed eyes, the shine of tears, the heart-wrenching pain.

"I stood by and let those people die," he said dully.

"That's not true." Remorse rippled through her as she scooted behind him and wrapped her arms around his broad torso. As his erratic heartbeat fluttered beneath her hands, she dropped her chin on his shoulder, her lips inches from his ear. "You didn't know what Rabbit and Kelly were planning to do. You thought they were going to call ahead."

He sagged back against her, the heat of his body warming her own. "I should have made the call myself. I shouldn't have trusted Rabbit to do it." A tortured noise flew out. "He *always* calls ahead, Bailey. I've seen the Dagger pull this same intimidation ploy dozens of times before, and they always make the fucking call! That bastard Kelly convinced him not to."

"So all those deaths are on Kelly," she said firmly. "Not you."

"That's bullshit and you know it. Hell, you *said* it."

The guilt returned. Hot and consuming, closing her throat right up. "I shouldn't have done that. I know it's not your fault. I just . . . needed someone to blame, I guess, and you were the most convenient target. But I'm sorry, Sean. I'm so damn sorry."

He twisted around to look at her. The tears in his eyes had dried, but the agony remained. "I almost got Morgan's men killed, too."

She shook her head. "They knew what they were getting into when they came to Dublin."

"Sullivan almost got blown up, Bailey."

"Nah." She smiled faintly. "The dude's invincible. And Liam called when we were driving back here, remember? He said Sully is all stitched up and resting comfortably."

Sean still didn't look appeased. If anything, his expression grew fiercer. "I have to kill him."

She tensed. "Kelly?"

"Him too. But I was talking about Flannery. If this is what he plans on turning the Irish Dagger into, then I'm damn well going to stop him."

"And Rabbit?"

"I don't know what to do about him yet." Sean sounded frazzled. "Something's going on with him. I don't know why he allowed that bomb to go off, but I could tell he wasn't happy about it. He's up to something. I need to find out what."

He was trembling in frustration again, but Bailey was there now, quick to calm him, stroking his hair until he went still. Her fingers were laced together against his chest, holding him tight to her body. He reached up and covered her hands with one of his own, his rough-skinned palm skimming over her knuckles.

"Kiss me," he whispered.

She gave a soft laugh. "You'll have to turn around for that. Unless . . . will any kind of kiss do?" She planted a fleeting kiss on the nape of his neck, and a shiver rolled through his body.

Before she could blink, he twisted around and pushed her onto her back, his mouth coming down on hers, rough and insistent. His tongue found hers and swirled around it, greedy, desperate strokes that left her gasping for air.

"I just . . . I . . ." He was breathing hard, looking like he was struggling for words. "I need you, Bailey."

She was already pushing her pants down her hips with one hand, using the other to undo his zipper.

"I'm here," she murmured. "Take me."

There was no foreplay, just deep penetration that sucked the breath from her lungs in a rapid whoosh. Sean's hips pistoned hard, driving his cock inside her in a frantic tempo that made the headboard smack against the wall, but Bailey knew he needed this. Needed to release the anger and adrenaline and guilt any way that he could, and she was more than happy to be the outlet.

Because hell, she needed it too. Those awful images on the news, the wreckage and the smoke and the frightened people. She wanted to shut out the gruesome sights, to lose herself in Sean's urgent kisses and wild groans.

He pounded into her body, each punishing thrust bringing her closer to the edge as she dug her nails into his back and held on for the ride. His skin was on fire, his thick cock stretching her pussy as he plunged as deep as he could go.

*"Bailey."*

He came with her name on his lips, and she groaned when she felt the sting of his teeth on her shoulder. The sharp bite was enough to trigger a blinding orgasm that made her convulse in spasms of pleasure. She clung to his sweat-soaked back, struggling to breathe, unable to move.

"I . . ." His breathing was anything but steady. "I don't deserve you."

As the aftershocks of her climax continued to tingle in her core, she slowly rolled their bodies so they were lying on their sides. Face-to-face, Sean still buried inside her.

"You give me too much credit," she whispered.

"You don't give yourself *enough* credit," he whispered back. "You're the most incredible woman I've ever known, Bailey."

Sean's cheek rested on the pillow and his green eyes were closed, giving her the opportunity to admire his face. His sharp cheekbones. Firm lips. A nose that for the most part was straight, except for the bump near the bridge. He must have broken it once or twice, most likely in a brawl he had no business being part of.

Bailey's curiosity got the best of her, prompting her to ask, "How many times have you broken your nose?"

One eye pried open, twinkling with amusement. "Not telling you."

"Why the hell not?"

"Because that means sharing details about my childhood and I've decided I'm not going to do that. If you don't share, I don't share."

She smiled despite herself. "So now you're blackmailing me into talking about my past?"

"Blackmailing implies that I have something you want to keep hidden. Not the case, luv, since you're already hiding." His voice went smug. "Well, I'm hiding now too."

"Ugh. You're so annoying sometimes. Just tell me how you broke your damned nose."

Sean cupped her right breast and tweaked the nipple. "Tit for tat."

She snickered.

"I mean it. You want to know about me, you have to tell me about you."

They were treading into a minefield here, but Bailey was confident she'd be able to navigate through it without setting off too many land mines.

"Fine," she agreed. "Tit for tat. How many times has your nose been broken, and why?"

"Twice. First time, I was sixteen, and it happened during a rugby game. Second time I was twenty-three . . ." He grinned. "Happened when I was beating the piss out of a guy who was flirting with Peggy."

"How'd he manage to break your nose if you were the one *beating the piss* out of him?"

"He didn't. Peggy broke it," he said sheepishly. "After she pulled me off his bleeding body."

Bailey burst out laughing. "I think I like this Peggy."

"Trust me—you don't. She was a real cocktease. And my cock wasn't the only one she was teasing."

He withdrew the cock in question from Bailey's core, and she immediately experienced a sense of loss. One muscular arm drew her closer so their faces were inches apart.

A sliver of concern sliced through her when she realized how vulnerable they were right now. Naked, tangled in each other's arms. Sean had banished her to the car earlier, but she'd still heard Kelly make his threats through the open window. What if he decided to act tonight? What if he sent someone to blow their heads off?

"Should we be worried about Kelly showing up?" she said in concern.

"He won't make a move tonight, luv."

"How are you so sure of that?"

"Because it's Dagger protocol. Twenty-four-hour cooling-off period, remember? They set off a bomb today, for Christ's sake. Rabbit won't let any of the men out of his sight until the heat dies down." Sean shrugged one shoulder. "Besides, Paige hacked into Kelly's phone and the satnav in his car, remember? She'll be able to see if he goes anywhere, and she'll give us the heads-up."

Bailey relaxed at the reminder. Although how Paige did half the things she did still amazed her. The woman really was a genius.

"My turn," Sean said as he stroked her lower back. "Why'd you sleep with Daniels?"

She hesitated.

"Hey," he chided. "You don't get to back out now."

A reluctant breath slid out. "Because I loved him."

Surprise flitted through his eyes. "Really? Shit. I was really hoping you'd say you did it to get ahead in the company or something."

Her skin prickled with insult. "Fuck you. You honestly think I'm the kind of woman who'd sleep her way to the top?"

"No, but I could've gotten on board with that. Because I honestly can't fathom how you could love a ninety-year-old man."

*"Forty-eight,"* she muttered.

"He was an old man, and you were practically a child," Sean shot back.

Bitterness rose in her throat. "Trust me, I wasn't a child even when I *was* a child." She turned the tables on him again. "Did you love Peggy?"

"Sure, when she wasn't doing my head in. Which was about, ah, ten percent of the time?"

"So she drove you nuts for ninety percent of the relationship?"

"Pretty much, yeah."

"Why didn't you end it, then?"

"Believe me, I tried." He laughed, deep and husky. "But every time I went to break up with her, she'd distract me with a blow job. And trust me, the girl sucked a mean cock."

Bailey narrowed her eyes. "Are you purposely trying to make me jealous?"

Sean looked genuinely startled. "No. Why would I—*aw*, shit. You got jealous."

"You wish," she lied.

Sean's laughter tickled her face. "You're totally jealous. You don't like the idea of another woman's mouth on my dick."

Bailey's cheeks hollowed in annoyance. "Isn't it your turn to ask a question?"

"Nice deflection. I'm gonna let it slide, though, because I do have another question." He raised a brow. "Why did you love Daniels? What was it about him?"

Discomfort rolled through her. "I don't know. He was just . . . he was good to me. At the beginning anyway. He recruited me, trained me, taught me how to defend myself. I thought I was a victim, but he showed me I was a survivor. He was my mentor. And then, when he showed a romantic interest in me, I . . . well, I welcomed it." She laughed cynically. "I guess it's the classic daddy-complex bullshit, huh?"

Sean's lips brushed the corner of her mouth. "We all have our issues, Bailey."

"Yeah, I guess."

"So what went wrong?"

"Isaac was a control freak," she admitted. "The two years when he was just my boss, he had no problem sending me out on assignments, no matter how dangerous they were. But once we became lovers, he got crazy possessive. It wasn't too bad for the first few years, but he grew more and more overprotective. He'd secretly send extra agents to watch me when I was on a job, which blew up in our faces a couple times. And he got controlling outside of work, too. Decided who I could be friends with, listened in on my calls—he *tapped* my cell phone."

Sean whistled softly. "Christ."

"It got to be too much to handle, so I ended it. Isaac didn't take the breakup well, and when it became obvious we couldn't work together anymore, I quit the agency and skipped town."

"Did he try to come after you?"

"Of course he did. It took him years to accept that it was over." She sighed. "Actually, he *still* hasn't accepted it. He's convinced that one of these days I'm going to come back to him."

Sean's fingers tightened on her hip, and his stubble abraded her chin as his warm lips found hers. "You're never going back to him, luv."

*Because you're mine.* The unspoken addendum echoed between them, and Bailey fought a rush of unease.

"Your turn again," she said abruptly. "I want to know something—was last year the first time you pulled a twin switch on a woman, or had you done it before?"

"A sexual twin switch? That was the first time. Every woman I've ever slept with has known exactly who was fucking her. But Ollie and I switched places all the time when we were younger."

Bailey tentatively touched his cheek, then gave in to temptation and stroked him. His whiskers scraped her fingertips, sending a shiver through her. He was so masculine. So addictive.

His eyes went heavy lidded as she explored his face, and she knew he was enjoying it. She rarely ever touched him outside a sexual context.

"Why would you switch places?" she asked curiously.

"Usually just to mess with people. Our parents, friends, teachers. If I forgot to study for a test, Ollie would take my place and ace it for me."

"Of course he did."

"Hey, I returned the favor," Sean protested. "Whenever he was too chickenshit to ask out a girl, I'd step in and save the day."

She had to smile. "It must be nice having a sibling. I always wanted a brother or sister."

"You're an only child?"

She nodded.

Sean's expression grew serious again. "Okay, my turn. What did your mother do for a living?"

"She . . ." Bailey swallowed as the memories resurfaced. "She was the US ambassador in Turkey until I was about ten. And then she got a post in Copenhagen. Before her diplomat days, she worked as the campaign manager for two presidents."

"Impressive." Sean paused. "And your father? What did he do?"

"He claimed to be a writer," she said bitterly, "but he never published a damn word, and I never saw him do anything other than drown his resentment in a bottle of scotch."

"He resented her, huh?"

"Big-time. He hated that her job was more important than his. He hated that she got all the attention when they went out socially. He hated that she was smarter than him, richer than him, *better* than him."

"So he hit her."

She nodded again.

His brow furrowed. "Why did she stay with him?"

"You'd have to ask her that." Bailey's voice cracked. "But whatever the reason was, she probably doesn't remember it now." She pressed her lips together to control the emotions trying to seep out. "I don't blame her, though. I never did. My father was a monster, Sean. He was so threatened by his own wife that he scrambled to find any bit of power over her. Mom was so strong in her professional life, but with him . . . she was weak. She was *scared.* It was awful to see her act one way in public and another in private."

"What happened to your father? Is he dead?"

"Yes."

"Did you . . . ?"

She gave a humorless laugh. "Nope. He found his way to the grave all by himself. That's what happens when you're a raging alcoholic—your body eventually punishes you for it."

Sean's voice went gruff. "I'm surprised *you* didn't punish him."

"He wasn't worth the effort it would've taken to kill him. And revenge isn't really my thing. I look forward, Sean, not back."

He fell silent, and she could see his astute brain working to absorb all the details she'd provided. Too many of them, damn it. Enough that all he had to do was open an Internet browser and he'd be able to fill in the rest of the blanks.

"I'll save you some time," Bailey muttered. "Because I know you're going to try to follow the trail of information I've given you."

"Bailey—"

"My mother's name is Vanessa. Vanessa Jones." Her belly went rigid. "Her husband's name was Terrance. And her daughter's name was . . . Tara."

Sean's breath hitched. "*Is* Tara," he said softly.

She rapidly shook her head. "No. That's not my name anymore. I stopped being Tara a long time ago."

His arms tightened around her. "I don't care what your name is, luv. And even though I'm glad you finally told me about your past, it never mattered to me, not in the way you thought. I don't need your name or your history or your bloody social security number to know who you are." Sean's mouth brushed hers in a fleeting kiss. "Because I've known you since the moment I laid eyes on you."

"Are you doing okay?" Liam set the remote control on the nightstand between the two beds in the hotel room.

His gaze strayed to Sullivan, who was lying on his side with his back turned. He knew his teammate wasn't asleep, though. Sully had been in visible pain all evening, groaning each time he moved his arm and turning green whenever he tried to stand up. Liam didn't think he had a concussion, but it was obvious the guy was suffering.

"I'm peachy, Boston," his friend muttered. "My arm's throbbing like a motherfucker, my head kills, and my stomach is churning from that sandwich you forced down my throat. Oh, and I've still got an adrenaline boner." A muffled groan echoed against the pillow. "Like I said, just peachy."

Normally the sarcasm would've made Liam grin, but the boner comment had filled the room with tension. It'd been easy not to think about the . . . *incident* . . . when he'd been playing nursemaid all day, because Sullivan was such a cranky patient, Liam wanted to slug him. As a result, Liam's mood today had alternated between annoyed and frustrated.

But now it was nearing midnight and Sullivan had dialed down on the Grumpy McGrumps routine, dozing on and off while Liam watched TV on the other twin bed.

*I've still got an adrenaline boner.*

Fuckin' hell.

But really, why should he expect Sullivan to censor himself? The man always blurted out whatever happened to be on his mind, no matter how inappropriate or absurd.

Besides, Sully was under the impression that Liam was over the . . . *incident*. He'd all but held up a neon sign on the flight from Portugal when he'd made that comment about putting the past behind him. And this whole time in Dublin, Sully had acted like everything was back to normal. He'd been Mr. Carefree and Impulsive, cracking jokes and talking shit and shamelessly flirting with Isabel.

So, yeah. Apparently Liam was the only one still thinking about it.

Fine, still *obsessing* about it.

"You'll feel better once the painkillers kick in," he said gruffly. "You took the two I gave you before my shower, right?"

"Nope. Didn't take the ones you gave me this afternoon either."

"Why the fuck not?"

"I don't like drugs, mate." Sullivan's voice was strained. "You know that."

Liam furrowed his brow as he searched his mind for a time when he'd seen Sullivan take a pill, which was . . . Shit, never. Not even an aspirin when he had a headache.

It hadn't occurred to Liam to ever ask him about it, but he did now. "Why is that anyway?"

"Just don't like 'em."

He waited, but the vague response was all he got. As silence fell over the room, Liam let out a breath, then reached over to shut off the light. "I'm turning in. It's been a long fuckin' day."

More silence.

Okay, then. Sullivan clearly wasn't in the mood to chat about—

"I had a bad experience with drugs before I enlisted, okay?"

The rough confession echoed in the darkness. Liam looked over, but Sullivan was still on his side, facing the wall. He'd pushed the blanket down to his waist, and Liam gulped when he made out his friend's long, sinewy back and the waistband of his white boxers.

He spoke through his suddenly dry mouth. "How bad?"

"I told you I lived on the streets for a while, right?"

"Yeah . . ." And before that, Liam knew Sully had lived at a church-run orphanage, followed by an array of shitty foster homes. But although his teammate often spoke about the homes, he rarely brought up his time on the streets of Sydney.

"Well, there're only two ways to eat when you're on the street, Boston. Beg, or deal. I chose the latter." There was a low chuckle. "This is so bloody ironic. I can't believe I'm fessing up to being a drug dealer in front of a former DEA agent."

"Hey, you know I don't judge. You did what you had to do to survive."

"Trust me—I would've had a better chance at survival if I just *sold* the shit. But I smoked it too."

"Weed?"

"Yeah, and I popped a shit ton of oxy. And then when my supplier—Hartley—added cocaine to his menu, I sampled that too. I was a raging coke addict by the time I was sixteen. I never stuck any needles in my body, though, thank God. But I know that if Hartley had been dealing in H, I totally would've hit that shit. I had no willpower back then, and I was impulsive as fuck. Didn't think about the future." Sully released a heavy breath. "I never expected to live past the age of eighteen, if I'm being honest."

"So what happened?"

"I got busted. But instead of getting hauled off to juvie, I got a slap on the wrist, and one of the cops who arrested me decided to make me his new project. He was a real do-gooder type. Brought me home, fed me, helped me get my high school diploma."

"That's really going out of his way for a kid he didn't know."

Even though Sully couldn't see his narrowed eyes, his friend picked up on the wariness in his tone.

"He didn't bugger me, if that's what you're thinking. Tom was as straight as they came. His wife and son died in a car accident a few years before he took me in, and I guess I was the replacement for his kid. But I'm not going to judge his motives. He helped me clean up my act, and he's the one who encouraged me to join the army."

"Is he still around?"

"Nah. Died about ten years ago."

"I'm sorry."

"Don't be. People die. Life goes on." There was a rustling sound. "Night, Boston."

He noticed that Sullivan had kicked off the rest of the comforter, which was now tangled at his feet. Liam had shared a room with Sully enough times to know that the guy never slept with a blanket. Claimed his body turned into a furnace when he slept.

Liam closed his eyes, trying to block out the sound of his friend's uneven breathing, but it was impossible to fall asleep when he knew Sully was awake and in pain. For the next hour, he lay on his back and listened to Sully toss and turn restlessly. Except every time the guy turned, he hissed in pain, as if remembering he couldn't lie on his injured arm.

Christ. Why didn't the stubborn ass just take the painkillers? They'd knock him right out.

*Not the only thing that'll knock him out.*

Liam's chest tightened as the thought slid into his head. It was true, though. He knew of one other thing that always made Sully pass out immediately afterward.

*Go to sleep,* a sharp voice commanded.

Yeah, he was thinking crazy thoughts right now. He squeezed his eyes shut, but they reluctantly flew open when another agitated groan sliced through the room.

Damn it. How the hell was he supposed to sleep when his best friend was suffering five feet away?

Liam got up as if possessed. No, got up because he *was* possessed. There was no other explanation for why he was walking toward Sullivan's bed. Why his chin had lifted in determination and his knees were colliding with the side of the mattress, which dipped under his weight as he stretched out next to Sully.

His teammate's shoulders stiffened. "What are you doing, mate?" Wary, alarmed.

Liam swallowed. Didn't help, though—his throat was still clamped shut.

He eased his body behind Sullivan's, making sure to keep his groin several inches from the other man's ass. Then he inhaled slowly and snaked his arm underneath Sullivan's, pressing his palm against the man's stomach.

A breath hissed out. "Liam . . ."

"Just . . . just shut up." His voice was barely a whisper, and thick with gravel. "It'll help you sleep."

His heart had never pounded so hard as his hand drifted over his friend's tight six-pack, inching lower, trembling as he reached the elastic of Sully's boxers. His mouth had turned to sawdust. His lungs had stopped working. But his fingers worked just fine, dipping beneath Sully's waistband, sliding lower, seeking.

Sullivan shuddered when Liam's fist enclosed his shaft.

Jesus.

He hadn't expected his friend to be so . . . big. Nearly the width of Liam's wrist. And hard. Sullivan was impossibly hard.

Liam's pulse went off-kilter as that monster hard-on throbbed in his hand, the heat of it searing his fingertips.

Holy shit, he couldn't breathe.

"Liam . . ." An unmistakable note of warning.

He ignored it. Gave a slow stroke that summoned a groan from his friend's lips.

And then Sully thrust into his hand.

Sweet Jesus.

A bead of moisture dampened the pad of Liam's

thumb as he swept it over Sully's engorged head. He used it to get his friend slick, making it easier to glide his fist along the man's length.

Christ almighty. He couldn't believe what he was doing. That Sullivan was *letting* him do it. And his own dick was so hard he felt like he was about to explode. Forbidden images flashed in his mind, all the things he could do with his body positioned behind Sullivan's like this. But . . . God. No. This wasn't about him. Or at least he hadn't thought it was. But he was wrong. So fuckin' wrong.

When Sullivan moaned, the husky sound sent a bolt of heat to Liam's groin.

His friend's hips moved faster.

Liam tightened his grip.

The room was quiet save for Sully's low groans. Their heavy breathing. The wet suction of Liam's hand and the soft squeak of the mattress as he worked his friend's cock.

"More," Sully rasped. "Faster."

Liam quickened the pace, pumping furiously, squeezing hard, until Sully's spine arched and he went still in his hand.

Sullivan's release coated Liam's fingers. He pumped his friend through it with long, lazy strokes, stopping only when Sully groaned and tried to ease away.

Liam felt weak and achy as he released his friend. He twisted toward the end table, reaching for the box of tissues there, his hand shaking so badly it took three tries before he managed to grab it.

His heart thudded as he wiped away the evidence of . . . of the biggest mistake he'd ever made.

"Uh . . . I . . ." Sullivan sounded sated. Confused. But his body had relaxed and his breathing had steadied, and when he spoke again, his voice was drowsy as hell. "Thanks, mate."

And then he fell asleep.

Liam could barely get up without keeling over, but somehow he made it back to his own bed and collapsed on top of it. His cock was hard. Painfully hard, but he was too stunned to dwell on that right now.

In the other bed, Sullivan was dead to the world, oblivious to the uncontrollable waves of panic spiraling through Liam's body.

He curled his fists into the sheets and stared up at the ceiling, his heart beating so fast he was surprised it didn't burst out of his chest.

Jesus Christ.

What the *hell* had he done?

# Chapter 20

"No way. You're not going." Bailey's tone was as steely as the glint in her eyes.

After the incredible night they'd had, Sean hadn't expected them to go right back to arguing in the morning. But then again, nothing was ever easy with him and Bailey.

They'd woken up fifteen minutes ago to find a text from Rabbit on Sean's phone. The man was requesting an audience. Though *requesting* probably wasn't the best way to describe it. He'd summoned Sean, pure and simple, and despite Bailey's more than obvious thoughts on the matter, Sean had every intention of going.

"I have to," he replied as he rinsed his coffee cup in the sink. "If we want to make a move against Flannery, we need to know where Rabbit's head is at."

"Then why can't I go with you?"

"Because he asked me to come alone."

Not only that, but Rabbit wanted to meet at a bar near the Docklands, when the man never conducted business outside his own establishment. If Rabbit was picking a place off the grid, that meant he had something of dire importance to discuss.

A frown touched Bailey's lips. "I don't like this."

"It'll be fine," he assured her. "D and Isabel will be watching me the whole time in case he tries to pull something."

Except now it was Sean's turn to frown. Oliver and Ash had left that morning on another fact-finding mission, and with Sullivan still on the bench and Liam refusing to leave his side, Bailey would be completely unprotected.

"Shit. You know what? D will back me up alone. I want Isabel to come here and stay with you."

"No way," she said again. "You need the assist more than I do."

He hesitated.

"I'm serious," she insisted. "I want D and Isabel with you. I'll be fine here by myself. This place is wired with motion sensors, and there's an entire armory in that back closet."

Sean relented with a sigh. "All right. But I want you to stay put. And when I get back, we'll figure out what to do about Flannery."

"Sounds good."

He moved away from the sink and was surprised when she blocked his path to the door, leaning on her tiptoes to kiss him. It was the first time Bailey had ever initiated a kiss, and damned if his heart didn't skip like a cartoon princess prancing through a forest.

He was so fucking whipped.

Sean couldn't resist slipping her some tongue, but just as the kiss got hot and heavy, Bailey laughed and pulled away.

"Go," she said firmly. "I want this over with as fast as possible."

Christ, so did he.

On the entire drive over to the waterfront, Sean

thought about all the crap they still needed to deal with. Like Flannery, who probably wouldn't be happy that Sean had left the Dagger again. And Cillian, who *certainly* wasn't happy and had already threatened to make him regret it. And then there was Rabbit, who was . . . hell, who knew what that man was up to.

And to top it all off, Sean had no idea if the woman he was head over heels in love with felt the same way about him.

Yup, he loved Bailey.

The realization hadn't hit him out of left field. It wasn't like *ding-ding-ding, you love the woman*. Something about her had captivated him from the start. Not just her looks, but her intelligence, her sarcasm, her fire. He'd always known his feelings for Bailey ran deep, but after last night, he'd finally allowed himself to give them a label—*love*.

He just wished he knew what she felt for *him*. She was definitely warming up to him. She'd told him about her family and her ex-lover. She'd spent the whole night in his arms. She'd kissed him just now. But he still had no clue where her head was at.

Twenty minutes later, he parked in the gravel lot outside the waterfront bar and turned on his earpiece.

"Just got here," he murmured. "Heading inside now."

Isabel's voice filled the feed. "I see you. D's already in position."

Yes, D certainly was. Sean spotted the man's close-cropped head the moment he entered the bar.

The huge merc sat at the splintered wooden counter, nursing a bottle of Stella, but neither D nor Sean gave any indication that they knew each other. Sean strode past the tattooed soldier and headed for the table in the corner, where Rabbit was waiting for him.

The Irish Dagger leader wasn't looking so good today.

His beard was more unkempt than usual, and there was a greenish tinge to his face, though maybe that was because of the neon green-and-blue sign glowing on the wall behind him.

"I wasn't sure you'd come," Rabbit remarked as Sean slid in the seat across from him.

"I told you I would." He couldn't stop the sardonic jab that followed. "Unlike some people, I happen to be a man of my word."

Rabbit heard the unspoken accusation loud and clear, because a crease appeared in his forehead. "It had to be done, lad."

"Why? Because Kelly said so?" The sarcasm continued to pour out. "Oh right, I forgot. Because it's time for us to enter the *twenty-first century*."

"No." Rabbit's tone was calm. "Because I needed to see how you'd react."

Sean faltered. "What the fuck is that supposed to mean?"

Rabbit wrapped his hands around his coffee cup. Steam rose from the rim and dampened his upper lip as he raised the cup to his lips. He took a hasty sip, and it became glaringly obvious that he wasn't well. His hands were visibly shaking, and his face *was* green.

"What the hell is the matter with you?" The question popped out before Rabbit could even address the first one.

But the man answered neither.

"I loved your father."

Sean shook his head in frustration. "No, we're not talking about my father right now. I don't want to hear about how much you loved him and how loyal he was and all that fucking bullshit. Why am I here, Rabbit?"

"Colin *is* the reason you're here. Your father was the best friend I ever had, Seansy. I could tell him anything, trusted him with my life. I always thought we'd grow up to be old men together." He shrugged. "Either that, or I'd die and he'd take over for me." Rabbit looked sad now. "I never expected him to die first."

Sean gritted his teeth. "Why. Am. I. Here."

"Your father can't take over the Dagger, Seansy, but *you* can."

He wasn't thrown for a loop often, but Christ, he hadn't expected *that*.

"Why would I do that?" Sean said in disbelief. "And why would you even want me to?"

Rabbit watched Sean over the rim of his cup as he took another sip. He swallowed, then set down the coffee.

"I have cancer."

Wait—*what*?

The shock caused Sean's jaw to hit the floor. He wondered if this was a joke. A ploy he didn't understand.

But Rabbit's brown eyes conveyed nothing but sorrow and sincerity. "I found out three months ago." The man tapped his chest, laughing harshly. "Lung cancer. Lovely, huh? Never smoked a day in my life."

Sean offered a wry smile. "I saw you puffing on your share of cigars back in the day, old man."

"Ya, a few, but I kicked that habit a long time ago."

When Rabbit exhaled, Sean didn't miss the wheeze in his breathing. Shit, maybe the man really was sick. It *would* account for the unexplained absences Sean had noticed since he'd rejoined the group.

"The doctors gave me six months."

Sean looked over in alarm. "That's it? What about chemo? Radiation?"

"Cancer's too far gone. Surgery's not an option either. Short of cutting out half my chest, the docs can't save me. I'm dying, Seansy."

Sean couldn't fight the sympathy that flooded his gut. Despite all the laws he'd broken and the people he'd killed, Eamon O'Hare had still been a major presence in Sean's life. The man had raised him alongside Sean's father.

"So . . . what, you want me to step up and take your place?" Sean said skeptically.

"Yes." Rabbit let out another breath, this one lined with exhaustion. "Kelly's not cut out for the job. I've been watching him for years, waiting for him to convince me that he's up to the task, but he's too ambitious, too prone to violence."

Sean snorted. "You want to talk about men who're prone to violence? Your group got its nickname because you *gut* people, Eamon."

"Always for the cause," Rabbit said, vehement. "I never killed innocents."

"You killed ten yesterday," Sean replied in a biting tone.

"It was a sacrifice that had to be made. I needed to see what you would do afterward."

Anger shot up his spine. "Jesus Christ. You're saying it was some kind of sick test?"

"Yes."

"Did you know all along that you wouldn't call ahead?"

"Yes. Cillian insisted on it." Rabbit leaned forward in his chair. "And that's when I knew for sure that Kelly isn't the man I want to take my place. He doesn't understand the Dagger. Doesn't appreciate our roots or respect the code we live by. But you do." Rabbit's intense gaze locked on Sean's face. "You endorsed the attack when you thought it would follow the rules. And when it didn't, you walked out. That tells me you know what's right."

Lord, this was priceless. Rabbit preaching about wrong and right after all the bloodshed he'd caused over the years.

"What if I'd stayed?" Sean challenged. "What would that have told you?"

"That you weren't the man I thought you were, the man your father was. But you didn't stay. You told me to shove it where the sun don't shine, then walked out the door." Pride filled Rabbit's eyes, shining as bright as the neon sign over his head. "You're the only man who can follow in my footsteps, Seansy. I need to know that when I die, I'm leaving my legacy to someone who deserves it. Someone who understands it."

Bloody hell. This meeting was not going at all like he'd expected.

"I know I let you down yesterday," Rabbit said gruffly. "I let *myself* down, and I'll be going to hell for it, don't you worry. But something good came out of yesterday's destruction. It confirmed my faith in you, showed me who the *true* leader of the Irish Dagger is. And it's not Cillian." The man raked a shaky hand through his gray beard. "So what do you say, Seansy? Will you take over the Dagger?"

*Hell, no* was the first response that came to mind.

But Sean knew he had to play it smart. Flannery wasn't going to let him get away with disobeying Cillian yesterday. Which meant that Flannery or Kelly or both would be coming after him. Which meant he might need an ally.

An ally like Rabbit.

"I . . ." Sean dragged a hand over his scalp. "I'd have to think about it."

"You will?"

"Why do you look so surprised? Isn't that what you wanted?"

A slight smile lifted the other man's lips. "Yes, but I thought you'd turn me down. I was prepared to watch you walk out that door."

"Believe me—I'm tempted." The ensuing lie came out smoothly. "But if my father were alive, he'd turn me over his knee if I walked out right now. He'd want me to say yes."

"Is that what you're doing, then? Saying yes?"

"No, I'm saying Da would have wanted me to. I still need to think on it." He sighed. "It's a dangerous life, Eamon. I've got my woman to think about, you know? Keeping her safe is my first priority."

Rabbit's eyes grew pained, and Sean knew he was thinking about his sister, yet another casualty of the cause.

"That's the reason I never got married," Rabbit confessed. "I didn't want the dark parts of my life to touch any woman I loved. But your lass is strong, Seansy. She's got fire beneath the surface. She can help you lead."

Sean thought about him and Bailey leading a terrorist organization together and bit back a laugh.

But he had to tread carefully.

"I'll need to talk it over with Bailey." He slanted his head, staring at his old mentor. "Is there anything else?"

"No. I've said everything I needed to say."

On a whim, Sean reached across the table and squeezed the older man's hand. It was cold to the touch and frailer than he'd expected. He'd been so focused on Flannery and keeping everyone he loved safe that he'd missed the signs. Eamon O'Hare was no longer the powerful force he once was. He was a dead man walking.

The depressing realization caused a pang of pity to tug on Sean's insides. Rabbit would die alone. No wife, no kids, nothing to leave behind except the fruitless cause he'd devoted his entire life to.

Sean never wanted that to happen to him. Christ. He would *never* follow that path.

"I'll be in touch," he said as he stood up.

Rabbit nodded. "Don't take too long."

*Because there isn't much time left* was the silent implication, and Sean's pity deepened, joined by a rush of sadness he hadn't expected to feel.

Swallowing, he left Rabbit at the table and forced himself not to look back.

Bailey was going to strangle every member of her mother's nursing staff. She really, truly would. She'd been arguing on the phone with Dr. Levinson for the past twenty minutes, but the stubborn old man still refused to approve the transfer unless Bailey signed the paperwork in person.

And to make matters worse, Daniels had texted her five times since Sean had left, giving her "updates" about his agents' movements. She was glad the spooks were watching the facility, but goddamn it, she didn't need to know every time one of them took a leak.

It was clear what Daniels was doing. The damn man was trying to weasel his way into her life again.

But she wouldn't let him. That chapter of her life was over. It had ended a long time ago, and it was time for Isaac to accept that. She would *make* him accept it.

Bailey opened her contacts list and scrolled until she reached Daniels's number, but just as she was about to dial, the security monitors across the room buzzed.

Her spine stiffened. Someone had triggered the motion detector in the lobby.

She hurried over to the screens but caught only a blur of black before the monitor revealed nothing but an empty lobby. Whoever had set off the sensor was now inside.

That didn't necessarily mean she had to worry, though. Sean's flat wasn't the only apartment in the building. It could have just been one of the other residents coming home.

Or not. Footsteps suddenly sounded in the hallway. More than one set of them. And they stopped right behind the door to Sean's flat.

Shit. She had visitors.

Her heart rate stayed steady as she shifted her gaze to another monitor. The camera over the front door provided a clear view of her uninvited guests.

Cillian Kelly. And two men whose faces she didn't recognize, which told her he wasn't traveling with Rabbit's entourage. This was a Flannery matter, then.

She flinched when a heavy knock sounded on the door.

"Open the door, luv," Cillian called from the hallway.

Yeah, right.

She swiped her gun from the desk and released the safety, palming the weapon as she examined the other security screen, which showed the alley at the bottom of the fire escape. Deserted. Cillian hadn't posted a guard out there.

Bailey's boots traveled silently on the floor as she headed for the window. She did a quick survey of the room, checking to see if she was leaving anything important behind, but she had her gun and her phone, and everything else was inconsequential. Sean had told her that if someone tried accessing any of his computers, the hard drives deleted themselves, and she knew he didn't keep any important files in this flat.

She started to slide the window up, but Cillian's voice stopped her cold.

"I suggest you let me in, sweetness . . . unless you want my sniper to put a bullet in your mother's head."

Panic rose inside her, but she forced herself to tamp it down.

No. He was lying. Daniels's last update hadn't mentioned any damn snipers. Bailey knew Flannery's thug was still staked out across the street from the nursing home, but all he'd done these past few days was watch and wait.

But . . . Daniels's update was also two hours old. Flannery could have dispatched more men during that time. The man had goons on speed dial, for God's sake.

Bailey's fingers trembled as she quickly typed a text to Daniels.

Possible sniper at Vanessa's facility. Please confirm.

"You've got thirty seconds to open this door, sweetness. Otherwise I make the call."

Kelly's voice contained a joyful lilt, as if the bastard *wanted* to order her mother's death. Well, hell, he probably did. Bailey suspected the man got his rocks off on tormenting people.

She didn't move. Didn't speak. She simply stared at her phone, pleading for Daniels to text her back. But he didn't.

"Twenty seconds," Cillian said in a singsong voice.

*Text me back, you son of a bitch!*

The screen remained blank.

God, she was wasting time. She should be climbing down the fire escape right now and getting the hell out of here. She had a car waiting on the next block, a bag of gear stashed in the alley. She'd prepared for this exact threat, but she couldn't do a damn thing until she knew if Kelly was bluffing.

"Ten seconds . . ."

*Text. Me. Back.*

"Five seconds."

Bailey's phone vibrated in her hand, and her heart sank to the pit of her stomach as she read Daniels's response:

Sniper confirmed. Take action?

She didn't reply.

She was already running to answer the door.

# Chapter 21

Sean slid into the driver's seat of the car and released the massive sigh he'd been holding. Shit. The meeting with Rabbit hadn't gone as planned. Instead of helping him figure out his next move, it had only complicated things further.

Or . . . maybe it hadn't.

Rabbit was dying. His men would need a new leader, and if Sean turned down the job, Rabbit would have no choice but to hand the reins over to Cillian. Who else was going to take over? Quinn? The man was too old, and he lacked the ruthlessness required to lead. O'Neill? Doherty? Doyle? None of them were leadership material.

How fucking ironic was that? Flannery was about to get what he wanted, and with no help from Sean. His own enemy was handing him the organization he'd been coveting. On a silver fucking platter. All Sean had to do was tell Flannery that Rabbit was going to kick the bucket in three months, the man would bide his time, and then Kelly would be the new leader of the Irish Dagger.

Except . . . Christ, Sean didn't think he could stomach it. Cillian had *let* that car bomb go off, damn it. He'd happily sat by with a pint of Guinness while all those people had been killed.

If Cillian Kelly took over the organization, who knew how many more innocent people would die.

Sean pressed his lips together, indecision twisting his stomach. He could rid himself of Flannery with one phone call, but that meant giving Cillian the opportunity to inflict terror on the country. The alternative was to go back to the original plan—eliminating Flannery and Kelly. Permanently. But that put his own life at risk, not to mention the lives of Bailey and Ollie and the others.

Fuck, he had to think it through. His whole life had been a string of rash decisions and impulsive acts, but he couldn't wing it this time.

He touched his earpiece to tell Isabel and D to meet him at the flat, but his phone rang before he could. When he checked the screen and saw Paige's number, he instantly answered the call.

"Hey, luv. Everything okay?"

"I'm not sure," she said slowly.

"What the hell does that mean?"

"I'm still tracking Kelly's phone, and . . ." Concern rippled through the line. "Kelly left O'Hare's about twenty minutes ago."

"All right. Where did he go?"

"Rathmines."

Sean's veins turned to ice. "Are you sure?"

"Yes. And the GPS in his car shows the same thing." She paused. "Of course, that doesn't mean Kelly is the one at the flat. Someone else could have his phone and be driving his car—"

"It's him," Sean said flatly. "Thanks for the heads-up. Call me if he goes anywhere else."

He hung up and turned the key in the ignition as a sense of urgency overtook him.

Cillian was at the flat.

*Bailey* was at the flat.

Alone, damn it. He'd left her *alone*.

"D," he blurted into the comm, "get your ass to the Rathmines flat. You too, Isabel." The worry spiraling through his chest flew into his throat, hoarsening his voice. "Bailey's in trouble."

Bailey threw open the front door just as Cillian Kelly was pulling a cell phone from his jacket pocket. He looked startled to see her, then broke out in a pleased smile. "Just in time. I really didn't want to have to kill that poor demented mother of yours."

"What do you want?" she said coldly.

"Can I come in?"

Her gaze rested on the two men on either side of him. They were dressed in all black, one lean, one stocky, both armed.

"Do I have a choice?"

"No." Cillian brushed past her, gesturing for his men to follow.

One of the thugs closed the door and flicked the dead bolt, then turned around and grinned at Bailey. He was one ugly bastard. Crooked teeth and gaunt features, his dark eyes set so deep in his face he resembled a ghoul from a horror movie.

Cillian propped himself on the arm of the couch, a silenced pistol held loosely in his hand. "We have a problem," he announced.

Bailey lifted an eyebrow. "Do we?"

"Your boyfriend has decided he doesn't want to do his job anymore." Cillian shrugged. "My boss isn't happy about it. *I'm* not happy about it."

She offered a shrug of her own. "Sorry to hear it. But if you came here to force me to convince Sean to change his mind, you wasted a trip. He doesn't listen to a word I say."

"Oh no, luv, I came here to change his mind all by my lonesome."

"Well, as you can see, Sean's not here. Come back later."

A sinister smile twisted his lips. "Trust me—Reilly will get the message whether he's here or not. I would've preferred he watch, but no worries. He'll get to see the final results."

Bailey tensed when the two thugs each took a step toward her. Shit.

Cillian chuckled when he saw her face. "Here's how it's gonna go, sweetness. I want you to fight. Gets me harder when they fight. Scream too, if you want."

Her fingers tightened around her weapon. She could shoot him. She could shoot all of them. Now, before any of them got their filthy hands on her.

But Cillian anticipated the move, because he whipped up his phone and turned the screen toward her. "Don't get any crazy ideas. The call's already been made."

Her pulse sped when she noticed the seconds ticking away on the display. The line was open, and whoever was on the other end of it could hear every word they were saying.

"I haven't given the order yet," Cillian added, his smile widening. "But if you think your CIA friends are gonna save the day, think again. They've been taken care of." He brought his mouth to the phone speaker. "Isn't that right, Devon?"

"Yes, boss," came a cheerful male reply. "Three dead spooks and a bottle o' rum."

As Cillian and his thugs laughed at the macabre joke, Bailey choked down a rush of horror.

Shit. Fucking *shit*. Flannery's people had taken out

Daniels's agents? She swiped her finger over her phone display in a discreet attempt to contact Isaac, but the goon with the crooked teeth suddenly yanked the cell out of her hand.

"You won't be needing that, baby." His voice was as ugly as his face. Raspy and nasally, rippling with menace. "I like my girls to pay attention to me when my dick is inside them."

"As you can see," Cillian said, "I've got all my bases covered—that's an American term you can understand, right? Bloody baseball—what a pointless sport *that* is. But anyway . . . if you try to run, I'll order my man to pull the trigger and you can say bye-bye to your mum. If you kill me, my man will hear it"—he waved the phone in the air again—"and you can say bye-bye to your mum. Have I made myself clear?"

"Crystal," she said tightly.

"Good. So now why don't you hand over that weapon to Leary? You know, just to eliminate any temptation of using it."

Reluctance lodged in her throat, but she didn't have much of a choice. Her mind was racing, synapses firing rapidly as she tried to come up with a plan. A solution. A way out.

These men weren't going to touch her. She'd die before she let them.

But her mother . . . God, her mother. Bailey pictured Vanessa in the suite she'd paid an arm and a leg for. She pictured her mother's gray eyes, her expression, which ranged from vacant to confused. Or tormented on the rare occasion she was lucid.

Cillian was on the phone with a man who could make those eyes go lifeless.

Kelly had to stay alive, then. She would *keep* him alive, for her mother's sake. But these other two . . . Her gaze locked with the dark, lust-filled eyes of Crooked Teeth, and every muscle in her body vibrated with rage.

The second man—Leary—took the gun that Bailey willingly handed to him and tossed it to Cillian. Then Leary and Crooked Teeth faced their boss, waiting for instructions.

"We'll start off nice and easy," he said with a decisive nod. "Leary, why don't you take our beautiful Bailey's clothes off? Except for the panties—leave those on. I want to cut them off her myself."

Bailey drew a calming breath. It was fine. She was fine. She'd dealt with men like these before. Sick men, violent men. Starting with her own father and ending with all the sadistic perverts she'd killed over the years.

It was just a matter of patience. Not revealing the upper hand too fast. Waiting until the right time to make a move.

Leary's hazel eyes burned with excitement as he took a step toward her. He wasn't a tall man. Only a few inches taller than her, and lanky rather than bulky. She could take him. Easily.

Bony hands reached for the hem of her shirt.

She waited.

He bunched the fabric between his fingers, licking his lips as he drew the shirt up her belly and exposed her bare breasts.

"Ah, look at that." His brogue deepened. "I'm gonna squeeze the hell out of these tits, baby. I'm gonna suck 'em and bite 'em and—"

She struck like a rattlesnake, spinning him around and wrapping one arm around his scrawny neck. Her free hand landed on his carotid with a precise karate chop, hitting the pressure point that made his entire body go limp. Before the unconscious man could hit the floor,

Bailey's arm twisted hard, snapping his neck with a sickly crack.

As Leary's lifeless body slammed into the hardwood with a thud, she turned to Kelly and smiled. "Who's next?"

Irritation flared in his ice blue eyes. "What the feck did you do that for?"

Crooked Teeth wasn't as composed. "You little *bitch*! You killed Frankie!"

He tackled her like a linebacker, slamming her into the wall behind her, and Bailey gasped as the wind was knocked out of her. Her fist instinctively shot out and connected with Crooked Teeth's jaw. He roared as his head was thrown back, then circled her neck with both hands and squeezed her windpipe.

"Let her go."

Kelly's sharp command boomed in the air, and suddenly Bailey could breathe again. Crooked Teeth staggered backward, breathing hard. His dark eyes glared bloody murder at her before shifting to his boss.

"She killed Frankie! We need to *gut* this stupid bitch!"

"No, we need to send a message to her boyfriend," Cillian replied evenly. "So calm the feck down, you sniveling asshole." His eyes narrowed at Bailey. "You broke the rules."

"You said I wasn't allowed to kill you. You didn't say anything about *him*." She pointed to the dead man on the floor. "He was fair game."

Either she was imagining it, or Cillian actually looked impressed, but his features hardened in the blink of an eye. "You'd make a great barrister, luv. But there're no more loopholes for you to exploit." He cocked his head at Crooked Teeth. "This one stays alive. No, this one stays *conscious*."

Shit, there went the karate-chop option.

A queasy sensation churned in her belly as she realized that left her with *no* options. If she took out Crooked Teeth, her mother would die. If she took out Kelly, her mother would die.

Oh God. Was she really going to stand by and let these men rape her?

No. *No*. There *had* to be another option. A way to keep her mother safe without sacrificing her body.

"Now, let's get back to the good stuff," Cillian said with a smile.

She was repulsed to find that he had an erection. The sight of the thick bulge poking against his fly brought bile to her throat. And Crooked Teeth was also hard. Hard and angry and downright gloating as he advanced on her.

Fear jolted through her as he ripped off her shirt and shoved her against the wall again. Fuck. She had to do something. Had to fight back. But no, Cillian *wanted* her to fight. He wanted her to scream and struggle and claw at Crooked Teeth's eyes. Sean had told her the violence excited him.

And God, now wasn't the time to be thinking about Sean and what he'd do when he found out that Cillian—

A thigh jammed between her legs, and Crooked Teeth grunted in pleasure as he ground his pelvis into her, rotating his hips, rubbing his erection against her mound.

"Oh yeah, baby, I can't wait to be inside you," he rasped.

Bailey went motionless. She met Cillian's gaze over Crooked Teeth's shoulder as the man rutted like a dog in heat.

"Fight him," Cillian ordered.

She didn't answer. Her mind was working overtime, frantically seeking a way out.

Crooked Teeth cupped one of her breasts, squeezing hard enough to make her gasp. His other hand traveled down her belly to her waistband, and her breath hissed out when he yanked her leggings down her hips.

She was naked now. Naked and completely out of options.

"Oooh-boy!" he crowed. "Boss, she's not wearing any panties. 'Fraid you can't cut 'em off her. But she's got the sweetest little pussy. Bet it's tight, too. Fuck, lemme find out."

The door flew open and Sean burst into the room.

# Chapter 22

Bailey's eyes locked with Sean's. Just for a split second. A heartbeat. Then his gaze landed on the male hand on her breast.

And all hell broke loose.

Sean lunged at the man and tackled him to the ground, his fists crashing down on the thug's face as red-hot fury flashed in his eyes. Bailey whipped her pants back up and stumbled forward to look for her shirt, only to halt in her tracks when Cillian raised his gun in her direction.

"Don't move, sweetness."

Sean's back stiffened, as if he'd just realized there was more than one threat to contend with. His heavy fist delivered a knock-out blow to Crooked Teeth, whose body went limp, head lolling to the side as blood streamed from his nostrils.

Sean flew to his feet like a gymnast, unconcerned by the gun pointed at him as he charged toward Kelly. "You gonna shoot me?" he spat out. "Go right ahead, you son of a bitch. Because the only way you're getting out of here alive is if you shoot me fucking dead."

Bailey experienced a shiver of fear. She'd never seen

Sean so enraged. He was seething, panting, practically foaming at the mouth. He was like a feral animal. Raw hatred and blind rage glittered in his green eyes, menace rolling off his body in hot, palpable waves.

Cillian cocked the weapon but didn't pull the trigger. Amusement flickered through his expression as he studied Sean's flushed face.

When Sean moved to attack, Bailey grabbed the sleeve of his black button-down, yanking him backward.

"No," she blurted out. "You can't touch him."

His head swiveled toward her in shock. "Are you fucking *crazy*? He—"

"He's on the phone with a sniper who's got a rifle trained on my mother's head," she interrupted. Softly, timidly, pleading at him with her eyes to stand down.

His chest heaved as he drew in ragged breaths. She could see him fighting an internal battle, struggling to gather the pieces of his broken restraint.

It was several seconds before his breathing changed. Steadied. He stared at the dead man near the wall, then the unconscious man at his feet, then looked at Cillian with fiery contempt that incinerated the air.

"I will kill you for this." Sean spoke in a calm, measured tone that sent a chill racing up Bailey's spine.

Cillian chuckled. "Maybe, but it won't be tonight. Unless you want your little bird's mother to die too. *Is* that what you want?" He held up his phone. "Because I can certainly accommodate you." When Sean didn't answer, another chuckle slid out. "That's what I thought."

Bailey kept a close eye on Sean, ready to step in if he tried to make another move. The last thing she wanted was to allow Cillian to walk out of here. She'd rather walk him out herself—with his head on a spike. But he hadn't left them much of a choice. Daniels's agents were dead, and her mother was unprotected.

Which meant that at the moment, Cillian was calling the shots.

"Well," he said cheerfully. "I've had a lot of fun, but it's time for me to go." He smiled at Sean. "I expect to see you at the pub tonight."

From the corner of her eye, Bailey saw a tic twitch in Sean's jaw.

"You'll be there, won't you, Reilly?" Cillian phrased it as a question, but they all knew what it really was—a threat.

"Yes," Sean ground out.

"Good boy."

With his phone in one hand and his gun in the other, Cillian strode forward. He tipped his head at Leary's body, then glanced at Bailey. "I'll leave this one here for you to dispose of. As my ma always said, you make the mess, you clean it up." His gaze lowered to Crooked Teeth, who was beginning to stir. "But this one—"

"Stays here," Sean hissed out.

Bailey's breath hitched sharply. "Sean—"

"He. Stays. Here." His jaw was clenched so tight she was surprised it didn't snap in half. "You made your point, Kelly. Loud and clear. I'll do whatever the fuck you ask of me. But if you think you're going to walk out that door and take this piece of garbage with you, then you're a helluva lot stupider than I thought."

Cillian looked at Crooked Teeth, whose eyelids twitched rapidly as he regained consciousness. He went thoughtful for a beat, before giving an apathetic shrug. "What the hell. Let's call it a show of good faith." He smiled again. "See, when you follow orders, you reap the rewards. He's all yours, Reilly."

After Cillian disappeared through the doorway, Sean moved to close the door. Then he picked up Bailey's discarded shirt and held it out without meeting her eyes.

As adrenaline thudded in her blood, she quickly covered herself up. Sean didn't look in her direction, not even once. It was like he was making a pointed effort *not* to, and distress fluttered through her as she took in the hard line of his shoulders, the inflexible set of his jaw.

"Sean," she said tentatively.

"No. Stay put," he muttered. "I've got it handled."

It took a second to realize he wasn't talking to her. He was addressing someone over the comm, his stiff fingers pressed to his ear as he barked another soft command.

"Damn it, D, maintain your position. I'll let you know when I need you to come up."

His hand dropped from his earpiece, and Bailey's pulse accelerated when Sean finally met her eyes. But he didn't say a word.

Bailey stalked past him and grabbed her Beretta, which Cillian had left on the arm of the couch. She set her jaw, then palmed the silenced weapon and aimed it at the unconscious man's head. She wasn't usually a bloodthirsty person, but her breast still bore the mark of Crooked Teeth's hand, and she wasn't going to lose sleep over eliminating the man. No, *man* was too generous. He was a monster, plain and simple.

"Put the gun down."

Her gaze flew to Sean. "What?"

"Put the gun down." His voice was eerily calm. "And you're going to want to leave the room now."

"No," she said tersely, "what I want to do is take care of this sick bastard."

Sean didn't answer. He simply knelt beside Crooked Teeth and lightly slapped his fingertips on the man's cheek. "Wake up," Sean coaxed. "There you go, lad. Open those eyes."

She blinked in alarm. "What are you doing?"

"Leave the room, Bailey."

"No." Every exhalation that left her mouth was laced with panic. She suddenly remembered the look in Sean's eyes when he'd burst through that door. When he'd seen the thug's hand on her naked breast. "He's my responsibility."

"Like hell he is," Sean said fiercely. "He's *mine*."

"Sean—" she started.

"There you go," he murmured to the rousing man. "Hello again."

A pair of brown eyes peered up at them, then darted toward the couch. When Crooked Teeth realized that Cillian was gone, fear flooded his expression and he frantically tried to sit up.

To no avail, because Sean immediately trapped him with the weight of his own body, straddling the man's thighs as he smiled down at him.

"Uh-uh, you're not going anywhere. I'm not finished with you yet." When the other man's eyes pleadingly sought out Bailey, Sean forcefully gripped the guy's chin. "Don't you fucking look at her, you piece of shit. She can't help you. No one can."

"P-please," Crooked Teeth begged. "I'm s-sorry. I didn't mean to—"

"To what? Put your filthy hands on my girl? Sorry if I don't accept your apology, mate."

Bailey started to feel sick. She had no sympathy for Crooked Teeth—not a goddamn iota of it—but there was a right way to do things, and then there was the wrong way. Sometimes torture was necessary. Right now? It wasn't.

"Sean, please don't—"

He cut her off without turning his head. "Get the fuck out of here, Bailey. You don't need to see this."

"No," Crooked Teeth blurted out. "Don't kill me! I was just following orders, okay? I—"

A breath flew out of Sean's mouth as recognition dawned on his face. "Oh shit. I *know* you." His eyes narrowed at the prone man. "You're the sick fuck who raped Jimmy Donovan's sister about ten years back. Son of a bitch. When'd you get out of jail?"

"I don't know what you're talkin' about! I didn't do—"

"Brian Butler." Sean snapped his fingers. "That's your name, isn't it? Brian fucking Butler, and you *did* rape that girl. She was fifteen years old, you bastard." His head tipped pensively. "Does Jimmy know you're out? Nah, he wouldn't. If he did, you'd already be dead."

Bailey's stomach churned. She had to stop this. The reckless glimmer in Sean's eyes scared the crap out of her.

And it clearly scared Crooked—*Butler,* she corrected herself. The man looked downright petrified as he stared at Sean. A second later, he abruptly changed his tune, contradicting his earlier pleas.

"You're right. I fucked that girl and I deserve to die for it." Butler went wild-eyed, each breath coming out shallow. "Just kill me, okay? Kill me now."

Sean's low chuckle made Bailey's blood run cold. "Nice try, Brian. But I don't think I want to kill you anymore. Not when Donovan will do that for me."

"No, *please*—"

"But we're not done yet, if that's what you're worried about. There's still plenty of fun to be had, Brian." Sean lifted one of Butler's hands and examined it. "Is this the one you touched her with? No, it was your left hand. I remember now."

Bailey swallowed a rush of nausea as Sean dropped Butler's right hand and picked up the left one. "Sean, don't," she whispered.

A crack ripped through the air as Sean snapped Butler's index finger. The man let out an agonized shriek, followed by three more as Sean broke his other fingers in rapid succession.

"There," Sean said, nodding to himself. "All done."

Butler whimpered, his hideous face contorted in pain.

"Oh, relax, Brian. The broken-bone portion of the day is over." Sean flexed both his hands before cracking his knuckles. "Now I'm just going to kick your ass."

Bailey's heart lodged in her throat, horror and anger and disbelief forming a lethal cocktail inside her. "Sean, don't do this," she begged.

He glanced over his shoulder, his features hard, upper lip curled. "If you're planning on staying, then save me the commentary. Otherwise, walk away."

Helplessness trembled through her, bringing the sting of tears to her eyes.

Without a word, she spun on her heel and hurried out of the room.

# Chapter 23

The morning from hell had turned into the afternoon from hell, which had promptly become the night from hell—and Sean knew it was nowhere close to being over. As he wearily climbed the stairs to his flat, he didn't need to check his watch to know it was past midnight.

He'd spent the whole night at Rabbit's pub, listening to the men discuss their next objective. By some miracle he'd sat next to Cillian without blowing the man's brains out, though not for lack of temptation. But he couldn't kill Kelly yet. Not until Bailey's mother was out of harm's way, and not until he dealt with Flannery.

But first, he needed to convince the woman he loved that he wasn't the monster she thought he was.

When he strode into the living room, he found Isabel on the couch, reading a tattered copy of Joyce's *Ulysses* that Oliver had left behind the last time he'd crashed at the flat.

Bailey was nowhere to be seen.

"Hey." Isabel lifted her head at his entrance. "How did it go at O'Hare's?"

"Fine, I guess." He bit the inside of his cheek. "Where's Bailey?"

"In the bedroom."

"Let me guess—she saw me on the security monitors and went to hide."

Isabel's lips twitched. "Pretty much, yeah."

"So on a scale of one to ten, how pissed is she?"

"Nine. Maybe nine and a half." Isabel sighed ruefully. "Did you really have to beat that man half to death?"

Sean met her eyes. "Yes. I did."

Just thinking about Butler brought his anger boiling back to the surface. Sean would never be able to erase the memory of that slimebag's hands on Bailey. The filthy lust flashing in Butler's eyes. The way Bailey had stood there, so utterly still, as if she'd been ready to let . . . *that* . . . happen to her.

His hands curled into fists, and suddenly he wished Butler were still here so he could work him over again. But the only traces remaining of the man were the bloodstains smeared on the hardwood beneath Sean's boots.

After taking care of Leary's body earlier that day, he and D had delivered the unconscious Butler to Jimmy Donovan. Saying that Donovan was shocked to open his door and find a bloody, beaten Butler at his feet . . . well, that would be the understatement of the year. But the deadly drug kingpin had gone from stunned to ecstatic in a matter of seconds, repeatedly vowing to Sean that he owed him one, even though Sean had no intention of ever coming to collect.

"You should talk to her." Isabel's hesitant voice broke through his thoughts.

"Yeah. I know." He swallowed. "He was going to rape her, Iz."

"I know," she said softly. "But she wouldn't have let him."

Disbelief pummeled into him. "She wouldn't have *let*

him? She was just standing there! She wasn't fighting back, damn it."

Isabel's voice rang with conviction. "If she wasn't fighting back, then it was part of her plan. Bailey *always* has a plan, Sean."

"Not this time, Iz. I could see it in her eyes. She didn't know what to do and she was *scared*."

"Maybe. But you got there in time. And Butler was incapacitated. You didn't have to torture him."

"What do you want me to say? I snapped, all right? I saw him touching her . . . no, *pawing* her, and I fucking snapped. A bullet to the head was too good for that bastard. He deserved what I gave him." Sean rubbed the day's worth of beard growth on his face, frustration rising inside him. "You can take off now, Iz. Head back to the hotel and get some rest. Tomorrow's going to be a busy day."

Her gaze sharpened. "Why? What's tomorrow?"

"We'll talk in the morning, okay? I promise, I'll fill everyone in. But I'm still waiting on a few things, and right now, I'm too bloody exhausted to recap all the bullshit that went down at O'Hare's tonight."

Isabel tucked her phone in her pocket as she stepped toward him. "Don't be a jackass to her, all right? She's exhausted, too. And she's not in the right frame of mind for an argument."

Sean waited until Isabel was gone before he headed to the bedroom. He rapped his knuckles on the closed door, then opened it without waiting for an invitation.

Bailey was lying on the bed with her head against the frame, her slim body clad in leggings and a baggy blue shirt that fell over one shoulder. Her hair was in a ponytail, pulled away from her face to emphasize those big gray eyes.

"Is Butler dead?" she muttered.

He sat at the foot of the bed, knowing she'd want him to keep his distance. "Maybe. Probably not, though. Donovan will want to prolong that." He hesitated. "Are you okay?"

"Am I okay how? Physically? Mentally? Emotionally?"

"All of the above," he said gruffly.

She shrugged. "Yes. To all of the above."

He didn't believe her. She was still angry. He could see the volatile emotion simmering behind her flat, indifferent expression.

Sean let out a soft groan. "You know, I think you might be the only woman on the planet who would get pissed off at someone for beating up the man who tried to rape her."

The anger breached the surface, lighting her eyes. "You lost it today, Sean. You *lost* it."

"Yeah, I did. That's what happens when you come home to find a man *trying to rape your girlfriend*."

"You broke his *fingers*," she burst out.

"You broke that other fucker's neck! How is what *you* did okay, and yet *I* committed the mortal fucking sin?"

"Because I didn't fucking *enjoy* it! I killed that man because I had to, and I would've killed Butler too, if you hadn't shoved me aside and decided he was *yours*. But I wouldn't have gotten any pleasure out of it."

Christ, it seemed like everything he did made him less than perfect in Bailey's eyes. What the *hell* would it take to prove his worth to her?

The depressing thought caused his frustration to spill over. "If I ask you to leave town because I want to keep you safe, I'm a controlling asshole. If I ask you questions about your past, I'm trying to have power over you. If I beat the shit out of a man who's *fondling* you, I'm a bloodthirsty psycho."

He shot to his feet, unable to control the surge of annoyance, the bite of resentment. "But I'm not any of those things, Bailey. I'm just a man. Yes, I've got flaws and I've got a temper, but that's all you ever see when you look at me, and I'm bloody sick of fighting with you." He sucked in a shaky breath. "I'm tired of apologizing for wanting to protect you. That's what a man does, goddamn it—he protects the woman he loves." He heard her breath hitch, but he plowed right on. "If you can't fucking understand that, then . . ."

Then what? He couldn't even finish his own bloody sentence. The events of the day had caught up to him, left him numb and cold and so angry he couldn't think straight.

"Guess what, luv—you have flaws too," he said hoarsely. "You're a control freak. You're stubborn as hell. You're terrified of letting anyone get close. You're terrified of letting *me* get close."

Her breathing sounded equally unstable. "That's not true."

"It is, and you know it. I've spent five years trying to get close to you. *Five* years, Bailey. If that doesn't convince you how I feel about you, then I don't know what else will."

"I've never questioned how you feel about me," she whispered.

"No," he said bitterly. "I guess not. I guess you just didn't want to admit that you might feel something for me too. Because I'm just a reckless, overprotective caveman—isn't that right? Just another bully of a man who wants to have power over you, right?"

He grew sick at the notion that he might actually be speaking the truth. That Bailey truly lumped him in with the men from her past. Her abusive father. Her controlling ex.

"I'm *not* like them," he choked out.

Her eyes widened.

"I'm not your father, and I'm not Daniels, and if you can't bloody see that, then there's no shot in hell of this ever working out." His throat squeezed painfully. "But what am I even saying? We were never going to have a future, were we, Bailey?"

When all he got was silence, his heart cracked in two.

Sean took a breath, then clamped his lips together. Gathered the pieces of his shattered composure. "I'll take the couch tonight," he mumbled. "You sleep here." He swallowed, but the lump in his throat only got bigger. "I . . . I'll see you in the morning."

"Sean."

Her wobbly voice stopped him as he reached the door. He didn't turn around. Didn't want her to see the devastation he knew was etched into his face. "Yeah?"

"I . . ." He heard her shaky inhale. "I . . . yeah . . . I'll see you in the morning."

"Have you seen Sullivan?" D poked his head into Liam's hotel room, an atypical flash of concern on his face.

Liam hoped *his* face didn't convey how queasy he was feeling. But Christ, just the sound of Sullivan's name twisted his insides and made him want to throw up.

He was a mess. Been that way all frickin' day. And the fact that Sullivan hadn't mentioned what had happened between them only made it worse. His teammate had passed the day resting and watching TV. Liam had spent it choking on wave after wave of panic.

He'd tried assuring himself that he'd just been helping a friend last night. Just a Good Samaritan who dispensed hand jobs to the injured. The frickin' orgasm fairy.

Except the explanation didn't hold much water. Good deeds were about giving to others without thinking about yourself. But Liam had been harder than steel last night, and if Sullivan had rolled over . . . if he'd so much as looked at Liam with even a trace of invitation . . . Christ. Liam knew damn well he would've done more than jack his friend off.

And that scared the crap out of him.

"Macgregor? Did you hear me? I can't find Port."

He swallowed his nausea and stumbled off the bed. "I thought he was with you."

"He was, but when I got out of the shower he was gone."

Shit. This wasn't the time for Sully to pull one of his disappearing acts. Reilly and Bailey were coming by in the morning to discuss whatever big plan Sean was brewing.

"Did you check Isabel's room?"

D nodded. "He's not there. I called Reilly and the rookie, too, and they haven't seen or spoken to him."

"Did you check the hotel?"

"Not yet. Figured we could split up and do a sweep."

Reluctance crammed inside Liam's throat as he grabbed his shoulder holster from the kitchenette table. He strapped it on, threw a Windbreaker over his T-shirt, and followed D out the door. "You check the dining room and veranda. I'll take the bar and lobby. Text if you find him. Otherwise, meet out front and we'll sweep the area."

"Sounds good."

They went their separate ways once the elevator doors dinged open. Liam kind of hoped D would be the one to locate Sullivan. He hadn't been able to look his teammate in the eye since the . . . *incident*. For fuck's sake, the incidents were just piling up, weren't they? And when you added them all up, you got one confusing clusterfuck Liam wasn't equipped to deal with.

He was *straight*, damn it.

His breathing grew labored as he strode toward the entrance of the hotel bar. He was straight, yet every fiber of his being desperately wanted to . . . find out for sure, he supposed.

The thought made him falter in his steps. Why *couldn't* he find out? Hell, college frat boys did it all the time. They fooled around with their buddies and—shit, what was that phrase he'd heard floating around Boston College? BUD? No, BUG. Bisexual until graduation.

He resisted the urge to rip his hair out by the roots. Jesus. What was he thinking? He wasn't going to fool around with another man.

But . . . fuck, if he was interested in addressing this little confusion problem of his, Sullivan *would* be the best candidate for the task. They were friends. They trusted each other. They—

*For fuck's sake. Stop this.*

Liam drew a ragged breath and entered the bar.

It took half a second to spot Sullivan.

"Grab a seat, hon, and I'll pop over with a drink menu," a pretty waitress chirped from the counter.

His gaze stayed glued to the back of the shadowy room, where Sullivan was leaning against the wall as a leggy brunette ground her pelvis into his. Sully's hands were clasped on the woman's hips, his blond head bent toward hers.

He didn't see Liam. Because he was too busy shoving his tongue down the brunette's throat. Too busy rubbing up against her and seductively caressing the swell of her ass.

"Sir?"

He wrenched his eyes off the raunchy scene. "Uh . . . no . . . sorry. I won't be staying."

Just as he turned on his heel, Sullivan's head lifted and

Liam found a pair of smoky gray eyes boring into his face.

Challenging him.

No. *Mocking* him.

Then Sullivan winked—he fucking *winked*—and refocused his attention on the woman in his arms.

# Chapter 24

It was difficult to concentrate on the discussion going on around her. How could she, when Bailey's mind was still spinning from her argument with Sean last night? Still reeling from the knowledge that he *loved* her.

Leave it to Sean to drop the L-word in angry passing, as if his feelings were a given. As if the fact that he loved her was no big thing. As if she'd *known*.

But she hadn't. Sure, she'd assumed he cared about her, at least in a professional capacity. And fine, a sexual one. But finding out his emotions ran so much deeper had come as a shock.

*We were never going to have a future, were we, Bailey?*

His sorrowful words continued to float through her head, along with the accusations he'd hurled her way. His claim that she was afraid to let him in, that she was a control freak who likened him to her father and Daniels. But she *saw* the similarities, damn it. The barely checked temper, the way he always had to remind her that she *belonged* to him.

*He's not like them, you fool.*

Bailey's throat clamped shut as the absurdity of that

sank in. Of course Sean wasn't like them. He wasn't cruel like her father, or vindictive like Isaac.

So what was she so damn afraid of?

And why was she so angry? Butler's torture hadn't been necessary, but Sean had still saved her from getting raped last night. What if Liam or Sully or any of the others had been the ones to come to her rescue? Would she have resented them too?

The thought gave her pause, and she bit her lip when she realized the answer was *yes*. She hated relying on anyone but herself. And that's who she was *really* angry with—herself. For letting Cillian Kelly gain the upper hand. For not finding a way to save her own skin.

"Jesus. Is the dude vying for the title of terrorist of the month or something?"

Liam's sarcastic remark jolted her out of her muddled thoughts.

Sean had just told the group about Cillian Kelly's latest brainchild, which the Dagger members had discussed at length the night before. Kelly's ambitious new plan was to drive a truck full of explosives into a government building splat in the middle of Dublin—tomorrow. On *Monday* morning, when the place would be crawling with civilians, inside and out.

Bailey hadn't been surprised to hear it. Kelly was a bona fide psycho—of course he'd want to follow up the Trinity car bombing with something even more destructive.

"And you said yes?" Ash spoke up, his normally relaxed face hard with disapproval.

"Don't worry," Sean assured him. "Rabbit has no intention of letting it happen."

"But he agreed to it too. You just said so."

"Yes, but only to shut Kelly up. Nobody's going to get

hurt tomorrow, Rookie. There won't *be* a tomorrow, not for Kelly and Flannery."

From his perch against the wall, D narrowed his eyes. "What's the plan? We taking Flannery out tonight?"

"No." Sean paused. "Rabbit's gonna do that for us."

Bailey's head turned toward him in surprise. "He is? How?" Worry flashed through her. "Shit. Does that mean you told him the truth, then? About Flannery coercing you to take Rabbit down? And that Cillian's working for Flannery?"

"Yes. Well, everything except the Cillian part."

Sullivan frowned. "You didn't out Kelly as the mole?"

"Nope," Sean said lightly.

"Why the hell not?"

"Because Rabbit would have gutted him. And I want to save that honor for myself."

Sean's ominous tone made her shiver. There he went again, displaying the ruthless streak that never failed to put Bailey on edge.

Except he wasn't the only one. The other men were nodding in approval, their eyes reflecting that same deadly gleam. Violent men surrounded her, and guilt pricked her skin as she realized that she didn't judge the others for it as harshly as she judged Sean.

Was she . . . damn it, was she *looking* for excuses to push him away? It sure as hell was starting to seem like it.

"I'm saving Kelly for later," Sean said with a shrug. "Tonight is all about Flannery. I set up a meeting between Flannery and Rabbit. It'll take place tonight—midnight—in one of Rabbit's warehouses near the port."

"Flannery agreed to this?" Liam said warily.

Sean nodded. "I told him Rabbit wants to strike a deal."

"And he fuckin' believed that?"

"Yup."

Isabel wrinkled her forehead. "O'Hare is actually going to show up? He does realize there's a good chance Flannery will take him out, right?"

"Yup. But Rabbit isn't too concerned about that." Sean paused. "Which is the other reason Flannery was so eager to agree to the meeting, actually. I told him Rabbit is dying."

Bailey glanced over in alarm again. This was the first she'd heard of it. "Is that true?"

"Rabbit told me yesterday when we met at the docks. He's got lung cancer." Sean's voice grew surprisingly pained. "Doctors gave him three months to live."

At the kitchenette, Sullivan nodded as if it all made perfect sense. "Ah. He's kicking it anyway, so he might as well take his enemy down with him. Gotta respect that."

"Rabbit asked me to tell Flannery that he's ready to deal. To hand over his organization in exchange for a few demands—money for his men, their necks are off-limits, et cetera, et cetera." Sean let out a tired-sounding breath. "But neither one of them will be walking out of the warehouse alive tonight."

"How does O'Hare plan on doing it?" D said brusquely.

Bailey didn't miss the look Sean exchanged with Oliver, who was leaning against the bathroom doorway. Something passed between the twins, almost like they were having an entire conversation in their minds, and then Sean broke eye contact and turned to shrug at D.

"Rabbit's got it covered." He paused again. "I'll be the one driving him to the meeting."

Bailey's pulse kicked up. "Wait, why? Why do you have to be the one to take him?"

"Because he asked me to. And because Flannery wants me there." When he saw the concern on her face, his tone softened. "I won't be there for the end, Bailey. Once I get the ball rolling and get them talking, I'm gone."

"Fine." She set her jaw. "Then I'm going with you."

"And we'll set up a perimeter," Liam said immediately. "We'll keep an eye on the warehouse when you— "

"No," Sean cut in. "No backup. That was one of Flannery's stipulations. He wants me and Rabbit to come alone, and he'll have men posted in the area to make sure we keep our word."

"But Flannery won't care if *I'm* there," Bailey pointed out. "He already knows we're a package deal."

Reluctance creased his forehead.

"I'm coming," she said firmly. "Even if I have to stay in the car and wait outside for you. It won't screw anything up, Sean. Neither one of them considers me a threat." She swallowed. "And I'd feel better knowing you have *some* backup."

Sean rubbed his chin, looking unhappy as he thought it over, but to her surprise, he didn't shoot her down. "All right. I'd feel better, too, if you were there."

He *would*?

*Since when?* she nearly blurted out.

"I'll give Rabbit and Flannery a heads-up, though," he said absently. "I can't spring any surprises on them."

The conversation continued, but Bailey was too preoccupied to focus on what the others were saying. She was still floored that Sean had willingly accepted her assistance, not to mention amazed at the very solid plan he'd formulated on his own. Involving Rabbit had been a risky move, but she couldn't deny it had paid off.

Sean had orchestrated a scenario that Bailey couldn't help but be impressed with. After all the years of hatred and violence that had fueled the flames of their blood feud, Eamon O'Hare and Ronan Flannery would finally be putting the fire out. Just the two of them.

Bailey couldn't think of anything more fitting than that.

Midnight didn't come soon enough for Sean. He drove into the east-end parking lot where he and Rabbit had arranged to meet, then gave a sidelong glance at Bailey, who sat in the passenger seat staring straight ahead.

They'd barely spoken all day. She'd spent most of her time chatting with Isabel or Liam, or on the phone with the director of her mother's nursing home, or on her laptop—pretty much doing everything but talk to *him*.

He could tell something was on her mind. Hell, he bet he knew what it was. She was preparing herself to end it. To kick him to the curb and disappear again, the way she always did after they crossed paths. The thought of letting her go tore at his insides, but he'd reached a depressing conclusion last night—he couldn't keep chasing her. If the two of them were ever going to have a future, she had to come to *him*. Freely, openly. She needed to deal with the messed-up issues that had skewed her opinion about him—no, about *men*—and take that first step.

"Are we sure Cillian won't show up and ruin everything?" Bailey asked as he put the car in park.

"Quinn promised to keep him busy," Sean answered.

"How?"

He sighed. "Private party. Kelly's probably balls deep in a prostie right now."

She made a face. "God. I hate that guy so much."

"Join the club."

Sean's gaze shifted to the petrol station where Rabbit had asked to get picked up. The front window was lit up, but there was nobody inside but the clerk. The pump area was also deserted, but Sean could sense Rabbit's presence. As if on cue, the man stepped out of the shadows at the side of the small brick storefront, emerging from the darkness and making his way toward the waiting car.

Rabbit slid into the backseat, reaching up to squeeze Bailey's shoulder. "Evening, luv. Reilly."

"Eamon." The sorrow in his voice astounded him. Not too long ago, this man had abducted his brother, and now they were sitting in the same car, and Sean was experiencing a genuine sense of loss at what Rabbit was about to do.

"Don't look so glum, both of you," Rabbit said gruffly. "This is a joyful occasion, remember?"

Sean met the man's eyes in the rearview mirror. "Yeah? How's that?"

"Because Ronan Flannery is about to die." Rabbit ran a hand through his beard. "You don't know how long I've been waiting for this day, lad." He ruefully glanced at his attire—jeans and a plaid shirt. "I shoulda rented a tux."

Sean grinned. "And tip off the enemy? You know better than that."

"Of course I do. Does it *look* like I'm wearing a fecking penguin suit?"

Bailey twisted around in her seat. "I bet you'd look handsome in a tuxedo."

"Ya?" Rabbit paused thoughtfully. "How 'bout you bury me in one, then?"

Just like that, the mood went solemn again.

With a sigh, Sean moved the gearshift and pulled out of the lot. The drive to the warehouse was a quiet one. Rabbit seemed preoccupied, his brown eyes fixed out the window, watching the city whiz by them. Sean slowed the car as they neared the industrial area behind the port. There was a full moon out, its silvery glow casting shadows on the rows of warehouses and the chain-link fences blocking off the structures.

Sean remembered visiting this particular warehouse when he was a boy. It housed the electronics imported by one of Rabbit's businesses, the merch arriving at the port, unloaded at this warehouse, and then distributed to stores around the country. The goods were hot, of course, and all the profits went to the laundry man, who cleaned them up nice and gave Rabbit a semblance of legitimacy.

"Flannery's already here," he said grimly.

An armored SUV was parked thirty yards from the steel doors at the warehouse's entrance, where two guards were already posted. Sean didn't need his humming instincts to tell him there were more thugs posted around the perimeter. He spotted several of them, and he was suddenly relieved that Morgan's men hadn't pushed the issue when he'd said no backup. If Flannery caught even a whiff of trickery, he'd be outta there faster than a bat outta hell.

Sean stopped the car farther out, near the fence separating the lot from the road. He parked but didn't kill the engine. "Leave it running," he told Bailey. "I won't be long."

Her lips parted, as if she wanted to say something, but then her mouth closed—and landed on his.

The kiss startled him. He hadn't expected her to lean in like that, to show affection after the way she'd shut him out since last night.

"Be careful," she whispered against his lips.

"I will," he said roughly, then glanced over at Rabbit. "Ready?"

The man nodded.

Sean brushed his lips over Bailey's again, stroking her soft cheek as he unbuckled his seat belt. "I'll be right back."

He and Rabbit got out of the car, pausing only long enough for Sean to surreptitiously slide a cell phone into Rabbit's hand.

"Speed dial one," he murmured, keeping his eye on the two men fifty yards away. He didn't think they'd seen the phone exchange hands, but he watched them carefully as he and Rabbit crossed the parking lot.

The guards stiffened at their approach, silenced pistols sliding upward to train on either man.

Sean offered a cool look. "Your boss inside?"

One of the men responded with a terse nod.

"Gonna have to pat you down," the other one informed them.

Sean and Rabbit were patted down. Neither of them was armed—another one of Flannery's stipulations—and Sean breathed in slow relief as the thugs cleared them for entry. Without confiscating their cell phones.

The interior of the warehouse consisted of one cavernous room with aisles of metal racks piled high with cardboard boxes full of DVD players, Blu-rays, flatscreens—whatever stolen goods Rabbit and his crew could get their hands on. The outer edges of the room were bathed in darkness, but the center was lit up, a dangling light fixture shining down on Ronan Flannery like a spotlight.

"I have to admit, I'm surprised you showed."

Flannery's voice reverberated in the enormous space, bouncing off the gray cinder-block walls and cement floor.

From the corner of his eye, Sean saw Rabbit tense up. How long had it been since the two men had been in the same room? He suspected it'd been a while. A very long while.

"I said I would, didn't I?" Rabbit grumbled.

The two men closed the distance between them and Flannery, stopping when only ten feet separated them.

Flannery's dark eyes focused on his brother-in-law. "So. Is it true?"

Rabbit knew exactly what he meant. "Three months," he said, a self-deprecating smile lifting his lips. "Jot that down in your calendar so you can start planning the parade."

There was a chuckle. "I'll be sure to do that."

Sean noticed that although Flannery's expression remained shuttered, a flicker of emotion peeked through that hard veil. Regret, maybe? Grief? It was too faint to decipher.

"Let's quit wasting time," Rabbit said abruptly. "Seansy tells me you're trying to take over my organization."

Flannery's cold eyes shifted to Sean. "Is that so?"

Chuckling, Rabbit waved a hand. "Don't be pissed at the lad. He didn't betray you. I already knew it was happening. That's why I came here tonight—to save all of us a bunch of fecking time. You don't have to steal my empire, Ronan. 'Cause I'm giving it to you."

"Is that so?" Flannery said again. "And why is that, Eamon?"

"You're gonna try to take it over after I'm dead anyway. Might as well make it easier on you." Rabbit smirked. "Besides, we both know the Dagger will run itself into the fecking ground the moment I'm gone."

Flannery hooked his thumbs in the waistband of his crisp gray trousers, which drew Sean's attention to the holster on his hip. Evidently the *come unarmed* law didn't apply to him.

"All right, I'll play along," the man drawled. "Let's say I take what you're *offering*. What's the catch?"

Rabbit assumed the same casual pose. "My men," he said gruffly. "Any of them wanna stay on, you let 'em. And you're gonna give 'em some cash. Half a mil each, even to the ones who decide to take off." His features hardened ominously. "And they stay alive, Ronan. Every fecking one of them. They become untouchable, y'hear me? You kill 'em off, and Reilly here will know about it, and he'll make sure you pay for it."

Flannery smiled. "Oh, will he?"

"Yes," Sean spoke up in a steely voice. "I will."

"And what's in it for me?" Flannery asked pleasantly.

"The Irish, you bloody moron." When Flannery's eyes flashed, Rabbit's amusement deepened. "My routes become your routes. My profits become your profits." He held up a hand. "But not if you decide to run the shite yourself. The locals won't want to answer directly to you. You'll have to allow Kelly to lead the Dagger."

Flannery's gaze flicked at Sean. "Cillian Kelly, huh? And you're certain Kelly will take orders from me?"

Sean knew a test when he saw one—Flannery was trying to figure out if Sean had tipped Rabbit off about where Cillian's true loyalties lay.

"He won't have a choice," Rabbit answered. "He'll be unhappy at first, but if you throw enough cash at him, he'll warm up to the idea eventually. But I ain't gonna lie—Kelly's not your biggest fan."

Flannery said, "I see."

Sean swallowed his relief, knowing he'd passed the test. Flannery believed he hadn't revealed Cillian as the mole, and it was all thanks to Rabbit, whose ignorance about Kelly's status had ensured that his words held nothing but truth.

With an indifferent look, Sean eased away from the men. "I'm afraid you two will have to hammer out the rest of the details without me. I have somewhere I need to be."

"No." Flannery's sharp voice stopped him. "You stay until we're through."

"No," he mimicked. "My girl's waiting for me in the car, and we have a flight to catch." He gave a pointed look. "We're heading to Colorado tonight. You remember who's in Colorado, don't you, Ronan? Bailey's mother, who, by the way, needs to be transferred to a different facility. One that isn't teeming with your snipers."

Flannery wasn't the least bit apologetic. "That doesn't sound like a very safe environment," he said with a smirk. "You're right to move her. Although . . . well, anywhere she goes, it'll leave a trail. I hope you realize that."

Sean acknowledged the barely veiled threat with a curt nod. "I'll be sure to leave you some bread crumbs." He turned to Rabbit. "I'll ring you when I'm back in Dublin. We'll catch a pint."

"Sounds good, lad."

Sean's gaze found Flannery's again. "I'll be in touch. And I mean that, Ronan. I promised Rabbit I'd watch your every move if you inherit the Dagger. I'll be watching the boys—Quinn and O'Neill and Doherty and even fuckin' Kelly—to make sure you keep your promise not to harm them."

"And if I break that promise?"

Sean just smiled.

"Fair enough," the man chuckled.

Sean walked off, keeping his strides casual as he headed for the door. But inside he was a ball of tension, painfully aware of Flannery's dark eyes fixed on his retreating back. He sensed suspicion in the air, but not a deadly amount of it. Not enough to indicate that Flannery was onto them.

When he stepped outside, he released the breath he hadn't realized he was holding, shooting an uncaring look at the guards by the door.

"Your boss and my boss are still negotiating," he told them. "A car will be here in twenty minutes to collect O'Hare. Black sedan, black rims. Do me a favor and don't shoot it up. Rabbit won't be happy if you fuck with his ride home."

One guard remained stone-faced, but the other cracked a smile. "Gotcha," he said.

Sean strode past them, battling a rush of amazement as he made his way back to the car.

Jesus Christ. He'd done it. He'd gotten out of there with his skin intact.

Now it was time for Rabbit to do his part.

"Is it done?"

Bailey's urgent inquiry greeted him when he slid into the driver's seat. He rested both hands on the steering wheel, released another breath of relief, and shook his head. "Not yet. But soon."

He jerked when a warm hand covered one of his. "Are you okay?"

Sean slowly met her eyes. He knew damn well that now wasn't the time to have this conversation, not when they were parked a hundred yards from the warehouse, but he couldn't stop the confession. "I love you, you know."

She blinked, and then a soft laugh spilled out. "Well. Look at that. You actually decided to *tell* me this time, instead of shouting it at me."

He shifted sheepishly in his seat. "I'm sorry. I know I shout at you sometimes, luv. But that's only because you do my bloody head in."

"No way, dude. I'm not taking responsibility for you being a brute."

There was humor in her eyes, but her words evoked a stab of frustration. "I know you think there's a lot of bad in me, but there's a lot of *good* in me too. I really wish you could see that."

Bailey's expression grew tortured. "I do see it."

"Do you really mean that?"

She nodded.

"Then I have one question to ask you. And your answer is going to determine whatever happens from this point forward." He breathed in deeply. "Do you love me, Bailey?"

"He's a belligerent son of a bitch, isn't he?" Ronan stared in the direction Reilly had gone before turning to chuckle at Rabbit.

He chuckled back, because feck, he couldn't deny it. Reilly was one of a kind. Smarter than he gave himself credit for, ruthless as shite when he needed to be, and so goddamn cocky it sometimes made Rabbit want to give the kid a hearty kick in the balls.

"Just like his father," Rabbit said with a grin. "Remember some of the stunts Colin used to pull? Before he married Leah? Shite, when he started that brawl over at Hannigan's that time? Got right up in that white supremacist's face and stabbed him in the gut with a broken billiards stick."

Ronan's lips twitched. "That bastard never did know how to handle his liquor."

They fell silent. The humor faded, replaced by the ever-present tension that had plagued their lives since they'd lost Maureen, God bless her soul. But before that, they'd been brothers. Rabbit hadn't forgotten, and when he looked into his old friend's eyes now, he knew Ronan hadn't either.

"I loved her, too, Ronan."

The other man's shock hung in the air, mingling with the silence that followed.

"Did you hear me?" Rabbit muttered. "I loved her, you bastard. Maybe even more than you did—because I can remember holding her in my arms when she was just a baby. Because she was part of *my* life long before you entered hers. She was my sister, and I fecking loved her."

Ronan looked shaken.

"She would whip us raw if she knew what we've become," Rabbit said sourly. "That's why I came here tonight—to end the madness. To end the bloody war that's been poisoning our lives since the day Maureen died."

Flannery's features hardened for a beat. Then he wheezed out a breath and spoke with such anguish that Rabbit's head lifted in surprise.

"I miss her."

Rabbit nodded. "So do I. Every fecking day." He swallowed. "But I'll be seeing her soon, y'know. At least if all those Hail Marys I said and all the rosaries I clutched secured me a place in heaven."

A cloud of sorrow floated through Ronan's eyes. "Give her . . ." He cleared his throat. "Give her a kiss from me when you see her, Eamon."

"I'll do that, Ronan." Rabbit reached into his pocket and fished out the phone Reilly had given him, pretending to check the time. "It's getting late. Whaddaya say I put you in contact with Kelly and the two of you can discuss among yourselves what to do after I meet my maker."

He tapped a finger on the keypad. Speed dial one, Reilly had told him.

"By the way," he said absently. "I did it again."

Ronan frowned. "What?"

"Only did it twice in the years I've been heading up the Dagger," he continued. "Including tonight, of course."

"What the feck are you talking about?" his former friend and oldest enemy demanded.

Rabbit held up the phone and smiled. "I didn't call ahead."

# Chapter 25

*Do you love me, Bailey?*

Sean's question hovered over the car like a canopy, dampening Bailey's palms and making her pulse race. But she shouldn't be this nervous. All she had to do was open her mouth and tell him—

The explosion that rocked the warehouse shook their car on its axis, sending Bailey's head into the dashboard. Pain shot through her forehead, but it wasn't strong enough to disorient her, and the shriek of her pulse in her ears didn't muffle Sean's loud expletive.

"We have to get out of here," he said urgently, and then his foot slammed on the gas pedal and the car went careening forward.

Bailey stared out the window with wide eyes. The warehouse was engulfed in flames. Chunks of cement cracked off the exterior and fell to the ground, along with pieces of the slightly slanted roof. All the windows had shattered, glass flying out in all directions and littering the asphalt in front of the building. The two men who'd been standing at the entrance were . . . gone. Bailey couldn't even see their bodies—the smoke was too thick, the flames too intense.

Tires squealed as Sean sped away from the conflagration. "Bloody hell," he burst out. A mixture of regret and amazement clung to his voice. "That son of a bitch did it. He actually did it."

She knew he was talking about O'Hare and the crazy sacrifice he'd just made, but Bailey was more concerned about the possible fallout. Flannery had posted other men around the perimeter, and if any of them had survived, they were no doubt chasing them at that moment.

But there were no headlights in the rearview mirror, no vehicles riding their bumper or gunshots being fired in their direction.

"Do you even know where you're going?" she demanded as the car hurtled down the dark road in the opposite direction from which they'd come.

Sean chuckled. "Course I do. Did I ever tell you about the time Ollie and I decided we wanted to haul cargo for a living? We used to hang around the port begging the dockmaster to hire us, so trust me, I know every inch of this—"

The other car came out of nowhere, smashing into the driver's side and sending their vehicle spinning. Bailey screamed as Sean lost control of the wheel, and suddenly the car was flipping, rolling, the crunch of metal and scrape of pavement deafening her ears.

The acrid scent of oil and gasoline stung her eyes, flooded her nostrils. The seat belt kept her plastered to her seat, but the forceful collision had caused her head to bounce against the window, blurring her vision.

She became aware of the silence. The stillness. The car was no longer flipping. It was back in the right position, wheels on the ground and roof up top.

"You okay?" Sean's frantic voice penetrated the fog in her brain.

She weakly turned her head, and relief pounded

through her when she saw that he was all right. Other than a streak of blood on his left temple, he didn't seem to be injured from the accident. His window was gone, though, only a few shards of glass still connected to the frame. The windshield was a spiderweb of cracks, and the side of Bailey's door was completely dented inward, but considering they'd just been violently T-boned, she was shocked the damage wasn't worse.

"I'm fine," she said in a shaky voice. Adrenaline continued to surge through her blood, making her fingers quiver as she unbuckled her seat belt. "No broken bones, but I bumped my head on the—"

Her door was wrenched open before she could finish.

Bailey yelped as her butt landed unceremoniously on the glass-strewn pavement. Sharp fragments dug into her back, bringing a sting of pain, but not enough to distract her from the danger pulsing in the air. Her gun had fallen out of her lap during the collision, so she made a mad grab for the pistol strapped to her ankle.

A heavy boot came down on her leg. "I don't think so, sweetness. You won't be needing that."

Cillian.

Bailey stared into the barrel of his gun, swallowing hard. From the corner of her eye, she saw Sean stumble out of the car, a Glock in hand, but his hand froze when Cillian dropped to his knees and pressed his gun muzzle to Bailey's temple.

"I suggest you lay your weapon down," he told Sean. "Otherwise I pull the fucking trigger."

When Sean hesitated, Bailey wanted to scream for him to ignore Cillian. To pull his own trigger and put an end to Kelly's psychotic reign of terror. But she knew Sean would never do it. Not when her life was on the line.

With a ragged breath, Sean lowered his weapon.

"Kick it over to me," Cillian said coolly.

Sean obeyed, setting the Glock on the ground, then kicking it in Cillian's direction.

Cillian swiftly snatched the pistol from Bailey's boot, then collected Sean's discarded nine mil and tucked both weapons in his waistband.

"Get up," he ordered, curling his fingers around Bailey's upper arm as he yanked her to her feet. "You," he barked at Sean. "Hands on the hood. You so much as twitch and I blow her bloody brains out."

Sean's shoulders sagged in defeat as he placed both palms flat on the dented hood of the car.

With his gun still jammed against Bailey's head, Cillian reached into his pocket and pulled out a set of flex-cuffs. "Cuff him," he told her. "If you try anything, I shoot you both, understood?"

She gave a terse nod.

"Hands behind your back, Reilly," Cillian snapped as he handed Bailey the plastic handcuffs.

Sean complied, and Bailey drew a slow breath as she came up behind him.

"Cuff him," Cillian repeated. "Quit wasting my time, bitch."

She reached for Sean's hands, giving them a brief squeeze before she fastened the flex-cuffs around his wrists. She kept one palm curled, shielding it from Cillian's view, and as she secured the cuffs, she slid something into Sean's right hand—the jagged glass fragment she'd swiped off the pavement before Cillian had hauled her to her feet.

She felt Sean tense, but only for a second. Then he went still again.

"Get over here," Cillian snapped at her.

Bailey edged away from Sean and approached Cillian warily. He kept the gun trained on her, but his mocking blue eyes shifted to Sean.

"I want you on your knees for this," he announced. "Get nice and comfy on the ground, Reilly. You're gonna want a good seat for the show."

Sean's green eyes flashed as he turned around, but he remained standing.

Cillian's lips curled in a sneer. "On. Your. Knees."

After a long beat, Sean silently slid to the ground. His arms were bound behind his back, but although Bailey couldn't detect even a trace of movement, she knew he was slicing the cuffs with the glass she'd slipped him.

"There you go," Cillian mocked. "Now we can get started."

Bailey flinched when he grabbed her arm. He drew her toward him, pulling her back flush to his chest. He ground his unmistakable erection against her ass, but she didn't have to twist her head to know he was still looking at Sean.

"I should've known you'd fuck me," Cillian muttered scornfully. "All you had to do was follow my lead, Reilly. Do Flannery's bidding and let us take over the Dagger. But no, you couldn't do that, could you, motherfucker? You had to go behind my goddamn back and scheme with Rabbit. You had to fuck everything up for me, didn't you?"

Sean was silent. Unblinking.

"I *needed* Flannery," Cillian said angrily. "Don't you get that? Rabbit's loyal little soldiers won't follow me now. Not without Rabbit vouching for me or Flannery backing me!"

Bailey's jaw tightened when he thrust his groin into her backside and rotated his hips. She met Sean's eyes, but his expression revealed nothing. Had he gotten free?

Couldn't he give her some kind of signal, damn it?

"I'll figure something out, though." Cillian spoke absently, almost as if to himself. "I'll find a way to get what I want without Flannery. But that's a matter for another day. Right now, it's time to teach you a lesson, Reilly." He jabbed his gun in the air. "I'm going to show you what happens when you *fuck me*."

Bailey gasped when Cillian's arm came around and his hand cupped her left breast. He squeezed it so hard her eyes watered.

"I'm going to fuck *her*," Cillian spat out. "Right in front of your goddamn eyes." His hot breath fanned against her neck, spittle splashing her skin.

Bailey stared at Sean, pleading with him to give her a sign that he was ready to make a move. With Cillian ranting behind her and his gun no longer pressed to her temple, it was the perfect time to spring to action.

"I'm going to fuck her cunt and her mouth and her tight little ass," Cillian was gloating.

Damn it, why was Sean *taking* so long?

"And you're going to enjoy every bloody second of it, Reilly. You'll probably come in your pants, just like I'll be coming when I'm inside your wom—"

Bailey had had enough.

She ducked out of Kelly's grip before he realized what was happening, her right leg slicing upward to knock the gun from his hand. He growled in outrage, his fist crashing forward—only to collide with the air.

Because Bailey was already crouched two feet away, gripping Kelly's fallen weapon in both hands.

"You little bit—"

She pulled the trigger and shot him right between the eyes, then twice in the chest for good measure.

He was dead before his body even hit the ground.

A second later, Bailey bounced onto the soles of her feet, spinning around to face Sean, who wore an amused look.

"Nice shot," he told her. "The first one anyway. The other two were overkill, don't you think?"

She shrugged sheepishly. "He really pissed me off."

Sean's husky laughter was music to her ears.

She knelt beside him, fumbling for his bound hands. "And I'm pissed off at *you*," she grumbled. "What are you, an amateur? I *gave* you a way out of those cuffs. You really couldn't—" She stopped short when her fingers collided with the loose scraps of plastic. Then her jaw fell open. "Seriously? Your hands were free this whole time?"

He grinned. "Of course."

"Then why the *hell* didn't you help me out?"

The irritated demand brought genuine confusion to his eyes. "Because you had the situation under control."

Bailey blinked. Then blinked again. "Wait—what?"

Furrowing his brow, Sean got to his feet and pulled her up with him. "You had it covered. There was no reason for me to step in."

She stared at him. "Are you fucking *kidding* me?"

His confusion grew. "No. Why?"

"*Why?* Where exactly was this infallible faith in my abilities the other day? You know, when you swept in and ripped Butler off me and then proceeded to beat him senseless?"

"That was different." Sean shrugged. "Because you *didn't* have the situation under control."

She gulped, unable to deny that she'd been grasping at straws when Butler had been pawing her. In that moment, she truly hadn't known how she would escape.

"That's what I thought," he said smugly. At her stricken expression, he softened his tone. "It didn't look good when I walked in, but you would have saved yourself, Bailey. I know you would've."

"At the expense of my mother? I don't know." Her voice cracked. "But I considered it. God, when Butler was touching me, and Cillian was just standing there enjoying it . . . I considered killing them both. Even though I knew it meant that the sniper would kill her." She swallowed and averted her gaze. "I'm glad you showed up and took the decision out of my hands."

"Are you?" he said skeptically.

"Well, I wasn't glad when it happened," she confessed. "I didn't like being in the position where I needed to be rescued. I've spent so many years taking care of myself, you know? I never accepted backup, not when I worked for Daniels, and not after I went private. I . . . don't like needing people." She bit her lip. "I needed you yesterday."

Strong hands cupped her cheeks, forcing eye contact, and then Sean's tender expression warmed her face. "That wasn't so hard, was it?"

"What?" she murmured.

"Admitting I might have done something right. Admitting that you needed help." His callused thumb traced the seam of her lips. "It doesn't make you weak, Bailey, and it doesn't mean you're letting someone have power over you. It just means that you're not a superhero." He chuckled softly. "Even superheroes have partners, you know."

Partners.

God, was that what they were? She'd spent so much time believing that Sean didn't view her as an equal, but she was stunned to realize that it was the other way around. She hadn't viewed him as *her* equal.

"But if we're ever going to have a chance of moving forward, you need to be honest with me," he said quietly. "You need to tell me what you're afraid of."

Her throat constricted. "I . . . don't know."

Sean touched her cheek, the epitome of tenderness. "Yes, you do."

"I . . ." Tears stung her eyelids and tightened her chest.

She took a breath, forcing herself to voice the truth that she was only now allowing herself to recognize. "I'm scared you'll hate me."

Shock filled his eyes. "What?"

"I'm scared that you'll resent me." The tears spilled over, leaving salty tracks on her face. "I'm strong, Sean. I really am. I needed help yesterday, but most of the time I can handle myself just fine. My mom . . ." She struggled for air. "She was strong too, and my father despised her for it. I know you'd never . . . do what my father did. I *know* that. But I'm so afraid you might hate me one day."

Oh God, she couldn't stop the words that were pouring out of her mouth. She felt weak and light-headed and mortified. She wanted to run away, but Sean didn't let her. He gripped her chin, the fierce look in his eyes holding her captive.

"I could *never* hate you, Bailey. Your strength is what I love most about you. Don't you see that? It's what blew me away the moment I met you."

She bit her lip harder, trying to stop another rush of tears. "What if that changes?"

"It won't. I'm serious, luv. I *love* knowing that you can kick my ass." His green eyes twinkled. "It's actually kind of a turn-on. I mean, how many men can say that their woman is capable of snapping a lowlife's neck with her bare hands? And don't get me started on that sharp brain of yours—if I ever need to plan a covert mission, you'd be the first person I—"

"Yes," she blurted out.

His forehead dipped in consternation. "Yes, what?"

"That's the answer to the question you asked me before." She pressed her palms to his cheeks and gazed into his eyes. "Yes, I *do* love you."

"You do?"

The adorable wobble in his voice made Bailey's heart squeeze. "So much it scares me," she whispered.

He swiped at her tears with gentle fingertips. "I promise you, as long as I'm with you, there's nothing you need to be afraid of."

She laughed through her tears. "Because you'll be there to protect me, right?"

"If you need me to," he said simply. "If you let me. But it goes both ways, you know."

"Oh really? You're saying you need me to protect you?"

"Fuck, yes. Someone needs to keep my reckless ass in line. Might as well be you."

"*Might as well?* God, you don't have a romantic bone in your body, Sean."

He flashed a cocky grin. "Maybe not, but there's definitely one in my pants."

She snorted.

"But I wasn't just joking before," he said, his expression going serious. "I *want* you to protect me. If I'm ever in danger, or in battle, or in pain, there's nobody else I want by my side, Bailey."

A hot rush of emotion flooded her chest. "Do you really mean that?"

"Bloody right I do."

"Good. Because now that I've decided I love you, you won't be able to get rid of me."

His answering smile shone brighter than the full moon above them. "Luv, that's the best news I've heard all day."

# Chapter 26

Sullivan grinned as he hung up the phone and glanced at Isabel. She was stretched out on D's bed but shot into a sitting position the moment he ended the call. "They're okay?" she asked.

"I think they're more than okay." He grinned harder. "According to Reilly, he and Bailey have decided they're madly in love, and they're now on their way back to his flat to consummate their eternal passion."

Isabel burst out laughing. "He did *not* say that." She paused. "Did he?"

"It's Reilly—what do *you* think?"

"God, he totally said it." She rose from the bed, her expression turning serious. "I can't believe O'Hare actually went through with it. I was sure he'd change his mind."

Sullivan's amusement faded. "I wouldn't have blamed him if he had. Christ. Nobody wants to die like that."

"Maybe he thought the alternative was worse," she said sadly. "Hell, maybe dying in a fiery explosion *is* better than withering away as your body is ravaged from the inside out."

"Jeez, love, way to depress the shit outta me."

Isabel reached up to ruffle his hair. "Nothing depresses you, Sully. In fact, I don't think I've ever met anyone who's so frickin' laid-back about everything." She grabbed her cell phone from the end table and headed for the door. "I'll pop into Liam and Ash's room to let them know Bailey and Sean are okay. Will you text D?"

He nodded. "Will do. Am I seeing you in the morning or are you flying out tonight?"

"Nah, I'm not leaving until noon. I paid extra for the breakfast buffet, and I intend to take advantage of it."

With a grin, Isabel slid out the door, leaving Sully to chuckle to himself, but once again, the humor didn't stick.

When his gaze shifted to his bed, his misery only intensified.

He couldn't look at that damn thing without thinking about what he'd *done* on it. With Liam. With the brunette he'd picked up at the hotel bar.

Both encounters had resulted in orgasms, but the latter hadn't screwed with his head the way the former had.

The latter hadn't turned his whole bloody world upside down.

Christ, he'd known he was attracted to his teammate, but . . . he hadn't realized just how *much* he was attracted to his teammate.

It went beyond an itch he simply needed to scratch, because he could do that anytime and with anyone. Sex was a game he excelled at. Hell, all it had taken last night were a few flirty remarks and a lady-killer grin and that brunette had been all over him, more than willing to indulge in a no-strings roll between the sheets. She'd scratched the itch, given him what he'd needed in that moment.

Liam had left him wanting more.

He turned toward the door when he heard the beep

of a key card sliding in place. Good. D was back. Sully had felt like such an ass when he'd kicked the surly bastard out of their room last night so he could get his rocks off. D had been forced to bunk with Liam and Ash, and Sully knew the guy was still pissed about it.

He pasted on the most apologetic smile he could muster as the door swung open, but his facial muscles froze when not D, but Liam, entered the room.

"Hey." Liam's blue eyes flickered awkwardly as he held up the room card. "D and I swapped key cards."

Sullivan kept his voice casual. "Why's that?"

"Because I'm bunking here tonight." The discomfort on Liam's chiseled face deepened. "We need to talk, and I figured it'd be easier if we did it without D or the rookie lurking about."

He swallowed a panicked groan. Liam wanted to *talk*? Sully had hoped his mate would sweep shit under the rug again, the way he'd done after Paris.

Damn it, he wasn't equipped to deal with this right now. He hadn't even finished sifting through his own messed-up thoughts about the issue.

But clearly Liam was determined to have a sit-down, because he literally sat down, sinking on the edge of the mattress as he met Sullivan's eyes.

"I don't know what the hell is going on with me, Sully."

He didn't answer. *Couldn't* answer. His throat was clamped shut.

"I lied to you this summer. After the . . . the whole thing with . . . fuck, I'm just gonna say it—after the *kiss*. It freaked me the fuck out, okay?"

"I know," Sullivan said hoarsely.

"No, you don't know," his friend retorted in frustration. "I freaked out on you and you thought it was because I was shocked and horrified by what you did, and then when you apologized, I *let* you. I let you think you'd done something wrong."

His lungs burned as a breath squeezed past his tight throat. "It *was* wrong."

"Was it?" The helpless tremor in Liam's voice ripped Sully's chest apart. "Because it didn't feel wrong. And last night, when I . . . when I . . . damn it, you *know* what I did." He paused. "That didn't feel wrong either."

It hadn't. Christ, it really, really hadn't. Sully couldn't remember the last time he'd come that hard.

But . . . no. He was *not* going down that road. Not with his best friend. Not with one of the only people who'd ever truly given a damn about him.

Liam stood up and took a step toward him.

Sully took a wary step back. "Where are you going with this, Boston?"

"I have no fuckin' clue," Liam said miserably.

He inched forward another step.

This time Sullivan remained frozen in place. At six-three, he towered over most other men, but Liam was the same height, and his vivid blue eyes were perfectly level with Sully's.

"Maybe we should . . . do this." That muscular body edged closer.

Apprehension lined Liam's features, those rugged movie-star features that made it impossible to look away, but then what he'd said registered, and Sullivan stumbled backward.

"Do what exactly? Screw? Because it ain't gonna happen."

"Why not?" Unexpected challenge lit Liam's eyes. "You're saying you don't want it?"

"It doesn't matter what I want. Any way you look at it, this doesn't end well." Sully sighed. "This friendship is too bloody important to me, mate."

Liam looked hurt. "And it's not important to me?"

"I'm starting to wonder, seeing as you're so willing to douse it with gasoline and light a fucking match to it."

Liam's hands balled into fists. "Damn it, Sully. I need . . . I *need* to do this." The helpless chord returned to his voice, echoing between them. "I have to find out if . . ."

An angry curse flew out of Sullivan's mouth. "If what, Boston? If you're bi? Gay? Well, forgive me if I don't want to be your sexual guinea pig."

"Since when?" Liam shot back. "When do you *ever* turn down sex, Aussie?"

Frustration burned a path up his spine. "This isn't about me turning down sex—it's about me caring about you too much to lead you down this path. You want an answer to your little problem? Fine, here it is: you're straight. You're going to marry a nice Catholic girl and have a dozen rug rats, just like your brothers and sisters. *That's* your path, mate. But hell, I'm all for you exploring. If you want to take a walk on the dude side and see what it's all about, go ahead. Just do it with someone else, okay? It *can't* be with me, because you know what happens after I screw someone—I walk away. And I don't want to walk away from my best friend."

He was panting by the time he finished, but his earnest speech fell on deaf ears.

"It doesn't have to be that way," Liam objected. "It doesn't have to change anything. Just . . . once. One time and then we . . ." He trailed off.

"We what? Pretend it didn't happen?" Sarcasm bit into his words. "Because you tried that approach with the kiss. How's *that* working out for you?"

Liam visibly gulped.

"Jesus, Boston. Are you really that naive? You think

we could take it further than a bloody kiss and it *won't* affect our friendship?"

Anger coursed through Sullivan's veins. Anger and exasperation and sheer disbelief that Liam actually thought this could *ever* be a good idea. The guy would never be able to handle it. He'd never be able to look Sullivan in the eye again, and damned if Sully would lose his best friend over something as pointless as *sex*.

The turbulent emotions eddying inside him spiraled to the surface and sent him charging forward.

He planted a hand on Liam's chest and shoved the other man against the wall. Liam's body collided into the hard surface with a thump, his eyes blazing with indignation, but Sullivan didn't give him a chance to speak.

"Is this what you want?" he hissed, grinding his lower body into Liam's.

Sullivan fought a groan when he felt a very noticeable erection straining against his thigh. His fingers touched the button of Liam's cargo pants, but he didn't pop it open.

"Well, is it?" he mocked. "Do you want me to undo your pants and blow you, Boston?"

Liam's breathing went heavy. He didn't answer.

Sully palmed his friend's package. "You want to screw me with this?" He squeezed that hard ridge, then grabbed Liam's hand and placed it on himself. "Or feel me screwing you with *this*?"

A strangled curse flew out. "Sully," Liam started.

He cut him off. "And then, when you're finished coming, you honestly think we'd be able to pretend it didn't happen and go back to being best buds?"

He abruptly released Liam and backed away from him. "Well, I'm not risking it. Maybe this friendship doesn't mean anything to you, but it sure as hell means something to *me*. And I'm not lighting that match. I'm not fucking doing that."

Ignoring Liam's stunned face, Sullivan stalked out of the room and slammed the door behind him.

Bailey struggled for breath as she collapsed onto Sean's bare chest, her body still tingling with the aftershocks of orgasm. The man beneath her was as breathless as she was, green eyes hazy with pleasure as he gazed up at her.

"I'm disappointed in you," he said with a grin.

Her eyes narrowed. "What the hell for?"

"For fighting me all those years." Sean tucked a strand of hair behind her ear. "Think of all the sex we could've been having. Five years' worth of orgasms, lost to us."

A laugh tickled her throat. "I'm sure we can make up for that. Actually, I bet we can squeeze in at least a couple months' worth tonight. Well, if you get some coffee in me."

He arched his hips and his still-hard cock stroked her inner channel. "There's no room," he drawled.

Bailey's laughter broke free. "You're incorrigible."

"Yeah, but you still love me."

God, she really did. So damn much. Now that she'd allowed those feelings to breach her heart, she couldn't seem to control them. She rested her head in the crook of his neck, breathing in the familiar scent of spice and man that never failed to make her light-headed.

"So what now?" she murmured. "Where do we go from here?"

"Literally or figuratively?"

She smiled. "Both.

"Well, relationship-wise—God, I love that word. *Relationship*." He stroked her cheek. "I plan on marrying you first chance I get, luv."

"I see. And do you plan on asking me beforehand?"

"I just did, Bailey. Get your head in the game."

A snort popped out. Yup, of course that would be Sean Reilly's idea of a marriage proposal.

"As for the literal *where do we go*—I'm putting you on the first flight out to Colorado."

Bailey didn't offer an argument. She was desperate to see her mother, even though Daniels had assured her Vanessa was all right. She'd reluctantly called him earlier to request he post more agents on the nursing home, but she needn't have bothered, because he'd already gone ahead and done that. Daniels hadn't handled the loss of his men well—he'd practically gloated when he'd told her that the second wave of agents he'd dispatched had eliminated every threat in the area. Flannery's men were dead, and with their boss also out of commission, there was nobody left to threaten her mother.

"Noelle's already sent a plane," she admitted. Then she paused. "I was hoping you'd come with me."

Sean's jaw dropped. "You want me to meet your mother?"

The awe in his voice made her shift in discomfort. "Unless you don't want to."

"I want to," he said instantly.

His eagerness made her smile. "Okay, that's set, then. Where will we go after?"

"I was thinking we could go to Costa Rica."

"So you can beg Morgan to take you back?" she teased.

"Yeah," he said sheepishly. "And I spoke to Ollie—he says he wants to join up with Morgan too, if the prickly bastard will have us."

"What about the Dagger?" Bailey asked. "There's no chance you want to stay here and take it over . . . is there?" Wariness rose inside her. Because God, as much as she loved him, she didn't think she could deal with that.

But Sean eased her worries by responding with an emphatic, "Hell, no." Then he sighed. "Actually, I had a talk with Quinn about it when you were in the shower."

"You told him about Rabbit and what happened at the warehouse?"

Sean nodded. "I also told him it's time to let go of the cause. The Dagger can't survive without Rabbit. It wouldn't have survived even if Rabbit had lived."

She arched a brow. "What did Quinn have to say about that?"

"He agreed with me. He knows they're fighting a losing battle. Hell, I think deep down he's relieved."

"So that's it? They'll just disband?"

"They might keep some of the rackets open, but I think their terrorist days are behind them. The younger lads will go off and do their own thing, and the older men—Quinn and Rory and the rest—they'll probably just end up retiring." Sean shrugged. "All right, that's enough talking. We've got too much work to do."

She wrinkled her forehead. "We do?"

A wicked gleam entered his eyes. He thrust upward and his cock hit a spot inside her that made her moan. "We're making up for lost orgasms, remember?"

Bailey leaned down and kissed him, running her palms along his broad, sculpted chest. "You're right. We'd better get started."

# Epilogue

The hotel bar was deserted, save for the bartender and one other patron at the far end of the long, gleaming counter. It was two thirty in the morning, but the sign on the door said the bar didn't close until three, so Sullivan wasted no time planting his ass on a stool and tapping the counter. The other customer paid him no attention—his dark head was bent over a cell phone, one hand playing with the stir stick poking out of his drink.

"Rum and Coke," Sully muttered. "Hold the Coke."

The bartender didn't even crack a smile. "Key card."

Aw, shit. He'd forgotten how insane this hotel was about security. Nothing got charged to a room unless a key card was produced, and Sullivan had left his upstairs. He could've paid in cash—if he hadn't left his wallet upstairs too.

But no way was he going back up there. He couldn't face Liam right now.

"I forgot my key and my wallet upstairs," he told the barkeep. "But you can still charge it to the room, can't you? Just type my room number into your little computer."

The man hesitated.

"Come on," Sully cajoled. "You know I'm a guest. You *saw* me here last night, mate. I know you did, because I saw you."

After a beat, the bartender muttered, "What's the number?"

"Two-ten."

Swift fingers moved over the keyboard on the register. The man scanned the screen and said, "Derek Pratt?"

Right, the room was under D's name. "Yep," Sullivan said lightly. "That's me."

A second later, a rum—hold the Coke—slid in front of him.

He took a long slug, letting the alcohol burn his throat and heat his insides.

Bloody Liam.

Why couldn't he have left well enough alone?

Sullivan drained his glass and slammed it down on the counter. He was about to signal the bartender for another when his peripheral vision caught a flash of movement. The dark-haired customer from the end of the counter slid onto the stool directly beside him.

"Derek Pratt?"

Sully's muscles tensed as he studied the other man. Skull-trimmed hair, shrewd brown eyes, a tidy goatee.

"That is your name, right?" the man prompted.

Sullivan nearly corrected him—until he noticed that the bartender was listening in. Not wanting to admit he'd lied, he gave a quick nod. "Yeah, that's me. What can I do for you, mate?"

Muscled forearms rested on the counter as the man clasped his hands together. "Mr. Pratt . . ." He chuckled. "You have no idea how long I've been looking for you."

Sully gulped. "Well. You found me."

"Yes." The man's deadly smile sent a chill through Sullivan's body. "I found you."

Want to encounter a sexy new kind of alpha group from Elle Kennedy? Read on for a special excerpt from the first book in Elle Kennedy's brand-new Outlaws series,

*CLAIMED*

Available from Signet Eclipse in October 2015.

She found an empty table and sat down, twisting off the beer cap and swallowing the lukewarm alcohol. She didn't like the taste of beer much, but she wasn't in the mood for anything stronger. She had to stay alert. And she definitely needed to find a place to sleep tonight.

Panic bubbled in her throat as she imagined spending the night outdoors again. She'd kept expecting bandits to pop out of the shadows, which had made it impossible to fall asleep. She'd been in outlaw territory for nearly a week now, and she wasn't even close to adapting to her rough, dangerous surroundings. She'd thought her training would help her survive out here.

She hadn't expected to be this damn afraid all the damn time.

Taking a breath, she glanced around the room. Despite the low chatter and occasional chuckles, nobody looked relaxed. Shoulders were stiff. Gazes were guarded. She was beginning to suspect this kind of behavior wasn't uncommon. Since she'd left the compound, she'd realized that nobody was immune to the Global Council's control. Even those who considered themselves free—the outlaws—continued to look over their shoulders.

When the GC had taken over four decades ago, they'd decided the only way to avoid another war was to rule with an iron fist. The Council members insisted that the devastation of the world would not have happened if a strong global regime had been in place, so they eliminated conflict-causing factors like class, religion, free will. The new system worked, to some extent. Hudson couldn't deny she'd been happy in the city, at least before Dominik had decided to turn her into a prisoner in her own life.

She supposed she was an outlaw now, too. A target, like the rest of them, and it was a culture shock to be thrust into this new world, surrounded by people who were determined to cling to whatever freedom they could.

Her gaze drifted to a table near the door, where four men spoke in hushed tones. They made a formidable sight. Gorgeous, masculine, oozing deadly intensity.

One in particular captured her attention. Late twenties, early thirties maybe, with cropped brown hair, cold hazel eyes, and muscles galore. He wore a fitted olive green jacket that most likely hid the slew of weapons beneath it, and everything about him screamed *warrior*. The broad set of his shoulders, the way his hawklike gaze swept over the room even as he carried a conversation with his companions.

Her breath hitched when the object of her perusal turned his head and looked at her.

Heat.

Holy crap. Nothing cold in his gaze anymore, just bold, undisguised fire.

He wanted her.

Ignoring the sudden pounding of her heart, Hudson wrenched her eyes away and gulped down some more beer. She felt flushed, her hair like a heavy curtain smothering her shoulders and back, but she didn't dare pin it up. Even though the tattoo at the base of her neck was buried under layers of makeup, she still wasn't taking any chances. If anyone so much as suspected who she was, she'd be killed in a heartbeat.

A high-pitched giggle sounded from the other end of the room, and Hudson turned to see a woman with blond hair and double Ds emerge from a dark corridor, flanked by a tall man with piercing blue eyes and a killer grin. He had the arrogant swagger of a guy who'd just gotten laid, and his companion's bee-stung lips and tousled hair confirmed it. The man gave her ass a playful spank, then sauntered over to the table Hudson had been observing.

Surprise, surprise. Sexy blond guy was with the sexy foursome.

As he sat, his gaze collided with hers, and a faint smile lifted the corner of his mouth. It faded when the dark-haired outlaw she'd been trying not to ogle muttered something that silenced the group.

Hudson sighed. Now definitely wasn't the time to get all hot for a sinfully sexy stranger. She had more pressing matters to deal with—so many of them, her head was starting to spin.

Find a place where she could lie low for a while. Scavenge some supplies. Figure out how to get the hell out of West Colony. Evade Dominik, who'd no doubt sent an army after her.

Maybe the folks who ran this place would help her find a safe haven—

"Down on the floor, assholes!"

She'd been so lost in thought, she hadn't sensed the danger until it was too late. She didn't have time to unsheathe the knife on her hip, because cold fingers grabbed her arm and yanked her to the dirty cement floor.

"Stay down, bitch!"

There was a blur of movement, loud expletives, and angry shouts as a dozen men stormed the bar and advanced on its patrons.

Bandits.

*Shit.*

The man who'd thrown her down had neglected to search her for weapons, so she still had possession of her knife, along with the rest of the sharp steel blades strapped to her body. She gripped the bone handle and slowly slid the hunting knife down to her side, lifting her head to assess the situation. She'd heard of bandits, but this was her first encounter with them.

They looked a lot like the homeless people she'd seen in her father's photographs of prewar Los Angeles. Threadbare clothing, dirty, reeking of booze. The Enforcers didn't differentiate between bandits and outlaws, but Hudson only needed two seconds to recognize the difference. Outlaws fought for freedom and, sure, they raided GC supply compounds when it was needed, but they were fighting against a government they opposed, not with one another.

These men were scavengers. Broken, desperate vultures who didn't belong, not in GC society and not among the rebels. She'd heard that bandits had no consciences, no remorse about robbing and killing and raping anything in their paths.

As her heartbeat accelerated, she stayed flat on the floor as the bandits manhandled the patrons in the smoky room, kicking anyone who so much as yelped. The leader of the band, a man with dark hair and a bushy, overgrown beard, hopped the counter, assault rifle in hand.

"We want all the booze," he snapped at the bartender.

Hudson slithered under the cover of the table. From the corner of her eye, she noticed that the five outlaws had remained seated and were watching events unfold with bored expressions on their respectively handsome faces.

"Get down on the ground!" shouted one of the bandits. He was a short, skinny man with a shaved head, his unimposing physique made deadly only by the gun he waved at the group.

"No, thanks," the outlaw with black hair and an even blacker scowl replied.

"You wanna die? Is that it?" The bandit cocked his pistol. "Because I'm perfectly happy to—"

The five men sprung to action. One second the table was upright, the next it was whipped on its side with two of them diving behind it for cover. Hudson saw a blur of arms and legs, flashes of steel and silver.

An outraged moan cut the air as the skinny bandit suddenly found a knife lodged in his upper arm. He staggered forward while his fellow robbers launched themselves at the men, their quest for alcohol forgotten.

It was a bloodbath. A gunshot boomed, sending one of the bandits crashing to the floor two feet from her head. More shots echoed in the room, making her ears ring.

She watched the scene unfold in morbid fascination. The outlaws didn't even break a sweat, and they were completely unfazed by the fact that they were outnumbered. Fists connected into jaws. Grunts heated the air. Another explosion of gunfire took chunks out of the cement wall.

A furious male curse made her wince, and she twisted her head in time to see the blond outlaw stumble backward. He lifted a hand to his neck in amazement, and even from across the room, she saw his hand come back stained with blood. He'd been hit. And yet he didn't even miss a beat as he raised his gun and fired twice, eliciting a shriek of agony from the longhaired bandit who'd been attempting to finish him off.

A thud. Two. The bandits were dropping like flies.

Silence finally descended over the room, broken only by the groans of those lucky enough to be alive.

"Well, that was fun," the man with the black eyes remarked. He sounded thoroughly bored.

A scuffed boot crossed her line of vision. She shifted in time to see the thick sole stomp on the chest of the bandit leader, the one with the beard. When she raised her gaze, she discovered that the boot belonged to the man with the smoldering hazel eyes.

"I suggest you round up your buddies—the ones who are still breathing—and get the hell out of here," he said coolly.

"Fuck you," was the strangled reply.

With a heavy breath, the man hauled the bandit to his feet. "Fine, we'll do it the hard way."

He grabbed the guy's arm and broke it with a sickening *crack*.

Hudson flinched at the bandit's shriek of pain, watching in amazement as the outlaw manhandled the injured man to the door. He stopped and glanced over his shoulder in an unspoken command, and his men wasted no time hauling the remaining intruders out of the bar.

Patrons slowly got to their feet. Dazed. The bartender rushed toward the blond man, but he brushed off her arm and continued toward the door, an unconscious man hanging over his broad shoulder.

Hudson stood up on shaky legs and stared at the bodies littering the floor. Eight in total. A bloody massacre. She wasn't surprised when a few customers made a beeline for the dead, frantically rummaging through pockets and looting the lifeless men.

She was sheathing her knife when the outlaws returned.

The blond had his palm clamped over his neck, and she could see blood oozing between his fingers.

"Everybody all right?" their leader asked gruffly.

The bartender hurried over. "Thank you," she blurted out.

He ignored the declaration of gratitude. "Two of my guys will stay here tonight in case those assholes decide to push their luck and come back. But I suggest you close up shop. Location's been compromised, which means you're bound to encounter more of this shit."

She nodded rapidly. "We will. We'll close up tomorrow."

"Good."

He glanced around the room, his hazel eyes resting on Hudson. Warmth instantly flooded her belly, traveling through her body until every inch of her felt hot and achy.

After a long moment, he broke the eye contact. "Let's move out," he barked at his friends. "Xander, you and Pike take care of the bodies and make sure these folks stay safe."

"No problem. Oh and, Connor," the other man added dryly, "get Ry cleaned up. He's bleeding like a stuck pig."

Connor. The name suited him.

Hudson couldn't take her eyes off him as he turned and marched to the door, providing her with a nice view of his taut backside. It wasn't until he disappeared through the doorway that she snapped out of her trance.

Ignoring the startled looks from the other people in the bar, she raced out the door, blinking to adjust to the darkness. The lights that had once illuminated the parking lot of the hospital had been knocked out, and parts of the pavement were black and cracking, most likely from the fires or explosives that had been set off by the looters all those years ago.

Everything beyond the walls of West City looked this

way—dead trees and blackened earth, crumbling buildings, and overgrown neighborhoods—and the coastal cities that hadn't ended up underwater were still flooded to shit.

Hudson stopped only to grab the duffel bag she'd stashed in the bushes, then raced across the parking lot. She caught up with Connor just as he reached the beat-up Jeep parked in the lot.

"Wait!"

He froze. Turned his head slightly, greeting her with suspicion.

She stumbled toward the vehicle, aware of how foolish she was being. How reckless.

But she knew without a shred of doubt that the answer to all her problems was standing right there in front of her. This man, with his warrior body and cold eyes and military precision—*he* was the solution.

"Yeah?" he muttered.

"You . . . What you guys did back there . . . I just wanted to . . ."

A soft chuckle sounded from behind her. She spun around as the blond guy with the bloody neck—Ry?—approached the Jeep, tailed by another dark-haired outlaw.

"See? I told you chicks got off on violence," Ry told his friend. He fixed his blue eyes on her. "But listen, gorgeous, don't bother with Connor. He's too bossy in bed. Me, on the other hand . . . I'll let you do *whatever* you want to me."

She couldn't help but smile. "Thanks, but that's not what I want from him."

"Your loss," he said lightly before hopping into the backseat.

"What the fuck *do* you want?" Connor demanded.

Their gazes locked, and a rush of awareness sailed through her again.

"Say whatever you want to say so we can get the hell outta here." Irritation crept into his deep, raspy voice.

"I . . ." She swallowed. "I— "

"Spit it out, sweetheart."

She opened her mouth, and four desperation-laced words flew out of it. "Take me with you."